Readers love *Arthropoda*
by XENIA MELZER

"I highly recommend this exciting page-turner and I will be a new follower of the Andi Hayes Mystery series."
—Queer SciFi

"If you like murder mysteries with a paranormal touch, if two tough guys finding ways to admit their vulnerabilities is your thing, and if you're looking for a suspenseful story with a few twists and surprises, then you will probably like this novel as much as I do. Absolutely fascinating reading!"
—Rainbow Book Reviews

"…the plot is [gripping], and the paranormal premise is superbly creepy."
—Paranormal Romance Guild

"The world that Xenia Melzer is building is a rich patchwork of people, places, and (creepy-crawly) things…. Still, from beginning to very satisfying end, it's a wild ride that you'll be glad you took."
—Parker Williams

By Xenia Melzer

ARTHROPODA
Arthropoda
Eruca

GODS OF WAR
Casto
Love and the Stubborn
Ummana
Braving the Storm
The Rules of War

Published by DSP PUBLICATIONS
www.dsppublications.com

ERUCA
XENIA MELZER

DSP PUBLICATIONS

Published by
DSP PUBLICATIONS

5032 Capital Circle SW, Suite 2, PMB# 279, Tallahassee, FL 32305-7886 USA
www.dsppublications.com

Eruca
© 2022 Xenia Melzer

Cover Art
© 2022 L.C. Chase
http://www.lcchase.com
Cover content is for illustrative purposes only and any person depicted on the cover is a model.
Author Photo
Photographer: Andreas Eirainer, bildwerk
Make-up: Kathrin Fuchsenthaler

Trade Paperback ISBN: 978-1-64108-322-5
Digital ISBN: 978-1-64108-321-8
Trade Paperback published February 2022
v. 1.0

Printed in the United States of America
(∞)
This paper meets the requirements of
ANSI/NISO Z39.48-1992 (Permanence of Paper).

For my father. When I was a child, you used to catch spiders with your bare hands and take them outside, even when they were so big we could see their eyes (shudder). To many, this might look like just some small act of kindness (or madness), but it has taught me respect and compassion for other living beings, no matter how alien and downright terrifying they are.

And for Schnurri, our family cat. When they moved, you ate them.

AUTHOR'S NOTE

DEAR READERS, thank you for returning to the adventures of Andi Hayes and George Donovan. While writing the second book, *Eruca*, I've realized something I failed to explain in the first book, and I hope no enraged biologists are going to come knocking on my door because of it.

The first book, *Arthropoda*, makes a generous use of the terms "arthropods" and "insects," as if they were synonymous, but strictly speaking, they aren't. Just as all German Shepherds are dogs, but not all dogs are German Shepherds, all insects are arthropods, but not all arthropods are insects. Commonly, "arthropod" is used as another word for insects, but accurately, insects are defined by having six legs. Spiders, who have eight legs, are arachnids but also arthropods. The same goes for pill bugs and centipedes. They are not insects but arthropods, and for the layperson there's no big difference between them because they all are creepy crawlers. I also took and take the liberty of using "arthropods" and "insects" as somewhat synonymous terms, not least because it allows me to diversify my writing a bit.

For the scientifically interested person, I want to stress again that arthropod is the term describing all animals with segmented legs, including insects, arachnids, chilopods (centipedes and the likes), Armadillidiidae (pill bugs), and crustaceans.

For example, the common honeybee would be described as Phylum: Arthropoda; Class: Insecta; Order: Hymenoptera (because of the wings); Family: Apidae (general for bees); Clade: Corbiculata; Tribe: Apini.

In the books, I don't go into such great detail; what's important is that all animals falling under the term arthropod are part of Andi's *geschenk*.

Andi is also able to connect with worms, which are Annelida, which means invertebrates.

All biologists reading this, please forgive me the liberties I took with the terms!

ERUCA

XENIA MELZER

PROLOGUE

THE WATER was cool, but not too much, a soft current enriching it with oxygen, making it perfect to grow in, rich in plankton and algae too small to be nourishment but so fertile, the prey fat and plenty, little fish and tadpoles swimming around, so many of them, easy to catch, and the larvae of the mosquitoes, a banquet, life consisted of waiting and grabbing and eating and growing, the exoskeleton fitting tighter every day, and then the current became stronger, a maelstrom swirling up the silt and the little pebbles and the rotting leaves and everything became obscured and the hiding place was exposed and the maelstrom didn't stop, became stronger, a second and a third one joining in, the water no longer nourishing but deadly, heavy, huge bodies falling, sinking, writhing, stirring, upsetting the balance with their thrashing, the larvae of the mosquitoes, precious prey, whirling around, out of reach, stones hitting the hiding spot, exposing the hunter to bigger predators, trout dashing through the browned liquid, snapping, chasing, collecting, the bodies causing smaller currents now, bubbles of oxygen drifting toward the surface, popping out of existence, the trout coming closer, no place to hide....

1. No Rest for the Wicked

"Come on, Andi, we've only been walking for an hour!" George sounded entirely too chipper for Andi's taste. Why he had given in to his partner's nagging and agreed to come on this ridiculous hiking trip on Swamp Fox Trail, Andi didn't know. They wouldn't be going the whole forty-seven miles, of course, just a few miles into it to enjoy the beautiful scenery of the swamps and then marching back, preferably before the mosquitoes had drained them. It was a nice morning in early fall, the solving of their first case by now almost five months ago. The wound in Andi's shoulder had healed nicely, and he and George had deepened their bond as partners over a few minor cases they had cracked within days, much to the vexation of Chief Norris, who still hated Andi, seemingly on principle. It was okay, though, because Andi didn't harbor any warm feelings for the chief either. In his opinion she was a career-driven greedy hag who put politics before victims, something Andi abhorred greatly, and he was here to relax, not get worked up about his stupid boss and her moronic prejudices.

Andi looked ahead to where George was waiting at a bend in the path, absentmindedly batting at mosquitoes—

Blood, lots of it, rich and good, promising nourishment for many eggs, with a sharp tang to it, repelling, but only superficial, the blood was fine, ready to be sucked, hunger, the need to lay the eggs, hunger, hunger, HUNGER!

—which were terribly unimpressed by the repellant they had generously sprayed on themselves, George promising, swearing it would work like magic. It didn't, thank you very much, and there was nothing they could do because they were in the middle of nowhere, surrounded by swamps and marshland chock-full of insects of all kinds. How on earth George thought Andi should be able to relax here would remain his secret. There were so many different images bombarding him from all sides, Andi was grateful he hadn't tripped yet. No more hiking trips with George. At least not when his partner was in charge of selecting the trail.

"Andi, what's keeping you? Come on, there's a beautiful little lake just over there!" George pointed excitedly ahead, reminding Andi of a puppy eager to play. The joy on his partner's face was what kept Andi from making a sarcastic comment. George had only the best intentions, and Andi knew he had worried him the last few weeks. Late summer was always a difficult time; insect activity reached several peaks then, and Andi wasn't always able to evade the thicket. Apart from the seemingly always present mosquitoes, the previous week had seen an infestation of love bugs on Stiles Point, where he lived, thanks to several of his neighbors not tending properly to their lawns and letting the thatch get too thick. Because of their neglect, Andi had spent most of the week trying to stay at the precinct as long as possible to not get completely buried under the frantic coupling and dying going on in the vicinity of his home. George had even offered to let him sleep on his couch until the worst was over. After seriously contemplating the offer, Andi had declined. He was grateful for George's understanding and his attempts to make things as easy as possible for Andi, but Andi was still determined not to get too attached to his new partner. George's days in Charleston were numbered, and Andi couldn't afford to lose his ability to fend for himself. He was already dangerously close to dependency on George. He didn't care if refusing George's offer made him an idiot of the highest order; he had to cling to some semblance of independence or the blow when George finally left would be even harder to bear.

So why was he on this trip?

Andi reached George, who beamed at him as if he'd found a diamond in his Christmas stocking. "Look, Andi, isn't it beautiful?"

Andi obligingly gazed in the direction George's outstretched hand indicated. The view was indeed breathtaking, a small lake surrounded by marsh grass and cypress trees, little purple and light blue flowers Andi didn't know the name of dotting the area, occasional rocks sticking out like crumbs strewn around by a giant, the water a rich brown color, the surface rippling gently in the soft breeze. Andi made a step forward, taking in the beauty of the place for a few heartbeats, before the incessant humming in the back of his mind took on a shape he knew only too well and he fell, dove deep into the water—

Temperature is perfect, getting colder the farther down he sinks, the deep brown strangely translucent, Andi can see farther than should be possible, but it's not him seeing, it's them telling him what is going on everywhere, larvae of mosquitoes and dragonflies, water beetles, pond skaters, providing him with an image in 3D, he's on the water and in it and under it and he feels the current and the different temperatures and the little swirls caused by fish—predator!—and the hunger and how ready he was to climb up that piece of reed to finally leave his underwater shell, and there's something in the water, something that doesn't belong, lots of fish around it, taking bites out of it, too much, poisoning the water, taking up space and getting bigger, little chunks falling off, not of interest, no food, at least for most of them, some are feeding on it, a feast, too many fish, and then Andi sees them, three bodies, on the bottom of the lake, half sunk into the sediments of rotting leaves, the gasses leaving them disturbing the water, their hands bound with something heavy and metallic, a bit like blood, what was the name, yes, chains, bound with chains and weighted with stones, their hair floating around in the tiny currents the fish create with their bodies, other images of them falling down, crashing into the water, going under, the whole lake in uproar, it could have only been a few days, the bodies still look kind of good, for water corpses anyway, probably because the water is so cool, and there's the mosquito larvae getting ready to leave their life underwater behind, Andi is dragged into the necessity of getting out of the shell, who is Andi, anyway, there's water here, and food and getting reborn is important and so much information, all in one endless stream drowning him with knowledge he doesn't need, doesn't know how to use, he goes under and under and under—

"Andi! What the hell?" George's voice was like a knife cutting through the veil around Andi's senses, freeing him of the grasp the agitated insects had on him, and he clung to George's arms like they were a lifeline in a troubled sea.

"Bodies. Three. Down there." He pointed in the direction of the lake.

"Are you sure?"

Andi just lifted a brow. George sighed. "This was supposed to be a getaway, not finding us new work."

"Hey, it's not my fault! Complain to whoever dumped them here."

"I know. I didn't mean it like that." George stared at the lake, which looked deceptively peaceful in the golden light of the sun. "Is this something we have to report? *Can* we report it?"

Two valid questions. In the few months they had been working together, these were the two most important questions Andi had taught his partner. He practically stumbled upon corpses on a daily basis, and not all of them could be reported, especially if Andi wasn't able to find a plausible story of how he found them in the first place. It wasn't as if anybody would believe he tripped over the skeleton under the concrete in the basement of an abandoned house by chance, for example. Since his *geschenk* was a secret—Andi had no inclination to be prodded by shrinks and curious doctors; oh no, his life was complicated enough as it was—there were victims for whom he could never find justice. It was one of the burdens he carried, one of the things he could ignore most of the time because, sadly, there were so many others who needed him.

"I think this is something we have to report. The ptomaine is poisoning the water, and I'm afraid the lake is too small to handle it. There is water coming in from somewhere, but not enough to spread effectively whatever nastiness dead bodies exude, and surely not of three of them. Sooner or later, somebody is going to notice, and you know chances are high we're getting the case then simply because Norris wants to see me fail, and I'd rather have Evangeline looking at the bodies while there's still a chance of getting solid evidence to back whatever we're going to find." This was another problem Andi faced regularly—matching the evidence the insects provided with what he got from the coroner and CSI. The older the corpse, the deeper the gap between what Andi knew and what science could prove. Sometimes it took serious storytelling on his part to explain some of his more outrageous conclusions—outrageous from the point of view of science, not from his own.

"What's our story going to be? I mean, nobody will believe we took a dip in there and just happened to find them." He shuddered visibly. "I don't want to think about knowingly going into water where three corpses are. Is there a chance they're going to float at some point?"

Andi shook his head. "There's chains and stones attached to them."

"Anonymous tip, then?" George shook his head. "We're using that excuse too often as it is. And who would give us a tip about three corpses in a lake on a trail where the chances of having witnessed the crime are practically zero?"

Andi hated and loved George's logic at the same time. An anonymous tip had always been his favorite excuse, and with Chief Renard, Chief Norris's predecessor, it had worked perfectly because he had valued Andi's solving rates more than the plausibility behind them. If anybody higher up got suspicious, Andi had always been able to count on Chief

Renard to smooth things over for him. Chief Norris, on the other hand, would gladly feed him to the wolves and have a party afterward.

They both stared at the water, thinking hard. When George spoke again, his tone was carefully neutral, which told Andi he wasn't sure if what he was suggesting was plain ridiculous or simply too dangerous for Andi to do. George was still finding his footing with Andi's *geschenk*, slowly learning the limits and no-goes of it.

"Do you think you could go down there once more? The way you were just now, I'm not happy even entertaining the idea, but I don't think we have any other options left."

"And what would I be doing *down there*?"

"Looking for something on the corpses we can perhaps pry loose with a long stick or a pole. Something that would float up and give us an excuse to call the authorities to investigate further."

"As ideas go, this one isn't too bad." Andi took a deep breath. Deliberately diving into the minds of insects was more difficult than just interpreting what they were offering on their own. It meant immersing himself even deeper than the usual level, and leaving was like walking through a sea of molasses that seemed to be reaching higher up his body every time he had to do it.

A soft touch on his right forearm had Andi looking up into the serious expression on George's face. "Is this truly all right, Andi? We can find some other way, or we can simply let nature take its course. Even if it means not catching the killers. Your well-being comes first."

More deeply touched by the words than Andi wanted to admit to himself, let alone his partner, he put his hand on the back of George's. "I will cope. We just have to sort out the logistics first, because I don't want to shift back and forth."

"How about I take that pole over there." George pointed to a thin but stable-looking stem of about sixteen feet that was lying close to the water. The flakes of bark peeling off the wood suggested the stem had been dead for some time now, thus probably being light enough for George to handle despite its length. It also had a conveniently pointy end, ideal to pry loose whatever Andi determined was worth the effort. He nodded, and George went to retrieve the stem, dragging it toward the grassy shore of the lake, promptly sinking ankle-deep into brackish water a few steps before he reached the lake. Cursing, George shook his left boot, the water laminating the hem of his trousers to the outline of the boot. Andi followed his partner, not caring where he stepped because they had to wade a few feet into the lake anyway. He grabbed George's free hand, dragged him into the cold brown soup until the small ripples were lapping at the area around their knees. The lake was not only small, but also shallow, the deepest part, where the bodies lay, only marginally deeper than Andi was tall. Thanks to the murky quality of the water, though, the bodies could not be detected by simply staring at the surface. Following Andi's directions, George positioned the stem with the tip facing toward the spot where the bodies were. Then Andi grabbed George's shoulder, his anchor to reality, dove in, opened his senses this time in a deliberate way, looking at the corpses in search of something they could use—

Cold, wonderfully dark, flakes of skin drifting through the water, too many fish, Andi was looking for something, something, he had to focus, the mosquito larvae were hatching, coming out of their shells, their wings still wet, waiting to dry in the sun, no, that wasn't where he should be, down, he had to go down to where the disturbance was, had to find food, no, something else, something useful, what was useful if it couldn't be consumed or eggs planted in it, something a blob needed, Andi was a blob, a cop, those were victims, he had to—take flight, before the fish found him—NO!— down, on the corpses, he wasn't a new mosquito, wasn't a dragonfly larvae, he was Andi, he needed to tell George where to poke with the pointy end, the stem, Andi latched on to it, using it as an additional anchor to George's body warmth, guiding him toward the corpses, they were bound tight, the chains digging into them obscenely because the flesh was already bloating, by now the corpses would be floating if it weren't for the stones weighing them down, the chains were slung around their bodies, no bits of clothing loose enough to get them up, and clothes weren't plausible anyway, cloth tended to sink, not float, Andi concentrated, found something odd on one of the bodies, out of place, even more than the chains and rocks, at least in the minds of the arthropods under the water, something that didn't fit with what the other two bodies had, hair, all wrong, not attached to skin, but something else, Andi knew what it was, he just had to find the right word... a toupee, that was it, hopefully it would swim, he started giving George directions, using his vocal cords, yes, blobs had those, they were used for communication, much like pheromones and visuals, not as precise but they had to do, more to the left, yes, forward, the stem was a little too short, one more step into the cold water, careful, the tip ripping through bloated flesh, causing a gash on the cheek, small bits of food floating upward, the fish going after it, forward, a little farther, yes, there it was, the water had already destroyed whatever had made the piece of hair stick to the skull, now it was loose, sinking down, not floating, damn, they needed it to come up, George had to catch it with the tip, dragging it toward them, it slipped off, landed in the sediments, now it was hard to see, it took some tries until George had it again, dragging it slowly, carefully toward them, over the ground, catching rotting bits of leaves in the strands, directing it toward the shore to their right, where Andi sensed a small current of water leaving the lake, making it plausible for the toupee to have drifted there, why was that important again? He needed to take flight, find nourishment, blood, there were two warm bodies nearby, ideal before mating, laying the eggs, he had to find them, no, not him, he wasn't them, he was Andi, he had to return to his body, taking in air through his lungs, not his trachea, there was George, touching him, anchoring him, guiding him back, Andi was back—

Andi took in a huge lungful of air, staring into George's light brown eyes, assuring himself that, yes, this was his body, his reality, and everything was fine. The worry in George's expression was mixed with a hint of triumph, because the toupee was caught on a small island of grass, where it was clearly visible from the trail. They waded closer to it, inspecting the piece of hair.

"I think this is our lucky day." George pointed at the hem of the toupee, where a visible chunk of skin was attached.

"Perfect. Now we have every reason to report this. Let's get rid of the stem and then call the police." Andi turned toward the shore, only to be stopped by George.

"Andi. Am I mistaken or is it getting worse? Some of the things you said—about taking flight and feeding—worried me."

Andi froze, kept his back deliberately to George. Yes, it was getting worse; it had been getting worse since the day he was born, but the speed had accelerated, his senses getting sharper, and he had problems keeping up with reinforcing his mental shields. It was nothing George could help him with, so he didn't want to talk about it.

"It's fine. I just have to meditate more."

2. WATER CORPSES

"IT'S FINE. I just have to meditate more." George would have loved to call BS, but the harassed expression in Andi's eyes just before he had turned his back on George was enough to keep his mouth shut. His partner was hurting, and there was little George could do apart from being there and offering his silent support. He was glad Andi had opened up to him as much as he had. Pushing his luck by pressuring his partner would only result in Andi going all hedgehog, shutting the world—and George—out with his prickles fully extended. Not being able to help his partner grated on George's nerves, activating a protective instinct he hadn't known he possessed until he met Andi. Knowing he had to tone it down until Andi was in a more receptive mood, George got his cell out to take some pictures of the toupee, as well as the area surrounding it. When dealing with drowned people, placement of potential evidence was crucial, even if it was deliberate in this case. Since there was no current to speak of and no connecting body of water where the corpses could have come from, it was quite obvious they hadn't moved a great deal. Still, it was necessary to have the chain of evidence as clear-cut as possible to gloss over the parts where they had to get creative. In the past months, George had learned a lot about ingenious report writing and the psychology of nudging a reader in a certain direction. They were skills he definitely wanted to know more about, and Andi was a true master.

Wading out of the water, the stem floating behind him, George watched as Andi talked to the operator on the phone. By the time George had gotten rid of the stem, placing it back where he had found it, Andi had ended the call.

"They're on their way, bringing divers and everything."

George noticed the dark circles under Andi's eyes, a sure indicator of his level of stress. At the moment, he was just this side of still functioning normally, more like an automaton than an actual person. Gently, George guided his partner back to the trail, put the blanket from his backpack on the ground, urged Andi to sit down, and started getting out the plastic containers with the food he had prepared for their trip. It was nothing fancy, plain old sandwiches made from sourdough bread with cheese and salami, two apples, and two bottles of water. Andi wolfed the sandwich down, guzzled the water as if he had just crossed a desert before he bit into the apple with a crunching sound. It put part of George's worries to rest, because with Andi, a healthy appetite was another positive sign of relative stability, meaning his partner was able to hold it together for the time being. George refused to think about the headache Andi would be nursing later that day.

"I wonder how they're going to haul all the equipment here." Andi had swallowed the bite from the apple and made a sweeping gesture with the hand holding the fruit. George looked around, the beauty of their surroundings reminding him why he had nagged Andi to go on this hike with him. Annoying mosquitoes aside, the Swamp Fox Trail was simply gorgeous, different kinds of warblers singing in the huge cypress trees growing majestically between patches of long brown grass and differently sized puddles of brackish water. The air had a clear quality to it, the scents riding on the soft breeze so much better than the stink of car exhaust and asphalt in the city. It had been a good idea to come here, at least in theory. Finding three dead bodies was not how he had envisioned their trip ending. Why couldn't people keep the murdering and dying to the cities and leave the countryside alone for stressed-out cops to enjoy in peace? It was an unkind thought, and George mentally chastised himself for having it. It wasn't the victims' fault they had been killed, and it also wasn't their fault that George was stressed. Operating in the area of tension between Andi and Chief Norris was taking its toll, the growing animosity making George wonder when Chief Norris would finally snap and go back on her word to help him once he left Charleston PD for the next step in his career. Since he hadn't given her what she wanted—dirt on Andi—she had started acting as if he was now under suspicion as well. Luckily for him and Andi, their solving rates were at a solid 100 percent so far, so there wasn't much she could do. Still, George would have preferred a more amicable relationship with his boss.

"I'm sure they have the right vehicles to do it." His reaction to Andi's comment was a little late. Andi took it in stride, one of the many things George liked about his new partner. Andi was so antisocial himself, he rarely got offended when George didn't act within the parameters of what other people would consider polite behavior. If George hadn't answered at all, Andi wouldn't have started wondering if George was angry with him or if there was another problem like almost every other partner or person would have. Andi would have just put it down to George not having anything meaningful to contribute, a correct assumption on his part.

Andi finished his apple while George chewed on his sandwich, listening to the birdsong and soft gurgling of all the water surrounding them. When Andi tensed next to him, George knew their break from the job was over. It still took another ten minutes until he could hear the rumbling of the engines of whatever vehicles were used to get to this place, time he utilized to get all their belongings back into their backpacks before hanging them on the sturdy branch of a cypress right next to the trail where they weren't likely to forget them. The first vehicle came into sight, an ATV with the emblem of the Palmetto Conservation Foundation at the front, followed by five ATVs from the Charleston PD. George hadn't even known the PD owned ATVs, but it made sense; they lived in an area where they did come in handy. All five of them had trailers attached, four of them with open beds packed tight with all the equipment the divers needed. The fifth had a closed trailer, presumably for the bodies. On first sight, it didn't look large enough to house all three of them, but George kept his mouth shut. Their story was about finding a toupee with bits of skin on it, which meant everybody was working on the assumption of there being one victim. He and Andi would have to be very careful regarding their reaction when the divers found three of them. With every day George worked with Andi, he understood better how very complicated it was to use his *geschenk* without tipping his hand.

The woman driving the ATV with the foundation emblem parked her vehicle close to where Andi and George had their picnic before she directed the other vehicles to different spots, obviously trying to keep the damage to the area to a minimum. When she was satisfied with the placement of every vehicle, she made her way over to them, followed by a tall man and Evangeline Melcourt, their coroner. Evangeline waved at them from behind the tall man, letting the woman do the introductions. She held out her hand, which was hard and warm in George's, the hand of somebody doing manual labor on a daily basis. There were laugh lines around her glittering brownish eyes, her blond hair was in a tight braid, and her smile was open and friendly.

"Hi, I'm Roberta Ingman, you can call me Berta, and this is Forrester Payne from the Underwater Response and Swiftwater Rescue Team." She indicated the tall African American man behind her who held out his hand to George, while Berta shook Andi's. "I believe you know your coroner."

George grinned. "Yes, yes we do. Hi, Berta and Forrester. I'm George Donovan from Charleston PD, and this is my partner, Andi Hayes. As he said on the phone, we were hiking this area and found a toupee with bits of skin over there at the edge of the lake." He pointed in the direction of the lake, effectively diverting the focus from Andi, who hated nothing more than having to meet new people, to the task at hand, namely finding three corpses he and Andi supposedly didn't know anything about yet.

"How do you want to proceed?" Forrester turned to Evangeline, who looked at Berta.

"CSI is on the way, and with water it's important to secure the area and search for any evidence before going in. What can you tell us about this lake?"

Berta shrugged. "There's not much to tell. As you can see, it's not big. The deepest spot is about seven feet, and there's no current to speak of because the water feeding it comes from several wells and smaller brooks. There is no flow; the water just trickles away into the surrounding soil. The weather during the last two weeks was good, no storms. Whoever has lost that toupee should be nearby. If the person died, that is."

Evangeline squared her shoulders. "Fine. Forrester, could you and your divers start searching the perimeter, everything within an eight-foot radius around the lake? I leave it to your expertise how many divers you send into the lake. I could imagine searching it is difficult because it's so murky. And please get me that toupee."

Forrester nodded. "I'm going to send two divers in. This lake is uncharted territory, because it's not attractive as a diving spot. We're doing a preliminary search based on the current that has placed the toupee where it is. With any luck, we'll find nobody."

"Yes, let's hope." Evangeline didn't look convinced. She had been working with Andi too long not to know that there was always a corpse when he called something in. Forrester and Evangeline returned to the ATVs, Forrester barking out orders while Evangeline started to prepare her own gear. Andi, George, and Berta were not needed at the moment and just tried to keep out of the way.

George made some light conversation with Berta, who was a very nice person with tons of stories about the Swamp Fox Trail, while Andi sat down on a fallen tree trunk, simply staring into nothing. George knew he was trying to shut out the images of all the arthropods who were disturbed by the vehicles and divers. When insects got agitated, it was harder for Andi to keep them out, and the kindest thing George could do for his partner in situations like these was providing him with the space he needed to concentrate on his breathing and mental shields. Berta didn't seem to mind. She glanced at Andi once or twice but had the decency to respect the invisible wall he had erected around himself.

It only took the divers half an hour to find the corpses, Evangeline calling in another ATV when it was clear there was more than one. CSI arrived at the same time Forrester's divers brought the first corpse out of the water, a grisly sight George could have done without. He'd always hated water corpses, their bloated bodies with the rubbery, shrunken skin and the veins shining through the flesh like ghastly roadmaps reminding him of a zombie film he'd seen as teenager. George had learned that evening that zombies were where his mind drew the line, and he'd slept with the lights on for the next six months, much to the amusement of his two older brothers. When he'd started in law enforcement, he had feared seeing corpses would trigger something, but it only happened with bodies found in water.

Andi was completely unfazed. He had once told George that because of his *geschenk*, he tended to see corpses in general as a source of nourishment. At first George had been appalled by the idea of viewing human remains as food. After working with Andi for almost half a year, he understood him better and could even see how dehumanizing the corpses helped Andi to compartmentalize the many deaths he was confronted with. And after listening to Andi describing corpses while he was actively linked to the arthropods in an area, George had started viewing them in a more pragmatic light as well. They were still humans, but only because he was human himself. Knowing there were millions of creatures who saw the very same thing in a completely different light was a sobering, humbling thought.

But water corpses were water corpses, and George had to force himself to inspect the first one, who was now put on a stretcher Evangeline had prepared. It was an elderly black man with a shock of thick white hair. He had no visible wounds on his face or body, as was often typical for water corpses because of the water dragging them over hard surfaces. The chains wound around his upper body down to his knees were weighted with stones that were attached to the chain links with small strips of leather.

Evangeline took several photos of the corpse before she closed the body bag and told one of her assistants to bring the body back to the city and into the fridge as quickly as possible. Water corpses tended to decompose at an accelerated speed once they were back on land, and if Evangeline wanted to preserve any evidence, she had to be quick.

George watched as the ATV with the corpse started in the direction of Charleston. About ten minutes later, two more ATVs appeared to transport the other two bodies while CSI combed through the area. It was getting dark, the whole ordeal having eaten up the entire day, and high-power beams were set up, the generators disturbing the peace of the area with their loud humming. Berta was less than happy and watched all the proceedings like a hawk, sometimes bellowing at people to be more careful. When the last body was on its way to the precinct, Andi and George decided it was time to head there as well. They walked back, using two flashlights they had borrowed from CSI. Once they were out of earshot, Andi started the mind game they always played when confronted with a new case. It was meant to force them to look at the facts without considering whatever Andi had already gained from his little informants, thus making the build-up of the case as solid and plausible as possible before they started following clues nobody else knew about.

"What do you think?"

George gathered his thoughts. "Three older men, bound with chains and drowned in a lake hardly deep and big enough to take the bodies. According to Berta there are no alligators here because the lake doesn't offer enough prey. It's information everybody could easily access by simply looking at the website of the foundation. According to Evangeline, the corpses haven't been in the water for long, four days max, and their clothes suggest they weren't poor. Some kind of drug deal gone wrong? But we don't have any big drug wars going on at the moment. Revenge? Weapon dealing? The possibilities are endless. I'd say it's most likely something shady. How did they get there? Why weren't their ankles bound as well? Did somebody force them into the water?"

It was a long list of questions, one that would hopefully shorten once Evangeline was done with the autopsies. Andi made a humming sound in the back of his throat. He always did that when he was going through options. George found it a little unnerving how well he knew his partner after such a short amount of time—with his previous partners, it had taken him a lot longer to get to know them even half as well. In most cases, he had been gone before he reached this level of familiarity. He blamed Andi's *geschenk*. Because his partner needed extra care, George was a lot more attentive when it came to his quirks and behavioral patterns.

"Whatever it is, it's big."

"I agree. Any thoughts?"

"Apart from what you said? No. I'm curious what Evangeline is going to find out."

"Yeah, let's hope she comes up with some substantial clues. It would be nice to work with some scientifically proven evidence for a change."

Andi mock gasped. "Are you saying you don't like the evidence I provide?"

"I love the evidence you provide, especially when it helps us catch a killer. What I don't like is writing reports filled with the equivalent of fairy dust and rainbows."

"I resent that. It's good for your creativity and teaches you to think outside the box." There was a hint of laughter in Andi's voice. He loved teasing George about his admittedly strict take on rules and the proper handling of things. Andi was much more relaxed when it came to writing reports and stuff, though George had to admit his partner was never sloppy. Just casual.

"I'm doing my best, and I dare say I've already gotten better."

"That you have." All amusement was gone from Andi's voice, leaving behind an earnestness George didn't know what to make of. They marched on in silence, both of them lost in their own thoughts.

At the precinct, Chief Norris was already awaiting them, her arms crossed in front of her upper body. She didn't look happy, and George wasn't sure if it was the late hour—it was now after ten in the evening— the fact they had brought in three corpses, or general annoyance with Andi and, by extension, George.

"Detectives, it seems your knack for finding trouble is getting stronger every month." It sounded like an accusation. As usual, Andi ignored the chief completely and left it to George to deal with her.

"We weren't actively looking, I can assure you. All we wanted was some peace and quiet."

"Instead, you got three corpses."

"Yes." George had found out it was best to let Chief Norris butt her head against a polite but firm wall until she gave up. Since she usually went home around six, she ran out of steam quickly.

"I'm expecting your reports tomorrow."

"Of course, Chief." George gave her a brief nod.

With furrowed brows, the chief left for her office. George followed Andi to their desks, where his partner had already fired up his PC.

"Let's write this stupid report and then go home. There's not much we can do until Evangeline is done with the autopsies assuming the chief is handing the case to us."

Which was a fifty-fifty chance. After the spectacular solve and busting of the human trafficking ring in spring, Chief Norris had used their excellent performance as an excuse to saddle them with what she thought of as the nastiest cases that came up, obviously secretly hoping they would either fail or make a mistake that gave her an excuse to get rid of Andi. Depending on who the victims were and how thin evidence was, she would decide who got the case. Chief Norris wasn't exactly subtle in her endeavors to establish other detectives as the stars of Charleston PD by giving them the slam-dunk cases, but had yet to be successful. Thanks to Andi's *geschenk*, they had cracked cases other detectives would have never been able to solve, had even made it look easy—which it was for Andi—and much to Chief Norris's anger and George's secret delight, everybody knew it. Her tactics weren't working, and it made her crankier every day. George was waiting for the moment when she finally exploded, already preparing himself for war with the chief because he was determined not to take any shit from her. He sat down at his desk, started his own PC, and got ready to spin a tale of plausibility.

3. A NEW CASE

THE NEXT morning, it took Andi only one look into Chief Norris's thunderous expression to know they had the case. She didn't even wait until they had taken off their jackets before she beckoned them into her office. George rolled his eyes and put on his pleasant face, a mask he wore a lot when he had to deal with people. Sometimes Andi wished he had such a mask himself, one that would help him get along better with the human population in general. Then he thought about how much energy it cost to keep such a façade going and was glad he'd given up on being amiable long ago.

In her office, Chief Norris motioned them to sit before she cut right to the chase, not wasting any time with fake pleasantries, which was the one thing Andi could appreciate about her. They didn't like each other, they both had acknowledged it, so there was no need to play pretend.

"Detectives, I just got a call from the mayor. Dr. Melcourt was able to identify the three victims, they were upstanding citizens of Charleston, and she wants the PD's best detectives on the case, which is you."

Andi wondered how much it had cost her to say those words and had no shame enjoying her discomfort.

"I'm sure it's superfluous to stress how important it is for you to be successful and finding the killer or killers as soon as possible." Now there was a hint of glee in her voice, telling Andi she had no problem with this high-profile case going south as long as she could blame him and George. What a stupid cow. Andi kept his mouth shut, though, letting George do the talking, which was the more peaceful option for everybody involved.

"We understand, Chief Norris. If there isn't anything else, we would like to get started right away."

The chief dismissed them with a wave of her hand. They deposited their jackets at their desks before heading to the morgue.

When they got there, Evangeline was waiting for them, the dark circles under her eyes telling them she had probably worked the entire night. Without a word, Andi handed her his herbal tea, which he hadn't had time to drink yet. She took it with a grateful nod, sipped a few times, and closed her eyes for a moment. When she opened them again, a little spark of life had returned.

"Good morning, gentlemen."

"Good morning, Evangeline." They said it in unison, almost as if they were at school. It provoked the ghost of a smile on Evangeline's lips, which was worth the embarrassment.

"*Aulelei*. Please follow me." She led them into one of the autopsy rooms, refraining from taking out the slabs as she usually did and instead attacked her tablet with sharp pokes until some X-ray images appeared on the huge flat-screen at the far wall. "You're looking at the skeleton of Harry Alexander McHill, sixty-nine, Caucasian, a businessman who made his fortune with real estate. These—" She swiped her finger across the tablet, causing the X-rays to change on the screen. "—are the bones of David Hector Portius II, seventy-one, Caucasian and senior partner at Portius, Dayson & Partners, a prestigious law firm here in Charleston and owner of the toupee that has led to finding them. The last one—" Again the screen changed. "—is Lawrence Miller, sixty-seven, African American, who's made his money in the stock market. None of them showed signs of abuse, no broken bones, no abrasions. If it weren't for the chains and rocks, I'd say it almost looks as if they went into the water voluntarily. I'm still waiting for the report on any toxins in their blood, though I don't have high hopes on any substantial finds. For that the bodies had been underwater for too long. The clothing is with CSI to look for any traces the water hasn't washed away. Unfortunately, the acidic nature of swamp water isn't in our favor. What does help is the short time they spent underwater. I still have to run some additional tests, but I'm fairly sure it was three days, four at the most. I'm hoping to get you a definite time frame, which, again, hinges on the evidence we can secure from the clothing and the chains. Any questions?"

Andi stared at the X-rays of Lawrence Miller, wondering what had happened to him and the other two men. The insects hadn't given him any indication how the victims had found their way into the lake, too occupied with them being *there*. Andi knew that at some point, he would have to go back to the crime scene and try to discern what went down, and he wasn't looking forward to it. He had felt some small ant colonies in the area who would at least be able to provide him with a frame of reference, murky as it might be because ants tended to sleep at night. The important information he would have to get from the larvae in the water and the flying insects around the lake, which was always harder than diving into the hive mind of social insects. Thanks to their strict hierarchies, social insects stored information in an almost orderly fashion, while the images provided by solitary insects were more random and harder to understand.

The names Evangeline had provided them were a good starting point for actual police work, which would offer Andi the chance to form a greater picture, and in turn made it easier for him to look for specific clues from his army of informants.

"No, not at the moment. George?"

His partner shrugged. "You gave us the names. We start from there and see what pops up."

"*Manuia ia te a'u.* I'll call as soon as I have the reports."

"Thank you, Evangeline. Get some sleep." Andi winked at her. She raised the cup with the herbal tea in a mock salute.

After getting back to their desks, George immediately went to his beloved whiteboard to write the names of the victims down. Andi started his computer, found the email with the information Evangeline had already sent them, and helped George get the details right. Then they started a search in the database, finding out everything they could about the three men. Each of them was what people would call a pillar of society, rich older men who donated generously to several charities in Charleston and could be found on every high-profile fundraiser happening in the city. Andi was instantly suspicious because, as the case with Jake Castain had driven home, having a respectable façade didn't mean you were a good person. All the victims were married, Lawrence Miller for the second time, and they each had a son. Andi started typing on his PC, looking at the Missing Persons databank. No entry for any of the three victims.

"George?"

"Hmm?" George was still engrossed, alternately staring at the names on the whiteboard and his screen, where he had pictures of them from some charity event this summer. Andi could practically see the gears turning in his partner's head. George may not have Andi's net of informants, but he was a damn good detective with great deductive skills.

"Look." Andi turned his own screen around so George could see it. His eyes widened.

"I'll be damned. They've been dead for three to four days and nobody called the police?"

"No."

"I wonder why."

"Me too." Andi turned the screen back. "I think we should pay the widows a visit. We have to inform them anyway, and I sure have some questions for them."

"Let's get going, then. The gossip pages aren't going to vanish any time soon." George grabbed his jacket and keys. "They all live in Berkeley County. Brings up memories." He grinned, albeit a little grimly.

"At least this time, we're going there with definite addresses and not on an 'anonymous tip.'" Andi put air quotes around the last two words, raising his brows at the same time. The grimness vanished from George's face, replaced by an amused smile.

"You can be amazingly funny if you put your mind to it. You should try it more often."

Andi didn't know anything about being funny. He had just made an attempt to distract George from the memories of their first case. If his partner thought it funny, Andi wouldn't protest.

"No. Otherwise people might think I'm becoming approachable, and I'm more than happy with the status quo." Just thinking about having to deal with the demands of other human beings had Andi shivering. It was just too much trouble and rarely worth it.

George snorted. "Believe me, nobody is going to think that."

Andi followed his partner downstairs and into the parking lot where George's Escalade was parked. These days Andi rarely drove himself, was picked up for work by George, rode shotgun during their workday, and when he had errands to run, George generally drove him as well. Andi had never asked George to do this for him but was insanely grateful for it. Driving had always been hard for him and afforded an amount of focus Andi had to fight for. With his *geschenk* becoming more intense, Andi driving himself was more a game of Russian Roulette than anything else. George didn't know just how bad things were getting; all he knew was that Andi didn't like driving, and the one time Andi had tried to thank him for it, he had simply shrugged and said he preferred his partner alive and, more importantly, able to help him acquire a flawless solving rate. Their driving arrangement was perfect as far as Andi was concerned, so perfect he didn't dare think what he was going to do when George finally left him.

During their drive to Berkeley County, they tossed some ideas around, talked about how the DA was finally getting ready to drag Castain and Harris, the two leaders of the trafficking ring, in front of a judge, and how much they weren't looking forward to being on the witness stand. It was the part of his work Andi hated most, and not only because he had to wear a suit and tie for it.

The first address they reached was that of Harry Alexander McHill. He lived—had lived—in a huge villa at the end of a long, winding driveway flanked by huge cypress and oak trees, very much like Castain's villa and probably every other home in this neighborhood. McHill's property was surrounded by an eight-foot stone wall. The iron gate through which George had driven had been apparently operated from the house; the camera zooming in on their ID was latest standard. The house itself was a monstrosity in white and peach, the style reminiscent of the old Southern planation homes, though with a modern touch that made it hideous instead of charming. George parked in front of the stairs to the main entrance, glancing at Andi with a teasing smile.

"Do you want to do the honors?"

Andi scowled. "Are you kidding me? I thought we had established that's the main reason I'm keeping you—not having to make the death announcements myself."

George laughed. It was a running gag between them—one with so much truth behind it, Andi avoided thinking too much about it.

George raised his hands. "It's good to know my place in our partnership."

"And don't you forget it."

They left the car. Before they had reached the final step leading to the front door, it opened, revealing the stick-thin body of a woman in a butler's uniform. She was about Andi's height, her graying hair swept up in an elegant chignon, her sharp dark eyes dissecting them, and her expression showing she found them wanting.

"What can I do for you, gentlemen?"

To Andi, it sounded more like "Go away and never come back, scum," but before he could start bristling, George stepped forward, his social smile number four—open but not too bright, indicating polite interest without being invasive—plastered onto his lips.

"I'm Detective George Donovan, and this is my partner, Detective Andrew Hayes. We're very sorry for the interruption, but we do need to speak with Mrs. McHill about her husband. It's urgent."

Andi had been watching the woman closely, trying to get a read on her body language. The way her eyes quickly darted sideways told Andi she did know something, though what that something was, he couldn't guess. He already knew from the arthropods that there were four other people in the house, two in the kitchen, one in what seemed to be a sunroom, spraying something nasty onto the roses, which the aphids hated, and one in an upstairs room. Nobody was stressed or worried, the silverfish and mites and spiders content. Harry Alexander McHill apparently wasn't missed. Interesting.

The woman was clearly weighing her options before she made a step back and sideways to let them in. "Please follow me."

She started marching along the corridor with its tiled floor until they reached an oak door. She opened it and gestured for them to enter. "Please, make yourselves comfortable. I'm going to get Mrs. McHill."

The butler was gone before either of them could say something. George walked farther into the room with two huge windows looking out into part of the garden—or rather park—and the four armchairs cased in soft blue brocade. The golden tassels at the front of the armrests were a bit over-the-top in Andi's opinion, as well as the coffee table with the golden inlays.

"What did you pick up on?" George had finished his round through the room, stopped next to one of the armchairs.

"Four more people in the house, no grief or stress, at least not recently. Everything is peaceful, except for the aphids dying in the sunroom right this moment. A serious case of mass murder."

Curiosity shone in George's face. "Does it bother you? When they die, I mean."

Andi thought about it. "Probably not in the way you think. Being linked to something alive means you do feel a sense of loss when it's gone. Mostly, it's annoying, because the sensations of them dying are intense, and afterward, there's a void where the moment before there was so much, and then other images fill the void like a high tide crushing in and I have to adapt again."

"I'm never sure what to say when you explain these things to me." George rubbed his hand over his face. "I want to help you and know I can't. It's—vexing."

"Don't worry. I'm used to it. And you can help me when it gets too much. That's more than I had before."

George sighed. "Doesn't mean I like it."

Andi didn't know how to react to this statement and was glad when the door opened to reveal the watchdog, aka the female butler who had brought them to this room. She entered the room, leading a typical Southern lady in. Sophia McHill was around five four, fifty-eight, with a body toned by a strict sports regimen, a face that had seen the help of needles and probably a scalpel, which gave her that eerie aura of looking old while at the same time kind of preserved, perfectly coiffed shoulder-length blond hair, and dressed in an elegant cream A-line dress and pumps, which made her look like part of the interior design.

"Mrs. McHill, these are Detectives George Donovan and Andrew Hayes. Detectives, this is Mrs. McHill." The butler turned to the woman. "Do you need anything, Mrs. McHill?"

The woman appraised George and Andi with a sharp look, no doubt trying to discern why they were here. Andi didn't get the feeling she was nervous or unnerved. If he had to guess, he'd say bored, which was probably the reason she hadn't called her lawyer yet. She shook her head. "Thank you, Christin, that will be all."

The butler—Christin—left with a nod. It didn't escape Andi that they weren't offered anything, not even a glass of water. A not-so-subtle hint how unwelcome they were.

"Detectives, what can I do for you? I'm sure you're aware how unusual it is for the police to just come over and demand entry." Sophia McHill's voice was a pleasing, carefully neutral alto, revealing even less than the Botox mask she had for a face. Her words also made clear how perfectly aware she was that she didn't have to tell them anything, one of the hassles when dealing with the obscenely rich.

George wasn't deterred in the least, his manners as polished as always. This time he was using his social smile number two, reserved for women not old enough to be grandmothers and no longer young enough to flirt with, infusing it with just enough wattage to make them feel flattered but well within the boundaries of propriety. Andi loved watching George doing this dance. It was always fun to see a master in action.

"Mrs. McHill, we're so sorry to inconvenience you, and of course we're very much aware how inappropriate our visit is, but I'm afraid we bring grave news. Perhaps you want to sit down?" George gently took Sophia's left arm to guide her toward one of the armchairs, effectively taking charge of the situation. She let it happen, her face still unreadable, her eyes softening a bit in the face of George's charm. Once she was seated, George took the opposite chair, while Andi kept standing, slightly out of the way to leave George room.

"What is the grave news, Detective Donovan? I have to admit you're worrying me."

George schooled his features into an earnest expression. "Yesterday afternoon your husband was found dead in a lake along the Swamp Fox Trail. You have my condolences."

Andi watched Sophia for her reaction, which was more difficult because of the Botox. The two spiders in the room didn't catch a flare in pheromones indicating stress. If anything, she was relieved. Her facial expression remained unperturbed; there was only a strange gleam in her eyes Andi couldn't interpret, especially not with the knowledge he had gained from the spiders. It was all rather strange.

"Oh my. This is sad news."

The understatement of the year, at least for a widow. George cocked his head, clearly unsure how to proceed. Usually this was the point where he offered some consolation and tried to get people to calm down enough for further questioning. Since this was moot, he needed a moment to get back on track.

"As I said, we're very sorry for your loss. We do have some questions for you, if you feel up to it."

"Thank you. And yes. I can answer some questions." Sophia McHill sounded distracted now, as if she were already planning her late husband's funeral or what to do with the money she would surely inherit.

"The coroner said your husband died about three days ago, and we're wondering why he hasn't been reported missing." George kept any and all accusation painstakingly out of his voice, infusing his tone with nothing but genuine curiosity. So far, Sophia McHill was cooperating with them, and the last thing they needed was for her to clam up and call the family lawyer. That would complicate things unnecessarily.

He probably needn't have bothered, because Sophia McHill didn't seem to pick up on anything. She was as calm as could be. "That's because I wasn't expecting him back until the day after tomorrow. He was supposed to be on a hunting trip with two of his friends, David Portius and Lawrence Miller. They try to meet at least once a month, and around this time of the year, they spend as much time as possible at their cabin at Lake Moultrie. They never bother calling because it's their 'free time.'"

The air quotes she put around the words "free time" made perfectly clear what she thought of the whole affair.

George briefly looked at Andi. That explained a lot. George turned back to Sophia. "Who else knew about this trip?"

She shrugged. "I'm afraid I can't say for sure. Tamara and Theodora, for sure. The staff at their houses. I don't know if they told anybody at work."

Tamara Portius and Theodora Miller, the wives of the other two victims. And the staff and potential acquaintances at work. So basically everybody who wanted to find out could have done so easily. Andi hated it when the pool of suspects opened up so wide.

"Thank you, Mrs. McHill. If you could give us the address of the cabin, that would be all for now. We'll contact you as soon as we have news."

George very carefully avoided mentioning the other two victims, and if Sophia picked up on it or the fact that they hadn't asked who Tamara and Theodora were, she didn't ask. Which meant she either didn't care in the least or knew already.

"I'll tell Christin to give you the address. Do you have an estimate for when I could plan the funeral? There is a lot to arrange, as you surely are aware."

"I'm sorry, Mrs. McHill, it all depends on how our investigation goes and how quickly we can get to the bottom of it all."

"Oh. So it wasn't an accident?"

This was the first time Andi heard something akin to interest in the woman's voice.

"We're not sure yet, Mrs. McHill. As I said, investigations are underway. We will keep you informed." George was smooth as always, blocking her without outright lying. If Sophia became a suspect—and Andi was inclined to put her on that list based on her reactions—she would feel safer believing they weren't sure about the death yet. Culprits who felt safe were better than panicking ones, at least at this stage of the investigation.

Mrs. McHill called back her butler, bid them farewell a little less frostily than she had welcomed them, and vanished in the depths of the huge house. Christin gave them the address of the cabin and saw them out the door. Back in the car, Andi waited till they were back on the road toward Lawrence Miller's house before he broke the silence.

"That was interesting."

"Oh yeah." George snorted. "Sophia McHill definitely has to work on her grieving-widow part. She didn't seem too upset about her husband's demise."

"She also didn't see a need to make us believe she was upset." Andi looked out the window. "If she had something to do with her husband's death, wouldn't she try to convince us how dear he was to her? And she didn't call her lawyer."

"Normally, I would say yes. But we're dealing with the upper crust here, and if Jake Castain has taught me one thing, it's that these people often feel invincible because of their status and money."

"True. She's definitely a suspect, though I think we should keep in mind that marriages are not always happy, and her indifference could be simply because she doesn't have any feelings for the man."

George nodded. "Let's see what the other widows have to say."

As it turned out, Tamara Portius and Theodora Miller were just as indifferent as Sophia McHill. They, too, let them in without calling the family lawyer, understandably at least in Tamara's case because her deceased husband probably *was* the family lawyer, and confirmed Sophia's story about the men being on a hunting trip. Theodora Miller was a little more polite than Sophia and Tamara, offering them iced tea and cookies. She also seemed a little more rattled than the other two women, seemingly not as used to masking her feelings as they were—which could be because she hadn't yet used Botox or other means to freeze her facial expressions—but overall, the stories and reactions of the women matched, perhaps a little too well.

It was already four in the afternoon when they returned to Charleston, but after a brief discussion, they decided to visit the sons of the victims as well, in the hopes of perhaps catching them unaware of their fathers' deaths. It was unlikely that their mothers—or stepmother in Lester Miller's case—hadn't contacted them yet, but even if they had, chances were the sons were rattled enough to slip. If there was slipping for them to do.

4. ESTRANGED SONS

GEORGE DROVE into the Park Circle area, looking for Sanders Avenue, where David Hector Portius III worked as a lawyer. That he wasn't in the same firm where his father had been senior partner made George wonder about the nature of the relationship between father and son. David wasn't part of a firm; he worked alone and advertised on the local TV channels, which put him far beneath the level his father had been on. It could be some twisted game of the son having to earn the merits his father's status could bestow on him, though George doubted it. When there was proving to do, why wouldn't David Hector II want it be done where he could see it directly? Perhaps the son simply wanted to make it on his own—unlikely, but not completely impossible. Or, and this was where things would get interesting, there was bad blood between father and son.

The GPS directed George to a building that had seen better days about fifty years ago, too new for the architecture to be considered charming, too old to be seen as desirable. This was also true for the rest of the neighborhood, which was still well out of the range of shabby and run-down but no longer pristine either. Mediocre. Just like David Hector III's legal services, if the short internet search Andi had conducted while George was driving was accurate.

"This guy looks so boring, I want to yawn just looking at his picture." Andi's voice had that aggressive undertone George had learned to associate with his partner trying to get used to the influx of the insects surrounding them. In an area like this, where old age had created prime living conditions for any kind of creepy crawlers, the barrage of images was usually worse than in newer places.

"Anything we need to be aware of?"

Andi shook his head. "Surprisingly, there's not a single corpse in the vicinity. A few days ago there was an accident close by, at least two, no, three people lost a lot of blood, cars were crashed, it was all quite noisy, and brutal enough to catapult brain tissue far enough for a colony of ants to profit from it. The blood was wasted, though."

The mention of insects feeding meant Andi was a little more open than George would have preferred at the moment, considering they were going to interrogate a potential suspect. He refrained from mentioning it, though, knowing Andi was trying hard to shut the arthropods out as best as he could.

George parked the car in front of the building, and they both got out and went for the entrance. It was a double door with faux oak inlays that were chipping, and a surely once gleaming brass plate to the right where the names of the residing businesses had been engraved. Now there were printed-out papers covering most of the plate, announcing the new inhabitants of the building, the old ones long forgotten. Mr. Portius III had his office on the second floor, where they went via the stairs. Another thing George had learned quickly was to never enter a lift Andi didn't want to set foot in. The staircase smelled of old food, a hint of mold, and some kind of detergent that obviously wasn't able to keep the tiled floor clean. Not surprising given how many cracks George could spot in the reddish stone. He didn't want to think about all the tiny legs hiding between and under those stones. When they reached the second floor, finding Portius's office was easy—there were only three doors, one with red-and-white barrier tape and a shield warning people to keep out because of ongoing repairs, the other with the name of an overseas company written on the glass upper half of the door. The third door down the short corridor was the charm, announcing the office of David Hector Portius III, lawyer for family matters. The letters looked new, as did the door itself, a thing with a light wood veneer that seemed strangely out of place amidst the washed-out green linoleum of the floor and the yellow-tinged wallpapers with water stains close to the ceiling.

George glanced at Andi, who had his eyes closed in preparation for this confrontation. He reached for the bell next to the door, the shrill sound exactly what George had expected in this place. The small speaker beneath the bell button crackled ominously, before a distorted male voice asked them in, followed by a buzzing that sounded way too important for its surroundings. George opened the door and stepped inside, leaving it to Andi to close the door. His partner liked to stay in the background, observing, connecting information he got both from his human and insect senses, while George provided the distraction and took over the human interaction, later comparing the results to what Andi had learned. The system worked perfectly and was much easier on Andi's mental well-being because he didn't have to waste energy to conform to societal norms.

The office wasn't big. There was a desk in one corner of the room and one open door to the right, leading into what looked like some kind of document storage room with high industrial shelves overflowing with boxes. Next to that door stood another small table with a Keurig on it, surrounded by several used mugs and coffee stains. The air was stale, though nothing opening the windows couldn't cure. George focused on the man sitting behind the desk. David Hector III was even more unremarkable in life than he had looked in the picture. His Asian heritage from his mother's side manifested itself in his sleek pitch-black hair and a slight slanting of his hazel eyes. The rest of his facial features as well as his build he had definitely gotten from his Caucasian father, as George could see when David Hector III got up to greet them. His suit was clearly not tailored, the sandy color not exactly doing him any favors. Neither did the light blue shirt, which could have given the outfit a bit more pep if only the person wearing it had been less boring. He didn't look like a grieving son, which either meant they had for some reason beat Tamara Portius to informing him, or he had about as much feeling for his father as his mother had shown earlier that day.

"Good day. How can I help you?" The lawyer's voice was as unremarkable as the rest of him, neither pleasant nor grating, it just was.

"Good day, Mr. Portius. My name is George Donovan, and this is my partner, Andrew Hayes. We're detectives with the Charleston PD, and I'm afraid we have to inform you about the death of your father, David Hector II. His body was found yesterday in a small lake."

While George flashed his badge, he kept a close eye on the lawyer, cataloging every twitch of his facial muscles. Or he would have, had there been twitches. Just like his mother and the wives of the other two victims, David Hector III was strangely unperturbed by the news of his sire's death. His mouth formed an *O* while he slumped back onto his desk chair, and that was it. No tears, no demands to be told what happened, no accusations, no joy or relief either, two emotions George had seen a few times too often when delivering the news of a death.

"We're very sorry for your loss." George added the phrase out of politeness, not because he felt it or thought it would do any good. David Hector III shrugged.

"Thank you, Detectives. We weren't close. I think the last time I saw my father was at Christmas, and then only briefly for afternoon tea. He had some function in the evening."

Providing an alibi already. Or the semblance of one. George didn't have to look at Andi to know his partner was regarding the lawyer sharply. Something about the man had all of George's internal alarms shrilling, even more than Jake Castain, and that guy was a grade-A douche.

"I assume from your words you don't know anything about you father's daily schedules or habits?" George still kept it vague. They hadn't mentioned murder yet, and he wanted to see if the man would eventually jump to that conclusion. It wasn't a far stretch by any means. The police didn't make a habit of sending detectives when there was a natural cause to a death, but George wanted to see if the lawyer could perhaps be tempted into saying more than he wanted to.

"As I said, we weren't close. In his opinion, I wasn't ambitious enough." The lawyer made a gesture that included the entire small office.

There was a world of hurt in that one sentence. George had no problem with continuing to poke, though. "Is that the reason you're not working in your father's law firm?"

The wounded puppy dog look with the tragic twisting of the lips could have fooled George. Unfortunately for David Hector III, George made his living detecting liars, and the lawyer was lying through his teeth.

"We don't—didn't—see eye to eye in many things. I needed to get out from under his thumb, and opening my own business was the logical step."

No in-depth information, no details, just enough to shut them up by hinting that their suspicions about a tragic father-son relationship were true. Andi shuffled at George's back, stepping closer to him, which created an intimidating front for the sitting lawyer. George glanced at Andi, who narrowed his eyes, giving an imperceptible shake of his head. His partner wanted the suspiciously unperturbed son to think they had bought into his story. George returned his attention to the lawyer.

"We understand. Families are a complicated thing. Did you know your father was on a hunting trip this week?"

David Hector III shrugged. "I didn't know it was this week specifically, but he always went on trips to the cabin during this time of the year. Usually with two of his oldest friends."

George nodded his thanks, pulling out his wallet to hand the lawyer his card. They couldn't ask for specific alibis yet, since they didn't have an exact time of death, one Evangeline would hopefully provide soon. "Thank you for your time, Mr. Portius. We have to ask you to stay in the area of

Charleston until our investigation is done. Should you think of anything that could help us in the matter, please don't hesitate to contact us."

David Hector III took the card without sparing it a glance. "I will. I wish you a nice afternoon, Detectives."

George and Andi left the office, waiting until they were back in the car before they started talking.

"It seems Southern hospitality is dead. At least in these three families." Andi made a face, as if he were appalled.

George snickered. "Would you have really wanted coffee or tea in one of those mugs?"

Andi shuddered. "No, definitely not. He hasn't washed them in weeks."

George started typing in the address of Lester Miller, who had his small marketing company on Wando Road, close to Palmetto Gardens. Once the GPS started giving him directions, he pulled back into traffic.

"Compassion also seems to be dead in these three families."

"Definitely. He was neither surprised nor bothered by the news of his father's death, very much like the wife." Andi stared out the window. "David Hector II didn't seem to be in line for Father or Husband of the Year Award."

"Absolutely not. But the son's not a helpless victim. This reeks of family feud." And family feuds were always messy. George had seen enough of them to know as much. "The question is how bad is it, and who was willing to commit murder to end it?"

"The family is always under suspicion." Andi chewed on his lower lip. "But I wouldn't dismiss outward sources yet. People who invoke so little feelings in their supposedly loved ones usually have a great pool of enemies to draw from, at least in my experience. And all three of them killed in the same manner? That's what keeps me wondering. If the wives acted together, how did they do it? And why? As far as I know, and I could be very wrong here, mind you, murdering your spouse isn't an appropriate topic for polite company."

George chuckled. "It isn't. Most definitely not. My own mother would be appalled if anybody brought it up over tea. If the men really have been friends for years, the women and sons must know each other quite well."

"Yeah. Though well enough to plot murder?"

Andi had a valid point. A lot of things weren't adding up in this case. George only hoped things would get clearer once they started digging deeper. The drive to Wando Road was blessedly short despite traffic thickening at this hour, and finding Lester Miller's office didn't pose any problems. It was a bit like déjà vu, walking into a building that had been around for some time, trudging through a corridor that had once been inviting, knocking on a door with bold letters telling the world this was the office of Lester Miller Marketing. There was no buzzer, the door was open, and when they entered, they were greeted by the kind of chaos some people thought of as creative. George simply found it annoying. In his opinion, everything in an office had its place and no business straying anywhere else. Lester Miller was standing in front of a whiteboard filled with the name of some brand in the middle and countless colored lines leading away from it. The man was about six feet, with a lean build that was already starting to show signs of a developing paunch around his middle. The artfully ripped black jeans and the band T-shirt gave the impression of a man desperately trying to appear young and hip. It was sad, really.

"Who are you?" The tone, on the other hand, was downright rude.

George flipped his badge, doing the same song and dance he had with David Hector III, this time getting a furrowed brow for his troubles.

"And what do two detectives want from me? Has my father finally done something that will get him into trouble?"

George felt Andi tensing next to him.

"What makes you think we're here because of your father?" George tried to sound bored. Perhaps Lester Miller was a little less guarded than David Hector III.

The man shrugged. "Simple deduction." He sounded so patronizing, George felt his fists twitching. "I haven't done anything, nor have my customers. I'm pretty sure of that. The only person I know who is likely to have trouble with law enforcement is my father."

"Well, you are right, insofar as we're here because of Mr. Lawrence Miller. I regret to inform you that your father was found dead yesterday. We're sorry for your loss."

While the phrases dripped from his lips, George kept a close eye on Lester. His eyes went wide, and then a small smile appeared on his lips.

"The old man has finally croaked."

"You don't seem to be very upset about this." George kept his voice even.

Lester Miller closed the cap on the whiteboard pen he'd been holding the entire time. "I'm not. My father and I haven't spoken in years, and the last time we did, we yelled things at each other no father and son should ever say. I'm not proud of how our relationship ended, but I've been free of my father ever since. His death means as much to me as if you told me a stranger had died."

The barely detectable trembling in Lester's voice told George he was a little more affected than he wanted to admit. The man was rattled, which was good for questioning.

"You really had no contact with him whatsoever? Not even with your mother?"

"If you mean Theodora, she's my stepmother, and no, we don't have any contact either. She's okay, but we had no reason to stay close. My mother, Angelica, returned to Haiti, to her family, after she divorced my father. We skype now and then."

"Did you know your father was on a hunting trip this week?"

"No. I mean, he always goes hunting this time of year, with his two best friends, but as I said, I haven't kept track of my father's affairs for a long time."

George shared a look with Andi. His partner shook his head. They were on the same page. "Thank you for your time, Mr. Miller. If you can think of anything that might be helpful, please don't hesitate to contact us." He gave the man his card and they left.

Back in the car, George looked at Andi. His partner drummed his fingers on the console of the car. "I don't like this. Lester Miller wasn't nearly as stressed as he should have been after hearing of his father's death. There was some sadness, but mainly anticipation."

George lifted a brow. "Can you read emotions now?" He'd meant it as a tease, but Andi was very serious.

"Only to a certain extent and when moths are close. They see the world mainly through pheromones, and emotions produce different combinations I can sometimes distinguish. It's not very exact, but combined with the visual input Lester Miller provided I'm pretty confident. Besides, anticipation has a very distinctive…." Andi started waving his hands in the air, clearly looking for the right word. Another problem with Andi's connection to the world of arthropods was how to convey what he experienced with words George not only knew but *understood* exactly in the way Andi needed him to.

"A very distinctive flavor, no, feeling, or better, the mixture of a flavor and a feeling, like when your leg has fallen asleep and starts prickling all over, only to me it's like a taste and a sensation…. I hate this!" Frustrated, Andi banged his fists on the console. George put his hand on Andi's shoulder. It was a light, brief gesture, stopping his partner's anger from building further.

Even though he didn't talk much, at least not to random people, Andi was always very to the point and concise with his words. Not being able to explain something that was natural to him grated on his nerves. They had started with building their own vocabulary in coherence with what Andi got from the arthropods, but it was slow going because of moments like this one.

"It's okay, Andi, I think I get it. Anticipation is distinct, and there were moths in the room. That's why you could pick up on it."

Andi's shoulders slumped in relief. "Yes. There's a crack between one of the window frames and the wall that leads into a cavity, and there were at least a dozen ash-tip borer moths in it."

"And they identified anticipation." George refrained from making it sound like a question, which would have upset Andi even more. His partner was slowly slipping into explanation mode, a much safer state of mind than the anger from a few moments before.

"Yes, yes. They were more or less asleep, they are nocturnal, after all, but their senses are always alert. Actually, it's easier for me when they rest, because then I just get the information without their interpretation of it."

The last sentence woke George's curiosity, but he didn't dig deeper. They had another suspect to question.

"Do you think we should try Dominic McHill's place of work or his home? It's getting late."

Andi glanced at the clock on the middle console. "I guess we better go to his home. He's a stockbroker and should be done with work by now. Let me find the address." Andi fumbled for his cell, that always seemed to be where he couldn't reach it easily. "Ah, here it is. He lives close to Summerville, which is about forty minutes from where we are. Let me put it in."

Andi typed the address into the GPS. Once the route was loaded, George started the vehicle and weaved back into traffic. On their way over to Summerville, George made a stop at a small deli to buy some sandwiches. It was getting late in the afternoon, and neither of them had had anything substantial the entire day. The sandwiches would tide them over until they could get some real food. Andi chewed his rye bread and cheese while he watched the buildings they passed, almost absentmindedly taking George's water bottle when he tried to put it back in the cupholder and giving it back to him before he was done reaching for it. It was one of the things George loved about having Andi as his shotgun. The man was intuitive to George's needs, probably without noticing it. They ate in companionable silence, mentally getting ready for this last meeting of the day.

Dominic McHill had a small house on Thrasher Drive that could do with a full renovation, including a new coat of paint for the façade. It wasn't what they had expected from somebody who made their money as a stockbroker. According to their research, Dominic wasn't top-notch. He apparently lacked the instinct for the right investments at the right time, but he still should make enough money to not live like this. George parked at the sidewalk in front of the house. "Same procedure as with the last two?"

Andi nodded. "Fine with me. Let's see how indifferent the young Mr. McHill is."

They marched to the house, and George rang the bell. It only took about a minute until somebody asked from the other side, "Who's there?"

"Mr. McHill? We're Detectives George Donovan and Andrew Hayes. Please open the door."

There was some shuffling at the other side before the door opened wide. Dominic McHill was on the shorter side, about five six with a shock of red hair that was thinning at the sides. He had the typical stature of somebody who worked in an office, didn't exercise much, but at least watched his eating habits.

"I guess you're here because of my father?"

Andi made the half step necessary to bring him to George's side instead of remaining behind him. "You already know?"

The man made a vague gesture with his right hand. "My mother called me. Was it murder?"

"We're still investigating. Can we come in, please?" George didn't wait for the affirmative; he simply stepped forward, forcing Dominic McHill backward with his mass alone.

"Of course. Please." The man hastily stepped aside, closed the door once they were inside, and led them to a living room with furniture so clearly secondhand, George just knew there was a story behind where the money McHill made was going. It clearly wasn't his home. The carpet was thin and so old, it was hard to tell its original color, though George suspected it had always been some kind of hideous brown, the wallpaper was peeling off in the corners, the sockets had that yellowish patina indicating they should be at least tested for safety at some point soon, and the way Andi was eyeing the couch told George all he needed to know about its cleanliness.

Their reluctant host gestured for them to sit down on said couch. After a short moment of internal debate, George decided he could always burn his clothes once he got home. They both sat down gingerly, keeping their butts to the very edge of the upholstery, which surely sent a strange message to Dominic McHill. Some things just couldn't be helped.

"Mr. McHill, let me first say, we're sorry for your loss." George rattled the phrase off, already anticipating McHill's response, and he wasn't disappointed.

"Thank you, but it's fine. My father and I weren't close." This was the third time they heard these words. It couldn't be coincidence.

"But you still had contact with him?" George lifted a brow.

Dominic McHill snorted. "If you want to describe a card on my birthday and one on Christmas as contact, then yes, I still had contact. Though I'm pretty sure my mother is the driving force behind it."

"You don't seem to mind too much." George was fishing now.

"I left minding behind me about six years ago. There is just no pleasing some people, and once I realized my father is one of them, I learned to let go. I'm not pretending it was easy or enjoyable, but I'm done with my father. Him dying has little to no impact on my life."

"Did you know your father was on a hunting trip this week?"

"Not this week specifically, but he always went this time of the year. Usually with his two best friends."

George felt the hairs on his nape rising. It was eerie how similar the conversations had been so far. Next to him, Andi shifted his weight just enough to have their thighs touching. His partner found this as disturbing as he did.

"Do you happen to know if your father had any enemies?" George spontaneously decided to add this question.

McHill laughed drily. "As you may already know, my father wasn't a pleasant man. He had tons of enemies. I'm not sure how many of them wanted him actually dead, but I can assure you, almost everybody he had regular contact with has wished him the plague at some point."

George had thought as much. He rose from the couch, suppressing the urge to swipe his butt. Instead he offered Dominic McHill his hand to shake. The man took it, his grip limp, reminding George of a dead fish wrapped in paper, without any force behind it. Definitely not an alpha male. He gave Dominic his card, telling him to call if he remembered anything that might be helpful. George was not going to hold his breath.

Back in the car, he stared at Andi. "Do I want to know what's in that couch?"

"Bedbugs. A healthy colony."

When George felt sweat forming on his forehead, Andi held up a hand. "Don't worry. We didn't take any with us. They were preparing to attack, and it wouldn't have been wise to linger any longer, but we made it out in time."

"I'm going to burn these clothes."

"I told you, there's no need." Andi glanced at him with that funny expression he always got when he thought George was being unreasonable.

"Believe me, there is. Just thinking about bedbugs has me itching all over."

"If it makes you happy. I'm telling you, though, it's a waste of perfectly good clothing."

"In this case, I don't care." George couldn't suppress a shudder. "Anything else I need to know?"

"Dominic McHill is an alcoholic. A heavy one. Which partly explains the state of his home. I'd say he's lost whatever control he had over his life some time ago."

George started the car. "Can you tell how bad it is?"

"You mean how long he has to live?" Andi sounded unbothered. "Something like that is hard to tell, but what I got from the ticks and mosquitoes, his liver has already started shutting down. Depending on how quickly his addiction has developed, he could have started early, like in his twenties, or only recently. Anyway, he's headed for an early grave if he doesn't get a handle on it, and I don't know about you, but he didn't strike me as the kind of person who has a handle on anything in his life."

"No, certainly not." George filed the information about the alcohol under "interesting to know." Addictions tended to complicate cases because addicted people rarely made logical choices. Neither did angry people or people who had been grievously wronged, and there were plenty of those to be found in this case. He thought it may be time to take a step back and think about it all. "It's already late. Why don't I drive you home and we'll see tomorrow if Evangeline has anything new for us."

"A great idea. We can both sleep on what we learned today. I see a lot of digging into the personal interactions of the victims in our future." Obviously Andi had come to the same conclusion, another sign of how well in tune they were by now.

George shuddered. "As do I. And I'm sure it won't be pleasant."

Andi simply nodded.

5. THEORIES

THE NEXT morning saw Andi and George early in Shireen's lair, where they hoped to get more information on the victims. Shireen greeted them with her usual disgusting cheer. The only reason Andi didn't hate her for it was because he knew for her it was as much an armor as his grumpiness was for him.

"Good morning, Shireen. What do you have for us?" Andi still wasn't sure if George was a morning person or not. When he picked Andi up for work, he had already done his early run, so for George it wasn't technically morning anymore. For Andi, morning could stretch well into the afternoon.

"I've got a lot for you." Shireen sighed. "Unfortunately, it seems to be only the tip of the iceberg. There's so much to unravel about these men, it's hard to decide where to start. I went for their financial information first because that's often the most telling." She started tapping at the ever-present tablet in her hand, making the large flat-screen on the wall flicker with pictures of documents. "At first glance, they are rich dudes who seem to be paying their taxes like they should, no shady business going on."

"At first glance?" George raised a brow.

"In my experience people with that much money are never clean, and I've already found some promising leads to dealings that are more dubious."

"What's going to happen with all the money now that they're dead?" It was a question every cop learned to ask early in their career. Money was one of the strongest motivators. Andi looked expectantly at Shireen.

"The testaments haven't been opened yet, but I'm pretty sure the wives are going to be the beneficiaries. The victims didn't have traceable contact with their sons, which led me to the conclusion they were estranged, and with what I've learned about the three men so far, I don't think we're going to get a surprise here. In Mr. Portius's case there is a possibility that part of the money goes to the firm, but I haven't verified it yet."

"Did you find enemies who stand out?" Andi still wasn't betting his money on the family alone.

"A lot of them. Mostly business related, though so far nothing that goes beyond the normal rivalries in their respective fields. I'll keep digging."

"Thank you, Shireen. Anything else we should know?" George had his forehead in a frown, a sure sign he was mulling the information over.

"Nothing that stands out. I've sent you everything I have so far."

Andi nodded. "Thanks, Shireen. When you're done with the victims, can you take a look at the wives and sons as well? I have a feeling this case is going to be more complicated than we initially thought."

"Aren't your cases always?" Shireen smiled sweetly at them. Just like Evangeline and Forard, she had learned to trust in Andi's abilities, even though she didn't know their true nature or extent. "You're going to crack this case like you always do."

Andi felt the weight of her trust heavily on his shoulders. Strange, how Chief Norris's ire didn't affect him nearly as much, but something so innocent made his knees almost buckle. Luckily for him, he now had George, who put a hand on the small of Andi's back as if he had sensed what was going on in his partner's mind.

"Yeah, Andi is going to crack this case, because he's no longer alone. He has me now."

Shireen's happy laughter resounded in her tech room. "I'm sorry, George, I didn't mean to leave you out. Andi can count himself lucky to finally have a partner, and one as reliable as you!"

George simply grinned and started leading Andi out of the tech room and along the floor toward the bullpen, where their desks were waiting. Shireen's comment reminded Andi that George's reliability was only temporary, that the man would leave him as soon as the next promising step in his career popped up. Strictly speaking, Andi couldn't afford to get too used to George's presence, and yet he already had, relying on his partner more than was good for him. He really should be maintaining his independence, but every time Andi tried, George somehow disarmed him and made himself even more invaluable in the process. So much that Andi had decided to simply go with the flow. He knew the end would be terrible, but he had come to the conclusion that since he couldn't change how bad it was going to be, he could at least enjoy what he had at the moment. There was no sense in ruining it all just because part of it was rotten.

They reached their desks, where George grabbed his beloved marker to add information on the whiteboard. Andi sat down, woke up his PC, found the files Shireen had sent, and started scanning them, reading the important bits out loud so George could jot them down.

"Okay, let's start with Harry Alexander McHill, married to Sophia McHill, formerly Sophia Ansel, an old family around here. Seems like Harry married for money and status. He made his fortune in real estate, apparently more successfully than a certain orange-skinned ex-president. According to the list Shireen sent, he has his hands in many pies, and not a small number have been baked by Lawrence Miller."

George made a snorting sound that had Andi looking up. "What?"

"I'm not sure if I love your analogies or if they're plain stupid. Baking, really?"

"You love my analogies, and you know it. Now stop with the snickering and draw a nice green arrow from McHill to Miller."

"So we are using green for business relations again? What happened to them being yellow?"

"Cut it out! I just thought it would be nice to shake things up now and then, but I've since seen the error of my ways! We stick to your boring old system. There, you've won."

Andi made a face when George threw his hands in the air and waggled his butt. The man could be so insufferable sometimes. After George had carefully drawn the green arrow between McHill and Miller, Andi kept on reading. "In the past three years McHill has started to withdraw himself from his company, giving his managers more responsibility. He has only done a few highly lucrative deals. There's no mention of his son in regard to his company."

"What about those more dubious dealings Shireen mentioned?" George had his red marker poised. Andi searched the pages.

"There's a few companies with a red flag, meaning Shireen wants to investigate them more closely. None of them ring any bells for me, though. Most of them seem to be in Africa and South America."

"Mmm." George drew two red arrows, marking them with A and S.A. "What else?"

"I'm sure this comes as an absolute surprise to you, but McHill's law firm is Portius, Dayson & Partners, and David Hector Portius II is listed as his personal lawyer."

Another green arrow appeared. "Let me guess, Portius is also Miller's personal lawyer?"

Andi changed documents. "Yep." He looked at the triangle in the middle of the whiteboard, now consisting of three green arrows for business relations and three blue ones for personal interactions. Andi followed a hunch and opened the file for Portius.

"Bingo. Miller also invested money for Portius." Another arrow was drawn, pointing from Miller to Portius. Andi scanned the pages again, looking for something else and finding it. "And both Miller and Portius have invested in McHill's company."

George drew yet another arrow. They both stared at the thick lines connecting the three men. "I think it's safe to say whoever killed them did it because of something they did as a group. How long have they known each other?" George changed to the black marker, ready to add the information. It took Andi some time to find it, because it wasn't money-related and therefore at the end of Shireen's preliminary report. "Practically all their life. They attended the same private schools, and all of them graduated from Harvard. They were members of the same fraternity, all of them in leading positions, of course. If I didn't suspect them of having been awful people, I'd say it's almost romantic. They even died together."

George shuddered. "I'm not sure I share your definition of romantic."

"Aw, come on, a relationship that spanned decades. If that's not romantic, I don't know!" Teasing George was fun.

"Speaking of relationships, what do we have about the marriages of the three?" And they were back to business. George had already written the names of the three wives, as well as Lawrence Miller's first wife, on the whiteboard.

"No public scandals. Not even when Miller divorced Angelica Worthington. He was, of course, represented by Portius, Dayson & Partners. There are no details about the settlement, but I guess we can safely assume it was either so generous Miss Worthington didn't have any objections, or they found something incriminating to keep her quiet. Chances are fifty-fifty."

"That would make her a prime suspect, even if her revenge was ice-cold." George stared at the blue lines connecting the wives with the victims. "And why would she go after McHill? I can't see what he might have had to do with the divorce, apart from being Miller's friend."

"Don't forget her son said she's in Haiti. I wouldn't cross her from the list of suspects, but she doesn't hold the pole position either."

George shook his head. "No, she doesn't. So far, we don't have contenders for it. Are the wives connected? Apart from their husbands being friends?"

Andi scanned the documents again. "Shireen hasn't put down a lot about them, but it doesn't seem so. Sophia is old money. Angelica was from Haiti, from money as well. Tamara's parents were immigrants from Asia who made it to upper middle class here. Theodora, Miller's second wife, is the only one who doesn't have a wealthy family at her back. It says here she was a teacher before she married Lawrence Miller."

"If they are friends, it's because of their husbands."

"Do you think they're not?" Andi didn't know much about relationships, apart from what he had learned through his work. And most of that was unpleasant.

"I think they surely are acquaintances, and perhaps they have formed some bonds, but probably more out of habit than anything else." Nevertheless, George connected the four women with blue lines, which created a wheel around the triangle of the victims.

Andi went back to the documents, searching for anything else they could put on their chart. To his dismay he didn't find anything substantial. Looking at the long list of business partners—and therefore potential enemies—Andi knew it would take Shireen time to get to the bottom of it all. Before he could voice his displeasure, his cell chimed with an incoming message from Evangeline.

"Let's go downstairs. Evangeline has some news."

George put the marker back, took a swig from his by now surely cold coffee, and fell in step next to Andi. "I hope she can shed some light on how exactly they died."

Andi nodded. Some light would be nice. Something they could work with. He dreaded what he'd have to do if there wasn't anything.

Evangeline greeted them with a little more energy than the day before. "*Ua mai le taeao.* You two look like you could use some good news."

Andi felt himself perking up immediately. "You know who did it? We just have to make the arrest?"

Evangeline's snort killed that pipe dream like a late frost did blooms. "*Aulelei.* No, I'm sorry, but I can't deliver your killer on a silver platter. I have yet to develop the power of divination."

"Then what are you good for?" Andi put some extra whine in his voice, knowing Evangeline liked the banter.

She put one hand in front of her mouth, her eyes widening in mock indignation. "What am I good for, he asks? Let's see if I ever again push to have blood tests rushed on your behalf."

"I didn't say anything!" George hastened to get some physical space between them, the traitor.

"Is it too late to say I'm sorry?"

"With you it always is because we both know you're never sorry." Evangeline huffed. "It's one of the reasons I like you. Now follow me." She led them into her office, where the desk was overflowing with documents as usual. With the precision of a magpie going after something glittery, Evangeline selected a binder from somewhere in the chaos and opened it. "The victims have been dead for three days. Estimated time of death last Friday. I'm almost certain it was some time after midnight, so early Friday. Very early."

"Almost certain?"

"Yes, Andi, almost certain. An exact time of death is hard to pinpoint with bodies found in water. They haven't been in there for long, which helps, and the way they died suggests it was after dark."

When George opened his mouth to ask something, Evangeline held up her hand. "Let me finish first, and then you can quiz me. The victims drowned in that lake. The water in their lungs is the same as the water they were found in. There are all the typical signs of drowning, like frothy fluid in the airways and over-distended lungs. I didn't find any defensive wounds on the victims, which led me to believe they were somehow sedated. Toxicology confirms traces of ketamine in the urine of all three victims. We were lucky you found them when you did, because ketamine can only be traced for a short time after it is taken. Death has slowed down the process of its breakdown, which we are thankful for. The most likely scenario I can come up with is that whoever killed the three men somehow managed to give them the first dose of ketamine and then used their disoriented state to take them to the lake. Depending on how far away they were from it, the killer—or more likely killers— must have given them several doses, because ketamine wears off after approximately fifteen minutes. And before you ask, no, I can't calculate how much ketamine they were given. It's impossible. The last dose was definitely shortly before they went into the lake, and it was an overdose to knock them out."

"They were unconscious while drowning?" Andi didn't know if that was a mercy or not.

"They were basically unconscious for the whole ordeal, I'd say. Ketamine causes a loss of awareness, one of the reasons it's used as a rape drug. I doubt they even realized they were brought to a lake. My guess is the killers guided them into the water until they came close to the deepest part. Then they gave them the last dose, easiest would have been a spray, and shoved them forward. The chains and rocks did their part, and the victims were dead."

"Your theory would also explain why their feet weren't bound. Whoever did this wasn't able or willing to carry them." George rubbed his forehead with his thumb, no doubt contemplating what this meant in terms of the kind of person they were looking for.

"How hard is it to get the right dosage of ketamine into somebody?"

Evangeline furrowed her brows. "You have to calculate, but it's not a secret or anything. Given the age of the victims it was probably a bit more difficult to get just the right amount to have them still functioning but docile, but the final dosage was easy because you just have to pump them full."

"Is it safe to say whoever did this had to have basic knowledge in chemistry and math?" George was trying to narrow their pool of suspects down, but one look at Evangeline told Andi it wasn't working.

"I'm sorry, George, I'd love to say yes, but anybody with access to the internet could have done it. There's fucking charts about the exact amount of roofies for certain bodyweights out there, some of them even considering the amount of alcohol consumed. All you need is the patience to visit a disreputable site and read up on it."

"Damn!" George threw his hands in the air. "You said the easiest way to overdose them in the water would have been a spray. Can you say how they got the first dose?"

Evangeline shook her head. "*Ua ou faanoanoa.* My best guess is the first dose was orally given because spraying three people at the same time is rather difficult. From then on it could have been spray or orally or per injection, though I didn't find any injection marks on their bodies, so it was probably spray."

"Thank you, Evangeline. Was there anything else?" Even though the coroner hadn't presented them the killer on a silver platter, she had still given them more to work with.

"Nothing directly linked to their deaths. All three of them were in remarkable shape for men their age, none of the usual problems with the heart or too much fat around the internal organs. They were as healthy as I would expect from men at least ten to fifteen years younger."

Andi nodded. This was the kind of information he liked to save in his mind. Not obviously important but maybe crucial at some later point when they were stuck. "You'll inform us if you find anything new?"

"*Ae sao fo'i*. I rushed the blood and urine samples, but everything I've taken from the chains and clothing is still processing. I'll keep you updated."

"Thank you so much, Evangeline." Andi waved at her while George said his own goodbyes. They went back upstairs, where George grabbed his keys. Andi couldn't help the small smile flitting across his features. It was always nice to be in tune with one's partner. "I'll get the address of the cabin they stayed in."

6. Clues and Puzzle Pieces

THE DRIVE to Lake Moultrie was silent for the most part, Andi doing his breathing meditation thing George knew was meant to prepare his partner for whatever insectoid input they were going to get. At the moment George felt like they were looking at hopelessly entangled balls of yarn, in different colors and with different lengths and thickness. There was no particular line they could follow, no piece standing out enough to grab it and yank without tightening the knot to a point where it could only be cut because there was no hope of ever detangling it. It was a normal state for huge cases with so many variables and so little distinctive evidence. It also meant they had their work cut out for them and that Andi's *geschenk* was more important than George would have liked. In the cases following the busting of the trafficking ring, they had been able to keep the use of Andi's *geschenk* to a minimum, mostly relying on it to point them in the right direction. Those cases had been a lot more clear-cut, even though two of them had been cold cases from over ten years ago. George was still amazed what a difference a tiny nudge in the right direction—concerning an investigation—could make. One little hint and a case that had appeared to be hopeless was wide-open and ripe for the solving all of a sudden.

This case, though, was bigger, and just looking at all the potential suspects and the media coverage the murder would receive as soon as the news got out had George shivering. They needed some clues, some results as quickly as possible. Andi knew this as well, and as much as George hated to put additional pressure on his partner, he still relied on Andi to provide those results where Evangeline and Shireen—and in extension he himself—met their limits.

They arrived at the cabin shortly after noon. The building looked more like a small chalet than anything George would have linked with the term "cabin." Which—for him—should be nothing more than one or perhaps two rooms built from roughhewn planks that had gone silvery from age. The simple life. Then again, the three victims had been rich, and there was no indication so far that they had kept a frugal lifestyle. The huge two-story building with the extensive wrap-around porch was built from wood, but there was nothing rough about it. The oak planks looked as well-tended as the broad gravel driveway that led to the cabin, cut into the surrounding forest with laser-like precision. The windows at the front, flanking the broad door, were floor-to-ceiling, and only the shades that were down kept them from getting a good look inside. Andi was already tense, the tendons in his neck twitching every time he swallowed. George hastened to get out of the car and close to his partner. When Andi got too immersed in the impressions bombarding him from all sides, he lost a great deal of his situational awareness. It was George's job to see to it his partner didn't trip or run into anything. Normally George would have preferred to have a look around before Andi tapped into the additional channels of information he had at his disposal, but the way his partner's body was coiled like an elastic spring made it clear this wouldn't be happening today.

"Andi, are you okay?" It was a moot question; of course Andi wasn't okay. George just didn't know what else to ask. Andi knew he was here to help him, and verbalizing *something* probably helped George more than it did Andi.

"So much upheaval, cars rattling the ground, heavy steps, the eggs were dislodged, loud, so loud, glass clinking and breaking, alcohol in the air, something leaking from a car, lethal, seeping into the ground, stench of gunpowder, sonic waves, blood, so much blood, dead things in the room without entrance, cold, pieces of tissue, fur, nothing substantial, loud, stomping, crashing, alcohol, smoke, thudding, more bodies, clinking, dragging over the floor, dust in the colony, too many vibrations, thud, thud, thud, down the stairs, something heavy and metallic in the sweat, no longer tempting, thud, thud, thud, down the stairs, thud, thud, thud, down the stairs, rumbling, rattling the ground, finally silence, then a humming, stomping again, more silent, more careful, stress, adrenaline, going round the rooms, going round and round, always careful, out of the house, the humming again, gone, silent, the night…."

Andi was breathing hard. His right hand found George's biceps, and he gripped him hard, as if he were drowning. "Food, blood bags for nourishment, I'm Andi, no, not so loud, they're hatching, don't draw attention, I'm Andi, can't get out of the web, prey, prey, *I'm Andi!*"

The shout startled George, and his worry for Andi reached new heights. He had known things were getting worse, but until this moment he had clung to the fragile illusion Andi had woven for him that it was manageable, that he had it under control; all he needed to do was meditate more. Looking at his partner's pained expression, George knew this wasn't something more meditating could alleviate. They were firmly in doomed territory, and he couldn't do much except try to help Andi to find his way back to himself.

"Yes, yes, you're Andi. You're here with me. I'm here, Andi, I'm here. Concentrate on my voice. You can do it."

The grip on George's biceps got more painful. Andi's eyes latched on to George's face. His gaze was strangely empty, so empty it made George shudder. He grabbed Andi's lower arms, dug his fingers in so violently, he was sure there would be bruises. The pain seemed to snap Andi out of whatever daze he was in. His gaze became focused again, and he loosened his hold on George's arm yet didn't let go, as if he needed the contact with human skin to stay anchored. George didn't let go either, providing all the help he could in an attempt to not feel useless.

When Andi's breathing finally started to even out, George took him in his arms, held him close, simply glad to have him back. "You have to stop doing this."

"I wish I could." Andi didn't try to wiggle out of George's hold.

"You said your grandmother was like you. Was it as bad for her?"

Andi shrugged. "I didn't know her that well, and we never really talked about the *geschenk* because she was a nasty old woman and I was a traumatized yet arrogant young man who had neither the intention nor patience to listen to what she had to say. I got the cliff notes—this is your destiny, it makes you special, use it as you see fit, blah, blah, blah, and I know she relied more heavily on her arthropod senses the older she got and the more her human senses deteriorated. I think she got more receptive over the years, but I have no idea if it came in waves as it does with me or if it intensified steadily or if she managed to gain any real control over it."

"You had episodes like this one before?" George couldn't hide his horror. And he hadn't been there to protect Andi. Nobody had been there!

"Yes. Not as bad, obviously, because my senses weren't as strong as they are now. The last one was while I was still a beat officer. It lasted four months, and at the end, I had already started as detective, my more astute perception helping greatly with the cases I was assigned to. Since then, I had good days and bad months, though nothing as intense as this. I think it started during our first case, when I tried to find Castain and had to connect to all the arthropods in the area."

That Andi was so forthcoming with information showed how rattled he was and in turn worried George even more. Right at this moment, his partner should resemble a hedgehog, rolled up in a ball, blocking everybody out, stubbornly declaring how fine he was. Andi showing his soft underbelly made the problem appear even graver.

"You should be trying to convince me everything is fine."

Still in the circle of George's arms, Andi snorted. "Believe me, I would try if I thought I could get away with it. But you heard me. You saw what happened. No sense in keeping up a lie I can't convince you to swallow."

"So what do we do now?"

"What we came here to do." Andi slipped from George's embrace, leaving an emptiness George didn't like but had to accept. "We're taking a look at the cabin. Then we call CSI to go over it with a fine-toothed comb. They were roofied and abducted here, and since the persons who did it were inside the house, we can hope for some traces." As if an internal switch had flipped, Andi was all business again, stomping toward the porch of the cabin/chalet. Shortly before he reached it, he veered to the left, where the garage was located. Following his partner, George reached him at the same time Andi opened the garage doors. Three cars were inside, a Jeep Wrangler, a Mercedes SUV, and a BMW X6. George whistled. "I'm not sure it still counts as a hunting trip when you arrive in this type of car and stay in a little mansion."

"Apparently it does." Andi entered the garage, stopped next to the BMW, and crouched. "There's an oil leak here." He extended a hand under the car, brought it back glistening with an oily film. "Fresh." Andi wiped his fingers on his jeans, at the same time venturing farther into the garage, to the back where George spotted a heavy steel door with a wheel for a knob. Andi turned it until the door swung open, revealing a cooling room with several deer carcasses hanging from hooks.

"Let me guess, the room with no entry and food in it."

Andi nodded. "Cooling rooms are notoriously well shielded against insects, for obvious reasons. This one is even better than most I have seen. They hate it."

"I can imagine." George watched while Andi closed the door again. They went back outside the garage and around to the front porch. The door was closed but not locked, another sign that things were wrong. Inside the air smelled stale. The huge living room with decadent leather couches arranged in front of an open-hearth fireplace was in disarray, bottles of beer standing and lying on the mahogany coffee table, pretzels and chips scattered on the ground.

"Looks like they had quite the party going." George was careful where he stepped as to not disturb any evidence. Andi's movements were more careless, indicating his channel to the arthropods was still opened wider than George would have preferred. His partner knew where the potentially important bits of evidence were located. He stared at the beer bottles with his head cocked to the side.

"I think the ketamine was given to them via the beer. It's the most logical course of action."

"Question is, how did the ketamine get into the beer, and how did the beer find its way here?"

"We can safely assume the victims didn't do any major cleaning or stocking of their own. We have to ask who prepared the cabin for their stay and who would have been responsible for cleaning it up afterward." Andi looked around the obvious chaos.

"It also gives us a timeline that fits the time of death. Their wives said they left for the cabin early on Thursday and were supposed to return tomorrow, so a full week of hunting. They spent the day killing those deer in the cooling room and then started to party. At some point they drank the roofied beer, which was the moment the killer or killers had been waiting for." George furrowed his brows. "The only thing I don't understand is why they would go to the trouble of herding them all the way out to Swamp Fox Trail when they could have drowned them right here in Lake Moultrie."

"The danger of being found out." Andi shrugged. "Think about it. Three pillars of society go missing during their hunting trip close to a lake. How long would it take until the first divers would be sent out? Plus, Lake Moultrie is comparatively crowded: fishermen, divers, people who go swimming or boating. You heard Berta, the forest ranger. The lake we found the victims in is too small for any of that. I'm just wondering if the killers were aware that the rotting corpses would poison the area and draw attention to it, thus wanting the bodies to be found at some point, or if they simply didn't know."

"As thorough as the whole operation seemed to have been, I'd say the first. They wanted the bodies to be found, but only after any kind of evidence was gone. Which awakes the small hope in me that there *is* evidence we can work with." George was inching back toward the entrance door. It was best to leave the crime scene to the pros. Andi followed him, getting out his phone to inform CSI they had another place to go over.

Instead of heading back to the car, Andi was walking around the cabin toward the woods, stomping over small bushes and into the gloom of the cypress trees. George followed hastily, Andi's swaying gait telling him his partner had been hit by another wave of information and would need George soon. Andi was mumbling, the words becoming clear once George reached Andi's side. "...too much input, no chance to find what I'm looking for, I don't know what it is anyway, information twisting and tumbling, all too complex, can't pull it apart, too many variables in that box, like a web, only stickier, I'm a fly, aren't I? Trapped, too many layers, holding me, can't get away, leave me be, need to find something, anything, not in the box, plop, heavy, strange smell, food, sex, where, down, up, outside, blobs here, three, no that was a week ago, two, yes, that could be the right day, something strange about them, something artificial overlaying something else, focus harder, it's important, moths are so difficult to read, see everything different than other species, must be the ketamine, I know what it looks like for them, what is this other thing, I can almost taste it, slippery, the moths know it so well, what could that be?"

Andi kept walking, farther away from the cabin, George glued to his side, trying to swat twigs and branches out of the way because his partner clearly didn't realize they were there. George wondered if he should try to snap Andi out of it, then dismissed the idea. Andi would never forgive him if he had to dive back in just because George was too chicken to listen to his ramblings, even if they were getting crazier by the second.

"What's that, metallic, there's more of the ketamine, click, click, all night long, where, it's close, need to find it, click, click, sharp, stay away, ah, over there, it's all here, the ketamine, the other thing, the females, the sharpness, metal, click, click...."

George had enough. He decided he could live with Andi's wrath, but not with the strange sounds he was making, no doubt trying to imitate whatever sonic input he was getting from the arthropods. Sometimes the difference between the worlds humans and creepy crawlers lived in was more horror story than anything else. George grabbed Andi's shoulder harder and shook him.

"Andi, snap out of it! Why are we here? What did you find?"

For a painfully long moment his partner simply stared at him with vacant eyes. George dared to shake him again, raising his voice. "Andi! Talk to me, man!"

Andi shook his head, put the palm of his right hand to his temple. "Sorry, I was frustrated because I didn't get anything useful from the cabin, too many people and things in there, and I could sense something foreign out here." He pointed to two cypress trees where George first couldn't spot anything interesting. On closer inspection, though, he realized something was attached to both trees, something in camouflage to mimic the trees' bark. Two little boxes, only visible once you knew they were there.

George went to the trees after he had made sure Andi was stable on his feet. He whistled. "Wow, it's a wildlife camera. And I can see footprints. But they could be from the person who set the camera up."

"We'll have to find out who it belongs to and contact them. Perhaps there's something on it." Andi was coming closer, veering a bit left, to a small evergreen. He bent down to retrieve something from the ground, using one of the rubber gloves they had with them. When he held it up, a triumphant smile twisted his lips. "And we have a winner!"

George went over to him to inspect what Andi had found. It was a needle. A used needle.

"Let me guess, ketamine?"

Andi nodded. "It's full of it."

George got out one of the small evidence bags he always carried in one of his back pockets. Andi carefully dropped the needle in, sighing when George closed it. The glove he stuffed back into the front pocket of his jeans, where he would probably forget about it until he had reason to reach inside the cloth again. Chances were the glove would get a nice little adventure in Andi's washing machine.

"That's at least something."

"Hey, don't be so hard on yourself. Nobody, least I, expects you to always find everything."

"I know. It's just, I'm kind of used to it."

George patted Andi's arm. "I understand, but you don't have to always provide the solution. Leave some work for me. Now let's take a picture of the sticker on the wildlife camera so we can get out of here."

ON THEIR way back to Charleston, Andi called Theodora Miller, asking her who was responsible for preparing and maintaining the cabin. With a new address, George drove into the Goose Creek area where Pérez and Sons had their office. After the two men had gotten over their initial shock about the police knocking on their door, they had been very helpful. As it turned out, they had been at the cabin on Wednesday, stocking it up with groceries and beer they had gotten straight from the brewery, a small crafts beer producer who was located in Berkeley County. A call there confirmed the Pérezes' story, establishing that the picking up was a pattern that had gone down whenever the three victims went hunting for the past two years.

"What do you think? Have Miguel and Santo Pérez suddenly decided to get rid of their employers?" George concentrated on the late-afternoon traffic, which was as thick as always.

"To be honest, I don't think so. They were at the cabin, just like they said, but only for the preparations they claimed. Now that I know what they look like to other arthropods, I can distinguish them from the other unknown people in the cabin. And if they wanted to get rid of their employers, I think they wouldn't have come up with such an elaborate scenario. They're both strong men, and there's easier ways to kill somebody than a trip to a lake in the middle of the night. Plus, they wouldn't have lost a needle full of ketamine in the woods at the back of the cabin. They went in through the front."

"And the cabin stood empty for at least ten hours after they prepared it and the victims arrived. Plenty of time to break in and doctor the beer."

"Yes. I did sense five other people there, four female, one male. Plus, the victims being there for an entire day would make pretty sure that any evidence for the break-in would be destroyed…." Andi sighed. "This whole thing reeks of careful scheming."

"It does. Which means not a crime of passion. Whoever did this had time to stew in their anger and plan every little detail. If you add the method of killing, it points toward the killer being female." George had paid close attention to his courses in criminal psychology and knew that women had a statistical tendency to murder with poison and to plan their crimes thoroughly.

"Yes. It's a high probability. The two people the arthropods sensed in the woods were definitely female, and they were inside the cabin as well. Question is, were they there on official business like the Perézs, or are they potential suspects? We should tell Shireen to look out for events in the victims' pasts. This could stem from an old grudge." Andi got his cell out and started typing.

"Or point toward the wives. Being married for so long gives you plenty of time to accumulate anger." George glanced at the clock in his car. "Though I don't want to dismiss the sons yet. None of them made the impression of being hands-on. I could definitely see them reverting to sneakiness."

"Not to forget they, too, had time to steep in their anger. I wonder if it was enough to motivate them to work together? Because I don't see one of them acting on his own and killing the other two respective victims as kind of a bonus. Too much hassle for one."

This thought put a damper on the theory, as George very well knew. So far they had had no indication that either the wives or sons had been particularly close. Or at least close enough to plan cold-blooded murder. Then again, George had seen stranger things in his time as detective, and people's motivations weren't always logical. "I guess we have to wait and see what Shireen digs up." He made the turn leading him to Stiles Point. "I'll pick you up tomorrow as usual."

"Thank you, George." Andi rubbed his face, the stress lines around his eyes deepening as if his body had finally realized that rest was in reach.

"Take an aspirin and try to get some sleep. I'll swing by the precinct to get the needle registered before I go home." George said it matter-of-factly, mixing in the information about what he would be doing to make it even more casual, as if they were talking about the weather. He had learned by now this was the easiest and most probable way to get Andi to listen to him. His partner made a waving gesture.

"Yeah, yeah. I need some sleep."

George stopped in front of Andi's house, waited till his partner was out of the car and then until Andi was through his door. He didn't like leaving Andi alone, probably as much as Andi didn't like being babied. They were even in that regard. Once the front door had closed, George had no reason to linger any longer, so he turned the car and drove home.

7. Give Me a Lead

THANKS TO the two aspirin he had taken, Andi had slept quite well, leaving him feeling almost refreshed. He still couldn't believe he had folded in such a spectacular way the day before. The barrage of information from the insects around the cabin had overwhelmed him like an avalanche, made it hard for him to find his way back. George's presence had helped a great deal, and Andi had been so glad, he had clung to his partner like a tick to a host. Since the Castain case, the amount of information he processed unconsciously had grown, which would have been a cause for celebration if the overall assault hadn't been getting worse. It was a pure self-defense mechanism on the part of his mind to protect itself from overloading. Everything was getting sharper, more detailed, more linked to the individual insect, which made it harder to discern the useful bits. Until four months ago, Andi had been able to filter through the things he didn't need with comparative ease. Now every piece of information was important, loaded, and finding what he needed without losing himself was getting harder and harder. He just hoped he would be able to get a grip on things soon. Or at least before George left him. Otherwise, he wouldn't know what to do. He had no contingency plan for his *geschenk* getting so out of control. Until now, the increases had come at a slow, manageable level with some intense months thrown in now and then. What he was experiencing at the moment was new and frightening, and he didn't know how to get it under control. Alcohol was looking more and more tempting, the only reason Andi hadn't reverted to it being that it brought another kind of loss of control. He sighed while he put on his jeans and T-shirt, shoved the gun in its holster, and clipped his badge to his belt—

There was a delicious scent of rotting meat in the air, a wonderful opportunity to give the larvae a perfect start into this world, the blossoms were rich, so much nectar for the hive, collecting bits of grass and tiny sticks to increase the nest, the fungi were doing great, growing fast enough to feed the colony, there was dung to be rolled, the humidity in the air whispering of rain to come, the scratching and munching and scraping of countless chitinous legs, like a symphony in his mind, telling of the worlds interwoven with his own, so close, so close, not at all far away like all the other blobs thought, he was there, all the time, knowing what was going on, getting lost in the sensations, no, he couldn't do that, he had to get back, stay, the nectar is good, food everywhere, the blobs provide it in numerous ways, get back, Andi, George is going to pick you up, rattling, the ground shakes, it's George, George is coming, Andi, get going!

Andi shook his head, trying to get his bearings. It was so strange, seeing himself through the eyes of the insects, feeling like one himself, talking to himself like an outside source. Wrapping his mind around this concept was headache-inducing.

The bell rang, saved him from dwelling deeper. Andi went downstairs, knowing George would use his keys to come in if he didn't react to the bell fast enough. It was another fail-safe Andi had created, using George like the miners had canaries. Not pondering about how he used his partner was another thing Andi was getting better and better at. He needed George at the moment, George was willing to help, he got a shiny solving statistic out of it, end of story.

When Andi opened the front door, George was already searching for the keys in his pocket.

"Ah, you're up and about. Good morning, Andi."

"Good morning, George. I'm not only up and about, I'm also ready to dive back into this wretched case. Let's see how far Shireen has gotten."

"Yeah, let's." In the car, George wordlessly handed Andi his cup of herbal tea and his plain bagel, which smelled even better when he remembered the stench of the dead mouse the burying beetles had found earlier.

After their arrival at the precinct, they went straight to Shireen. "If you guys had troubled yourself with checking your emails, you'd know I've found something interesting."

"A good morning to you, too, Shireen. Perhaps we just wanted to see your beautiful smile." George could be snarky with the best of them. "And you know we love hearing good news directly from you." He winked, which made Shireen actually blush a little. The man was also a charmer.

"Fine. You win. Just as you asked me, I dug a little deeper into the victims' pasts, and there's two things standing out. The first are bills indicating each of them had had at least two affairs in their life which, to be frank, doesn't surprise me. Harry Alexander McHill seems to have been the busiest. So far I've found four mistresses over the years. David Hector Portius II was more of a one-night stand man and premium member of a high-class escort service here in Charleston. I can't tell how many of his escorts he slept with, though I guess it's fair to assume he didn't let any opportunity go to waste. Lawrence Miller had had two affairs I could find, one while he was still married to his ex-wife, Angelica Worthington. The other is still going strong as far as I can tell. The juicy bit is his mistresses are misters." Shireen pulled up the pictures of two men, both in their late thirties. "The hunky Latino on the right is Juan Alvarez, personal trainer and ex-boyfriend of Lawrence Miller. Before you ask, he lives in Spain at the moment, with another man, dare I say sugar daddy?" A smile flitted across Shireen's features. "Anyway, the yummy dark stud on his way to hot silver fox is Jeremy Fisher, professor of chemistry at the University of Charleston, Virginia, currently working in a private lab here in our wonderful city. The topic of his research is strictly confidential, but rumors have it he's part of a team that tries to find a way to dispose of plastic in environmentally safe ways."

At the mention of chemistry, Andi and George shared a look. This was good news. Not just the thing with the plastic. The chemistry was a lead.

"Before you go chasing the man down, I found something else. It was hidden very well, and I would have missed it if the *Cambridge Gazette* hadn't decided to digitalize all its issues, starting in 1910." The flat-screen changed pictures and they were staring at an old newspaper page with the picture of a young man who looked into the camera with huge soulful eyes. The title read "Student in Wheelchair after Fraternity Prank." "Meet Gideon Gartner. He was a freshman at Harvard and wanted into the fraternity Miller, Portius, and McHill were in. They set the usual ridiculous tests, one of them going into an abandoned house that was supposedly haunted as a dare. Apparently Miller, Portius, and McHill had prepared the house to make it spookier. Because of their tampering, the structure of the stairs was affected, and Gartner fell from the second floor down. He broke his back and has been in a wheelchair ever since. The fathers of Miller, Portius, and McHill made it all go away, though how, you have to ask Gartner, because financial transactions from that time are hard to track. Not everybody believes in digitalizing." Shireen sounded so sad Andi felt compelled to pat her on the back.

"It's fine, Shireen. You found us something, and we'll take it from here."

"I wish you good hunting." She smiled at them. "I'll keep digging."

"You're the queen." Andi waved before he turned to follow George out of Shireen's domain. He felt energized and ready to tackle the two new suspects, so it was only natural for Chief Norris to choose this moment to summon them to her office with an imperious gesture of her head. Andi sighed and trotted after George, who had already assumed his position as Andi's shield against whatever the chief would spew. Andi was perfectly capable of defending himself, but he did acknowledge that, thanks to George, he hadn't yet said something to the chief which could not be taken back or forgotten.

"Detectives, please tell me you've made some progress with the case. The mayor has been asking. She wants to have something to tell the media once this gets out, which, as you're hopefully well aware, is only a question of time."

Andi kept his mouth firmly shut, leaving the explanations to George. Of course the chief was only asking because the mayor needed something to look good in the public eye. Next year was the election. While George made nice with the chief, Andi thought about the case and the ever-growing pool of suspects. It wasn't surprising, really, with men as old and rich as they were. It would have surprised Andi a lot more if they'd had no enemies and no secrets. Still, so far, none of the suspects made sense once he thought more closely about them. The sons and wives were automatically suspicious simply because murder, especially when money was involved, often happened among family members. As much as Andi would have loved to put his hopes on Jeremy Fisher or Gideon Gartner, his common sense already told him it was unlikely. For Fisher the same reasoning applied as did for the sons and the wives—even if he had a grudge against Lawrence Miller, why would he murder the other two men as well? As for Gideon Gartner, he was in a wheelchair. It was impossible for him to haul three men, even when they were drugged, along Swamp Fox Trail and into the water. If anything, he might be complicit, but before he had even met the man, it was pure speculation on his part. They would follow those leads nevertheless, because anything that shed a light on the life of the three victims could help them unravel the case.

"Am I boring you, Detective Hayes?" Norris's voice cut through his thoughts like the wailing of a foghorn. Andi looked up to see George and the chief staring at him.

"No, of course not, Chief Norris. I'm just eager to get back to the case." Andi didn't try to hide the sarcasm in his voice, knowing full well the chief wouldn't buy his bullshit either way. Her gaze turned dark, and she opened her mouth, no doubt to say something sharp, when George interrupted her. His tone was way more genuine and conciliatory than Andi would have ever managed.

"My partner is right, Chief Norris. As I said, we're looking at an uncomfortably large number of possible suspects, and time is of the essence if we want any hope to solve this murder."

For a moment the chief seemed to contemplate her options. Andi could almost see the gears turning in her head, weighing if she should indulge herself and pick on Andi some more or let them get back to the case so she could tell the mayor things were progressing. The chief's need to strengthen her position with the mayor won out, and she sent them away with a dismissive gesture. On their way back out to the car, George scolded Andi in that mild-mannered way that made Andi's fingers itch to clock his partner.

"You really should try to play a little nicer with the chief, Andi. She's not perfect, but also not the devil you make her out to be."

"That's what you think. I'm not sold on the not-devil part." George snorted but thankfully stopped harping about how things would be easier if Andi were more amiable toward the insufferable chief. They got into the car, and Andi leaned back, enjoying the relative quiet inside the vehicle. The thrumming and scratching and trilling of the insects was slightly dulled in this metal box into which none of them had found their way yet.

"Where to first? Gartner or Fisher?" George's hand hovered over the middle console, ready to type in the address of either man.

"I think Fisher. We should be able to get him on campus. If he has anything to hide, apprehending him at his place of work could rattle him enough to slip."

"You're a calculating bastard. I like that."

Andi just huffed. When George was done feeding the GPS, he pulled into traffic. The drive to Bluebird Road where the private lab—Earthlabs Inc.—was located, was blissfully quick, Maybank Highway for once being empty enough to drive at a reasonable speed and not having to move at a snail's pace. After they parked directly in front of the main building, they went inside, looking for Jeremy Fisher's office. It was on the second floor at the end of a long hallway, and luckily for them, the professor was in. He asked them to enter, and Andi—

—sadness heavy in the air, oppressing, down, the sweat not tantalizing, too saturated with grief, new blood bags, better food, the need

to find an opening, belly heavy with eggs, nourishment needed, laying would happen soon—

—was immediately bombarded by Fisher's grief. Even before George could introduce them, the professor spoke.

"I assume you're here because of Lawrence?"

George quickly glanced at Andi, who decided this was one of the rare occasions where he should be taking the lead in talking to a suspect.

"You already know?"

Fisher shrugged, the downward turn of his lips suggesting he was fighting hard for control. "Theodora called as soon as she heard."

Andi could feel his brows shooting to his hairline. The wife had informed the lover, but not the son? The sudden tension in George's body next to him told him his partner was as surprised by this turn of events as Andi was.

"Please, take a seat." Fisher gestured to the two chairs in front of his neatly organized desk.

"First, let me tell you we're very sorry for your loss. And please forgive me for being so forward, but Theodora Miller informed you about the death of her husband?"

The ghost of a smile appeared on Jeremy's lips. "I know, it sounds strange. Which very aptly describes my entire relationship with Lawrence." He looked out of the floor-to-ceiling window with a wistful sigh. "It was a very good strange, though."

"Could you please enlighten us? As you may have guessed, this is a murder investigation, and even though you don't have to talk to us, it would help us a great deal." Andi kept his tone neutral, trying to get Fisher's help by appealing to his sense of justice, which, given his palpable sorrow, had to be running high at the moment. Surely the man wanted his lover's killer or killers brought to justice.

"Well, Lawrence was in an open relationship with Theodora. Or more precisely, he was in a relationship with me and kept Theodora as his beard."

"You want to tell us Lawrence was with you before he married Theodora?" Andi didn't try to keep the disbelief out of his voice.

"Yes. You can ask her; it's all in her prenup. After Lawrence had his divorce from Angelica because of my predecessor, and after he broke up with him *because* of the divorce, he had learned his lesson. When he met me, it was clear from the beginning that we would never be official, but I was fine with that because I had my own career to think about, and our arrangement was perfect as far as I was concerned. After a while and when the gossip about his new bachelor status reached the point where he had to do something, Lawrence found Theodora through a matchmaking service. She was a good deal younger than him, but their goals matched. He needed a wife he could parade around at social events, thus shutting up all the old hags who love nothing more than a juicy scandal, and she wanted financial security. Not having to fulfill her duties as wife in bed was an added bonus for her. She signed an NDA, and in case of a divorce the amount of money she would get was not only clearly outlined but also very generous."

"And what would you have gotten if you had broken up with Mr. Miller?" This whole conversation was so bizarre, Andi decided to just ride it out.

"I've got my own money. I don't need his. Lawrence did install a trust for me in case of his death. It was his way of showing how much he cared." The slight wavering in Jeremy Fisher's voice showed clearly how much *he* cared.

"You really loved him." It was a statement from Andi's side, not a question.

Fisher shrugged. "What can I say? He was an asshole, just like me. Probably the reason we got along so well." He rubbed his face with his left hand. "I'm fully aware how weird our relationship must look for you. In the past few months, Lawrence had started thinking about making us official, but I'm not sure how serious he was. Times have surely changed a lot, and he certainly could have gotten away with it."

"Did Theodora know?"

"Yes. You may not believe it, but Lawrence had a relationship of equals with her. And she's the most pragmatic woman I've ever met. As long as her financial bottom line wasn't endangered, she couldn't care less what Lawrence did. Her words, not mine."

"We're going to verify this with her, of course." Again, there was no threat in Andi's voice. It usually took him longer to be sold on a suspect's story, especially when his occupation was such a perfect link to the way the crime was conducted, but Jeremy Fisher's grief was real, and the way he talked about the entire arrangement he had had with Lawrence and Theodora Miller suggested it was genuine. Of course, the man still wasn't completely off the hook; nobody was until the case was solved. He had lost the number one spot, though. Now that the actual interview was over, Andi left the polite chitchat to George. This eventually led to them leaving the labs on their way back into town and to the office of Gideon Gartner, which was located in the Downtown Charleston Historic District. It took them less than five minutes to find the office in one of the historic buildings, not enough time to talk in depth about the bombshells Jeremy Fisher had just dropped on them.

When they entered the building, Andi stopped dead in his tracks. The sudden silence crashing into him with the force of a freight train was a shock to his system. George was at his side immediately, clasping his upper arms and staring directly into Andi's eyes with so much worry, it would have touched Andi a lot more if he hadn't been so busy cataloging what was going on with his senses. The entrance door was closed, and there was no underlying humming, no barrage of anything. Just his own sense of smell and sight and touch and hearing. Nothing was amplified, nothing distorted, no strange signals he had to translate in order to not get crazy from their constant impact on his brain.

"Andi! Andi! Is everything all right? How many are in here? Should I take you outside again?"

Andi put his hands on George's where they rested on his biceps. "No, everything's fine. It's quiet in here. Completely, blissfully quiet."

George furrowed his brows. "You mean there are no insects in here?"

Andi nodded.

"But you once told me they're everywhere, all the time."

"They usually are, especially in a building as old as this one. My guess is they had the entire structure fumigated. Recently. The day before yesterday, otherwise the first ones would already be back."

George let go of Andi's arms. "I don't know if I should be happy about the reprieve you're getting or afraid for my health because of all the poison surrounding us."

"Well, it's a tie. I'm sure you can make it up by doing some extra miles and downing more of that disgusting green smoothie shit you're so fond of."

"If only you would try them, you'd see how good they are for you."

"Thank you, but no thank you. Let's go find Mr. Gartner." Andi walked with a definite spring in his step, enjoying the silence in his mind. He had to admit he felt a bit empty, the absence of the insects in his head almost deafening in its hush. It was weird, too, seeing the marble steps and just registering, yep, steps, made from pretty stone with an interesting pattern. Nothing more. So good. No unwanted information about the structure of the building, about all the nooks and crannies nobody really wanted to know about. They reached the first floor, where a polished brass sign announced the location of Gartner & Partners to be on the second floor. Again, Andi took the stairs. Because there were no insights from the arthropods, he wasn't willing to take the risk of a faulty elevator.

On the second floor, they were greeted by a wide hall with marble tiles on the ground, a subdued yellow paint on the walls, which went well with the dark oak doors—or was it walnut? Pine? No, pine tended to be lighter. Andi found himself thinking about the strangest things. It was of no consequence what kind of wood the doors were made of. Not to their case and certainly not to him and George personally. And yet he couldn't shake the feeling of being bereft, of lacking vital information. He shook his head. Of course, such was his luck that the one time he got a reprieve—however short-lived it was—from his *geschenk*, it turned out to be a double-edged sword. It also showed him how much he subconsciously relied on the things the arthropods told him. A sobering thought and one that made him angry, frustrated, and afraid at the same time. Not a good combination when they would be meeting a potential suspect.

The first door to their right was open, another brass plate telling visitors to check in here. Andi went over the threshold and into a warm room with a counter made from some dark, gleaming wood—he wouldn't waste time guessing what kind, oh no—a thick carpet with a beautiful pattern in different shades of blue, and two receptionists, one of them screaming stereotype with her immaculate blond chignon, the sharply shaped body of somebody who had been missing a lot of meals in her life, and enough makeup to cover any and all signs of possible age. The other one was a young man with dark hair and eyes, a manbun that somehow managed to look respectable, and a tailored suit in a light gray. The man stepped forward with a smile.

"Good day. How can I help you, gentlemen?"

Andi didn't even have to look at George. He felt his partner next to him, all calm and confident despite being confronted with that mixture of arrogance, snobbism, and class that made Andi's lips twitch with the urge to say something rude and very inappropriate. When the receptionist wore a tailored suit, you knew you had breached holy ground.

"Good day. We are Detectives George Donovan and Andrew Hayes." Andi dutifully pulled his badge out when George did the same.

The receptionist inspected them closely, made quick pictures with his cell before handing them back. "We're here to talk to Mr. Gartner."

The receptionist nodded. "Mr. Gartner is here, but I'm not sure if he's free. Please give me a moment to talk to him." The young man picked up an old-fashioned phone, dialed once, then waited. Neither Andi nor George tried to pressure him. Working where he did, he surely knew he didn't have to do anything for them without a warrant. It was best to stay polite. They could always get the big guns out later.

"Yes, Mr. Gartner." He put the receiver back onto the phone. "You're lucky, Detectives, Mr. Gartner is available and willing to talk to you even though your visit was unannounced. Please follow me."

The receptionist with the perfected passive-aggressive attitude stepped around the counter to lead them out of the reception room and along the hall to a door that also marked the end of the floor. After a short knock, the young man opened the door and motioned for them to enter. George went in first, taking the lead. Gideon Gartner's office reflected perfectly his station in life, namely at the very top. The walls had a light wood paneling where they could be seen between ceiling-high bookshelves stacked with leather-bound tomes. The desk behind which Mr. Gartner resided took up a good quarter of the room, all heavy and dark and gleaming. There were two screens on it, as well as a quill and inkwell. The contradiction between old and new fascinated Andi. As did Gideon Gartner, who looked at them with the same soulful eyes Andi had seen in the newspaper picture. His hair had once been dark, and a few strands still stubbornly clung to their original color while the rest displayed a distinguished silver. The man had aged well, not too many lines marring his angular face. He motioned toward the two leather chairs standing in front of his desk.

"Please, gentlemen, take a seat. Can Gary bring you something to drink?"

George and Andi both declined with a shake of their heads, after which the receptionist, Gary, left, closing the door behind him. Before George could start with the usual introductions, Gartner started speaking again. He was clearly used to taking charge. Being a lawyer for international law, he had to be or else he wouldn't be sitting at such a dignified desk, owner of his own law firm. Behind the thing, Andi saw only glimpses of Gartner's wheelchair, but it looked very high-class.

"What can I do for you, Detectives? It's not every day I get a visit from local law enforcement. I hope none of my clients were naughty." He chuckled softly, as if he'd just made a very funny joke. Or one only he was privy to. Lawyers had a strange sense of humor.

"Well, it's not every day three men are found dead in a lake, so I guess we get a pass?"

George sounded as jovial as Mr. Gartner. With a mother who was a judge, George probably knew all the lawyer jokes in the book.

"Three men dead in a lake? I'm impressed. That is a huge thing. May I ask where I come into play?" There was a furtive quality to Gartner's expression now, one Andi wasn't sure how to read. Was the man simply curious, already knowing it couldn't be good, or was it that he knew why they were here and was trying to gauge how much they knew?

George didn't let himself get derailed. "The victims were Harry Alexander McHill, David Hector Portius II, and Lawrence Miller."

Andi kept his eyes glued to Gartner's face, hoping for some tells. The man's shoulders slumped, and he leaned back in his wheelchair. "Oh. To be frank, I'm surprised you found the connection to me. Back then their fathers did everything in their power to make the whole incident go away and hide all traces."

George shrugged. "Small digitalized newspaper."

"Ah, the joys of the technological age." Gartner chuckled, albeit not in an amused way.

"You said incident. Wasn't it more like grievous bodily harm?" Andi threw the question in, waiting to see if Gartner took the bait. He was definitely rattled.

"That's what I would be going for today, after decades of experience in the courtroom. Back then, when I was a young man without any money or connections, it was an unfortunate incident where the execution of hallowed traditions ended in tragedy." Gartner's lips twitched in clear amusement. "The outcome would have been the same, though. Me with more than enough money to be settled for life and the subtle backing of three powerful men to help me with my endeavors."

"You're not angry about what they did?" George kept his tone light, as if they were making small talk about the weather.

Gideon Gartner sighed and rubbed his face with his left hand. "Dissecting everything I feel about the incident that robbed me of the use of my legs and the violent death of the three men who are to blame for it will take more than the short time we have together. It's going to cost me another two years at counseling at least and will make my psychotherapist richer than she already is. The short version is, a part of me hates them for what they did and will never stop until I die. Another part of me, the pragmatic part, knows very well I probably wouldn't be where I am now if it hadn't happened. I was in Harvard on a scholarship that didn't cover food, clothing, and housing, and the only reason I tried to get into the fraternity was because they offered cheap rooms to members. Still, the chances of me finishing law school were slim from the beginning, and even if I had made it, I didn't have any of the connections necessary to get a real start. After I left the hospital—all bills paid, no questions asked—I had a private room with a part-time assistant lined up for me on campus. I still worked very hard to keep the scholarship, though it wasn't necessary anymore. The trust in my name saw to that. It also saw to my parents getting the medical help they needed after years of hard labor, and it saw my two sisters through school. After graduation, I was invited by one of the most prestigious law firms on the East Coast to start working with them. That wouldn't have happened if Harry Alexander McHill's uncle hadn't been one of their senior partners. From there, my only way was up." Gartner steepled his fingers on the gleaming surface of his desk. "I'm not going to cry a single tear over their deaths, and I'm not going to send flowers to their funerals. I'm also not going to do a happy dance over their demise, and not just because of the obvious reasons. I guess I simply don't care."

"Fair enough." George nodded. "Nevertheless, we need to know where you were last Friday. The entire day."

"Of course. I'll prepare a written statement Gary is going to send to your email with all the receipts and other proof I can find to corroborate my story. Would that suffice?"

"Most certainly. We hope we don't have to inconvenience you again, but you know how these things sometimes go." George got up, and Andi followed suit.

"I know all too well. You're welcome anytime, Detectives. It's my pleasure to aid the police. Have a good day."

"Thank you for your time, Mr. Gartner."

They left the building, neither of them commenting on Gideon Gartner's overly friendly attitude. When they entered the street, the barely there hum Andi had started to feel inside after the initial shock of absolute silence had worn off turned into the usual roar of images. It hit him hard even though he had anticipated it, and he was glad George drove them back to the precinct.

8. Impossible to Unravel

After a short stop at a deli to get some sandwiches, George and Andi were back at their desks in the precinct, George standing in front of the whiteboard with his black marker at the ready. He stared at the numerous lines and names crowding the space, none standing out yet, with a cluster of arrows pointing toward them. Andi was slumped in his chair, nibbling on his sandwich without much appetite, which could be because of the quality of the sandwich—though that rarely deterred Andi—or more likely, because he was back to having the full arthropod surround-sound. The change in his partner when they left the fumigated building had been subtle but telling. The stress lines around Andi's mouth and eyes, which had evened out a bit during the half or so hour with Gartner, had returned with full force, and the air of constant tension was back surrounding him. Andi had once told him his usual circle of awareness was about half a mile, like a background noise he could never turn off. It was overlayed by his immediate surroundings, which always had the strongest impact. The building certainly wasn't half a mile wide, but George assumed the absence of the battering of images in his direct vicinity had been the same as absolute silence. People were surprisingly good at ignoring sounds or images they got on a regular basis, like when living close to a railroad the rumbling of the trains didn't register anymore, while new or different impressions or the absence of sounds they were used to were experienced as more impacting than they actually were. It didn't help to alleviate his worry about Andi, who very pointedly ignored that he had admitted to having trouble and tried his best to do business as usual. George was experienced enough to give Andi some line before he tried to haul him in again. Hence his focus on the whiteboard.

"We have eight people close to the victims who had reason to off them, and only one showed any signs of true sorrow." George drew a pink circle around Jeremy Fisher's name. "He's also the one suspect who had the easiest means to get his hands on the ketamine that aided in killing the victims."

"I don't think he did it." Andi was playing with a ballpoint pen from his desk, slowly unscrewing it. By the end of their brainstorming, it would be in its individual parts, which Andi would then proceed to break. George made a mental note to buy a new bulk set. They were running low. "Yes, his profession means he is the ideal candidate, but his emotions were genuine, and he had no reason to kill the other two."

George uncapped his black marker just to give his hands something to do. "He wouldn't be the first killer to regret what he did, but I agree with you. Why the other two? Unfortunately, that goes for all the wives and the sons as well. The only one who had reason to go after the three of them was Gartner, and he's in a freaking wheelchair. Even if he has the best model available, I doubt the thing would be versatile enough to herd three grown men into a lake."

"He could have had help. Or hired somebody."

George mulled this over. "He could. Why did he wait so long, though? Why didn't he kill them in their prime?"

"Perhaps he wanted to wait to make sure they couldn't be traced back to him? You saw and heard him when you told him how we found him. He hadn't thought anybody would make the connection."

"True. By waiting he eliminated the chances of being found out." George drew a red circle around Gartner's name. "Could he have used a contract killer?"

"That's what I would have done if I were him." Andi was now pulling at the spring inside the pen, turning it into a straight piece of cheap metal. He had blue stains on his fingers. "Then again, if I were him, I would have hired a contract killer much sooner and told him to make it look like an accident or natural causes. Plus, a contract killer would never go through the trouble of tampering with their beer, then hauling them up to the lake and drowning them."

"Unless he was told and paid to do so." George tapped the pen against his chin. "Until now we have assumed they were roofied to keep them docile, but what if that's not the case? Or more precisely, what if that's just a nice bonus and the whole thing is more about symbolism?"

"Keep talking." Andi was done with the spring and now busy pulverizing the plastic casing by breaking it repeatedly with his hands.

"Do you agree that this wasn't a murder on impulse?"

"Absolutely. It has none of the classical signs, and the insects didn't report any of the anger that usually goes with this kind of murder. Which makes it so hard to distinguish between all the people who have been at the cabin."

"If a murder is committed in cold blood, it's either done by a pro or well planned. In this case, it could be both. What if Gartner gave the contract killer he hired clear instructions how to take the victims out?"

"I'm with you, George. But why have them roofied? What kind of symbolism is that? Wouldn't Gartner rather have their backs broken?"

"Too obvious. On the off chance the connection between him and the victims would be found. Perhaps he wanted them to be as helpless as he felt back then? He said it himself—he had no money, no connections. There was no other choice than to accept whatever the fathers of the victims were offering."

"I could get behind that reasoning. Can you also explain why he had them brought to the small lake? If he wanted them found, the probability would have been higher in Lake Moultrie. It was pure chance we found them when we did." Andi was done with the plastic, his fingers pushing the sad remnants of a once proud pen over his desk, using the straightened spring to plow lines into the bits.

"Don't forget, Berta said they would probably have found them eventually because the lake is too small to hold three corpses without the poison affecting the surroundings. Perhaps that was factored in?" George drew a line from Gartner's name outward, made a circle with a question mark and wrote "contract killer" into it.

"To get rid of the ketamine. Makes sense. And Gartner would have the means to find a pro to do the killing for him."

"You don't sound entirely convinced." Actually, George liked that about his partner. Andi was a skeptic and always willing to poke holes in theories. Others' as well as his own. Andi reached for the bin next to his desk to sweep the dead pen into it.

"I'm still a bit hung up about the time factor. Even if Gartner wanted the victims' deaths to have symbolic value, he could have had that sooner. And a pro would have no problem hiding the bodies long enough for any evidence to be gone or to see to it there wasn't any to begin with. So why now? What has changed?"

"That's something we definitely have to look into." George drew a clock next to Gartner's name. "We also have to ask Shireen to search the darknet for any contracts on the victims."

"She's going to be so happy with us." Andi yawned. A quick glance at his watch told George it was time to call it quits for the day. He capped the marker.

"Let's get you home. You can send Shireen a text message in the car."

Andi grinned. "Good thinking, man. She won't be able to complain to us until tomorrow morning."

After shutting their PCs down, they went out into George's car. The drive to James Island was swift. Andi looked like he would fall right into his bed when he left the car, and George had to suppress the urge to follow his partner into the house and make sure he got upstairs all right. There were days when Andi allowed and appreciated such a gesture, and there were days like this one, when he didn't. Being able to tell them apart was one of the greatest accomplishments George had made in the past months. After the door to Andi's house was closed, George turned the car to drive back to his own home, deep in thought. Not only about the case but also about Andi and where their partnership was going. George was as good at avoiding topics he didn't like as Andi, and just like Andi, he had moments of weakness or clarity—he wasn't sure which term he wanted applied—where he had to face the facts.

The partnership with Andi was the deepest one he ever had with a partner. George was aware the main catalyst for that was Andi's *geschenk*, the huge, unbelievable secret George was now helping him to hide. Such a thing tended to bind people together. But that wasn't all there was to it, which worried George. He genuinely cared for Andi, not only as his partner but also as a friend. He wasn't sure if Andi in turn saw him as a friend. He wasn't even sure if Andi was familiar with the concept. George could also feel how Andi was trying to maintain a certain distance between them. It didn't take a genius to realize Andi was waiting for George to leave him. Which he would do. Definitely. He had a career to make, goals to achieve. Yes, he had.

George thumped his forehead against the steering wheel, hitting the horn in the process. Luckily, he was already parked. A quick glance around showed nobody was paying him any attention. Sighing, he got out of the car. For a long while, he just stood next to it, wondering why what had been meant to be just another stepstone in his career was suddenly becoming so much more. He needed to go on a run, he decided, to clear his thoughts. The air was still reasonably warm for late fall, and it would be light outside for at least another hour and a half. With new determination,

George went into his apartment, put on his running gear, grabbed a bottle of water, put in his earbuds, and started his favorite running music, a vicious mix of German Power Metal bands and some Epica and Nightwish thrown in for good measure. His feet hit the asphalt outside his apartment, and for the next hour George lost himself in the pounding of his heart and the steady rhythm of his feet eating the miles. Back home, he managed a shower and dinner before the thoughts came back with a vengeance. The whole thing had been bothering him on and off for the last three months. It seemed it was time to grab the bull by its horns. George knew he had to talk to somebody about it, and that somebody was his brother Daniel, a member of the MP and currently stationed in Hawaii. He answered the phone on the third ring.

"George, my sweet little brother! I thought you had gone and died in a ditch."

"You could have called as well, you know."

"Yeah, I just wanted to give you some mom vibes here." Daniel sounded as if he was in a ridiculously good mood. Well, George could remedy that. "How are you?"

"If everything were peachy, I wouldn't be calling."

"I'm fine, thank you very much."

"You're in Hawaii."

"Aloha. Now, joking aside, why are you calling your favorite brother?"

George sighed. It was one of the things he loved about his brother—well, the only thing—he did banter, but he knew when to get serious as well. Or at least how to attempt to get serious.

"I'm sorry, Daniel. I just need somebody to listen."

"Ah, so it's about your partner, the infamous Andi. Seriously, man, you have to introduce us."

Daniel was also perceptive and annoying. And the only person he could call. Damn. "Yes, it is about Andi, and no, I won't be introducing you. You can't be trusted."

"He would love me."

"He would kill you... come to think of it, I *should* introduce you."

"Aww, George, you would be sad without me around, admit it!"

"Not as sad as I am now pissed."

"Fine, tell me about your latest problem with the partner I'm not allowed to meet." Daniel made a clucking noise with his tongue.

"I'm going to leave him, and I don't know if I like it." There, his whole problem summed up in one sentence.

"What do you mean, you're going to leave him? I didn't know you were together in the first place! Have you been holding out on me?" The teasing tone made clear Daniel didn't mean the nonsense he was spouting. George very firmly kept himself from losing even one thought on how much he liked the fact that Daniel could see him and Andi as a couple. That was forbidden territory, like Chernobyl forbidden.

"You're an ass."

"Right back at you."

"Our partnership is going to end when I leave Charleston."

"Which won't be for another year. You told me you were thinking about staying at least two years if not three because Andi makes your solving statistics look good. Very clever idea, by the way."

"I'm not exploiting Andi!"

"I didn't say so. Now why do you feel like you don't want to leave him? Have you gotten addicted to solving every case? Have you forgotten the importance of being pruned now and then to stay humble?"

"He needs me."

"Oh." There was a moment of silence before Daniel started talking again, all teasing gone from his tone. "Has this to do with his special talent?"

After George had found out about Andi, he had talked to Daniel, not revealing Andi's secret—he would never betray his partner's confidence—but calling his *geschenk* a special talent. Daniel assumed Andi was some kind of autist with a special knack for putting clues together. As a stand-in it worked well enough to allow George to talk more freely about Andi and the things he did.

"Yes. He's finally started to rely on me, which in turn makes working together run more smoothly. And if I leave, he'll be alone again."

"He's an adult. He'll find somebody else if he needs to."

The idea of Andi trusting anybody but him with his secret was in equal parts hilarious and gut-wrenching. George realized he was way more involved than he had initially thought. "I'm not sure he will. And I can't stand the thought of it."

"Easy, then. Stay. You can make a career in Charleston as well."

"Not the kind of career I want. You know that."

"George, to be honest, I'm not sure the kind of career you're aiming for is what you truly are or need. You're driven, yes, and I'm sure you'll make a damn fine chief one day, but the way you're going about it...."

"You're doing the same."

"Yes, and there are days when even I question the sanity of the path I have chosen, and I don't attach as easily as you do."

"I attach easily?"

"It's one of your more endearing talents. You can grow roots everywhere. Me, I'm not good at that, which is why all the gallivanting around the States comes easy to me. But on you it's hard, and don't try to tell me otherwise. I know you too well."

George had to think about that for a moment. Daniel was right. He had an easy time getting homey in places. He needed it too. It gave him a sense of stability and purpose he otherwise missed. Which was the reason he had never stayed in one precinct longer than a year and a half until now. Just thinking about prolonging his stay in Charleston was taking him into territory he had subconsciously avoided so far.

"You think I should consider staying here for longer? Seriously?"

"You're calling me because you're worried about leaving a partner you've been working with for what now, six months? Before Andi, I could call myself lucky when I found out your partner's name before you transferred to the next precinct. Hell, I know more about Andi than about any other person you ever had in your life, apart from family."

"What about my plans?"

"Plans change, George. They can be altered, as you well know. And see it like this—if you decide to stay longer, you get some breathing space to examine your feelings and goals. Perhaps something has changed and you haven't noticed because you were so busy trying to fulfill your five-year plan."

George mulled this over. It was too big a leap to simply embrace it. He would have to sleep on it, catalogue it, examine his feelings, as Daniel had put it. At least he had a plan now.

"Thank you, Daniel. I needed to hear that. I guess I have a lot of thinking to do."

"Try not to overdo it. I don't want to be responsible when your brain explodes."

"And I'm not grateful anymore. Have a nice evening, you ass."

"Love you, too, little brother. Call me anytime."

"Love you, Daniel. I think."

The line went dead, and George stared at the blank screen of his TV. It was a good thing he had been running, otherwise he wouldn't be getting much sleep tonight.

THE MORNING wasn't good. George hadn't slept as well as he had hoped, Andi was staring tight-lipped into his herbal tea, the dark circles under his eyes indicating his night hadn't been any better, and Shireen was already waiting for them in the hall, motioning them to follow her into her lair. After a slurred "Good morning" from Andi, Shireen went straight to the heart of the matter, not even complaining about the additional work they had unloaded on her the day before.

"Good morning to you too. And before you ask, I haven't found anything on the darknet yet. But Mrs. Ingman from the Palmetto Conversation Foundation has sent me an email with some lovely pictures. I contacted her after you sent me the info about the wildlife cameras. Apparently two biologists are researching the movement patterns of the wildlife in the Lake Moultrie region, and they have several cameras in close vicinity to the cabin because they want to see how human settlement affects the animals. The two searched all the cameras and sent me everything non-animal they found from Wednesday through Friday."

"Your satisfied smile says there was something of interest?" George longed to hear something that would help them.

"Yes. I hope. It definitely qualifies as a lead." Shireen pulled up several images of a bulky-looking dark green car, the first four in color, the next in varying shades of gray, as was typical for pictures taken during the night. "This car, a BMW X1, was caught by two of the cameras, both times coming and leaving. On Wednesday it drove toward the cabin at around five o'clock and left about an hour later. On Thursday it came in at eight in the evening and left only twenty minutes afterwards. I understand this coincides with the cabin being empty before the victims came and then with the night of the murder."

George looked at Andi, who was staring at the pictures with furrowed brows. "The first time span fits. An hour is enough time to break into the cabin and doctor the beers, then leave again. But twenty minutes isn't enough to get three grown men, no matter how drugged they were, out of the cabin and into a car. Are there any pictures where we can see who's inside the vehicle?"

Shireen shook her head. "Sorry, George. The cameras' position is too low for that. But it's just the right height to catch the license plates."

"Which you did." Andi was still staring at the pictures.

"Which I did because I'm the best, you wanted to add." Shireen winked at George, not the least bit offended by Andi's absentmindedness. She changed the picture on the screen, showing two names and an address. "Meet Tabitha Clemént and Josephine Garr, the owners of that beautiful beemer."

Shireen tapped some more, and two license pictures popped up on the screen. One showed an African American woman with short hair, the other a stockier-looking Caucasian woman with dark hair, eyes, and skin complexion that hinted at Mediterranean ancestors. Her hair was pulled into a ponytail, and her round face with the sharp nose didn't show any traces of makeup. "Tabitha Clemént, forty-three." Shireen enlarged the picture of the African American woman. "A lawyer for family law with Dexter & Partners. She's one of the senior partners and lives in East Cooper in a pricey house she shares with Josephine Garr." Shireen changed pictures to the other woman. "Josephine has a PhD in chemistry and works for a skin-care company, Natural Beauty, here in Charleston. They produce high-end stuff, and Josephine is in charge of their research department."

"Any connection to the victims?" George was wondering what a family lawyer and a researcher had to do with three business sharks.

"None I could find yet. The women both graduated from Yale, and they seem to have known each other before. I have to dig some more."

"Do that, but could you concentrate on the immediate family? We're going to pay these two a visit now, see what they have to say."

George didn't have to look at Andi to know his partner was with him on this. Tabitha and Josephine would either be additional suspects on their seemingly endless list, or they would be able to dismiss them, an option George would prefer. They left Shireen to her hacking and got into the car.

HOBCAW BLUFF Drive in East Cooper was lined with beautiful houses varying in style from respectable Southern Belles to modern buildings with flat roofs and plenty of glass and steel. The driveways and front gardens of these houses were beautifully groomed, showing a wide variety of autumn blooms such as Angel's Trumpet, Autumnal Blues, Balloon Flowers, and Belladonna Lilies. Their rich colors were like a last rebellion against the upcoming cold season, very much welcomed by the arthropods, who not only fed from the plants but also used them as shelter as George had learned by now. Naturally Andi was a well of information about the living habits of creepy crawlers and their abilities to adapt to almost every environment, which never ceased to amaze George.

The home of Tabitha Clemént and Josephine Garr was very modern, the driveway with the gray pebbles lined with rhododendron and baygall bushes. Two huge gray pots housed pyramids made of willow branches on which Black-eyed Susans climbed upward, accentuating the steel construction in the background with their bright yellow beauty.

George drove by very slowly, giving Andi a chance to take a quick internal peek. "Anybody home?"

Andi nodded. "Yes. We have to be careful."

George tensed. He hated it when they couldn't move freely. The closer they could get to the house, the less the strain on Andi's body and mind when he opened himself to the arthropods, but also the higher the chance they were detected before he could find anything useful. With a sigh, he parked the Escalade two houses down.

"Here, I brought ibuprofen. Perhaps it helps if you take them beforehand." He leaned over to the passenger side to open the glove compartment where he had stored two bottles of water and four ibuprofen. When he handed them to Andi, his partner was staring at him with a strange expression.

"What?"

"Nothing." Andi selected two of the pills, getting them out of their casing with a cracking sound. "It's just, you're always thinking ahead. I could get used to this." The implication was clear. Andi knew George would leave in about eighteen months. Deliberately, George ignored the subtext, as well as the little voice in his own head demanding he finally face reality. Instead, he uncapped the water bottle for Andi and held it out to him. "If I were really thinking ahead, I would have come up with this idea sooner." He frowned. "Why didn't you think of it?"

Andi shrugged. "Easy. The pain pills always make me a little woozy. Doctor said they have that effect on some people, and I'm part of that lucky and illustrious group. When I was still working alone, I preferred the pain over a delayed reaction time. Especially when I had to get home somehow. Car accidents are nasty."

"You don't have to worry about delayed reaction times anymore. I'm here."

"I know. Thank you." Andi swallowed the two pills and washed them down with half the water from the bottle. "I'm good to go."

Conveniently for them, a small alleyway separated the house from its neighbor on the right, the shed in the garden with its back to the fence providing excellent cover. Andi leaned against the decorative stone wall guarding the house from the alleyway and closed his eyes. Even if somebody came by and wondered what they were doing, it simply looked as if Andi was exhausted and they were taking a break, enjoying the autumn sun in the process. George stayed close to his partner, waiting for the oral tour through the house and lives of Josephine Garr and Tabitha Clemént. It didn't take long. Andi's expression got that faraway quality George had learned to both welcome and fear, meaning his connection to the arthropods in the area was now fully open and working.

"The soil is good, there were blobs bringing new earth, dark and rich, new flowers, sleeping, it's getting cold, there's spaces in the wood, planks, it's warm there, safe, two blobs in the house, moving, moving, stress, loud, the colony was disturbed, acid in the trash, everything ruined, no food, contaminated, bad, no cocoons, there should be cocoons, why should there be cocoons, prey, the net is broken, a breeze from above, lazy, cold, poison in the kitchen, they destroyed the nest, death, all gone, empty, where to hide, the flowers taste good, need to feed, the dead season is coming, so tired, must go underground, where the cold can't reach, the host is dead, find another one, rot, decay, a feast, mating, I'm caught in the net, can't get free, prey, finally, food, warmth, the breeze is too strong, need to, need to, the blobs left in the dark, they never do this, late, I need to dig, the wood's too hard, there's something in it, bad, the clothes are wet, drip, drip, drip, strange water, not the one from the faucet, what's a faucet? Dripping, cold, it's broken, where do I go now, deeper down, stone, death, no hiding—"

George decided it was time to end this. Andi's speech pattern was getting more and more distorted, losing all coherence, resembling the chaos Andi described to him as the natural state of his connection to the insects. He grabbed Andi's arm to shake him out of his stupor. Sweat was beading on his partner's brow, and his skin looked even paler than usual. It took him what seemed like an eternity but couldn't have been more than a few minutes to yank Andi back to him, back into reality, all the time calling his name and murmuring reassurances that he was there, that Andi could come back, that it was safe. Finally, Andi's eyes lost the daze and focused on George. He shook his head like a cat that had gotten wet.

"They were definitely there. At the cabin. In the cabin. I recognize them more clearly from the woods. And there was this strange substance again, not the ketamine, though they had some in the house at some point. Something else. I wish I knew what it was. I have a feeling it's important." Andi's shoulders slumped. "Or maybe I'm just confused."

It broke George's heart to see his partner so dejected. Intellectually he had known their cases wouldn't always be as clear-cut as the Castain case, with them knowing the culprit way before they had enough evidence to prove it. As George was learning bit by bit, too much information was a problem when you didn't know what exactly you were looking for. It was like fishing for sardines. There were so many fish, you could never hope to concentrate on just one, constantly being distracted. At least they had confirmation that the two women had both been at the cabin and that they had ketamine in the house. How they would prove that George didn't know yet. He offered Andi his hand to help him up, and his partner took it.

"Let's go and talk to them."

9. ABYSSES

WHEN THEY rang the bell, it took some time until Tabitha Clemént answered it. Andi felt her moving through the house—

Rising from the chair behind her desk, the wood no good, not real wood, the fake one that neither provided food nor nesting space, to the door, down the steps, heavy footfalls, she wasn't careful, slippers slapping against the tiles in the floor, slap, slap, slap, loud, vibrating through the house, coming closer, stopping at the intercom, a crackling, the air in waves, unsettling—

"Who is there?"

George stepped toward the little camera on top of the bell, showing his badge. "This is Detective George Donovan from the Charleston PD. I'm here with my partner, Detective Andrew Hayes. If you have time, could we perhaps ask you some questions?"

Nervous, her adrenaline spiking, shuffling—

"I don't think so." Short and to the point. George wasn't one to give up easily, though.

"Please, Ms.—is it Ms. Clemént or Ms. Garr?" Smart move, showing her they already knew something, but not whether it was her or her friend inside the house, giving her the illusion of an advantage she didn't have.

"It's Mrs. Clemént." She sounded grudging, ready to cut them off.

"Mrs. Clemént, we're truly sorry to disturb you, but we're investigating a murder, and we have photographic proof you were close to the place where it happened. We were hoping you could perhaps provide us with some information to help us?" George was a very clever man, subtly telling her they had the means to link her to the crime, at the same time making clear she wasn't a suspect by appealing her to help. Andi didn't know how much of it she was buying—the woman was a lawyer after all—but her stress levels went down considerably. She still didn't open the door, though.

"What do you want to know?" Still grumpy, but she was cooperating.

"We understand you were at Lake Moultrie last Wednesday afternoon. May I ask why?" George acted as if it was perfectly normal to conduct an interview via the house intercom. Then again, the man had worked in Narcotics. Drug addicts tended to be highly suspicious of cops.

"We go there regularly. Hiking."

A valid reason. And most probably true because Tabitha Clemént was now calm as could be. She was telling the truth.

"It seems to me you chose a rather interesting parking spot." No accusation from George, no direct question why they would park off a rarely used side road when there were huge parking spaces available in the area. Mrs. Clemént huffed.

"When we go hiking, we like to be alone. In the afternoons, the parking lots are usually full." True and plausible. If it hadn't been for that strange substance Andi had felt in the house, outside, and now everywhere in Tabitha and Josephine's house, he would have believed her.

"I understand. Did you see anything unusual? More cars parked outside the parking lot, perhaps other people hiking there?"

"No. Nothing unusual. A few people around, don't remember how many. Two runners with their dogs." Tabitha was apparently intent on being as uncooperative as possible while still speaking to them. George demonstrated once again that he was a saint.

"I see. Now why did you go back there Thursday night?"

A pause, the spiders inside the house telling Andi the stress levels were rising again.

"Josephine lost her bottle. It was a new one, quite expensive. We decided to look for it but couldn't make it before it got dark."

The stress levels were sinking; she had gotten her footing back.

"You were looking for a bottle in the dark? Did you find it?" There was now a hint of disbelief in George's voice. Andi wondered if his partner was annoyed by the plausibility of everything Tabitha had said until now or if he was trying to push her a bit.

"It's a large bottle with metallic painting. We figured it would even be easier to find it with the flashlights because we would immediately see it, even from a distance."

Which actually made sense. Andi shook his head at George. They wouldn't be getting anything out of Tabitha Clemént, not today and not with the little information they had.

Still, George tried one more time. "Did you notice anything out of the ordinary when you looked for the bottle?"

"No. It was dark, and we were concentrating on finding the bottle."

George gave up. "Thank you, Mrs. Clemént, for your help. We appreciate it."

All they got was a clucking sound before the intercom crackled out.

"Seems like this case is going to fill our quota for meetings with hostile women." George winked at Andi on their way back to the car. They climbed in, and Andi got out the second water bottle from the glove department. He offered it to George, who took a generous gulp before returning it to Andi. They drove back to the precinct in silence, both lost in their own thoughts. Back at their desks, they saw they had no new messages from either Shireen or Evangeline, just a short note from CSI that the needle they had found had indeed been used to inject the ketamine through the beer caps and that they had found a partial fingerprint they couldn't match, though they kept searching.

George stared at the whiteboard. "Two more suspects." He wrote the names of Tabitha and Josephine down. "With no connections whatsoever."

"No connections we know of," Andi corrected. "But you're right, this is strange." He leaned back in his chair. "You know we have to go back to the lake, don't you?"

George pressed his lips into a thin line. "I don't like it."

The worry in his partner's tone warmed Andi's heart. "Me neither. But we need to get some sort of order established, and we can't do that without having all the facts. At the moment we're like chickens with their heads cut off."

"Are you sure you're going to get any facts? So far we have too much input, and the one that's standing out you can't place." George's voice was soft, taking the edge off his words. Andi wasn't offended. George was right after all. So far, his tiny informants had added to the chaos instead of thinning it out. He only hoped what he would find out at the lake was worth the migraine he would get. "I'd say we drive up there tomorrow. Too late today."

George closed the cap on his whiteboard pen. "I really don't like it."

TWO FRUITLESS hours of staring at the whiteboard and discussing possible theories later, George was ready to call it a day. After they swung by a deli to get dinner for Andi—George wanted him to have something substantial in his belly for the task the next day—he drove his partner home.

George told Andi to get as much rest as possible, which his partner acknowledged with an eye roll and a "Yes, Daddy." The gentle tone, though, told George how much Andi appreciated his worry. And worry he did. Was it really necessary for Andi to do this, to risk his sanity just so they could solve the case more quickly? Would they be able to solve the case without Andi's *geschenk*? George was honest with himself. The chances were twenty to thirty percent of them solving it without help. There were too many variables, too many suspects, and they had just started scratching the surface! From experience George knew things got uglier the longer one kept digging, and with the victims being so ripe in years and so powerful? Nobody got that far and stayed ahead without stepping on toes. And there were so many things not adding up, like the wives who didn't even try to pretend they were grieving or the sons who openly admitted to not having much or any contact with their fathers, the way they lived so humbly compared to the mansions and lifestyles their fathers had. Then there were Tabitha and Josephine, two unknown players with seemingly no connection to the victims. George felt his head spin from all the possibilities stretching out in front of him. And they hadn't even started on the contract killer theory, which was plausible enough to not be dismissed. No, Andi needed to do it, because the victims deserved justice. He just had to be there for his partner when the inevitable breakdown followed.

On his way home he stopped at a small clothes boutique with a *Sale* sign in the window he spotted while waiting on a red light. They had beautiful cotton sweaters in different colors, ideal for the upcoming fall. George didn't know if his gesture would be appreciated, but he had the burning desire to do something nice for his partner, something that showed his appreciation without him saying all those words Andi never seemed comfortable hearing.

Deciding which sweater to get Andi proved difficult, because George was the first to admit that fashion wasn't his strong suit. He had long ago learned what looked good on him and stuck to his color palette. Knowing Andi wouldn't care if the color and style of the sweater suited him or not made it somehow even more important to choose something good. Luckily for him, the sales assistant seemed to receive his vibes of sheer desperation and came over to him.

"Sir, can I perhaps help you now?" she asked with a polite smile. When George had entered, he had said he was just taking a look, which she had accepted with a nod.

"Yes, please. I'm looking for a sweater for my partner and am a bit lost as to what I should get him."

"Ooh, that's sweet! Is it an anniversary?" Her smile was so broad now, it almost reached her ears. While George appreciated that she was neither racist nor homophobic, he couldn't let her believe that he and Andi were a couple.

"Uh, no. He's my partner in the police force. We're both detectives, and his clothing style is—questionable."

"Pardon me. I shouldn't have made assumptions." She seemed flustered, and George hated the dejected look on her young freckled face. He also realized he had kind of liked her thinking he and Andi were an item. No, no, no. He couldn't go there. Shouldn't. Bad idea.

"It's okay. I could have been clearer, and besides, I think it's wonderful that you are supportive."

Those words perked her up again. "Your partner, what does he look like? Do you happen to know his size?"

George started to sweat. Buying clothes for himself was a lot easier. "Uhm, he's smaller than me, reaches up to here." He indicated with his hands where Andi's head ended below his collarbone. "And he's leaner than me." He held his hands apart to show how broad Andi was in the shoulders.

The shop assistant nodded and smiled. "So most probably a size forty."

George nodded. That sounded right. "I'm a size forty-two/forty-four for jackets and sweaters."

"Wonderful. Now, what's his hair and eye color? If you happen to know." She didn't sound hopeful, and George couldn't blame her. He wondered how many men walked into the shop not knowing such vital information. Well, he wasn't one of them.

"His hair is kind of a dirty-blond with lighter strands at the top. He keeps it quite long because he doesn't like going to the barber. His eyes are this mixture of blue and gray with a little green thrown in."

The utter surprise on her face made George's chest swell with pride. He did pay attention to detail, no matter what his mother claimed.

"That's quite accurate. I rarely have customers who know these things at all." She rushed over to one of the pyramid squares where all kinds of sweaters were displayed and selected a few. George immediately knew Andi wouldn't go for the bright red and probably not for the apple green either. The gray-purple one, though, could be a winner. As well as the caramel-colored one. George pointed at the two sweaters in question. The gray-purple had a V-neck and close-fitting cuffs. The caramel had loose cuffs and a turtleneck. Both were unbelievably soft to the touch.

"They don't chafe at all, you can put them in the washing machine, though not the dryer, and they're among the sturdiest we have. Plus, both of them are sixty percent off." The shop assistant smiled brightly.

George looked at the price tags, trying to decide which one he should buy. They were both gorgeous. After a moment, he handed the shop assistant both. It might be reckless, but he felt kind of wild today. Or perhaps it was his worry about what Andi would be doing the next day that he needed to soothe somehow. It didn't matter. The sweaters were good quality, Andi could definitely use them, and the price was reasonable.

"I'll take both."

Her smile became even brighter, and she hurried to the cash register, as if she was afraid he would change his mind at the last minute. After George had paid, he went home with his new purchases, already wondering how he should go about giving them to Andi.

10. A Dip in the Past

ANDI WOKE up knowing he had to prepare his bedroom for the afternoon when he came back from their trip to Swamp Fox Trail. After a quick visit to the bathroom, he got the bucket, placed it right next to the bed. A box of ibuprofen went on the nightstand, together with two bottles of water and his sleeping mask, which would help him keep the light out. The window was tilted, letting fresh air in. Andi rubbed his face with his right hand. He really wished he didn't have to do this, but their choices were slim. Even without Chief Norris just waiting for them to fuck up, they desperately needed a nudge in the right direction to know on which suspects from the ever-growing pool they should focus. The insects around the house were quiet this morning, a small mercy Andi gladly accepted. He went into the kitchen to drink some orange juice before George arrived. His partner was always super-punctual, which left Andi about three minutes to get his juice. Andi had just taken the first sip directly from the carton—he lived alone, so it was perfectly okay—when he heard George's car in the driveway. Opening the door, Andi saw the surprise on George's face.

"You're up."

"Yes, I'm up." It wasn't *that* rare for him to be at least vertical when his partner arrived. Andi was just about to get his jacket when he realized George was fidgeting. He was also holding a paper bag in his left hand.

"What's that?" Andi pointed his chin at the bag. George gulped, his Adam's apple jumping like a frog in a swamp.

"Uh…. You see, when I went home yesterday… uhm…." George changed the bag from his left to his right hand, then back again. He hesitated for a moment before thrusting it toward Andi as if he wanted to get rid of whatever was in there. "This is for you. It was a sale, no big deal."

Curious, Andi looked inside the bag. He spotted a nice gray-purple sweater. When he took it out, a second one came into sight, this one caramel. George was scratching the back of his neck. "Yours are all a bit—outdated, and I thought you would like something new."

With sudden clarity, Andi knew George was unsure about his reaction. As if there was any doubt. Without any effort on his part, Andi was now in possession of two brand-new gorgeous sweaters that would save him from having to expend the energy to get them himself. It was a bit like having his own fairy godmother.

"Thank you so much, George. I like them. You don't happen to have some jeans for me as well?"

Andi had meant the last comment mostly as a joke to lighten the mood, though one could always hope, he figured. The way George's face lit up like a Christmas tree told him he had said something right.

"No, but I can totally get you one or two. You see, the boutique where I bought the sweaters, they're having a sale, and I've seen some jeans which would look good on you—"

"That sounds wonderful, George, but you have to let me pay for them."

The relieved expression on George's face puzzled Andi. "Did you think I'd let you pay for everything?" He had more than enough money.

George shook his head violently. "No, no, that's not it at all." He sighed deeply. "You see, all the way from my place to yours I've been wondering how you were going to take this present, if you'd get angry because I overstepped, and I know you don't like going shopping and I thought this is something I can help you with…."

Andi forced his heartbeat to slow down. George was being nice, but George wouldn't be here forever. "I'd appreciate it. Going shopping means talking to people." He gave an exaggerated shudder.

"I can take care of that for you." George smiled, the nervousness from moments before completely evaporated. "Are you ready?"

"To go and listen to Chief Norris? Never." Andi put the bag with the sweaters on the small table he had in the hall, slipped on his jacket, and closed the front door. He spent the drive to the precinct eating his bagel, because when he had to deal with the chief first thing in the morning, he needed all the energy he could get.

Norris was as unpleasant as always; after a short "Morning," she went right for their throats.

"I'm still waiting on reports about your progress, Detectives. I assume there is progress?" The way she lifted her brows made perfectly clear she knew there was nothing noteworthy so far.

"We're still pursuing several avenues regarding possible suspects. The victims were very active members of society, and the list, I'm afraid, is rather long," George explained smoothly.

"In other words, you have nothing." There was a hint of satisfaction in the chief's voice that made Andi's dislike of her go up several notches. "May I ask why your famous instinct hasn't kicked in yet, Detective Hayes?"

"Oh, don't worry. It's kicking like crazy. Would be even more so if we could do our work in peace." The words weren't outright disrespectful. They were just challenging enough to warrant a reaction. Andi could see Chief Norris gearing up for exactly that when her phone started ringing. One look at the caller ID and she shooed them out with narrowed eyes, her gaze promising she wouldn't forget what had just happened.

"Saved by the bell," Andi commented as they walked to their desks to see if either Shireen, Evangeline, or CSI had any news for them.

"She's escalating." George threw his keys on the desk. "We have to be careful, Andi. And I think it would be a good idea to start writing things down. Every interaction we have with her."

"You think it's that bad?" Andi didn't like the woman, but he couldn't believe things had progressed so far. Especially since George had advised him to be more amiable toward her only a few days ago. Had his partner just tried to shield him then, or was this worry about the chief something new? Maybe it would be a good idea to pay a bit more attention in the future, no matter how distracted he got by his *geschenk*. Another thing he knew would be getting worse over the years—while his awareness of his surroundings, his view of the world, would take on even sharper edges, his perception of other humans, especially the social part of them, would deteriorate to the point where he would test the patience of those who knew him to the breaking point, while strangers would simply wish to kill him for his terrible manners. He had seen it all play out with his *Oma*, and she had had the excuse of old age to afford her a lot of leeway.

George was booting his PC. "Let me say it like this. I'm not sure how much longer her desire to look good to her superiors will outweigh her animosity toward you and, by now, me as well." Back to the problem at hand.

"I'm sorry you have to put up with this. You had other plans." It galled Andi to even mention those other plans.

"She asked me to investigate whether you used shady means to solve your cases. You don't, I reported as such. It's neither your nor my fault this woman can't accept the facts. If she doesn't learn to work with the realities of life, she's not going to get much further than her current position."

"I love how you can put everything into perspective." Andi didn't try to hide the hint of sarcasm in his voice, knowing full well George would interpret it as aimed at the chief, not his own aspirations. As predicted, his partner laughed.

"It's a talent." He peered at his screen. "There's no news from either Shireen, Evangeline, or CSI." He reached for his mouse. "I guess we don't have a reason to stay here any longer. Unless you want to go over the whiteboards again?"

They both glanced at the two white spaces with all the lines and names on them. They were a visual manifestation of how little they had found out while at the same time drowning in information.

"I think the whiteboards can wait till tomorrow. Let's go to the crime scene."

George switched his PC off again. "Do you think we should inform Berta?"

"I don't like to, but we're going to need one of her ATVs to get to the lake. I checked yesterday, and the ATVs belonging to the PD are all in use today." Andi would have preferred not having to rely on anybody for their visit of the crime site. Unfortunately, he knew that he stood no chance getting back on foot like when they had found the bodies, and he didn't want to burden George with hauling him home. Before the Castain case, he would have been able to recuperate on site enough to walk back under his own steam. Now it wasn't an option any longer. He would count himself lucky if he was conscious after connecting with the arthropods at the lake, depending on how far he had to cast his senses. The whole thing was even more difficult because the crime had happened at night. There were just as many insects about in the dark as during the day, but the social insects, the ones he relied on for providing a time frame, rested during the night, which complicated things. He only hoped the three victims and their killers had made enough racket to disturb them in a way they noted.

"I'll think of something to keep her from coming with us." George opened his cell to call Berta. It was a blessedly short talk, and from George's end of the conversation—"No, that's no problem at all, don't feel bad about it. We're fine going up there alone—"Andi already knew Berta wouldn't be accompanying them. George ended the call with a grin. "She's busy somewhere else. There's an ATV we can use. The keys are in a key safe she gave me the code for. It's just going to be the two of us." He waggled his eyebrows in an exaggerated way that had Andi smiling.

"Can't wait for it."

They found the key safe and the ATV where Berta had said. George took a few minutes to familiarize himself with the vehicle before he asked Andi to hop on behind him. With an adventurous roar, the ATV started them on their way to the lake. The trail was devoid of people, not uncommon for this time of the year and on a weekday. George's body was radiating warmth, helping Andi to relax and prepare for his task.

Despite his mental shields being newly enhanced by a long meditation the day before to prepare him for the aftermath of today, Andi already felt the sensual input from the arthropods in the area battering against his mind. The closer they got to the lake, the more he purposefully opened up in the hopes of catching onto something useful, relying on George to help him down from the ATV and keep him from tripping or running into trees and stuff—

The air was getting colder, sleeping season, less activity, not now, though, now there was more, the dragonflies hunting, mating, getting the next generation underwater, so much going on, the soil so rich with dying leaves, a feast, the larvae getting fat, the wasps already dying, their queen looking for a hiding spot to hibernate, he had to dig deeper, go back in time, difficult, not that many social insects here, time was for blobs, there were blobs here, so often they ignored them mostly, except for the mosquitoes and ticks, they loved the blobs being here, the wasps remembered the night, the noise had disturbed them, now he had the right day, comparing it to what the other insects contributed, flashes of light in the dark, heavy stomping, the sweet smell of sweat, five blobs, three of them swaying, perhaps dying, they could be useful, the other two smaller, limber, more stomping, the splashing of water, three blobs gone, two leaving, the moths tasted female, two women, there was something strange about them, something artificial overlaying almost everything else, he tried to focus harder, moths were so difficult to read, their perception of chemicals so different from other species, no other drugs, just the ketamine, he would now forever know what it looked like, but what was that other thing, just like at the cabin, and the house of the two females, the moths knew it well, it didn't register for them as prominently as the ketamine, what else was there about the female blobs, the spiders didn't sense any poison, they wore dark clothes, their sweat was tantalizing for the mosquitoes, they left more silently than they had come, the stress in their scent completely gone, they were tranquil, the moths could taste it like that other thing, the one he couldn't place, several anthills on their way, it was night, dark, the ants inside their nests, no reference for

Andi, he was looking for something else, anything to help them, he needed to think about what he had found out, why was that important, there was no reason to think, just get that fly into the nest, the bark was ideal to hide away during winter, the nest was empty, just a few dying wasps left, the last brood starving in its cells, a dung beetle was rolling its pill through the grass, the dead season was in the air, how did insects know it was the dead season, no, Andi knew that, he knew why a dung beetle's pills always had the same diameter, the beetle couldn't know, it just wanted to lay eggs, hunting that butterfly was easy, the dragonfly was standing in the air above the water, the four wings working separately, like a helicopter's, no, the helicopter worked like the dragonfly's wings, why was that important, knowledge helped, he had to find a secure place to weave his cocoon—that was important, why, he was safe underneath the surface, the soil warm and dark and nourishing, digging his path, he needed to go back, no, the soil was good here, plenty of dead leaves to feed from, what was that on the females, why did he care, the sap of that plant was delicious, there was a blob in front of him, familiar, important, not as important as the dead bird, no, more important, he was a blob, this blob was… this blob was…. George, this blob was George, his partner, he needed to tell him, had to get back—

Andi grabbed George's arms and held on to him as hard as he could.

"It's fine, Andi, everything's fine. I'm here, hold on to me. Deep breaths, you can do it. I'm here."

Andi focused on the voice, on George's voice that was drowning out whatever the insects shared, muted it, he could return to his own body, forget about the feeling of having four wings or no feet at all, getting his own limbs back under control. He didn't know how long he stood there, clinging to his partner with the desperate need for an anchor. Suddenly, his stomach rebelled against the overtaxing of his entire system, and he stumbled aside, losing everything he had had that day. At his right, a bottle of water appeared. Andi took it to cleanse his mouth of the vile taste before he gulped some of it down. Not too much or he would go back to heaving immediately, a lesson he had learned a long time ago. He took another few minutes to regain his senses before he blindly reached out with his left hand. George took it, helped him up, his arm coming around Andi's waist to give him additional support. Andi hated being so helpless, couldn't do anything against the warm feeling spreading in his chest when George gently steered him toward the ATV, murmuring reassurances Andi didn't catch, making sure Andi was seated comfortably before he got on the vehicle himself, driving them back to the cabin that was Berta's base. George saw to it that the ATV was parked correctly, the keys back in the key safe, Andi bundled away in the car. He stared outside, trying to make sense of what he had glimpsed. When George sat down behind the steering wheel, Andi was ready to share the gist of the information.

"It was two females, but neither Tamara Portius nor Sophia McHill." He closed his eyes. "And I'm almost sure it wasn't Tabitha Clemént and Josephine Garr either."

"How do you know?"

"No poison. Tamara and Sophia are both botoxed up to their hairline, and the insects didn't catch anything like that. With Tabitha and Josephine, I'm not entirely sure. Though the image I got from the arthropods in their house doesn't completely match with what I saw up here." Andi frowned, remembering the other substance the moths had picked up on.

"Which leaves Theodora Miller." George drummed a short beat on the steering wheel.

"I'm eighty percent sure it wasn't her either. As with Tabitha and Josephine, the way the insects in her house perceive her is different from how the ones out here see things, but there were no hints she was one of them."

"How is it different?" Andi knew George wasn't just asking out of curiosity but also in the hopes of finding some clues. It never ceased to amaze Andi what his partner could discern, just from the inadequate descriptions he was giving him.

"You already know how I see people as multilayered pictures from the different ways arthropods are aware of their surroundings."

George nodded solemnly. He had caught onto that concept quickly.

"When I'm searching for somebody, I basically compare the way certain arthropods, like mosquitoes, ticks, silverfish, or any social insects, see them with the images I get from other insects. That's why I'm always grateful when somebody has a place they frequent regularly, because that gives me a clear picture with many nuances. It's also the reason I couldn't get much from the cabin because I didn't know any of the people who were there before. The picture I have of Theodora is vivid because she spends a lot of time inside her home. Which is good because the arthropods here at the lake, especially the ones who are active during the night, have a very different outlook on blobs. Luckily for us, there were some mosquitoes around when the victims were killed. They see humans similarly to ticks, and by comparing those two images, I can be fairly sure it wasn't Theodora up here. Or Tabitha and Josephine. What they showed me was so vaguely familiar it could have been any woman I've met the past few days."

"Hmm. This gives the contract killer theory a push."

"Kind of. But two female contract killers working together?" Andi thought it was rather far-fetched. Then again, the most likely female culprits from their list of suspects were all crossed off now.

"Stranger things have happened. I wouldn't dismiss it entirely, though I agree with you it's unlikely." George was on the highway now, pushing his Escalade to go faster. "Unknown players? Because I can't remember any other female suspects sticking out. The enemies the victims made in business seemed to all have been male. The joys of a patriarchal system."

Andi gripped the base of his nose between his thumb and forefinger. The migraine was on its way.

"Pills are in the glove department. Water too."

"Thank you, George." Andi found the pills and swallowed two, buying himself the time to get home before the pain really hit, or so he hoped.

"There was something else about them, a substance the moths registered, just like at the cabin and Tabitha's house, but I don't know what it is. If we could find out, it could perhaps nudge us in the right direction. Or at least help me identify them."

"Like with Castain?"

"Yeah. Like that. I hope. Problem is I have no clue as to what it could be." Andi groaned, the headache pulsing more insistently against his temples.

"Don't stress it. We can find out once you're feeling better." George shot him a worried glance. "We'll be at your place in less than fifteen minutes. If you have to puke again, warn me."

"Will do." Andi closed his eyes, leaning back in his seat. His stomach was empty, reducing the danger of him soiling George's beloved car to a minimum.

Andi did register when the car parked in front of his house, but he had no recollection as to how he got inside and into his bed. The pain in his head had grown to a steady pulsing, drowning out anything besides the wish to push his brain out through his ears. Warm, strong hands held him up while he swallowed another two pills, washed them down with water. Those same hands laid him down on his bed, the sheets soft and cool, helped him out of his jeans, and pulled the comforter over him. He heard a whispered, "Sleep tight," and then everything went blessedly dark.

11. DIGGING AROUND

GEORGE PUT a cold washcloth over Andi's forehead, pretty sure his partner didn't register and happy about it. Andi was out like a light and hopefully getting the rest he so desperately needed. George went downstairs to retrieve his overnight bag from the car. He hadn't told Andi he would be staying with him because he was sure his partner would have been against it. Better to ask forgiveness than permission in this case because there was no way George would be leaving Andi alone and vulnerable. He'd seen the aftermath of what the *geschenk* could do to Andi more than once and was determined to be there for his partner this time and every time in the future. George brought his things into the small guest room on the first floor, where he could hear Andi should he need anything during the night. Then he drove to the next deli to buy everything for chicken broth, something light he could feed Andi in the morning. Back at Andi's house, George checked on his partner, saw that he was still sound asleep, and went down into the kitchen to prepare the broth. He ate some grilled cheese sandwiches and salad before he put on the nature channel. Watching how eiders raised their chicks gave his eyes something to do while his mind went through all the possible scenarios of their murder case. He had hoped for Andi to recognize one or more of their prime suspects on the scene, but of course things rarely were that easy. George was fairly sure they had done a thorough job unearthing the pasts of the victims so far, which made him wonder what they had overlooked. Two strange females Andi couldn't connect to any of their suspects gave the case a twist they didn't need.

George sighed and leaned back on the sofa, putting his feet up. It looked as if they had to start from scratch, which heightened the killers' chances to get away with it. He waited till the eider chicks were safely grown before he went to bed, the worry about both the case and Andi forming an anxious ball in his stomach that kept him from sleep till long after midnight.

BECAUSE OF his bad night, the blare of the alarm on his cell was particularly unwelcome. George seriously considered staying in bed until he remembered why he wasn't in his own bed to begin with. He quickly got up, went to the bathroom to get ready for the day, and on the way toward the kitchen, he made a stop at Andi's bedroom. His partner was still asleep, though his restless movements meant he would wake up soon. George hurried to get tea and coffee going and to warm the broth, which wasn't exactly what he considered breakfast food but smelled nice enough to make him hungry. Just when the coffee was done, he heard movement upstairs. Moments later, Andi came into the kitchen, his hair tousled, the T-shirt he had slept in wrinkled. He wore no pants and was barefoot, which gave the whole situation an air of domesticity George found vaguely disturbing for reasons that had absolutely nothing to do with Andi being male.

"George?"

Andi sounded so confused, George had to make a conscious effort not to find him adorable.

"I've made tea." George offered Andi a mug. "And chicken broth. Something light. Are you hungry?"

Andi sat down at the small breakfast counter, cradling the mug with both hands. "I think I could eat. It smells great."

"Thank you." George filled the two bowls he had already placed next to the pot with the soup. "Here you go."

Andi accepted the bowl and the spoon, took his time to stare into the liquid while it cooled down.

"Did you sleep here?"

It was a surprisingly lucid question, considering the time of the day and Andi's mental condition.

"Are you angry?"

Andi looked up in surprise. "No, not at all. Just wondering." He took a spoonful of soup. "Where did you sleep?"

"In the small guest room upstairs. I didn't enter your grandmother's room." It was one of the things George had learned quickly—to leave the bedroom of Andi's beloved grandmother alone.

"I should clear it out." The world of hurt in his partner's voice was like a fist gripping George's heart.

"No. Not when you're not ready. You have so much on your plate, Andi, it's only natural you want to cling to one of the few positive things you had."

"Now I feel truly miserable." Andi tried a grin, only to wince and press his thumb and forefinger against his forehead. George rushed to one of the cabinets, getting Andi two Tylenol, which he swallowed with a huge gulp of his tea. "Thank you."

"You're welcome. How about we eat, and once you feel a little better, we can talk about what you've seen."

Andi nodded, then immediately turned to his bowl of soup. They ate in silence, savoring the broth, even though it still wasn't a proper breakfast dish in George's opinion.

When he was finished, Andi put the spoon down. "I assume you've already pondered what I told you yesterday?"

George took the empty bowl and spoon from Andi, placed it on top of his own. "Yes. And I'm afraid we're kind of fucked."

"Your estimation is correct." Andi furrowed his brows. "I dissected everything I experienced yesterday, and except for that unknown substance, there's nothing else sticking out. We have two female killers who may or may not have been at the cabin but are otherwise complete strangers to me, and the only way for me to find them would be to open myself up like I did during the Castain case."

"No. Absolutely no. This here is bad enough, what with your *geschenk* getting stronger. I remember how you were after you looked for Castain. And if the women really are contract killers, they're most probably no longer in the area. You could be risking your sanity for nothing." George shook his head vehemently.

"Unfortunately, you're right. I won't be doing it, since I honestly can't estimate what it will cost me, but we may have to face the possibility of not solving this case."

With Chief Norris breathing down their necks, just waiting for them to make a mistake or fail, that was an even unhappier thought than just accepting letting a killer go unpunished. "There have to be more clues, things we haven't considered yet. Shireen is still digging into the victims' pasts, unraveling their finances. Perhaps she will find something that'll point us in the right direction. We're not giving up so easily. We're detectives, and even without your *geschenk*, we're damn good." George hadn't meant to go into pep talk mode, and he wasn't sure who needed it more—he or Andi. His partner was staring into his tea mug, his eyelids slightly drooping.

"You know what? You go back to bed and get some more rest. I'll drive to the precinct to see if Shireen or Evangeline have found something new. If yes, we can follow up on that tomorrow. If not, we concentrate on that substance you sensed. I'm sure there's ways we can narrow down what it is."

Andi looked up at him with a weak smile on his lips. "We'll see. I *am* tired, though. Thank you for the soup."

"I'll be back later. Let's see if we can't get you to eat something more solid then."

"Sounds tempting." Andi slowly got up from his stool. Watching him walk toward the stairs with slightly hunched shoulders, George had to quell the urge to run up to him and offer his help. Instead, he put the dishes into the dishwasher, cleaned the kitchen, and went out to his car.

AT THE precinct, George first went to Shireen, who didn't have any news for him. Untangling the lives of the three men proved to be more difficult than they had anticipated. Evangeline didn't have anything either, and after staring at his two whiteboards for another half hour without any kind of inspiration hitting, George decided his time would be best spent back at Andi's place, where he could contemplate the case as well as look into how to best find out what substance Andi had sensed. If he hurried a bit, he could also cook lunch, because the broth hadn't filled him the way a real breakfast would. He got his keys, ready to leave, when the door to Chief Norris's office opened. She beckoned him inside with a barked, "Detective Donovan, in here."

George mentally braced himself for whatever rant was coming his way, glad that Andi was at home and couldn't make things worse with his challenging comments.

"I see you're here without your partner today, Detective Donovan." Chief Norris didn't even wait until George was fully seated.

"Detective Hayes is at home with a migraine, as I called in this morning." He kept his tone very matter-of-fact, determined not to rise to her challenge. George knew there was little chance they wouldn't clash before he left Charleston, but today was not the day. He had more pressing matters at hand.

"Then let's hope he gets better soon." Norris steepled her fingers on her desk. "I trust there is progress with the case?"

ERUCA 97

"There is. We're still pursuing different alleys, but we were able to dismiss several suspects already. It's narrowing down." There, that was satisfyingly vague while still giving her something that was *true*. She didn't need to know their new suspects were completely unknown. George started to understand Andi better and better. It was vexing, being able to know and/or identify the killer in a case while at the same time *not knowing them*.

"It had better narrow down quickly. So far, the mayor is not impressed."

And you did nothing to protect us, George thought bitterly. He had worked with hostile superiors before, though never under such difficult circumstances, having to look out not only for himself but also for a partner who neither had a clue about political schemes nor the inclination to take part in the dance. It hardened his resolve to keep a more detailed record of his dealings with the chief. Until now, he had simply made notes of her more aggressive comments, complete with date and witnesses, usually Andi. He was determined to write his first memory protocol today as soon as he was back at Andi's.

"I'm sure the mayor is aware that solving a crime is not a race."

"What the mayor is most aware of is that next year is an election year. She needs something to show, especially with the victims being such upstanding members of society."

What Norris really meant was rich members of society. George was too used to the double standard applied to crimes depending on who the victims were to make this into an argument. "We're working on it. But we want the case to be airtight before we start pointing fingers."

Norris nodded. "Just don't take too long; that's all I'm saying. You may go now, Detective Donovan."

George got up with a curt nod. He didn't enjoy being dismissed like some lowly underling, but he had learned a long time ago to choose his battles wisely. "Goodbye, Chief Norris." He left before his mouth let something slip he really didn't want her to hear.

On his way back to Andi's house, he stopped to get everything for a light chicken stir-fry, one of the few recipes his mother was able to cook. Even though, or perhaps because, they'd had it very often while growing up, it was still a favorite for him and his two brothers. Back on James Island, George checked on Andi, who was sound asleep again, a good sign that made George hope he would be functioning the next day. George was almost done with the stir-fry when Andi came into the kitchen, already looking better than he had in the morning.

"What smells so good in here?" He inhaled deeply.

"Chicken stir-fry. A family recipe. I thought this was something you could stomach."

"I'm definitely going to try. Anything new from the precinct?"

"Except for Norris hounding us to solve the case yesterday? No. Neither Shireen nor Evangeline were helpful this time, though Shireen is very busy digging deeper into the lives of our victims. She said it takes longer because there's so much." George added some herbs to the stir-fry.

"Norris really has it out for us. I'm sorry, George. That's not what you need." Andi sounded exhausted, and George wasn't sure if it was an aftermath of yesterday's trip or something deeper.

"I'm fine, Andi. Don't forget, I'm an adult and I can take care of myself. As is the chief, who should know better than to pursue personal vendettas just for the heck of it. Speaking of which—" He made a face. "—I need to write a memory protocol about today's meeting with her."

"That bad?"

"Let's just say I think it's a good idea to get our ducks in a very neat row." George got out plates and forks and ladled generous portions of the stir-fry onto them.

"Which makes it even more important to find our killers."

"Don't start stressing over it, Andi. Now let's eat, and you can tell me exactly how you know what heroin or crack look like when you see it through the eyes of your creepy crawler friends." George put the plates on the kitchen bar, motioning for Andi to sit down. "Are you well enough to talk to me, or should we wait until tomorrow?"

"I'm good." Andi took the first bite of his food and moaned happily. "Do you want to move in?"

George grinned. "As tempting as that offer sounds, I'm afraid we'd kill each other within a week."

"What makes you think that?" Andi raised a brow. George wasn't sure if he was teasing or genuinely interested.

"Well, for one, I'm afraid our view on tidiness differs too greatly, and no amount of good cooking on my part will make you put up with me constantly nagging you to pick up after yourself."

Andi took a moment to chew and swallow his food. "You could just pick things up yourself, you know."

"I'd be your roommate, not your cleaning service."

"There's no chance you'd want to be both?" The longing in Andi's voice could have fooled George if he hadn't seen the twinkling in his eyes.

"Uh, let me think about it... no. I do my housework, but I don't like it."

"And it was such a good idea," Andi murmured. "You would save on gas as well."

"It's not worth the potential fallout, believe me."

"You're probably right." Andi started eating in earnest. When his plate was half-cleared, he looked up at George again, who had done his best to fill his own stomach as well. "Okay, we can start. What do you want to know?"

"You already explained to me how you learned to recognize all kinds of drugs and some diseases through knowing what it was and then comparing it to what impressions the insects gave you. Like Dominic McHill's alcohol addiction. Though I'm not sure if that's a disease or a drug."

"Both, I'd say. And yes. The first drug I learned to distinguish was heroin. There was this huge raid we did when I was still a beat officer, just fresh from the academy. The warehouse was chock-full of mosquitoes, termites, ticks, pill bugs, spiders, flies, and moths. Each of them has a different way of recognizing chemical signatures, and from what I gleaned from them, I was able to get a 3D model of the drug. It's similar to how I can recognize humans. A bit like one of those pictures where you can see different things from different angles. Heroin, I know from almost every angle. The same goes for crack, weed, LSD, angel dust, and some others. I also know quite a lot of pills and diseases. Hospitals are great places to learn." Andi shuddered.

"Okay. I get that, I think. Can you tell me *what* it is you see?"

Andi hesitated. "I can try and put things into terms you would be able to work with."

George nodded encouragingly.

"Okay. So let's take weed. It's not artificial but something that has grown. I can always sense that. It's not something I can put into words at all, just a feeling I get. Insects are very good at distinguishing between natural and artificial, and they don't use a sense I can pinpoint. They just seem to kind of know?"

"That actually makes sense. I mean, our senses are very different and probably not as fine-tuned, but we can tell, for example, if a cloth is sheep wool or cotton or polyester." George looked at Andi, asking him silently to either affirm or negate his words.

"It's close. And yes, their senses are much finer. But that's how I know the substance is natural."

"Good, that's good. Now, when you identify something, like weed, what else do you see?"

Andi started drawing circles with his fork on the empty plate. "You know how there's different ways to represent an element or a chemical compound?"

George nodded. "You have the name, like oxygen, then you have O2, and those complicated patterns of letters and lines to depict what it looks like." George made a face. "One of the worst chemistry tests I ever had to do."

"Yes, exactly. Now what I get are combinations of the three or a completely different picture altogether. Usually, my only chance to learn is when I can directly compare it to what the substance is for me." Andi sighed. "Which throws us back to square one."

George shook his head. "Not necessarily. We already know it's not artificial. Can you tell if it's an element or a chemical compound?"

Andi furrowed his brows. "The moths knew it very well, as if it was a part of them or some kind of memory. Not something they had learned…. It's a compound."

"Good. Can you identify parts of it?"

"I'm not sure. For moths, things are based on scent, pheromones. The substance smelled—good? God, I hate this! Why can't I see this more clearly?" Andi put the fork down with enough force to make the plate vibrate.

"You're doing great! Don't sell yourself short. I mean, you're trying to translate from a language that not only uses different words and letters but also a completely different view of the world." George took the plate to rescue it from breaking. "You know what's probably the most important thing I learned from you? How small a human's view of the world is. You opened up my sight, and I don't want to imagine how hard it must be for you to constantly mediate between the two. Now back to the problem at hand. Did you sense anything you recognize?"

"There was something familiar about the substance. Something that had nothing to do with why the moths knew it." Andi furrowed his brows in concentration. "It's something I've seen before…. Oh my God, I'm so stupid!" He slapped his hand against his forehead, then winced. The headache obviously wasn't gone completely. "It's a protein. I sensed the structure of a protein!" Andi shook his head. "And not just any protein. It resembles the silk spiders use to weave their nets."

"Wonderful! We're getting somewhere." George got his cell out and opened the search engine. *Silk protein that resembles spider silk.* The list of hits was seemingly endless. The one standing out, though, was the silk of caterpillars. George clicked on the most promising-looking link and was faced with a complicated sequence of letters connected through lines. Underneath it said *primary structure of fibrin.* "Does that ring any bells?" George showed Andi the screen.

"Actually, it does. I recognize a part of the structure." A slow smile spread on his lips. "I think we found it!"

"Which brings us right to the next question—what was it? I only know silk as clothing or very expensive cloths."

"They didn't wear it. Their clothes were a mixture of cotton and polyamide. The usual for most people."

George started typing into the search engine again. *Use of silk.* He stared at the screen. "Silk is used in skin-care products. Did you know that?"

"No. But it's a possibility. And Josephine Garr works for a skin-care company." Andi started drumming his fingers on the bar. "Which would explain why I sensed it in their house and, since they definitely were in the cabin, also there. But the two weren't the ones herding the victims into the lake. The traces were weaker on them, perhaps because of their clothing. If it was contract killers, they would have worn something sturdy and practical and thick enough to keep evidence like hair from falling down."

Which made everything vague again. George wanted to curse while knowing he had to keep his cool, and not just for Andi's sake. "Okay. There're a few things we can say for sure. The substance is silk as produced by insects." He hesitated. "Wait a moment. There are tons of butterflies around here. Which means a lot of caterpillars. You should know what that looks like, shouldn't you?"

Andi groaned. "I *know* what silk looks like. For caterpillars and butterflies. And ants and wasps. Moths are different. I could only make the connection because moths get caught in spiders' webs all the time, which was my frame of reference here."

"Oh. I see. That complicated, huh?"

"You have no idea."

"Sorry." George stared back at the screen of his cell. "We know it was silk from caterpillars on the women, most probably from a skin-care product. It also wasn't clothing in any shape or form."

"Yes, and my guess is they use it on a daily basis, because while it wasn't the most prominent thing, it was still strong enough for the moths to register with the women at the lake. On Tabitha and Josephine, it was a lot stronger, which means their exposure is greater in whatever shape it happens." Andi started rubbing his temples, a sign that he needed to get back to bed.

"Probably part of Josephine's job." He put the cell down. "You go back to bed, and I'll write down what we've found out." He made a face. "And I have to write that damn memory protocol."

"I don't envy you." Andi was already on his feet. "I'm sorry. I really should lie down."

"Go." George made a shooing motion. "I'll wake you for dinner."

Andi left the kitchen with a weak smile on his face. After George heard the door to Andi's bedroom shut, he took care of the dishes, then sat down to do his homework.

12. TRACES AND LEADS

IT WAS a wonderful evening, the air was already cooling down due to the cold season coming, though still warm enough for Andi to enjoy it before he had to go underground for hibernation, that's what his kind did, they were the exception, not dying like the other crickets, though how he knew that he couldn't say, he was on the ground, the soil a bit dry and crumbly, hard to walk on it even with six legs, he wanted to get to a more vantage point, where his song would carry farther, going up the small hill where he had dug his tunnel for the winter, his back legs already rubbing against each other, producing the typical sound of a summer evening, but summer was over, these were the last flares before everything slowed down, he would go to sleep, deep in the earth, unaware of everything around him, just wonderful darkness, unconsciousness, nothing to worry about, no pain, no pictures and images and sensual input, just rest, how wonderful that sounded, he hadn't rested in ever, couldn't remember what it felt like to be at peace, it was all too much, had been for a long time, he really should go underground, close his eyes and wait until the spring sun woke him again to new life and a new cycle and perhaps a new chance, but not for him, there was a shadow, a rushing of wings, Andi felt his life wink out, was catapulted from the mole cricket back into the world, and he hated it, how it overwhelmed him with everything, he just wanted to sleep, he needed to sleep, to get rest, he—

"Andi! Wake up! You're dreaming!" George's voice cut through the promise of darkness and peace, yanked him back like it had done so many times before, and what would he do once George left him and his grip on reality thinned even more? His *Oma* had died at the ripe old age of ninety-five, had been a part of life till the end, but her family had known, had been able to help her, had admired her, while he didn't have anybody, except for George who would be leaving soon and....

"Andi! If you don't wake up right now, I'm going to put you under the cold shower! I mean it!"

"That's so mean."

"I'd do it, though!"

Andi slowly opened his eyes. George was leaning over him, his eyes full of worry, one hand on Andi's shoulder, ready to shake him out of his stupor. "Are you back?"

Andi sighed. "Unfortunately, yes. I had such a wonderful dream."

"You were twitching like somebody electrocuted you."

"Um, yes, the end of the dream wasn't perfect. The mole cricket got eaten."

"I'm just pretending what you just said doesn't make the kind of sense I'm afraid it makes. Come, I've made grilled cheese sandwiches for dinner."

Andi's stomach took this moment to remind him that food was actually a good idea. Especially food he didn't have to work for. "I'm coming."

He got up and followed George downstairs. There were already two plates on the kitchen counter, heaped with grilled sandwiches, chips, and a small salad. The red of the cherry tomatoes made a beautiful contrast to the gold of the melted cheese. "Remind me again why you're not moving in with me?" Andi sat down, only half joking. It was nice having somebody in the house and even nicer to wake up to cooked food.

"We already agreed it wouldn't be a good idea." George's voice was calm, with only a hint of amusement tinging it.

"I can't remember agreeing to anything."

"Must have slipped your mind." George bit into his grilled cheese sandwich, a single drop of cheese fat collecting in the corner of his mouth—

The blob was delicious, healthy and vibrant with life, such a good meal, not too loud either, getting used to him was easy, he didn't stir things up too much, and he cooked, leaving morsels of food outside, nourishment to collect, his body was a mixture of colors and scents and forms, all molded into the familiar shape of George, *who was there, with Andi, also his blood tasted good, no diseases, no drugs, perfect—*

"Uh, Andi? Are you still with me?"

Andi shook his head. "Sorry. Got some input just now. Thank you for cooking."

"It's no problem. Actually, cooking for two people is easier than for just one person. Feels less like a waste of time." George speared a cherry tomato with his fork. "Do you think you can go back to the precinct tomorrow?"

"Yes. I feel a lot better already. One more night of sleep and I should be as good as new. Or as good as I can get."

George grinned. "I really shouldn't find this funny but, yeah. I'd love to have you back as grumpy and growly as usual."

Andi shrugged. "That's my natural charm."

They ate in silence, Andi consuming the calories his body needed so desperately, just slowly enough to not look like a pig. When he was done, he put his fork down and leaned back. "What's our plan should Shireen not have anything for us?"

George took his time to noisily crunch the last of his chips, his brows furrowed in what Andi hoped was serious contemplation. "I think taking a closer look at the sons isn't a bad idea, no matter if and what Shireen finds. We can at least cross them out for good with a valid explanation for the chief."

"I hate that we have to dance around her. The old chief was so much better."

"Harry Renard. I've heard only good things about him." George gathered the plates. "He didn't mind your methods?"

"Not in the least. And he always protected me, and he never ever doubted what I did and how." Andi sighed. "Paradise."

"It certainly helps when your superior is fully behind you."

"Like you wouldn't believe."

Andi got up and took the dishes to the kitchen. A quick glance into the dishwasher and he decided it was time to let the old girl do her work. "Do you want to have a beer?" he asked George. "We could see if something interesting is on TV." Out of the corner of his eye, Andi saw an interesting mixture of fear, relief, and happiness playing out on George's face. He also felt it, the surge in pheromones that enhanced what he had read on his partner's face.

"Sounds like a plan."

"Of course, you'd have to stay the night, because I can't let you drive intoxicated." Andi smirked.

"One beer is hardly enough to intoxicate me, but as an officer of the law, I have to set a shining example." George started moving toward the living room. "Plus, I think it's a good idea if I keep an eye on you. Just to be sure you're fine."

"You're so good to me." Andi went to the fridge to get two bottles of beer. For a short, paranoid moment he feared it might have been tampered with, unconsciously dipping into the memories of the arthropods in the house, who showed him no strangers at all. They had by now accepted George as part of the scenery, another reminder how dependent Andi was on him. He opened the bottles and brought them to the couch, where

George was already channel surfing. They agreed on the rerun of a hockey game and spent the evening in companionable silence, nursing their beers and cheering the goals, no matter which team scored.

THE MORNING was nice. After a real breakfast with bread and cereal, they drove to the precinct, where Shireen was already waiting for them in the hall, motioning them to follow her into her lair. Her face had that grim expression she always got when she had found something truly ugly. She didn't bother with a "Good morning." Instead she started talking immediately, her tone clipped with a hint of sharpness Andi rarely heard from her but remembered well from the few times he had.

"It's an awful morning. And before you ask, I haven't found anything on the darknet yet. But I pieced together other things. Terrible things." Shireen's brows were furrowed; even the ever-present clinking of her jewelry sounded dulled. George nodded at her to continue. Andi had his nose buried in his tea, waiting for Shireen to hit them with whatever she had found. Given how agitated she was, it couldn't be good. Shireen took a deep breath.

"There are hospital bills for Sophia McHill, dating from the time she was newly married to Harry Alexander until about three months before her son was born. Broken bones, two times it was the ribs, open wounds in the area of the head that had to be sewn, a knocked-out tooth. When she was six months pregnant, she was in the hospital for two weeks because she was in danger of having a preterm birth after falling down the stairs. After the birth, no more hospital bills." Shireen sounded angry, and rightfully so. As members of the police force, George and Andi were all too familiar with those kinds of injuries. They didn't paint a happy picture of Sophia McHill's marriage.

"Shortly after the son was six months old, Harry Alexander took his first mistress, some A. L., as he calls her in his documents." When she saw their raised eyebrows, Shireen shrugged. "I already told you he didn't keep them secret. Had a folder and an account for every one of them. And the hospital bills for them always coincide with some big purchase of jewelry. You're looking at an abuser, gentlemen, a violent one who has obviously gotten away with a lot."

"You mean all those mistresses have every reason to want him dead?" Andi heard the dread in George's voice as the mountain of suspects started growing again.

"Yes and no. Some of them stayed with him quite long, for years, and as far as I can see from his finances, he paid them very generously for their silence and acquiescence."

"Hatred can fester for a long time." Andi made that statement matter-of-factly.

"Yes, it can. The question is whether a check with seven zeros can purge that hatred." Shireen showed them the copies of several checks written for different women. Harry Alexander McHill had been as generous with his money as he had been with his fists.

"Do you think he simply let them go when they wanted?" There was a certain resignation in Andi's voice. Sadly, the victims of domestic abuse often put blame on themselves or simply weren't able to leave their abusers.

"Yes, he did." Another document popped up, showing the photo of a legally binding contract between Harry Alexander and one Susan Ferrier. "You see that paragraph here? It states that when the woman decides to end the relationship, she has the right to a certain amount of money paid directly and in full to her. If he ends the relationship, aka grows bored with her, the sum doubles."

"Let me guess, those contracts were drawn by David Hector Portius II." George did nothing to keep the disgust from his voice.

"And the participant gets a hundred bonus points. I have more, though." Shireen started tapping her tablet. "David Hector II wasn't a choir boy either. He didn't weigh himself down with mistresses. He had two high-end brothels, one here in Charleston, the other in New York, which he frequented, according to what I could find in his finances and from the brothels themselves. Really, these places have immaculate bookkeeping. I know some huge companies who should take a leaf out of their book, if you get my meaning—" The way Shireen talked made it clear she didn't think her joke was that hilarious. She just wanted to fill the space between one piece of disgusting news and the next with something a little lighter. "Anyway, he paid both establishments a pretty six-figure sum per year to keep him in barely legal company. He wasn't picky either. As long as they looked young, he didn't discriminate between gender, skin color, or looks."

"I wonder why he wasn't a customer of Jake Castain?" Andi was fiddling with his cup of tea. What he was learning about the victims made him want to take a long hot shower and clean himself with a steel brush.

"I wondered the same and cross-checked, but it seems Portius wanted to maintain some kind of—respectability, I guess?" Shireen scrunched up her nose. "He always paid, he always made sure his company was legal, even had a contract with both brothels that if they ever provided him with somebody who was underage, they'd have to pay back the equivalent of three yearly payments."

"And of course he made it look as if it were legally binding." George huffed.

"He was a cutthroat lawyer. What do you expect?" Shireen turned the huge flat-screen on the wall dark. "That's it from me for the time being. I'll keep digging and inform you as soon as I find something new."

"You're the best, Shireen. Thank you." George made a little bowing gesture. "If you could compose short papers on every mistress and whore Harry Alexander and David Hector II had dealings with, that would be wonderful."

"The mistresses are easy, but the sex workers…." Shireen shrugged. "Even though the brothels are exceptional with their bookkeeping, they didn't use their employee's legal names. It's going to take some time to find them all." She tapped her chin with her right index finger. "That sounds like a job for our rookie. Timmy!"

"Yes, Shireen?" A young man of perhaps twenty-five years came running from the other end of the room. If he'd had a tail, Andi was sure it would have wagged like crazy. Shireen didn't seem to notice. "I've got a job for you." She gestured to one of the desks, where Timmy immediately went. George and Andi waved Shireen goodbye, which she acknowledged with a nod before she concentrated on Timmy.

Andi followed George out of Shireen's domain and down the hall to the stairs leading to Evangeline's kingdom. For a moment Andi pondered how the two women had managed to make the IT-center and the morgue their own when there were others working there as well, but the answer was really simple. Both Shireen and Evangeline were the kind of women misogynist men feared the most: strong, capable, intelligent, unbending. In other words, everything Andi would have wished for his own mother to be.

On the stairs, George broke the silence. "What do you think? Do we visit the wives again, or do we invite them to the precinct?"

Andi was pretty sure he knew what his partner wanted to do. "I'm tempted to invite them to the precinct, but we both know they won't cooperate then. We'll have to visit them in their homes, where they feel safer. And we have to give them notice. They won't talk to us without their lawyers this time around. Not when we're going to ask such personal questions."

George nodded. "Yeah, I'm still surprised they did the first time."

"I guess we caught them by surprise." Andi shrugged.

They reached the door to the morgue. George lifted a brow. "I'll let you handle this."

"You've seen me do it before. Don't you want to try?"

"No. Not yet. Perhaps never. I know what we're about to do is technically not illegal, but for some reason, the words manipulation of evidence keep echoing in my mind."

Andi huffed. "It's not manipulation. It's gentle nudging in the right direction."

"Yeah. Whatever. I want you to do the nudging."

"As you wish." Andi held the door open for his skittish partner. Sometimes George really was a bit of a crybaby. They found Evangeline in her chaotic office, where she greeted them over the rim of a mug of steaming tea. "Detectives, *malo lava le taeao*. What can I do for you?"

Andi sat down in one of the two chairs standing in front of Evangeline's desk. Her thick dark hair was in a messy bun on top of her head, indicating the previous days had been rough. "A good morning to you, too, Evangeline."

The coroner merely took a sip of her tea when George closed the door to her office before sitting down as well, wishing her a good morning.

"What do I need to look for, Andi?"

Andi smiled at her, grateful for her quick mind and willingness to help him out. "Silk protein. The kind caterpillars produce. Unless you or CSI have already found it since the last report we got?"

Evangeline put her mug down. "No. It's not something we usually look out for unless it's clothing, because it's quite useless and insignificant in terms of practically everything. I gather it's neither useless nor insignificant for this case?"

"It could be the breakthrough we need."

She sighed. "Don't hold out much hope for anything on the victims. Silk protein and water don't mix well."

"It doesn't have to be on the victims, although that would be perfect. If it's in the cabin, we could work with it." Andi gave her what he hoped was a pleading look. Evangeline waved her right hand.

"*Ua lelei, ua lelei*, I'll see what I can do. Just don't expect any miracles."

"Thank you, Evangeline, you're the best." Andi got up.

"I know. Now out of my office. Apparently, I've got work to do. If I find your silk, I'll even come up with a good reason why I tested for it in the first place."

"I love it when you give me a good backup story." Andi wasn't foolish enough to blow her a kiss, but he did incline his head to indicate a bow. Evangeline waved them off.

"*'Aua le popole*. No worries. You make me look good. It's the least I can do."

They left the morgue and took the stairs back up to their own office. "See, that wasn't so bad, was it?" Andi couldn't help but tease George a bit. His partner looked at him as if he had swallowed a lemon.

"I don't know what bothers me more, your nudging or the promptness with which Evangeline, Shireen, and Forard react to it."

"You heard Evangeline, and I think Forard has mentioned it as well—I make them look good. And there's little risk for them when they follow my 'hunches.' Worst-case scenario, it doesn't pan out. People will still think they're just being very thorough, which isn't a bad thing in our profession."

"No, not a bad thing at all." George held the door to their floor open for Andi. "So, now we're going to call Sophia McHill and Tamara Portius and see if we can visit them this afternoon. Come to think of it, let's see if Theodora Miller is free as well. I don't know about you, but I'm still not entirely sold on her being fine with her husband's affair with a man."

"Me neither. What do we do until they agree to see us? If they agree to see us." Andi knew very well how quickly the upper crust could clam up when dealing with the police.

George sighed. "I hate to say this, but we should probably work through our lists of remaining suspects, seeing who we can cross off without relying on your very true and very unprovable information that it was two women who killed the victims."

"Fun times." Andi shuddered. "Perhaps we should get something to eat first?"

"Now you're stalling. We just had breakfast." George pulled his keys from the front pocket of his slacks. "Let's go. You can call the wives while I drive."

Grinning happily, Andi followed his partner outside.

13. A New Web

THEY WERE lucky, at least George said it was luck that all three women agreed to meet with them this afternoon. They went to Theodora Miller first, partly because talking to her with what they knew now would be the easiest part of their day, partly because she was the only one who said she didn't have to call her lawyer and was free at 1:00 p.m.

The widow led them into the same room as on their first visit. Once they were all seated, she looked at them expectantly, her perfectly coiffed hair falling down on her shoulders in soft waves, her expression as neutral as it had been when they told her about her husband's death.

"Thank you for making time for us again, Mrs. Miller." As always, George tried to be polite, even though the raised brow of Mrs. Miller clearly stated how unimpressed she was by his gratitude.

"It's always a pleasure." If there was a hint of sarcasm in her reply, George obviously chose to ignore it. Andi was once again glad he was doing the talking because he would have already lost his temper with the woman.

"We're here to talk to you about the contract you had with your late husband."

"I know. Jeremy called to let me know you would be coming."

George was surprised. He had half expected for Jeremy Fisher's story to be false. "So what he said is true?"

"About the contract? Absolutely. I have it here, assuming that's what you wanted to talk about." She pushed a clear plastic binder that had been hidden under a small tablecloth across the table to them.

"You seem to be getting along well with your husband's lover." Andi took the binder.

Theodora Miller shrugged. "I admit I didn't care much about Lawrence. He was a bona fide asshole." She looked down at her hands for a moment. "Jeremy kind of is as well. An asshole, I mean." She sighed. "But he's also the reason I won't ever have to worry about finances, which means I'm inclined to cut him some slack."

"Did you know your husband was thinking about leaving you and making his relationship with Jeremy public?" George clearly hoped the question would rattle her a bit, but they had no such luck. The woman was as cold as a dog's snout.

"Yes, of course I did. I have to say it would have been beneficial for them both. These kinds of relationships are all the rage today, and their careers are so settled, there wasn't much risk to it."

"And it didn't bother you in the least?" Disbelief was heavy in George's voice.

"I think you're making a wrong assumption here, Detectives." Theodora Miller smiled softly, as if she were a mother knowing so much better than her children.

"Do enlighten us, please." George motioned for her to talk while Andi stared at the contract, deeply fascinated.

"My relationship with Lawrence was pure business from beginning to end. We married, yes, a small ceremony with the excuse of him already being too mature to go for something big, even though I guess most people in his circle knew already about his inclinations. It's a real shark pool out there, you know. Anyway, we didn't even have a honeymoon. I went on a lovely spa holiday with two of my friends while he was on a cruise in the Caribbean with Jeremy. We only had intercourse once, to seal the marriage, which was more for my benefit than his since it would have been my bottom line that was threatened if people started doubting the legality of what we had. We've lived in the same house, but we led so vastly different lives, we barely saw each other except for the official functions where I acted as his beard. When he started thinking about divorcing me, we discussed it at length, and we even had a preliminary contract written down. I wanted to show it to you as well, but it seems Lawrence kept it at his office in the city because I couldn't find it here."

"The contract looks legit." Andi put the plastic binder down. His gaze turned sharp. "One more question, Mrs. Miller, and we're out of your hair for the time being."

Theodora nodded gracefully.

"How did it feel, signing that contract?" Andi tapped his fingers against the thing.

Theodora smiled, the first genuine expression on her face Andi had seen since he first met her. "It was liberating. I felt free and happy."

Andi nodded thoughtfully. It made sense, in a twisted way. He then got up, and George followed him out of the house.

"Let's see if Tamara Portius was as understanding of her husband's tastes as Theodora." Andi very much doubted it.

TAMARA PORTIUS greeted them with the same arrogant indifference she had shown them the first time, introducing her lawyer, one Jake Dyson, obviously David Portius's partner since they looked close in age. The man was the epitome of a rich, arrogant lawyer who was doing them all a favor with his mere presence. He also didn't seem to be too happy about being here, and Andi couldn't blame him, because according to the nervous signals Tamara Portius was broadcasting, she had a lot to hide. It was a stark difference to the first time they had met her, when they had told her about her husband's death. Back then she had been calm, hardly bothered. Now she was a bundle of nerves, and the entire house was in uproar—

Creaking and moving and scraping and thumping and stomping, stomping, stomping around, everywhere, loud, no rest, ever, wood splintering, so old, a perfect hiding place, broken, paper moved, anxiety whirling in the air, saturating everything, anger, stinking hot acidic anger, stomping, pacing, feet on the ground, vibrating all the time….

"Mrs. Portius, we have a few questions, if you don't mind?" George had picked up on her skittishness as well. Ever the gentleman, he infused his voice with just enough care to give the woman a deceptive sense of security, all under the watchful eyes of Mr. Dyson. Tamara lifted a hand to her face, presumably to push a strand of hair out of it, seemed to reconsider, let her hand fall down at her side, then gestured wildly for them to follow her. There were no house personnel in sight, and Andi couldn't sense anybody but the four of them in the house. Interesting.

They sat down in what he assumed was the living room in these posh villas, a monstrosity of a room with perfect white leather couches, white carpets, white tables, white everything, bland and boring, steel and leather, not interesting for any purpose, a fairly useless room except for the wooden ceiling, there were some cracks there, good hiding spots, the spiders loved them, if only the blobs wouldn't dust off their nets so often—

Andi felt a hand on his shoulder and only narrowly avoided flinching back from the touch. It was George, who looked at him with worry in his eyes. He had been spacing out again when he should have been paying attention to his surroundings. Andi gave a tiny nod, conveying with one movement that he was sorry and okay. The little twitch of George's left eyelid told him he accepted the nod for now, but there would be a talk later. They both focused on Tamara Portius and her lawyer again.

"Mrs. Portius, I'm really sorry to be so blunt with you, but did you know about your husband's—extramarital activities?" George tried to be delicate, which wasn't needed, as it turned out. Tamara huffed and lifted her jewelry-laden hand to her face again, this time putting that strand of hair behind her ear, deliberately ignoring the warning throat clearing of the lawyer.

"You mean if I knew about his whores? Oh yes, I did."

"And you weren't happy about it, I presume?" George still spoke with a certain aplomb, which made her answer seem even cruder. Mr. Dyson tried to stop her before she could start talking, but to Andi's and George's joy, the woman was faster, completely ignoring her lawyer. Andi started to understand why the man seemed so constipated.

"Not happy? I was fucking humiliated!" The outburst was sudden and more violent than Andi would have expected, and it ended almost the same moment it happened. Tamara Portius took a deep breath, schooled her features, and put on a fake smile that had to hurt her jaw. Next to her, Jake Dyson made a sour face, rolling his eyes.

"Please excuse my language. I don't know what came over me. Must be the stress of David being murdered and trying to get his affairs in order." She folded her hands in her lap, the very picture of a dignified rich lady. Andi didn't miss the sharp glance she shot her lawyer when she mentioned her spouse's affairs. "My husband had certain interests he couldn't fulfill in our marriage. His solution was to seek help outside our home, and as long as he returned to me, I was willing to look the other way when it came to his infidelity."

That sounded like something the lawyer could have written up. Considering his pleased look, Tamara was finally acting according to script. How unfortunate for them. George didn't let it deter him, though.

"Did you know that Lawrence Miller and Harry Alexander McHill had affairs as well?" Andi was curious how she would answer that. The little tidbit about settling affairs, he stored in his brain for Shireen to have a closer look. Could be interesting. For a moment, Tamara's entire body seemed to freeze. Jake Dyson lifted his right hand from where it had been resting on the upholstery to his knee. It was his only visible reaction to the question. Then Tamara caught herself and sat even straighter on the pristine leather couch, her dark skirt and blouse a stark contrast to the clinical white. She glanced at her lawyer, this time openly, who seemed to be trying to convey something with his facial expression and failing. He cleared his throat and spoke for the first time since they had been introduced.

"I'm not sure what the possible extramarital activities of other people have to do with Mrs. Portius's marriage."

George nodded, as if he totally agreed with Mr. Dyson. "Under normal circumstances nothing, but the three men were killed together, and that does make us curious."

"I wasn't aware my client was under suspicion of murder." Jake Dyson furrowed his brows and shot Tamara Portius a dark glare.

"She isn't." George was smooth and quick, mostly because it wasn't a lie. At this point, they knew—not officially, but without doubt nevertheless—that she hadn't been the one to kill the three men. If she was guilty of conspiracy to murder wasn't clear yet, but that was something neither Mrs. Portius nor her lawyer needed to know at the moment. "We're merely trying to build a frame of references for our investigation."

George's honest smile must have reassured Mr. Dyson, or perhaps he simply wanted to get out of there as soon as possible. Andi didn't know, but the lawyer gave a slight nod to Tamara, who looked down her nose at them.

"What you need to understand, Detectives, is that in our circles, nothing is really secret. We are all in each other's pockets, especially here in the South. We just don't talk about dirty laundry—we delight in whispering about it behind our hands, happy that at least others are as miserable as we are ourselves. Yes, I knew about Harry Alexander's mistresses, as did everybody else in the country club. He even took them there sometimes. Distasteful, if you ask me. David at least had the decency to keep his whores where they belonged. And yes, I also knew about Lawrence's boyfriend or lover. I never understood how Theodora could be so calm about it, but she did marry him for his status and money, and I guess for somebody from her class, he was like a lottery win no matter who he bedded."

Andi wasn't sure if Tamara was a homophobe, a class snob, or simply never had to think about how her words could be perceived. The phrasing sounded harsh and vitriolic, but her tone was pleasant, as if she was simply stating facts. There was no real menace behind it. This was the reality in which she lived, and she had merely described it—or not. Andi had learned to be distrustful of words and tone in equal measure and to be doubly careful when the two didn't match.

"How would you describe your relationship with Theodora Miller and Sophia McHill? Your husbands were best friends, so you probably met often." Andi was curious what her reaction here would be. Interestingly, Mr. Dyson didn't try to intervene. He almost seemed curious himself.

"Our husbands were friends, yes, we're members in the same country club, though Theodora rarely goes there, we see each other regularly at all the charity functions throughout the year, but we almost never met in private with our husbands. They always preferred being amongst themselves, no doubt to combine business and pleasure without having to be considerate of us."

It all sounded so arrogant and sad at the same time. Andi didn't know if he should be angry about Tamara Portius or have pity. He decided to squash both emotions and go for a direct approach.

"You don't seem to be too sad that your husband is gone, Mrs. Portius."

The same thing happened as before, when George had mentioned the sex workers her husband had bedded. Like a ripple on a peaceful lake, anger rushed over Tamara Portius's face, made her eyes flare with a fire Andi easily identified as strong enough to kill. And just like before, Jake Dyson tensed next to her, clearly expecting another outburst. He appeared to know his client very well, already opening his mouth to intervene. But just as quickly as the storm had come, it was all gone, leaving behind a mask cultivated during years of being a member of the upper crust and frozen with Botox. Tamara Portius gave a dramatic sigh, keeping Jake Dyson from whatever he might have wanted to say. Andi was happy because clients were so much more likely to slip up than an old warhorse like Dyson.

"I can see how things are hard for you to understand, Detectives." Her condescending tone wiped out any pity Andi may have had left. "Let me explain. Did I love my husband? No. Most certainly not. Like almost every marriage in our circles, ours was one of tactics and to unite money with money to get even more of it. My family was wealthier than his, but he was a lawyer, which my father could use for his businesses. The arrangement was made, we had a beautiful wedding, a child, my father got legal advice for practically free, and David climbed new social heights, which in turn helped his law firm along." At this, she subtly turned toward Dyson, who actually squirmed a bit. Andi had a suspicion that Tamara Portius held more sway over the man than he had assumed. Clearly more than Jake Dyson was comfortable with. Another thing Shireen would have to look into. Tamara kept on talking.

"We both lived our lives, with the promise to be discreet in our less socially acceptable endeavors. I kept my end of the bargain, he didn't. Now he's dead and I'm left to deal with the aftermath."

It was the second time she mentioned affairs she had to take care of. They had to be unpleasant enough to get to her, or else she wouldn't mention them, however marginally. It would also explain the nervous activity he was getting from the arthropods, not to mention the rapid blinking of Jake Dyson, who was getting more uncomfortable by the minute. Whatever it was, it was tied to the law firm in some way. Asking her about it now would only make her lie and alert Dyson, two things they didn't want at this point. Sometimes it paid to let people steep.

Andi leaned back, silently asking George to end the conversation. His partner got them out quickly, and it was a tie who was more relieved to see them leaving, Tamara Portius or Jake Dyson.

On their way to Sophia McHill, they discussed the things Tamara Portius had said. George glanced at Andi.

"What was it you picked up on when we were there?"

"What makes you think I picked up on anything?"

George chuckled. "You want me to spell it out? Firstly—" He lifted the index finger of his right hand. "—you spaced out. Secondly—" He put the finger back on the steering wheel and lifted it again. "—you were trying to get a rise out of her. You usually do that when you have something too unspecific to directly inquire. You were fishing. Well done, by the way, with her lawyer present. I don't think he suspected anything. He did seem a bit nervous, though."

Andi couldn't help the smile forming on his lips. No matter how dangerous it was that George was getting to know him so well, it was also very nice. And him being so sharp made him an excellent partner.

"Superb detective work. Remember when we met her the first time to tell her David Hector II was dead? The house was bustling with people. Today, we and the lawyer were the only ones there. And there has been a lot of hectic activity during the last few days. Frantic searching, if I read the impressions correctly."

"Which you always do. Lost testament, do you think?"

"Definitely something important. You heard her. She has to deal with the aftermath. I'm pretty sure she wasn't just talking about the funeral. Something has gone wrong for her, and the way she acts, I bet my money on, well, money. And Jake Dyson is part of it, up to his neck, and not in a way he enjoys."

"You have such a talent with words." George sighed dreamily.

"Ass." Andi punched him on the thigh, not too hard, he was driving after all. "Let's see what Sophia McHill has to say."

At the McHill mansion they were led into the house by Christin, the butler. Sophia was as immaculate as at their first meeting; if anything, her face was even more masklike. She, too, had a lawyer present, a woman named Hilda Doran who Andi guessed to be around fifty. She was more pleasant than Jake Dyson, though that wasn't too hard, and interestingly enough, she didn't work for Portius, Dyson & Partners but came from another firm. Sophia McHill looked at them with fake interest.

"Detectives, what brings you back? Do you have good news regarding the killer of my husband?"

George shook his head. "I'm afraid not, Mrs. McHill. There are a lot of people we have to talk to." George made a meaningful pause. "Which brings us to you, Mrs. McHill. The things our IT department found out led us to believe your husband had a tendency toward domestic violence."

Andi watched the words sink in. Sophia McHill had a phenomenal grip on herself; Andi had to give her that. All he spied was a slight widening of her pupils and one intake of breath that was a little sharper than the ones before and after. She did look at her lawyer, who cocked her head.

"Your IT department seems to employ some very clever people, Detectives." Hilda Doran's voice was calm, neutral.

Waiting for the other shoe to drop, Andi thought.

"We always thought so." George lowered his voice to a soothing tone, turning back to Sophia. "Were they right?"

Sophia McHill's posture got even more rigid, and she stuck out her chin defiantly, again looking at her legal counsel. Hilda Doran shrugged. "It's up to you if you want to answer that question, Sophia. I would advise against it, on the assumption that it could always be used against you."

"We wouldn't be invading your privacy like this if we didn't think it would help us solve the case," George added in an attempt to sway her.

Sophia closed her eyes for a moment, clearly pondering her options. Her stress levels were rising, as the spiders confirmed. Andi felt bad for dredging up such horrible memories. Nobody deserved to be abused and treated like shit.

"I guess, since you already know. Yes, they were. But it's been years since he last touched me in anger." Sophia's voice was hollow, resigned.

"When you were pregnant." George was so good at playing the understanding cop.

"Yes, when I was pregnant. I almost lost my son. That's when my father intervened. Beating the wife was totally fine according to him, but he drew the line at harming his grandchild and potential heir. There were some threats, harsh words between my husband and my father, and after my son was born, my husband decided to set his sights elsewhere. I can't say I was sad about his decision."

"You knew about his mistresses?" George kept the soothing tone. Sophia McHill seemed to be in a talkative mood, which, being the excellent detective he was, he didn't want to disturb. Hilda Doran, on the other hand, wasn't as happy. She put her hand on Sophia's shoulder.

"That I definitely wouldn't answer, Sophia. It's one thing to admit to having been abused, especially when there's evidence, and quite another to acknowledge information about potential mistresses. One makes you a victim, the other a potential suspect." She stared at George and Andi. "Is my client a suspect, Detectives?"

"Not anymore," George announced smoothly. "Of course we suspected Mrs. McHill initially because, as you are surely well aware of, Mrs. Doran, family members are always under suspicion, especially when so much money is involved. The fact that neither of the victims was a saint—" Sophia actually snorted at this comment, a very unladylike sound she tried to cover up by holding a hand in front of her mouth. "—makes it even more likely for the murderer to come from their own family. But we already know it can't have been Mrs. McHill for various reasons we can't disclose yet. We wouldn't mind getting her alibi for Thursday evening, just for our reports."

Hilda Doran didn't look convinced. She turned to Sophia. "I still recommend you don't say anything."

Again Sophia McHill pondered her options. She inhaled deeply. "Do you think one of his mistresses could have done it?"

"We're investigating in all directions," George answered.

"Well, then. I guess it doesn't hurt to tell you. I did know about the women in my husband's life." There was a hint of amusement in her voice. "He made sure I knew, flaunting them under my nose, how perfect they were for him, how they weren't as delicate and fragile as me. In his mind, I should have been begging him to focus on me again when in truth I thanked God every night for these women who were foolish enough to think they could take my place." Now Andi saw a real smile on her lips. It was the nasty, cruel kind he had seen so many times on his *Oma's* face. The smile of somebody who was suffering but knew they still had the upper hand. Knew there were others out there who suffered even worse. "They never understood that my husband would have never divorced me. My money and social standing are too valuable. Sometimes it was almost funny, watching as he strung them along, getting more and more violent until they finally realized what a monster he was. Then he would pay them a hefty sum to keep their mouths shut and go looking for the next one."

Sophia McHill reminded Andi of a fat spider, sitting in the middle of her web, controlling more than she let on, maybe even waiting to bite off the head of the male.

"I gather from your words you didn't mind his affairs?" George was reiterating the obvious. Hilda Doran didn't object to this question. Her body language telegraphed she'd rather have Sophia shutting up completely, but the hint of dejection in her eyes told Andi she knew that wouldn't happen.

"No, not in the least." Absolute sincerity rang in Sophia McHill's words.

"Are you friends with either Theodora Miller or Tamara Portius?"

Sophia seemed to think about this. "It depends on how you define the term 'friends,' I guess. Our husbands were best friends since forever, and Tamara and I went to the same school, though different years. Theodora is a good ten years younger than me and Tamara. We rarely did those couple nights where the three families met. Our husbands preferred to be among themselves. Of course we see each other at the club and all those social functions, but we never meet privately, and I wouldn't think to confide in them." She tapped her chin with her right index finger. "No, we're not friends. Close acquaintances through regular exposure, I'd say."

That was one way of phrasing it. Andi was impressed. George glanced at him, his gaze asking if he should go on or wrap things up for the time being. Andi shrugged almost imperceptibly. She was surprisingly forthcoming, something they should take advantage of in his opinion. The next time, her lawyer might have gotten through to her, and then she wouldn't be so helpful anymore. George turned his attention back to Sophia McHill.

"Even though you weren't friends with them, Mrs. McHill, did you know about the affairs both Mr. Portius and Mr. Miller were having?"

At this question, Hilda Doran relaxed a bit in her seat. Incriminating others was usually fine for lawyers. Sophia raised one brow, or at least it looked as if she was trying to. The Botox turned it into some kind of nervous little twitch. "I did. Just like they knew about my husband's extramarital activities and his penchant for violence. We never talked about it, though. That would have been—wrong." The word sounded strange from her lips, as if she had been searching for a better one and not been able to find it.

"Wrong?" George dug deeper.

Sophia McHill thought about it for long enough to make Andi think she wouldn't answer. When she finally did, it was in a monotone voice, as if she were reciting something she had once heard. "They were open secrets, but still secrets. These things only become real when you admit them out loud. Until then, everything can be glossed over with small talk and shut out by simply ignoring it."

Andi didn't know if this statement was deep or just plain sad. Probably both, depending on who looked at it how. After that George ended the conversation fairly quickly, getting them away from the two women and back on the road within ten minutes.

The silence in the car lasted for about half a mile before George started speaking.

"That wasn't as helpful as I'd hoped. We have three wives who have no love for their late husbands, no problem admitting it, perfect reasons to kill them, and who claim not to know each other too well."

"We do know it wasn't them," Andi pointed out.

"We know they weren't the ones to pull the trigger, so to speak. We don't know if they didn't pull any strings in the background." George sounded thoughtful.

"No, we don't. Then again, could you see Sophia McHill going on the darknet and hiring a professional killer?"

George drummed a rhythm on the steering wheel. It was tight, the beat of Vivaldi's "Summer" from the *Four Seasons*. Andi knew because

George had made him listen to the entire thing when Andi had asked what song he was always drumming when he was thinking.

"Not really. Doesn't mean she didn't do it. Sometimes people surprise you in a bad way. I'm inclined to take Theodora out of the equation. If what she says is true, she never suffered because of her husband, quite the contrary—he's the reason she can lead a carefree life in comfort. She didn't strike me as a person who would secretly pine for something she can't have. She's too pragmatic for that. And she went into the marriage knowing what she was getting."

"Unlike Tamara and Sophia. You heard them. And they never use their husbands' names when they can avoid it. That says a lot about the relationship they had." Andi stared out of the window—

Drying soil, a breeze too light to be dangerous, dead roots, food, small cadavers, mating, eggs, the pulsing of change within cocoons, humming, whirring of wings, the bustling inside an anthill, the earth giving way, a new tunnel, food, food, food, eating, flying, building the net, mating....

The images zipping through his mind at the speed the car was going, never lasting, just flashes of something, no context, not important, or important, but not to him, not at the moment, he was talking about the wives, would they kill, or had they gotten used to the way things were as they said?

"Yeah, the kind bad soap operas are made of." George snorted, pointedly ignoring the gap in their conversation, or perhaps it hadn't been such a great gap and Andi just hadn't realized it.

"The screen writers have to get their ideas from somewhere."

"It just sounds so far-fetched." George set the blinker to get them on the highway. "And I'm not convinced they had anything to do with it. There's too many things not adding up. Just like with Gartner. Why would they have waited until now? I bet they had tons of chances to make it look like an accident. Why did it have to be now, and why in the way it happened? There was nothing easy about the kills."

"Perhaps we have been too focused on the possible killers. It makes sense with all the things we've found so far. And eliminating the closest family members as suspects is always a good idea, which is why we definitely have to talk to the sons again. But perhaps it's time to take a very close look at the way the victims were killed?"

"You mean like going through the evidence Evangeline and CSI have so far again and trying to come up with a plausible timeline in which we then try to fit our mysterious female killers?"

"It's a start. And real police work." Andi had to admit he sounded self-deprecating.

"What you do is real as well." George glanced at him with visible worry. "It's just not officially accepted."

"A very fine distinction."

"And a very good one as well." George's hands tightened around the steering wheel, telling Andi to stop putting himself down.

"It is. It just doesn't help us with Chief Norris breathing down our necks because the mayor is riding her ass."

"And we're back to your poetic use of words." George laughed. "I don't want that either, but some things just can't be helped. Besides, if we do real police work, as you call it, you don't have to ruin your mental health, which is more important to me than any hounding the chief could do."

"Thank you. That means a lot." Andi glanced at George, infusing his words with enough sincerity to show his partner he wasn't joking. George put his right hand on Andi's thigh for a moment, a reassuring gesture that shouldn't have felt so good.

The first thing George did when they were back in the precinct was to get a second whiteboard. They were the only ones using them, so nobody complained when George arranged the second one in a ninety-degree angle to the first one, creating another wall between their desks and the rest of the office, shielding Andi's workspace completely. It almost felt like having their own office. Andi booted his PC and opened the files CSI and Evangeline had sent them. George was already waiting with his black marker at the ready. At the top of the board, he had written TIMELINE. Knowing his partner needed for things to have a certain structure, Andi refrained from making fun of him. And even though he would never admit it, the tidiness of George's fact gathering helped Andi to think. He glanced at the other whiteboard, which was a mess of colored lines and huge circles with names on it. Perhaps tidiness was too big a word for it.

"Okay, let's start with the date. Time of death was last Friday between two and four a.m. Cause of death was drowning in the body of water the victims were found in. Tox screen says they were drugged with ketamine and their blood alcohol was at approximately one per mill for each of them, which hints at them having roughly the same speed when drinking."

George wrote it all down, the time and cause of death more to the right of the board, while the alcohol and ketamine got spaces closer to the middle. George cocked his head.

"We know from their wives they went to the cabin early on Thursday and spent the day hunting."

"CSI confirms that the deer we found in the cool house was from that day." Andi scrolled down the document while George put "departure from home" at the very left of the board, followed by "arrival at cabin" and "hunting."

"They had a successful day, killed some innocent creatures, decided to start with the beer the Pérezes have stored there on Wednesday."

George inserted "beer + ketamine" in the space between "hunting" and "ketamine."

"Now you've got ketamine twice," Andi pointed out.

"Alcohol as well." George glanced at Andi. "Do we have confirmation the ketamine was in the beer?"

Andi scrolled some more, finding the line he was looking for. "Yep. Several bottles of the beer had been tampered with. They have a special cap designed specifically for this brewery. The cap is thinner than the usual crown caps and has a loop for easy opening. There were six caps with tiny injection sites found in the trash and on the table and under the sofa. CSI also found six more bottles with injection sites, which makes two crates at the very top of ten crates in total, stacked at five."

"Whoever did this wanted to make sure they got the doctored beer on the first evening. Sensitive schedule?" George furrowed his brows.

"Probably. The sooner they died, the more time they would spend in the water destroying any and all evidence before they were even reported missing."

"Which brings me back to the professional killer. This is something a pro would definitely consider."

Andi leaned back in his chair. "You're right. Or somebody who had gone to the trouble of finding out everything about ketamine, how it works, and how quickly it leaves the human system. You said it before: this whole setup reeks of meticulous planning. Of somebody who had the time to ponder all eventualities."

"Which would shoot our theory that the point in time is somehow important. It could have just been that the killer or killers were finally done with the preparations." George put the black marker down, getting the red. He wrote "TIME?" above "departure from home."

Andi opened his drawer, found a ballpoint pen in there, and started dissecting it. While his fingers were busy, the analytical part of his brain pondered the possible scenarios. "We have either a pro at work or somebody with a grudge and the patience to enjoy their vengeance served frozen."

George got a green marker and made two double lines under the initial timeline. The first he labeled "Pro," the second "Amateur." He tapped the back of the marker against the whiteboard. "I'm a bit out of touch with the going rates of professional killers. What would a three-person kill with such specific instructions cost?"

"I'm not sure. A simple kill these days is at around 50K I think, if you're turning to a pro. If the targets aren't protected somehow. Three people, 150K. A complicated kill like that? Probably a quarter million if not more."

"Do I want to know why you're familiar with the rates of professional killers?"

"I went by the break room a few weeks ago and Shireen was in a full-blown discussion with some beat officer about the costs of being a professional killer and how their rates are quite sensible when you included gear, living costs, retirement plan, insurance, health care, safe houses, and I don't know what else. It sounded all very logical." Andi shrugged.

"Except for the part where Shireen knows about the life necessities of professional killers." George had a point, a good one, though Andi would never tell him why.

"She spends more time in the darknet than in real life. She's bound to know things we'd rather not."

George seemed to mull this over before he focused back on the whiteboard. "Anyway, a quarter million eliminates a whole bunch of suspects." He pointed at the other whiteboard where they had two circles with "business rivals." In the first one, there certainly were some names who had enough money to pay for a professional killer without it affecting their bottom line, but the reason for most of them to hate the three victims—and for being in the second circle—was because they had lost money to them. Lots of it. "I don't think Tabitha Clément and Josephine Garr would have the cash to pay a contract killer, let alone two. And they wouldn't have been at the cabin themselves if they had paid somebody to kill them. It does keep Gideon Gartner and the wives in the pool, though." George wrote their names between the first two lines. Then he pointed to the lines below. "Gartner is out here. Which still leaves Tamara Portius and Sophia McHill."

"Could be. I'm writing Shireen a message to see if the wives had any contact beyond what they've claimed."

George started twirling the marker in his fingers. "Somehow I just can't picture any of the wives killing their husbands like that. I can totally see Theodora haggling with a contract killer about the price for Lawrence Miller's death, but I can't imagine why she would pay for the other two. Unless she was in cahoots with Tamara and Sophia, though I doubt it. Tamara, on the other hand, she strikes me as the type who would have done something drastic, like castrating Portius or something like that. She may try to keep her anger under a lid, but we've seen it boil over. No way would she have the patience to hire a professional who then drugs her husband and guides him out into the swamp if she could just bludgeon him to death herself where they were standing. And Sophia, she's the type who would go for poison. She doesn't want any unpleasantness."

"Probably would ask her butler to do it for her." Andi shared George's assessment of the women. None of their personalities fit the way the murders were conducted. Then again, people lied all the time, and perhaps they were simply phenomenal actors.

"Tell Shireen to go digging about Portius's finances as well. Perhaps this is something we can use." George had put the marker down and was back in his chair, still staring at the whiteboard.

"Excellent idea." Andi started typing. "How about we call it a day? I need to digest all this information."

"You mean this indigestible chaos of leads and suspects not fitting what we know about the crime? Good luck!" George started gathering his things.

"Perhaps once it's all settled down in our brains, we can find a pattern?" Andi wasn't optimistic. There were just too many things not adding up. They needed some kind of break soon, otherwise he would have to try and find the two women from the lake, which was nearly impossible because he hadn't seen any distinguishing features in them he could use as a guideline. If they really were contract killers, they had probably left the state already.

After George had gotten him home, Andi went outside to do his mediating in his gazebo. The air wasn't as warm as just a few days before yet still pleasant enough. He did put on thick socks because his feet were always the first to get cold. Standing on the dark blue yoga mat, Andi went through the mixture of yoga, Pilates, and qui-gong movements that loosened his entire body, especially the area around his shoulders. Once he was sufficiently warmed up and his mind had started to settle down, focusing on the movements more than on his thoughts and the images coming from the insects, he sat down in a half lotus, closed his eyes, and started concentrating on the walls protecting his mind. Their thinning had halted, which meant he could now try to rebuild them. As mundane as it sounded, imagining them as actual walls like in an old medieval castle helped him with the task. The input from the arthropods was like the ocean churning against the stone, chipping at it, sometimes taking chunks out of it. He felt them, their minds—because for him they had minds, no matter what science tried to tell him—like little dots of light in the endless sea of impressions, each of them seeing and interpreting them differently, like a prism, only the other way round or, no, like a prism where you put in different lights and got out something else entirely, and he had to catalogue it, put it in the right regard, give it priority or ignore it, more often than not without really understanding, just guessing, he was doing so much guessing, and he had his own list of references, he could tell apart most drugs like cocaine and heroin, even the batches, and then he thought he had it figured out until he experienced something totally different and there just wasn't anything he could relate it to, and it was so hard to forget these things, to dismiss them and concentrate on what he knew, because he was curious, oh yes, it was part of being a cop, a requirement, and too much curiosity killed the cat and one day he wouldn't come back from one of his inquiries, and he always wondered how it would be, if they would find his catatonic body or if he would still be functioning somehow, going through the motions without anybody being in the driver's seat, or if he would end up in a mental facility, pumped full of drugs that fulfilled the same purpose as alcohol only with different side effects, and would he realize the loss of control he feared so much or would he be grateful because he could finally let go, and what kind of life would that be, would he even be aware of being trapped in his mind or just lost in the consciousness of thousands of tiny minds, tiny lives, flaring up and winking out in a steady rhythm, like a heartbeat, his own, perhaps, and where were the lines, what was reality and what was them, only they were real, too, even more so than many of the blobs, no, humans, he interacted with, and how would it feel to forget all about social necessities and just follow your instinct, and why was he here in the first place, he needed something to do, there was stone, hard, unyielding, yes, the walls, he had to reinforce them, because the *geschenk* was getting stronger, he was becoming more and more like them, just like his *Oma* had, and she had once told him something, it was important, he thought, something about *being* them, about embracing it all, stupid old woman with all her nastiness and her cold heart, seeing human beings as things, obstacles, blobs, like *they* did, having no compassion because she wasn't one of them anymore, and looks could be deceiving, couldn't they, making you believe one thing while another was true, like the stripes on the back of a mimic fly, pretending to be a wasp while really being harmless, only his *Oma* had never been harmless, poisonous, in words and deeds, never helpful, telling him to accept what was ruining all his chances at being normal, and when you had no choices you made the best of what you were given, only it rarely worked, and those walls looked ready to crumble, no longer fit to keep anything in or out, so he better started putting new stones in, so much work, and the sea outside was crashing against them, but he could do it, had to do it, he didn't want to give in yet, there were things he still wanted to do, life was still sweet enough to not be consumed by the bitterness of being more than one, of being born and dying and living all the time without a break, building his wall to keep that other reality at bay for a little longer....

14. LIKE FATHERS, LIKE SONS

GEORGE SERIOUSLY contemplated putting Andi back in bed. If he even had been there the last night. It certainly didn't look like it. His partner was wearing yoga pants that could have been black at some time. Now they were this washed-out gray, the cloth at the knees almost see-through and not in a sexy way, the hems at the legs fraying. The thick woolen socks seemed to be hand-knitted and had turned to felt in some places. A sweater of dubious color and form rounded out an outfit that perfectly matched the tired expression in Andi's eyes. He stepped aside to let George into the house.

"I'm sorry. Didn't hear the alarm. Can you give me five minutes to shower?"

"Take fifteen, and don't break your neck on the tiles. Should I make tea?" George tried to sound nonchalant and was doing a terrible job. Andi rolled his eyes.

"I got kind of lost yesterday, okay? The good news is, I was able to strengthen my mental shields, but it took longer than I thought."

"Okay." It was far from being okay, not the way Andi looked as if he'd been on a three-day binge with more alcohol than one person should be able to consume. Knowing Andi hadn't touched a drop of the stuff made it even worse. George hated to ask the question, but he had to. "Are you even able to go to work today?"

Instead of getting angry, which would have been George's cue that Andi could go to work, his partner seemed to think about it. "I'm tired." Andi yawned as if he wanted to stress his words. "I can go, though. Let's just hope Shireen has found something good for us to wake me up properly." With that, Andi went toward the stairs.

George stayed in the kitchen with nothing else to do but set the water to boil and rummage in the cupboard over the sink for some tea. He found a blend of peppermint, sage, and lemon balm which he knew Andi liked. He did have the obligatory cup of herbal tea from Starbucks in his car, which Andi could drink later. This moment called for loose leaves, and besides, George needed to occupy himself. Otherwise he would have stormed upstairs to check on Andi, which he was sure would not be appreciated. While the tea was steeping, George wondered how he could help Andi. The gaps in their conversations when Andi's mind wandered elsewhere were getting more frequent and long enough to draw attention from outsiders. George was still able to gloss it all over, but they had to find some kind of solution soon. Even those who were used to Andi's weird ways, namely Shireen, Evangeline, and Adam Forard, the leader of one of the SWAT teams, had started to regard Andi with worry, which told George that his partner had never before been this bad. How he should breach the subject without getting his head bitten off, George still wasn't sure. He definitely had to wait until Andi was in a better mood than now.

"Oh, smells great." Andi was coming down the stairs, his dirty-blond hair tousled. He had changed into one of his threadbare old jeans, which only stayed on his hips because of the worn leather belt that also held Andi's badge. His attempt at looking like a respectable detective by wearing a shirt and jacket was hampered because the shirt looked like something George's grandfather might have worn, and the jacket seemed to have been there when the supercontinent Gondwana broke apart. When they had first met, George had been appalled by Andi's lack of care for his looks. Now he would have found it endearing if he hadn't known that it was simply another side effect of the *geschenk*. Andi only had a limited amount of strength at his disposal, most of which he used to keep his mental shields up. The rest was for solving cases. There simply wasn't room for something as mundane as going clothes shopping. George wondered if their relationship had by now progressed far enough for him to follow his suggestion from a few days before and buy Andi a wardrobe. He understood how it could seem like he was patronizing his partner when in truth all he wanted was to make Andi's life easier. And his partner had reacted positively to the two sweaters. Watching while Andi put an obscene amount of honey into his travel mug with the tea, George decided to just go for it. If Andi decided he didn't like it after all, he could always return the stuff. Yes, that was a good idea.

After Andi was done stirring the tea, they went to George's car. At the precinct, they found several messages from Shireen in their email inboxes. One was actually from Timmy Delain, the newbie Shireen had tasked with composing the reports on the mistresses of Harry Alexander McHill, as well as the sex workers David Hector Portius II had met. The list of the mistresses was complete, and much to George's dismay, none of them stood out. It appeared they all had been given quite the money to keep their silence, not to mention the airtight NDA they all had signed when entering their respective relationships with McHill. Three of them hadn't been in the country during the time of the crime, and the other four had ironclad alibis. None of them had the financial means to hire a contract killer without it being noticed, and unless Timmy or Shireen found out they had somehow been in contact with each other, they were out of the investigation. The sex workers Portius had frequented were a more difficult matter; there were too many to expect Timmy to have dossiers on all of them. Their sheer mass was also what dismissed them as prime suspects—Portius's contact with them seemed to have been on a purely business level, and the crime screamed personal.

The first message from Shireen was sobering. It said she couldn't find any closer contact between the three wives than the necessary calls and short texts needed when on the same committee to organize a charity. Unless they had used burner phones or smoke signals, they had told the truth about not being close. The second message told them to come into Shireen's lair because she had found something.

With all the honey from the tea coursing through his system, Andi appeared to be a little more awake, which was more than George had dared to hope on their way over. Shireen greeted them with a cheerful smile. "Rejoice, dear Detectives, I have good news."

"You found a contract on the darknet?" Andi sounded almost alert now.

"No. If there was a contract out for the victims, it's either already deleted or very well hidden. Rather the former than the latter."

"Then why are you so disgustingly happy?"

"You really are a ray of sunshine, aren't you? Couldn't you have given him some sugar when you picked him up?" Shireen stared pointedly at George.

"Any more sugar than he already has ingested and he could go into a diabetic coma," George deadpanned.

"Oooh, so it's one of those days."

"Could you two please stop talking about me while I can still hear you?" Andi's tone was close to getting impatient, something George liked to avoid at all costs. He motioned with his head for Shireen to proceed. The hacker was well enough acquainted with Andi's moods to understand the silent nudge.

"Well, despite me being super busy with all kinds of important stuff, you know, something got me thinking about the sons of your victims. I mean, isn't it strange that three young men, sons of highly successful fathers and with the best education money can buy, aren't at a more elevated state in life? One of them could be written off as a normal family fallout. But all three?"

That got George's attention. They had briefly toyed with the same question and the idea that the sons could have been involved in their fathers' killings, but with so many more likely suspects they had put the sons on the back burner.

"You have a point. What did you find?" George was curious now, as well as Andi, who had made a step toward the huge flat-screen on the wall.

"That's just it. Nothing. One moment they were their daddies' darlings, going to the same alma mater, spending their time in the same fraternity, all busy being rich sons, the next they were all on their own, trying to get a scholarship for their last semesters at Harvard. If it weren't for a secret benefactor paying for them, they would have dropped out for lack of money. Their trust funds dried out more quickly than spittle on a hot stove, all thanks to Portius, Dyson & Partners, and there wasn't some lavish traveling after getting their degrees or high-paying job offers as you would expect for people with their fathers' kinds of connections. And now David Hector Portius III is working as a second-rate lawyer who has problems paying his rent and loses most of his cases because his grasp of the law is flimsy at best, Lester Miller has never held a job longer than a few months, has already founded and crashed two companies and is now busy doing the same with the third, all due to a terrible lack of understanding for finances as his accounts suggest, and Dominic McHill is so up to his nose in debt that his monthly paycheck evaporates the moment it hits his account. These three men are sad, weak shadows of their fathers' glory, and even if we assume the fathers knew this and were disappointed, why didn't they at least try to help their own offspring?"

"You're telling us there was some kind of fallout. Something big because it involved all three of them." George and Andi exchanged a long glance. This was interesting indeed. "You don't happen to know what they did to fall from grace?"

Shireen sighed. "I'm still looking. It's the things I didn't find that made me suspicious in the first place. It's as if the last semester before they were estranged hasn't existed except for their names being in the official documents."

"Like fathers, like sons?" George asked, staring at Andi, who nodded.

"It's definitely worth considering. Question is, what did they do?"

"I'll keep digging. If I was able to find out about Gideon Gartner, I should be able to find out whatever the sons did, right?" Shireen had that determined line between her brows, telling George to not contradict her.

"Absolutely, Shireen. You're the best." Andi, too, knew how to read their resident hacker. "Have you found any signs that the sons had contact with each other?"

Shireen shook her head. "No contact through their phones, and none of them is on social media. No Facebook, Twitter, or Instagram for those three." She furrowed her brows. "Almost as if they're hiding…." Her tone took on a faraway quality. After a moment of intently staring at nothing George could see, she started typing on her tablet.

"Did you have a chance to take a look at Portius's affairs?" Andi queried, even though Shireen seemed to be engrossed in what she was doing.

"Huh?"

"Portius's affairs? I sent you a text. His wife is concerned about something." Andi was patting the back pocket of his jeans, searching for his cell.

"Ah yes, I remember." Shireen kept typing. The flat-screen flared to life again. "She has every reason to be concerned. It seems David Hector Portius II changed his will without telling her. A great chunk of his money goes into a trust to enable children from lower-class families to go to college. It's airtight as far as I can see and one of the few good things this man ever did."

"So she'll get nothing?" George thought that was a valid reason to be agitated.

"Well, nothing is a big word here. She won't get as much as she probably expected, but I don't call two villas and a seven-figure fortune, mainly in bonds, nothing." Shireen tapped her index finger against her chin. "Compared to the eight-figure sum that goes into the trust, it is nothing, though. Numbers are always about the right relation, you know."

George looked at Andi. "Back to Tamara Portius?"

Andi nodded. "Back to Tamara Portius."

"Thank you, Shireen, you're the best!" George blew her a kiss, which she caught, examined, and then stuffed into the front pocket of her dress or whatever the bag-like thing in bright violet and pink she was wearing was.

TO SAY Tamara Portius wasn't happy to see them was an understatement George didn't want to make. They had given her a call telling her they would be coming over because they had some more questions. Tamara Portius had been terse, saying something along the lines of doing what suited them. George and Andi had decided to take it as an invitation to just drop by. Before they had rung the bell, Andi had informed him that today there were four people inside the house with her. Two of them in the kitchen, one in the laundry room, and one upstairs with a vacuum. It was safe to assume they were all servants. No sign of Jake Dyson, which probably meant Tamara Portius wouldn't talk to them at all.

To George's surprise, she opened the door herself, staring at them as if she had forgotten they would be coming.

George nodded at her politely. "Good afternoon, Mrs. Portius. May we come in?"

Tamara Portius made a huffing sound at the back of her throat, her eyes narrowing to small slits. She looked upset and agitated, and when she stepped aside to let them in, her body language spoke volumes about how much their visit was inconveniencing her. She didn't even invite them to sit down. Which was fine by George because he was more than ready to take the gloves off. He had felt pity for her because she had obviously drawn the short straw in the husband department, just like Sophia McHill, but that didn't give her the right to be such an impolite bitch.

"Mrs. Portius, we'd like to talk to you about your husband's will. Will Mr. Dyson be here shortly?"

Tamara Portius managed to turn her expression into a mask of pure fury despite the Botox hampering her efforts. "That's not his will. Not the real one, anyway. The money is mine. And Dyson won't be coming to this house. Never again!"

And there it was, the ugly face of greed and anger. "I gather from your reaction you didn't find out about the will until recently?"

She balled her fists at her sides, making George worry for a moment that she would attempt to punch him. "He named Jake Dyson the executor of his will, and that old son of a bitch enjoyed telling me how most of the money, my *family's money*, is going into a fucking trust for underprivileged children. *After* you were gone the last time, that sniveling, slimy asshole had the gall to sit there and patronize me about how to handle the police, and then he advised me to get legal counsel because Portius, Dyson & Partners wouldn't be representing me anymore. But the last word hasn't been spoken!"

Suddenly, Dyson's twitchiness during their last visit made sense. The man had been waiting to dump Tamara like a share that had gone bad. Why she would agree to see them without new counsel was beyond George, but he wouldn't look a gift horse in the mouth. It could very well be she was simply fighting on too many fronts to think about such comparatively small fish like having the police in her home without a lawyer present.

"Your husband was a lawyer. I can't see how you think you could stand a chance fighting his will." George was goading her on purpose, hoping to get her riled up even more. Any information they were getting now was true. When they were angry, most people forgot to lie, and without legal counsel present to stop her, the chances of Tamara slipping up were rising.

The vicious smile appearing on Tamara Portius's face made George shiver. "Yes, he was a lawyer, and he thought himself the smartest motherfucker walking this planet."

Anger also made people forget their manners and language, George noted.

"But I'm not just a pretty face taking care of our social standing. When we married, he signed a legally binding contract stating that he got more than two-thirds of our starting capital from my father and that, should he die before me, two-thirds of everything we have acquired would go back to me. As soon as I find that contract, the will is worthless."

"What makes you think he didn't destroy it? Since you can't find it, I mean." Andi's voice was dismissive, as if he didn't care either way. Which he probably didn't.

"Oh, he definitely destroyed the original. It wasn't in its place." Tamara looked ready to breathe fire. "But I made copies of every single document concerning our marriage and me. I had them notarized and kept them hidden from him. Unfortunately, the hiding spot was—untidy. It's just a matter of time until I find it, though." She was calming down, a sign that she was sure she would be finding the document in question.

"Do you know if your son has any contact with Dominic McHill and Lester Miller?" George asked out of the blue. He figured he had exhausted the topic of the will. Tamara wasn't as startled by this abrupt change of gears as George had hoped.

"No, I don't know. I rarely talk to my son these days." She shrugged dismissively, as if not having contact with one's own son wasn't worth mentioning.

"Can you tell us about the fallout your son had with his father?" Andi followed George's vein of questioning. This got a reaction out of Tamara Portius. She shut down like a clam.

"It was a father-son thing. They had some—disagreements over certain things."

"Could you be a bit more concrete perhaps? In case you haven't noticed, this is a murder investigation, and not answering our questions could mean the killer will walk free," George reminded her in a stern tone. He was done being polite.

Tamara Portius tried to make a face as far as the Botox allowed, conveying without words how little she cared about finding her husband's killer. She answered nevertheless, apparently not concerned about telling them anything they shouldn't know. She was either truly innocent or damn sure she wouldn't be caught. "My son and husband argued about my son's duties toward him. It got ugly, words were said, my husband decided to show my son who was in charge. My son didn't like it. End of story."

"Thank you." George wanted to bet his salary this wasn't all there was to it, but for the moment, it was enough to work with.

After a brief goodbye, he and Andi left the Portius mansion. On their way back, they stopped at Theodora Miller's and Sophia McHill's homes, asking them the same question and getting equally evasive answers. Theodora had the most plausible, stating that she and her stepson had never been close, and neither did she know nor care what he was up to. When his father cut him out, it technically meant more money for her, so she didn't argue. Sophia McHill referred them to her lawyer, Hilda Doran, who stated that Sophia's son and her husband had a big fight about what was expected from Dominic. Sophia did her best to stay out of it, and with Harry Alexander McHill's history of violence, George could understand.

"We're sure the sons did something the fathers had to cover up, aren't we?" He glanced at Andi while he was waiting at a red light. His partner furrowed his brows.

"We are. It can't be coincidence that they all fell from grace at the same time. What I wonder is if the wives really don't know or if there's something they're not telling us."

"Oh, I'm sure there's a lot they're not telling us. But I believe them when it comes to this." George focused back on his driving when the light turned green. "First of all, none of them is stupid. They have to know we're asking each of them, and since we're operating under the assumption that they're not friends with close contact, they can't know if one of them isn't going to spill the beans. Second, each of them has good reason not to be interested. Theodora is just the stepmother, and she married Lawrence Miller when Lester was already in his first year in college. I bet she barely knows what he looks like. I also have the impression that Sophia McHill tried everything to stay out of her husband's way. I can't see her taking an interest in something that could potentially attract her husband's focus back to her, especially when she wasn't close to her son. As for Tamara, she's so full of open hatred, I can see her enjoying her husband's anger over something he couldn't control."

Andi sighed. "I agree. None of them is the motherly type. I can't imagine any of them defending her offspring like some mothers would. My impression was that having a child was something that's expected in their circles, and once they had ticked that particular box, they went on with their lives. What has whatever the sons did to do with their fathers' deaths, though?"

"You don't think there's a connection?"

"To be honest, I think these men were such scumbags we're going to find a lot of connections the longer we dig. This whole case is like a spiderweb with the victims at the center. And all the lines are intertwined somehow. We just have to find out where." Andi blew air upward, letting his bangs flutter. It did look kind of cute, even if applying that word to Andi felt wrong on so many levels.

"They certainly weren't the kind of people I would have chosen to surround myself with."

"No, definitely not. With cases like this, I sometimes wonder why I even bother solving them. The way I see it, those three men got what they deserved."

George swallowed hard. He had always known he and Andi had differing opinions on law enforcement and justice in general, but they were usually good at skirting the loaded parts. It seemed Andi had just opened one of them up for discussion. George would have preferred not to talk about this to keep the peace. He wasn't somebody who backed down from an argument, though, and he knew Andi wouldn't want that. He just wasn't sure if this was the time and place for it.

"You mean being drugged out of their minds, then led into a lake and left to drown?"

From the corner of his eye, George saw Andi glancing at him. "Do I detect a certain amount of sarcasm here?"

"You do. Listen, Andi, I totally get why you're feeling the way you're feeling. Every cop gets there at some point. What we can never forget, though, is that we're not judges. We're the ones who find the culprits so judges and juries can speak their verdict. There's a very good reason for division of power, and you know it."

"Spare me the police academy talk. I've been there, same as you. And same as you, I've learned the hard way how unjust justice can be." Andi wasn't quite yelling yet; his voice was still calm, but there was an undertone of steel creeping into his words. Just enough to get George's hackles up as well. This case was drawing out, they had too many suspects, he was worried about Andi, his own career, the way he was getting more and more attached to his grumpy partner, and he was also tired. Not the best premise for an in-depth discussion of such a loaded topic.

"It doesn't matter. History has shown us that it always goes wrong when cops take justice into their own hands."

"What about all the justice that never happens? All the people who are dead and whose bodies will never be found? Justice is an illusion society has created to keep up a semblance of order. Problem is, there is no order, no higher legitimacy. There's just people. And some of them get justice while others don't, whereas we stand at the sidelines, operating in a system that has more holes than a cheese from Switzerland. I'm so fucking tired of it all."

George was so shocked by this outburst, he set the blinkers and parked the car at the curb somewhere on the outskirts of Charleston. His anger started to fade in the face of Andi's obvious distress. Instinctively George understood this wasn't about justice at all—or perhaps only marginally. This was about Andi being backed into a corner he couldn't escape, and George had made it even worse by speaking so harshly to him. He could have slapped himself.

"I'm sorry, Andi. I don't think it's a good idea to keep talking about this. I'm going to drive you home. I'll call in and tell them we're following a lead that has suddenly come up." George reached for his cell to do just that. Andi was staring at him with glassy eyes, his Adam's apple bobbing up and down when he swallowed hard. He looked angry and confused and torn, and George could see his walls coming down. Then Andi leaned back in his seat, his eyes closed, his voice that monotone he always had when he was explaining what he got from the arthropods, and George knew his partner didn't want to share, didn't even want to experience anything, but didn't seem to be able to stop it.

"It's all a maelstrom, emotions and feelings and images, and I'm caught in it, I want out, I don't want this, don't want to know, I can never escape, oh why is it so hard to get out, so impossible, I'm trapped again, so many pictures, so much info I can't place, I need to get back to solid ground, only where is it these days, always gone, never where I need it to be, and I'm so hungry, and the spider has caught the fly and the butterfly was hit by a car while the caterpillar eats away the leaves of the flowers and the pill bugs cower beneath the sink and the roaches roam the gutter, finding food and shelter and nourishment, and why am I up here when it's so much safer down there, where it's cool and dark and nothing can touch me, but I'm too big, why am I too big, and why would I go down into the earth, when I have the sky to take to, with its breezes and clouds and sun, sun is good, warm, though fading, I could hide in the walls, plenty of wood there to gnaw on, to build tunnels, to reproduce, I never wanted children, the danger of passing on the curse is too great, the curse, the *geschenk*, the root of all my problems and suffering, the net is torn, why am I here, the bumblebee is exploring a hole in the ground, a good place to spend the winter, I—"

George felt guilt and shame creeping up his spine. He had done this, he had pushed his already mentally fragile partner into this, this… episode simply because he wanted to be right, and now he had to deal with the aftermath, had to pull Andi back from whatever world he was losing himself in. He grabbed Andi's shoulder and shook him violently.

"Andi! Come back. I'm sorry, Andi, I'm sorry. I didn't mean to aggravate you like that. Please, come back to me."

For way too long Andi stared at him blankly, his eyes open but clearly nobody was home. George thought he heard the dry rasping of chitin on stone, the buzzing of an angry fly. Then Andi twitched, shook his head, was back.

"What?"

"It's okay. I'm going to get you home. You need to sleep, Andi." George started the car to get back into traffic. Things were escalating so quickly, he didn't know how to react. He needed some time to think, to clear his head. The last thing they needed right now was arguing with each other. It took George another twenty minutes to get to Andi's house, twenty minutes during which they stayed mostly silent, Andi appearing to meditate while George was worrying himself sick about his partner.

As soon as they arrived, George saw to it that Andi had a light dinner—it was only 5:00 p.m., but that counted, didn't it?—and then went straight to bed. When his partner started snoring, George finally had time to freak out. He went downstairs and out into the garden to get some fresh air and a little distance to his partner, who had been close to giving him a heart attack. Andi had said his *geschenk* had started to calm down. He had assured George—or made him believe, as he now realized—that there was nothing to worry about. And to be honest, George knew Andi's breakdown—shutdown? Meltdown? Spacing out?—was directly related to the stress of having Chief Norris harassing them all the time and George's own harsh reaction to Andi's implication of maybe letting the killers go unpunished. George was also adult enough to admit that 90 percent of his irritation about Andi's viewpoint didn't stem from righteous indignation— it *sure* played a part, but George had been on the force too long already to not have been tempted—but mostly from the desire to show Chief Norris up and maybe, hopefully, get rid of her sometime soon, because the prospect of being forced to deal with her for another two and half years—George very pointedly didn't think about his growing desire to prolong his stay in Charleston for even longer—was about as compelling as having a root canal. He could do it if he had to, but not without proper sedation.

In his desperate need to get his thoughts in order, he called Daniel, hoping his brother was available. Daniel picked up after the fourth ring, his voice a little distorted. "Hey, dearest brother. What can I do for you?"

"Hey, Daniel. I could use some advice."

"Shoot. Though be warned, I'm in an area with bad reception. We may be cut off."

"Are you okay? Am I interrupting something?"

"No worries. Technically I'm on duty at the moment, but practically we're having a break, so you're good." The exaggerated cheer in Daniel's voice was just palpable enough to ring George's alarms, but he knew better than to ask. Daniel was even worse at expressing a need for help than Andi.

"What I'm telling you now has to stay between us, Daniel."

"Scout's honor."

"I'm serious."

"Me too." And Daniel was, as George knew. He might hide it behind a light tone and seemingly careless banter, but his brother could keep a secret. To this day, neither their mother nor their oldest brother Griffin knew who was responsible for the *mysterious disappearance of the chocolate Easter eggs*. Admittedly, the bribe had been substantial, but the silence had been worth it.

"Okay, here it comes. Andi and I are working a huge case at the moment, and we have so many suspects we could start a yard sale with them. The chief is breathing down our necks to close that case ASAP because the mayor wants it, so as you can imagine, tensions are riding high at the moment. We just drove back from interviewing some suspects when Andi suddenly started talking about how much the victims deserved to die, which led to a heated argument, and it upset him so much I had to get him home."

"Ah, I see, one for the ethics and philosophy classes."

"Daniel!"

"Calm down. What was your first reaction?"

"Honestly? That I can understand him. My second thought was that I want the person responsible to pay for the crime."

"Mmm. And Andi thinks just letting it slide would be preferrable.... From what you told me about him, I wouldn't have pegged him as somebody who takes the easy way out."

"He doesn't. It's just that he has a very unique way of seeing the world. And our perspective on things doesn't always match."

"Okay, George, I can see how this is a difficult situation for you. Now take a deep breath, and we try to detangle what's going on here because I think you have your priorities all mixed up. First, what is the main reason you called me? Because you don't know what to do about the case or because you had a fight with your partner?"

George opened his mouth to answer, then closed it, before opening it again. "Because I had a fight with Andi. That upsets me more than anything else." It was a staggering truth.

"If you put aside whatever tumult Andi's differing of opinion has put you in, what are your feelings about the case?"

George swallowed hard. "I don't want to just let it slide because no matter what terrible assholes the victims were in life, they deserve justice. And I don't want the chief to have the gratification to see us fail."

"Fair. If you put your personal animosity, as justified as it is, aside, what are your thoughts?"

"That the police shouldn't be judges because it's just not *right*."

"Good. What else?"

"I can totally relate to Andi's point of view, and it scares me while at the same time riles me up because it goes against everything I was taught to believe in and everything our family stands for."

"Have you tried explaining this to Andi?"

"No. I kind of started yelling first."

"Kind of?"

"Fine, I got my hackles up and pushed him into what I think was a minor breakdown, and now I feel bad."

"Bad enough to consider going with his suggestion?"

"No. He wouldn't expect or even want me to. I know him well enough to say this with absolute certainty. He's got no problem with me seeing things differently and expressing my view. There's just so much playing into the topic, I get the feeling it isn't *mine* no matter what I do."

"This is fucked-up, even for you, brother."

"Thank you very much. I'm aware. Now help me."

There was a sigh on the line. "Me just listening to you didn't help?"

"It helped a lot. Now tell me what to do."

"So you can ignore it?"

"Basically, yes." Getting Daniel's advice was good, because it helped George decide what he absolutely wouldn't do.

"I distinctly remember you ignoring my advice and falling into a river in mid-March."

"I was ten, and it was the only time you were ever right about anything!"

Daniel tsked loudly. "What if this is the second time?"

"I'm going to risk it. Now stop stalling."

"Fine. I see several problems here, George. First, there's your personal entanglement with Andi, and don't you dare deny it. You feel responsible for him, which fucks with your usual pragmatic take on situations like these. Then there's your beef with the charming Chief Norris, a problem you know you'll have to address sooner rather than later and which I trust you have under control. Both things influence your way of thinking. Then there's the fact that our parents raised us to be citizens so upstanding, we could as well have swallowed a broom."

At that they both chuckled, their parents undoubtedly having left a mark on them.

"From what you've told me—and I'm sure you're leaving a few crucial points out—"

George winced audibly. "I'm sorry, I…."

"It's fine, I get it. I'm in law enforcement as well, remember? From what you've told me, I can see how not solving the case would be a way out. Yes, it would hamper your precious solving statistic, though none too badly, but your partner would get a much-needed break and the chance to catch a breather."

"I would also have to live with the fact that I let a killer go unpunished."

"Yes. It's a question of priorities and ultimately what you value higher—your integrity, which only you know about, or your career, which is for the world to see, or your partner, who is so important to you."

George gulped. He hated to admit it, but the choice wasn't as clear-cut for him as he would have wished or thought of himself. Interpreting his silence right, Daniel went on.

"You don't have to decide right now, brother. I assume you have at least the night to sleep on it. Go for a run. You do your best thinking when you're exhausted."

Since he didn't know what to say, George went with, "Thank you, Daniel."

"You're always welcome. And you have to introduce me to Andi one of these days."

"I'll think about it. Take care of yourself. And Daniel?"

"Yeah?"

"If you ever need me to listen to you… you have my number."

"Let's just hope it never comes to that."

"Asshole."

"It's my pleasure." Daniel laughed. "Thank you, George. I may take you up on your offer. Bye."

The line went dead before George could properly say goodbye. He stared at his phone for a long time, wondering what he should do. Then he decided to heed at least part of Daniel's advice for once, namely to go on a run. First, though, he had to make sure Andi was sleeping well before he could start the drive home.

15. ENTANGLED

THE NEXT morning, Andi was woken by the delicious smell of pancakes. Knowing this was George trying to mend whatever he thought had been broken the day before, Andi got out of bed and hurried through his morning routine. The arthropods in the house were content, if a bit giddy because cooking always meant feeding, something that didn't happen too often when it was only Andi. George, on the other hand, was a reliable source of food, not just for Andi. When Andi entered the kitchen, George looked up from the stove with a guilty expression Andi didn't like seeing on his face. Before his partner could utter a word, Andi started.

"I'm sorry about yesterday. What I said about the victims deserving death—well, I still think they did, but I could have phrased it differently. Not made it so offensive for you."

George's shoulders slumped. "I'm sorry too. I shouldn't have gone off like I did. I admit it's kind of a hot topic for me, because my family has rigid views on the law. Nevertheless, that doesn't mean I should dismiss other opinions the way I did yours."

Andi chuckled. "Look at us all being adult and reasonable and stuff. I'd say we put it behind us. Can I have my pancakes?"

George grinned, his relief radiating off him in waves of pleasant pheromones as the moths in the ceiling and the spider in the corner attested. "Of course." He put a plate stacked high with golden baked disks and fresh strawberries and melon in front of Andi. After he had prepared his own plate, he sat down next to Andi at the kitchen bar, throwing him a sideways glance. "Can we talk about the other thing that happened yesterday?"

"I guess it's too much to ask for you to just forget about it?" Andi put the first fork of fluff into his mouth and chewed slowly. George shook his head, placed a strawberry slice on his pancake before eating it.

"I'm sorry I worried you." Andi stared at his plate. He knew he needed to say more, give an explanation of some kind. The problem was, he couldn't even remember everything he had said when the input from the arthropods had become too much. His defenses had been low because of the argument—another reason Andi hated people, interacting with them distracted him, though he couldn't hate George, never George—and the switch from slow-boiling anger to being swamped had been too sudden for Andi to exercise any control. He was aware that his own thoughts were mixing with what he got from his surroundings more and more, and it was hard for him to decipher what he had really said, what had just been in his head, what had come from the arthropods, and what was mere memory. "Sometimes I get kind of tripped up in what I receive."

George snorted, no amusement in his voice. "Tell me about it." He turned in his seat, looked directly at Andi, the worry in his gaze hitting Andi hard. "I've seen you go deep with the crawlers before, Andi, and I'm aware how ugly it can be, but yesterday—you lost control yesterday, and none of what you said made a lot of sense. At least not to somebody who doesn't know you. And it was me who triggered it. Your own partner."

"To be honest, I'm glad it was you and not somebody else. Otherwise I'd be in a padded cell now." Andi tried to sound nonchalant, though he knew very well this would be the harsh reality for him if things kept escalating at this pace.

"I don't even want to think about it." George took a piece of melon, chewed it thoughtfully. "What are the chances this is going to happen again?" He was now using his pragmatic tone, the one indicating he was looking for a solution. Andi was insanely grateful and, at the same time, wary. Any solution would involve George and therefore be short-term. Yet he needed his partner if he wanted to have any chance at keeping his life running smoothly—or as smoothly as he could hope for—after George was gone. Which meant he had to be honest. Suddenly the pancakes tasted like ash in Andi's mouth.

"They're pretty high. I told you, I'm going through a phase, and I'm trying to adapt. It's just taking some time."

"I wish I could help you."

The words were so heartfelt, Andi realized his throat was constricting. "You do help me. More than you realize. Without you, I would have had to call in sick or take an extended leave of absence half a year ago."

"Which is still a possibility." George sounded bitter, as if Andi's problems were his fault. He probably saw it that way.

"Yes, but just that, a possibility. Not inevitable."

"I don't like it." George glared at what was left of his pancakes.

"Me neither. We'll have to work with it, though. You think you can do that? Or will you dump my crazy ass the next time I slip?" Andi was going for teasing. The way George's shoulders tensed, he wasn't too successful. His partner forced a smile on his lips.

"I'm a Donovan. We don't back down from challenges. Never. Your crazy ass is safe with me." The mixture of pain, determination, gentleness, and despair in George's voice summed up their situation accurately.

"Then let's finish breakfast and get our sorry selves to the precinct. Hopefully there's something new from either Shireen or CSI. Otherwise, I'm afraid we're stuck at the moment."

"Which sucks on so many levels." George took a huge gulp of his coffee. "Why can't we just get the perfect suspect served on a silver platter, who made one crucial mistake which allows us to arrest them?"

"Because that would be a fairy tale, and we live in harsh reality land." Andi ate his last pancake, thinking it would be nice to have a fairy tale case now and then. Or none at all, come to think of it.

AFTER THEY arrived at the precinct, they went directly to Shireen. The resident hacker greeted them with gleaming eyes, her countless pendants clinking as she moved about excitedly.

"I'm the best," she said by way of greeting.

"We never doubted it," Andi answered. "Tell us something good."

"Oooh, you're going to *love* this!" Shireen started tapping at her tablet, motioning with her chin to the flat-screen on the wall. "It wasn't easy to find. They hid it well, and don't get me started on digital security in the nineties and how much hacking I had to do." She made a face. "Prepare to be thoroughly disgusted."

Andi and George shared a look. So far, nobody in this case—victims and suspects alike—had been especially endearing to them. "We can't wait." George's tone was dry as a desert. Shireen opened a window on the flat-screen showing the pictures of the victims' three sons in their early twenties. "These charming young men you already met were accused of drugging and raping two female students during one of their fraternity's parties. I had a hard time finding the names of the women because the fathers did a damn good job of erasing everything from public records." She looked at them, her expression unreadable all of a sudden. "The names of the victims are Josephine Garr and Tabitha Clemént."

George whistled, expressing Andi's thoughts exactly. "That puts a new spin on things. Damn bastards! Let me guess, they were never convicted for their crimes?"

"The whole thing didn't even make it into the courtroom." Shireen's eyes were murderous. "Guess who saw to that."

"Portius, Dyson & Partners." Andi spat the names like they were a curse. It wasn't hard to figure out.

"Exactly. They did their best not to leave the slightest trail, but something like that can never be completely contained. I'm currently searching the databases of all hospitals in the vicinity for two female victims matching the age, date, and, of course, crime to get a more substantial background for you to work with." Shireen blew a strand of hair out of her face. She looked serious. "I have to admit, I'm not a hundred percent comfortable with digging for details, even though I know it's necessary, but perhaps there is a chance they'll get a late kind of justice?"

The look of hopefulness in her eyes made Andi wince. Justice wasn't the most dependable of mistresses, as he knew only too well. When it came to cases of rape, justice was a downright whore who favored the person with the deepest pockets, which, sadly, were rarely the victims. Why Shireen was still so naïve after everything she had gone through and all the years she had spent in law enforcement remained a mystery to Andi. He suspected it might be due to a certain stubbornness that refused to accept reality.

"We'll see what happens once we've talked to them. Thank you, Shireen. This is very helpful."

"You're welcome. I'll contact you as soon as I know more."

Andi followed George out of Shireen's lair to their own desks. The two whiteboards with their countless names and lines seemed to mock them. Instead of going straight for a pen and adding the next lines to the complicated web, George let himself fall heavily into his chair.

"Fuck."

That about summed it up as far as Andi was concerned. "How do we proceed? Do we pay them another visit, or do we invite them to the precinct?"

"I think we might fare better if we went to their home. Judging from our last encounter, I'll bet they clam up if we apply too much pressure. Besides, we already know they weren't the ones at the lake."

"No, they weren't. But they were at the cabin, and now we know they had every reason to hate both the victims and their sons."

George got up to step to the whiteboard. "The same question applies as with the other suspects. Why did they wait until now? Especially if they had hired a contract killer. Or killers. And why would they go for the fathers? No, that's obvious. They were the ones who got their sons out of trouble. Of course they would hate them." He started drawing red lines from Tabitha and Josephine's names to the triangle of the victims. The web grew another spoke, making it look more like the blotchy sheets some caterpillars wove to hide themselves from hungry birds. Andi sighed. It was a successful strategy and much harder to dissect than a spider's web.

"I'm going to call them."

Getting Tabitha Clément to agree to a meeting in the afternoon took forever, and she only relented when Andi told her point-blank that they had found out about the rape. There had been a long silence at the other end of the line, then a dejected "Fine, at five," before Tabitha hung up. Andi wasn't happy about using the most traumatic experience of her life to threaten her into talking to them, and he felt disgusted with himself. The only reason he went through with it was because he hoped they could strike them from their list of suspects. In view of the circumstantial evidence they had so far—the pictures from the wildlife cameras and the shared ugly history with the victims, not to mention Josephine's chemistry degree—they were among the top contenders. Tabitha and Josephine could count themselves lucky that one of the detectives working their case already knew they were at least partly innocent. And unless they had substantial sums of money stashed somewhere Shireen hadn't been able to find it, it was unlikely they were the ones who had hired the killers.

The time until they would meet with Tabitha Clément and Josephine Garr was spent updating their reports and staring at the whiteboard, willing it to impart some clues they had missed until now. At 3:00 p.m. they got an email from CSI telling them they found traces of silk matching the one used in the products sold by Natural Beauty on the beer crates. It was good news because it meant they now technically had reason to arrest the two women. Practically, Andi and George both knew what a good lawyer would have to say to their evidence, and applying pressure when a gentler approach would potentially garner them more information was simply stupid. Andi also felt unease pushing the two women who were victims themselves.

Their arrival in East Cooper and the ringing of the bell was accompanied by the plethora of images coming from the arthropods inside the house. They were in uproar, mirroring the anxiety of the blobs living with them—

Up and down, up and down, back and forth, back and forth, round and round and round, muttering and crying, so many tears, old and worn and tired and angry, crashing, crunching of glass, more crying, the tears heavy in the air, saturating it with salt and bitterness and why were they here, causing so much distress and pain, it wasn't right, never would be, they had to find the killers, it was important, why, they were crying, it was wrong, everything was wrong—

Andi shook his head, trying to focus himself back into reality where George was waving his badge in front of the camera of the intercom. After a moment, the door opened, revealing Tabitha Clément. She was an impressive woman, almost as tall as George, her hair was cut short, and she was wearing a white A-line dress and bright red lipstick. Her gaze was sharp, her face all hard lines, her entire body language screaming defense.

—so lost, so angry, the pain was like a knife in the air, cutting through everything else, even the salt from the tears—

"Good day, Ms. Clément, and thank you for seeing us on such short notice."

Tabitha's mouth twitched angrily. "It's not like you left us much of a choice, Detective Donovan."

She stepped aside to let them in, and judging from the tension emanating from her in waves, Andi felt reminded of running the gauntlet, waiting for her to stab them with something sharp. She didn't do it, instead leading them into a cozy living room with huge sliding doors leading into the garden. Josephine Garr stood next to a dark blue sofa with fluffy-looking pillows in shades of turquoise and sea green. She was a curvy woman, a little smaller than Andi, her dark hair pulled back in a ponytail. Her face, devoid of all makeup, showed lines around her eyes and mouth that seemed to be too deep for a woman her age.

—sad, anxious, silk, so much silk and no cocoons, no caterpillars, just the silk, how was that possible, it was there, and not, he could sense it but not find it, all wrong, all wrong—

He held out his hand to her while George did the introductions. "Ms. Garr, this is Detective Hayes, my partner. Thank you for speaking with us."

"Tabitha says we have to." The tone was flat, not betraying anything, with a hardness underneath that spoke of a will of iron.

"We're really sorry to bring all those bad memories up. If we could somehow avoid it, we would." George was doing his best to sound empathic. Judging from the way Tabitha had put her arm around Josephine and was glaring at him, he wasn't too successful. The two women remained standing, creating a hostile atmosphere. Andi couldn't blame them.

"The problem is, we do have pictures of your vehicle at the crime scene, both on the day the crime happened and the day before. CSI has found traces of silk they can connect to Natural Beauty, Mrs. Garr's workplace, on the crates with the doctored beer, and then there's the rape."

"Why don't you arrest us, then?" Tabitha challenged.

George sighed, and Andi wasn't sure if this was part of the role he currently played or if he really had sympathy for the two women. Andi thought it had to be a mixture of both. As righteous as George could be, he was also a sensitive man.

—the pain sharp and clear, pheromones spiking, stress, so much stress, worse than before, mixed with something else, the silk, food in the kitchen, a rotting apple, they hadn't found it yet, behind the cabinet, so delicious, soft and juicy, decay in the house, in his mind, no not his, or was it, he needed to stay alert, alert, it all fell apart in his hands, in his head, everywhere, the silk, the tears—

"You're a lawyer. You know."

Tabitha relaxed a tiny bit. "It's all circumstantial. The silk could be from anybody who uses the products made by Natural Beauty, and it was the sons who raped us, not the fathers."

George nodded. "Exactly."

"Why did you come?" A hint of curiosity laced Tabitha's voice.

"Because we need your help." George kept his hands loosely at his sides, appearing as nonthreatening as was possible for a man of his size. Andi stayed in the background, observing, waiting. The women weren't as anxious as when they had arrived, which was good.

"Look, we know you didn't kill the victims." Not a lie; they hadn't been the ones to lead them into the lake. "We also know that all the ugliness we've unearthed so far is somehow connected to the death of the victims. And while our IT department was able to find out about the rape, we don't know any details, especially of what happened afterward. I know how hard it must be for you to talk about it, but perhaps there is something that will help us catch the killer, which would also exonerate you regarding your presence at the crime scene. We could write it off as coincidence."

The two women looked at each other for a long time, communicating without words.

Determination, sadness, pain, it all flittered across their faces, hung in the air for Andi to taste, clung to the surfaces of the furniture, filling the house.

Finally, Tabitha gestured at the sofa. "Perhaps we should sit down."

George took a seat on an armchair opposite the sofa. Andi sat down on the armrest, while Tabitha and Josephine took the sofa, staying close together, no doubt drawing strength from each other. After a long period of silence, George gently said, "Whenever you're ready."

Josephine gripped Tabitha's hand harder, visibly shivering. Tabitha took a deep breath, her eyes hard as flint. "If we cooperate, you will keep our names out of the final report, and you will make clear that our presence near the cabin had nothing to do with the crime."

George nodded. "You have my word. We will treat everything you say with the necessary discretion."

"I guess that has to be enough. Well, then." Tabitha straightened. Andi could feel the shift in her demeanor; she was now a warrior ready to go into battle.

—*blood and gore and bones, hunger and death, decay and rot, all there, all feeding the arthropods, the screams so sweet, they promised food, the Valkyrie riding, killing, slaying her enemies, adrenaline heavy in the air, Andi could taste it, could hear the battle cries, the crying of the wounded, the dying, it didn't matter, on and on it went, never stopping, always, always, the hunger, the greed—*

"I assume you wish to know what happened afterward?"

George nodded. "We don't need details of what exactly happened to you. The fact that it was hidden is proof enough how serious it was."

Josephine snorted. Her eyes were wet from unshed tears.

—*so many tears—*

"When we realized what had happened, we went to a hospital where all the necessary things were done. After that, we contacted the police. We had just given our statements when two lawyers from Portius, Dyson & Partners appeared to talk to us." Pure thunder stood in Tabitha's eyes. "They made all kinds of threats, insinuated we had been asking for it, going to a fraternity party, dressed like we were, that we didn't have the money to get a decent lawyer, that we'd never be able to see this through, blah, blah, blah."

Andi perfectly understood the pure hatred and resignation in her voice. The way courts treated rape victims was an especially ugly stain on their system of justice. To think that rape victims were no longer forced to marry their abusers was a major improvement made Andi's head hurt.

"And you believed them?" George sounded gentle, but Andi could hear the anger he was trying to hide.

"What do you think?" Tabitha laughed harshly. "We were young, both studying on a scholarship, me a woman of color and Josephine looking Mexican enough that it made no difference that she's actually Italian. Nobody would have cared for such subtleties. Not when it was against the sons of such rich fathers. We retracted our statements, applied for scholarships at Yale, and tried to leave it all behind."

"Did you ever have direct contact with any of the fathers?"

"No. Only with their lawyers. Believe me, that was enough." Tabitha shuddered.

"Do you know what the sons are doing at the moment?" George kept his tone casual, laced with empathy. If Tabitha chose to answer, this one could be interesting. She hesitated for a long moment.

—*a spike of satisfaction in the air, the enemy not slain but dying, suffering, so pathetic, the anger soothed a bit, overlayed with spitefulness, silk, the apple emitting its juices, so sickeningly sweet, so good, he felt his stomach revolting, the stench—*

"We do check in on them occasionally." A small smile flitted across Tabitha's face. "I can't say their current position in life bothers us much."

"Believe me, I can relate." George allowed himself a grin as well. "Thank you again for talking to us. This helps us a great deal. Would it be okay to contact you again if we have any questions?"

"I'd rather we never hear from you again, Detective Donovan, but yes, you can call." Tabitha very pointedly didn't say she would cooperate. Smart woman.

They said their goodbyes and were out of the house as quickly as their visit had been unwanted. Back in the car, George fumbled with the radio for a while, his way of getting his thoughts in order.

"Do you think we can cross them off?"

Andi rubbed his forehead with the palm of his right hand. "I want to. I'm sure they had something planned for the three men, something unpleasant, considering it was most likely them who put the ketamine into the beer, and they were thwarted by whoever killed them. But we do know it wasn't them at the lake, even if we don't have proof we can write in the report. What we can do is keep them in mind but concentrate on the more likely suspects. Move them down from the top spot, can't we?

"Yes. Unless we find out they hired the contract killers or were somehow helping them."

"Which is unlikely."

"But not impossible."

"No, not impossible. It would certainly explain why they came back the next day. To watch how the victims were taken away." Andi stared out the window, listening to Dolly Parton's "Jolene" while the city raced by. He had never understood why somebody would want a man who couldn't be faithful, but to each their own.

"Do we ask the sons to come to the precinct tomorrow?" Andi was eager to get those bastards into an interrogation room.

"Don't you think it would be wiser to visit them?"

"No, I want to see them sweat." Andi knew he sounded vindictive.

"It's tempting," George admitted. "And if we put them together in one room, we can rattle them some more."

"You're evil."

"You love it."

Andi just huffed, not wanting to admit how much he loved George's evil side. Or any side of George at all. No, it wasn't love, no, no, something else, kinship perhaps, though nobody could be kin with him, not with a freak like he was, he had to stop this train of thought, right now. To break the awkward moment, Andi took out his cell and called the precinct, asking them to invite Lester Miller, David Hector Portius III, and Alexander McHill to come for some questions, giving them different times of arrival so they couldn't talk before George and Andi were with them.

Then George brought him home, telling him to eat something before he went to sleep. It was sweet and annoying at the same time, making Andi smile while he watched from his window as George drove off.

16. Sins of the Past

GEORGE HUMMED while he shaved in front of the mirror. The morning run had done him good, allowing his mind to empty completely before he and Andi would confront the sons of the victims today. Sleeping in his own bed again still felt both nice and strange. Nice because he was back in his own space, where he could relax better, and strange because he missed the feeling of taking care of Andi. Or somebody. Yes, somebody, not Andi specifically. Dangerous territory and all that. He just hoped the sons would provide them with a lead to their killers, or at least point them in the right direction. They could certainly use it. After he had put on his favorite aftershave, some fancy organic stuff his mother always got him for Christmas, he left the bathroom. The bags with the clothes he had bought for Andi were waiting by the door.

The day before, after he had left Andi at home, George had stopped at the nice little boutique again, giving in to his need to get Andi a decent wardrobe. Their sale was still on, and the nice saleslady from last time had been more than happy to help him again. George had chosen four pairs of jeans—they were high quality and a breathtaking 70 percent off—and he had somehow allowed the sales lady to talk him into buying eight T-shirts in varying shades of dark blue and charcoal, which, he was sure, would make Andi look a bit more put-together, especially when combined with the new jeans. Then he had thrown bundles of five pairs of socks each into the mix but had balked at getting underwear for Andi, since he thought that might be a bit too invasive. Then a picture of what his partner thought of as perfectly serviceable undergarments had risen before his inner eye, and before he could talk himself out of it, he had added eight simple black boxer shorts made from extra-soft material to the pile on the counter. The sales lady had been very pleased with him and added another pair of high-class merino wool socks to his purchase for free. George eyed the bag he knew contained those socks. He was still torn about giving them to Andi. His partner could definitely use them, but George knew how to really *appreciate* the fine cloth. With a heartfelt sigh, George picked up the four bags, left his apartment, and went to his car. Andi would be paying for these purchases, so it was only fair if he got the extra socks.

On James Island, Andi was already up and about, opening the door to his house before George had left his car. He went to the trunk to get the bags, enjoying the peaceful morning in this fancy neighborhood. His own apartment wasn't too shabby, but the surroundings were definitely livelier than the serenity he found here.

Andi eyed the bags suspiciously. "What do you have here?" he asked instead of a morning greeting.

"Clothes." George felt nervous all of a sudden. Had he gone too far? "You said you wouldn't mind, and the sale in the shop where I got your sweaters was still on…." He trailed off, holding the bags out to Andi.

The suspicion on Andi's face morphed into puzzlement before a smile took over. "Wow. Thank you. I never thought you'd really go for it. This is so much better than having to go shopping myself!" He snatched the bags from George's hands. "Oooh, you got me jeans and T-shirts. Perfect." Andi rummaged through the two smaller bags containing the socks and underwear.

"If you think this is too personal…." George trailed off when Andi made a dismissive gesture.

"You've seen me in my underwear more than once. Hell, you have emptied my barf bucket twice already. Buying me new underwear is pretty tame in comparison. Thank you again, and what do I owe you?"

"Receipt's in one of the bags, I think with the jeans. And you're welcome." George didn't specify to what Andi was welcome. The thing with the throw-up bucket was definitely gross, the only saving grace being that Andi usually didn't eat much when he knew he would be connecting with his crawling spies in a more active way, and wasn't that a sad thought? When Andi started searching the bags, George interrupted him. "You can look for it tonight, when you try everything on. You can pay me once you've decided what you're going to keep."

"Are you kidding? If those clothes fit, I'm going to keep them all. If things go well, I won't have to go shopping for *years* with this stash."

Well, George thought, *nobody can accuse Andi of being wasteful*. His partner put the bags on the floor of his hallway, closed the door to his house, and went to George's car. He seemed to be more chipper than usual at this time of the day, and George wanted to believe it had something to do with his offering of clothes.

At the precinct they had one hour to kill before the three sons of their victims would arrive, which they used to plot the whole interview. A lot of it would hinge on the reactions of the men, though there were some things they could control. Like the interrogation room they were going to use. In room four, a healthy colony of silverfish had established their home behind the plastic molding on the ground, and several cracks in the ceiling had allowed for spiders to claim the place. As far as lie detectors went, they weren't as ideal as moths or ticks or mosquitoes because they were neither relying heavily on pheromones nor were they fixated on blood, but they still picked up a hell of a lot more nuances than two simple human detectives ever could. George was proud of himself that by now he could think along those lines without feeling the urge to contact a shrink.

The room was prepared with three chairs on one side of the bolted-down table and two on the other side. The camera was ready to roll, and the receptionist had instructions to inform them as soon as the first man arrived. When they had been called the other day, the officer had given the men different times, asking Lester Miller to come at nine sharp, Dominic McHill to come at ten past nine, and David Hector Portius III to arrive at twenty past nine. The plan was to bring Miller directly into the interrogation room, storing McHill in another room until Portius arrived and then bringing them together. For a moment they had contemplated just watching them for a while, but with Portius being a lawyer, even if he wasn't top-notch, the chances that they would clam up the moment he got his wits about him and advised them accordingly were too high. Better to have them all rattled with no chance to come to an agreement.

It all went down without a hitch, Miller stewing in the interrogation room while they waited for McHill and Portius. Asking the lawyer to come in last had also been on purpose. An angry lawyer who had time to contemplate his next move was more difficult to deal with than one who was immediately thrown into action upon his arrival. Once Portius had arrived, George escorted him downstairs, meeting Andi, who had gotten Dominic McHill at the door to the room. He could see both David Hector Portius III and Dominic McHill tensing the moment they saw the other, a tension that rose a few notches when they were ushered into the room by Andi and George, seeing that Lester Miller was already there.

"Please, gentlemen, take a seat. Do you need something to drink?" George was acting all polite, as if the men had nothing to fear. Which was technically true since they probably wouldn't be able to nail them down for the rape they had committed some twenty years ago. While the statute of limitation for rape was twenty years, with the count starting when the victim turned thirty, they would still be well within the time frame, but sadly, once a crime like that had been dormant for so long, it didn't have high chances of making it into court. Even with a full confession it would be difficult, and more so when the victims of the crime had taken their statements back. Not to mention that Tabitha Clemént and Josephine Garr probably didn't want to dredge up such a traumatic event in their lives. They had made it more than clear that they wanted to be excluded from the investigation as soon as possible. It didn't mean he wouldn't try to get the men to confess, though.

George's soothing tone didn't seem to work, because the three men were telegraphing worry and fear that was slowly morphing into anger, a typical reaction for people who knew they had done something very wrong.

"I'm sure you know each other, since your fathers were such close friends and you went to Harvard together." George kept playing the jovial detective while Andi was watching the men like a hawk, at the same time dipping into the consciousness of the insects in the room. George made sure to seat himself at a slight angle next to his partner to be able to pick up on his clues and reactions. They had done this many times by now, and George still marveled how much easier interrogations went when you had somebody with you who could so easily stir the pot, or suspects. He did feel a little worried after Andi's meltdown during their argument, but his partner had assured him he had everything under control, which George hadn't wanted to argue, though he had his doubts. He decided to be extra vigilant and keep an eye on Andi in case things got out of control.

"We do know each other, though I have no idea why you would want to talk to us all at once." Ah, so Portius was taking the lead, something he wasn't necessarily used to, as the slight tremor in his voice showed. He was already sweating, small beads slowly running down his neck into the hem of his pristine white shirt. McHill seemed to be shell-shocked, while Miller had narrowed his eyes and folded his arms in front of his chest. George wanted to bet his next monthly check on him being the leader of this small group—or at least he used to be. He didn't seem happy to leave the talking to Portius but wasn't stupid enough to not let the lawyer be in charge. Interesting already. George glanced at Andi, who gave a slight nod.

"Well, as we've told you, gentlemen, we're investigating in all directions concerning the deaths of your fathers. As you can imagine and have already hinted at when we talked to each of you, we found out some alarming things about the ways your fathers conducted their businesses and private lives."

All three men nodded automatically, confirming George's assumption that they knew quite a lot about the things their fathers had been up to.

"That's no surprise. What I'd like to know is what it has to do with us. It's highly unusual to put witnesses into an interrogation room." Portius was suspicious, and rightfully so. George smiled at him before dropping the bomb that would hopefully get them some new insights and perhaps even a hot lead in the case.

"Tabitha Clemént and Josephine Garr."

It was a small satisfaction to see the expressions of the three men freeze for a moment before their eyes widened in horror. Served them right.

"As it turned out, your fathers weren't the only ones with dirty secrets." George leaned slightly forward, which caused the three men to instinctively lean backward before they seemed to realize what they were doing. Miller instantly moved his upper body forward again, the motion subtle enough to not be seen as a threat but still clear. This man was used to manipulating people, it seemed, and skilled in the art of body language.

Portius just froze where he was, trying for a stern look and ending up giving the impression of a deer caught in the headlights instead. A leader he was not. McHill just kept sagging against the backrest of his chair, as if his spine had decided it was time to give up its service.

George let a sharpness bleed into his voice he usually reserved for hardened criminals. It worked like a charm on these fuckers, who had thought it was okay to roofie two women and rape them. "Tell us what happened after the rape. We know your fathers tried to sweep it under the rug, and we want to know how they went about doing that."

McHill was staring at the table, probably hoping it could somehow save him from George's ire or imagining what it would feel like to be chained to it once he was officially arrested. George found it hard to say, because the man's face was turning more into a mask by the second. Miller was looking at Portius, who tried to sit up straight and project confidence. He wasn't overly successful.

"There was no rape." He didn't elaborate, didn't protest with fancy words. He was saying it like a man who hoped the words he spoke would become true simply because he wished for it. The other two just sat there, shaking their heads as if to give the words more weight.

"Oh, then why did your fathers see the need to interfere? Or more precisely, why did they think they had to send in the lawyers?"

"They didn't want a scandal, and the situation back then was quickly becoming volatile." Portius sounded a bit more secure. George saw Andi shifting in his seat, silently telling him to poke a bit more.

"How was the situation becoming volatile?" George loved throwing their own words back at suspects. It was a reliable method to get them riled up. It worked on Portius as well. Having to explain himself clearly rattled him. McHill and Miller remained suspiciously quiet. They both had beads of sweat forming on their foreheads. McHill's silence didn't surprise George, he seemed like the type who always followed, and with his alcoholism, he probably didn't have too many functioning brain cells to rub together. For him, silence was the safest option. Miller clearly had to restrain himself from saying anything. George had to give him some points for self-control. Portius cleared his throat.

"It was the early nineties, everybody was big on women's rights, our fraternity already had eyes on it for some minor transgressions, and our fathers decided to nip it in the bud. End of story."

George smiled. When people tried to shut him up like that, his hunting instincts roared to life. Andi slightly leaned his upper body forward, like a bloodhound straining against its leash. A clear sign for George to go for the throat.

"You mean your fathers decided to make the accusation of rape go away. Must have been difficult, with the situation already being *volatile*."

"I told you, there was no rape! They took their statements back!" Portius snapped, revealing why he wasn't reeling in the big bucks as a lawyer, slipping up not ten minutes into the interrogation. George allowed a small, unpleasant smile to form on his lips.

"And we all know once a statement is taken back, it's as if the accusation never existed, don't we?" He put his hands on the table between him and Andi and the three men who were now visibly squirming. "Tell me, what did your fathers do to intimidate the two women?" George already knew from Tabitha and Josephine, but he wanted to hear what the sons had to say.

Miller kept staring at Portius, while McHill kept his gaze firmly fixed on the table in front of him, very pointedly not looking at George and Andi. Portius stuck out his chin defiantly, not saying a word. George sighed dramatically.

"You know we're going to find out anyway. This is related to the murder of your fathers, and we do have the means to get our hands on whatever file Portius, Dyson & Partners has about the victims. Granted, it will take us some time, but we're going to read it. If you talk to us now, we won't have to charge you with obstruction of justice. Not that we'd feel bad about doing it. It's just such a waste of time, don't you think?" Actually, George wasn't entirely sure if they would be able to construe this as obstruction of justice, but it was worth a shot. Portius didn't give the impression of being well-versed enough in the law to contradict George's statement. He let his words sink in for a moment before he pressed on. "Now tell us what's in the file and what exactly happened. We know all three of you had your fallout with your fathers shortly after."

Miller narrowed his eyes. "I want a lawyer. Now."

McHill just kept staring down, as if his worst nightmare was playing out right in front of his eyes, his lips moving as if he were mumbling to himself. Portius huffed. "I *am* a lawyer, in case you've forgotten, and I hate to say it, but Detective Donovan is right. They will get their hands on the file one way or another." His shoulders slumped. "And you know as well as I do that what's in there won't make us look good."

"Fucking damn." The words came out like a hiss. Miller put a hand over his face. "Tell them."

Portius turned back to George and Andi, furrowing his brows in a clear attempt at concentration. "After the incident that could have been misconstrued as rape, which it definitely wasn't, Miss Clemént and Miss Garr wanted to press charges against us. As soon as we heard, we informed our fathers, and they took matters in hand. They sent two lawyers from my father's firm to explain to Miss Clemént and Miss Garr how unwise it would be to take the matter to court. And because our fathers never did anything for free, not even for their own family, they froze our trust funds to punish us." Portius made a face, as if he still couldn't understand why his father had done such a terrible and unreasonable thing. For a brief moment, George felt something akin to respect for the three old men, but it winked out when Portius kept on talking.

"Miss Clemént and Miss Garr took their statements back and left Harvard shortly afterward. We thought our fathers would relinquish control of the trusts after a few months, once we had suffered enough in their eyes." Portius pouted. "Instead, they saw to it that the trusts were dissolved, which took about six years, and the money channeled into their own pockets. They left us with nothing, saying we had to earn it back for having been so stupid, as if they had never made any mistakes." Again he made a disgruntled face about the perfidy of it all. George had to fight the urge to throttle the man. He saw an opening in his last statement, one that could potentially lead to somewhere interesting.

"Your fathers made mistakes?"

"Quite a lot, and they always tried to hide them, but somebody with an inquisitive mind could find out a thing or two." Portius now sounded almost hopeful, clearly picking up on George's interest. He probably thought he could divert the focus back on the misdeeds of his father and his friends. Miller shot him a sharp look, while McHill was rubbing the tips of his forefingers together.

"And may I ask what you did find out?"

Portius hesitated. "What do we get if we tell you?"

As attempts at negotiating went, this one was pathetic. George gave it the consideration it deserved. None.

"You can go to sleep at night with the knowledge that you helped in the investigation of the murder of your fathers."

Miller huffed, and Portius made a face. There was no reaction from McHill, who seemed to have slipped into a world of his own. George waited. After roughly two minutes, Portius relented. He really was a terrible lawyer.

"Our fathers weren't squeamish when it came to conducting their businesses. They have left many angry people in their wake, which you surely already know. They also had their own transgression during their time at college, one that cost their fathers, our grandads, a lot more than what they had to pay for our mistake."

George felt bile rising in his mouth when Portius referred to the rape as a "mistake." A little sharper than he had intended, he asked, "You're referring to Gideon Gartner?"

"You know about him?" All the wind left Portius's sails. He must have thought this piece of information to be some kind of ace up his sleeve.

"Yes, we do. What I'd like to know is how you know about him. Your grandfathers did a very good job sweeping it all under the rug."

"Yes, our grandfathers." An ugly smile appeared on Portius's face. "It's interesting, the things a man with dementia can remember."

He didn't have to say more. George could imagine very well what had happened. It seemed David Hector Portius III did have a nasty streak in him.

"Did you know about this as well?" He turned to the other two men, who had been very silent. McHill just nodded, still rubbing his fingertips, his eyes focused on the repetitive motion. Miller shrugged.

"You already know our family life was difficult. Any ammunition we could get, we took."

As sad as this statement was, it explained a lot. George wondered if he should try to pry some more names from the three men, though he was sure they wouldn't know more than Shireen had found. He glanced at his partner. Andi shifted in his place, slightly changing the angle of his body. He wanted George to change directions. "Who paid for the last semesters of your tuition? After your fathers cut you off?"

A sharp intake of breath from Miller and some nervous shuffling from McHill. Portius seemed resigned. "You found that out as well?"

"What can I say, our IT department is on top of things."

"We honestly don't know. The money came through university channels, though the dean made it clear it was specifically for us. We didn't question our luck, though."

"Could it have come from your mothers?"

At that, Miller snorted. "Surely not. Theodora would have never wasted money on me, and Sophia and Tamara… just no."

"Did they know what you did and were appalled?" George insisted.

Miller opened his mouth, but Portius beat him to it. "I have to say it again, we did nothing, and no, our mothers didn't know. Our fathers thought it best to keep them in the dark about most things, and they preferred it that way." He started fiddling with his tie. "We always suspected the money was coming from old acquaintances of our grandfathers. Even though my own grandfather had dementia at the time, he still had his lucid moments, and Lester and Dominic's grandfathers were still fit for their age."

"And they did this for their grandsons out of the goodness of their hearts?" George couldn't believe it.

Portius laughed, the sound hollow and resigned. "What are you thinking, Detective? Of course not. If it really was them, and we don't have any proof of that, they did it because otherwise we would have had to drop out, which would have stained the family names."

It actually made sense. Protecting the family was important to the three grandfathers, as the incident with Gideon Gartner proved. George could see how they wouldn't want their grandsons dropping out of university without a degree. He glanced at Andi, who shrugged. It fit what they had found out about the three families until now. Sometimes it still surprised him how dysfunctional some marriages and entire families were, even though he saw proof of humanity's imperfections on a daily basis.

"Let me sum this up. After you raped Tabitha Clemént and Josephine Garr, your fathers saw to it that the two women retracted their statements with the police. They cut you three off, froze your trusts, and dissolved them in the end. Even though your fathers bailed you out, your relationship to them died completely after that because you felt they were treating you unfairly while they thought you had to pay in some way for your stupidity, and your mothers didn't know what had been going on. Some mysterious benefactor, probably in the shape of your grandfathers, paid for the rest of your time at Harvard, but you don't really know who it was, though you're sure it wasn't your mothers. Am I correct?"

"In everything but the rape," Portius confirmed. George was a little disappointed. He had hoped to get them with this. It seemed Portius was perhaps a better lawyer than he had originally thought—or more likely, he simply was hypersensitive when it came to this special topic. Andi was leaning back in his seat, sharing George's opinion that they probably wouldn't be getting anything else from the three men. Dominic McHill seemed to have lost his speech completely, and Lester Miller was again making a visible effort to keep his mouth shut.

"Well, thank you for your time, gentlemen. We're asking you to stay in Charleston for the time being in case we have more questions. Let me show you outside."

He got up, waited for the three men to follow his example before he led them out of the precinct. George stayed just inside the main door to see if they were talking to each other. McHill just left as quickly as he could while Miller and Portius did talk for a while. Judging from the wild gesturing and agitated body language, it wasn't something positive. After ten minutes, the two men parted. George went back to their desks, where Andi was already waiting. A quick glance around showed they were almost alone in the bullpen, and the few other detectives present were at the other end of the room, focused on their computers. George sat down on his chair, grabbing one of his trusted markers.

"What do you think?"

Andi pinched the bridge of his nose. "That we didn't get as much as we hoped."

"You don't like it." It wasn't a question. George didn't like it either. He had really hoped for some solid lead. Something. Anything.

"No, I don't." Andi closed his eyes. "I mean, these men are assholes. They have roofied and raped two women, and their biggest concern about the whole thing was that they lost their trust funds. And Tabitha Clemént and Josephine Garr, they had something terrible done to them, and then they were forced to give up justice. I don't know about you, but a part of me thinks the way these three men died was too nice."

"Which brings us right to the questions." George got up to stand in front of his whiteboard, glad he could steer the topic away from justice and fairness. As he had seen before, he and Andi had differing opinions on the matter. He didn't want a repeat of this discussion now, not only because it wouldn't help their case but also because he could understand Andi's point of view a bit too well for comfort, especially after talking to both Tabitha and Josephine and the three men who raped them. George found it hard to defend his own views when he could comprehend those of his partner so easily. Needless to say, he'd always been last to be chosen for the groups in debating society.

"In light of what we found out, I get why Tabitha and Josephine would go after the fathers, not the sons." He looked at the names of the two women on the whiteboard, that was already a chaos of lines and colors. He had hoped he would be able to erase their names or at least get some other names to replace them or a semblance of order into the chaos. No such luck. "They clearly had plans when they went to the cabin. What I don't get is why they waited so long."

Andi was rummaging through his drawer, reminding George of the pens he needed to buy. Apparently there were none left because Andi came up with a paper clip. He started bending it even before he had settled back in his chair. "Perhaps the same reason we suspected with Gartner. They didn't think we would make the connection. Which if it had worked, would have been beautiful. The victims' own maliciousness would have protected them. We know they didn't kill them. What I'd love to know is what they had planned. And we have already established that it could still be they were involved somehow."

George wrote "time" on the whiteboard, underlining it. He had to admit Andi was right. It would have been a warped kind of justice if the cruelty the victims had shown the women would have made it impossible to find their killers.

Andi was forming a spiral out of the paper clip.

George tapped his pen against the whiteboard. "What about the three sons?"

"Dominic McHill has added heroin to his alcohol abuse since we've last met him. His days are definitely numbered. Lester Miller and David Hector Portius III were both highly agitated. Their pheromones and blood pressure were all over the place. They did rape these women, and they know it."

"Then why didn't Tabitha and Josephine go after the sons? Or just the sons? No, it's like Tabitha said, the sons are not in a good place. It would make sense to kill the fathers because they screwed them over." George was staring at the whiteboard, still fixated on the extensive timeline. "Now who beat them to it?"

"That's the bonus question. We know it was two females, most probably professionals unless we find another pair of women gravely wronged by Portius, McHill, and Miller, and they must have had eyes on the victims as well. No hitman worth their money would forgo watching the mark." Andi threw the spiral, formerly known as a paper clip, into the trash and got up. "How about we get lunch, and then we can pay Shireen a visit, see if she's found something new."

George was very much on board with this idea. Anything to get away from the depressing whiteboards with their abundance of leads and suspects. "I could eat. Let's walk over to that little bistro with the delicious pizza. We can take some panna cotta for Shireen when we return."

"Smart man, bribing her with sweets."

"I've learned from the best." George patted Andi's shoulder when he passed him.

17. FINDING SUSPECTS

AS IT turned out, bribing Shireen wasn't necessary. The hacker was practically vibrating out of her skin when they found her in her usual place in the middle of the IT department. "There you are! I was thinking about texting you. Oh, is that for me?"

She tucked her tablet under her left arm to grab the box with the panna cotta George was holding out like a sacrifice for an angry god.

"It's all yours."

"Thank you." Shireen managed to open the lid without losing her tablet. "Oooh, panna cotta. And you brought a spoon!" She almost squealed when George handed her the wooden spoon.

"You said you wanted to see us?" Andi reminded her gently. Shireen could get a bit sidetracked when offered sweets.

"Oh yes, I did. Hold that for me, would you? But don't touch it!" She gave George a warning glance. He took the box and the spoon back, keeping them at a respectable distance from his body to show he didn't even think of touching the sugar. Seemingly satisfied, Shireen grabbed her tablet from under her arm and started the familiar swiping and typing. The flat-screen came to life, showing a website Andi easily recognized as one from the darknet.

"I'm pretty sure I found your killer."

"You did what?" George put the panna cotta down on a nearby table. Andi couldn't have said it better.

"Well, you did suspect it could be a contracted kill, and I'm sorry it took me so long to find it, but the darknet is a big and scary place."

Says the woman who has hacked it all at least once, Andi thought. Aloud he said, "Tell us what you found."

"Sooo, there's this one website in the darknet that's so shady even most of the people who use the darknet stay away from it. Some of the most terrible deals ever have been made in its darkest corners, and I mean terrible for those who were affected by them. The security there is usually pretty tight, and to be honest, it's sheer luck the contract for your victims was booked by a new broker who's still inexperienced enough to leave doors open for inquisitive minds to walk through." Shireen shook her head. "Enough with the bad comparisons. Our broker was stupid and left the contract negotiations in the chat. It's a very private chat, but practically everything can be hacked, and here you are."

She did some more typing, and Andi and George saw a long column of back-and-forth between two parties. Thankfully, Shireen had highlighted the interesting bits. "As you can see, the broker established contact between a man named Peter LaFarge, fifty-three, from France but living most of the time in the US, here in Charleston, and one Phantom, aka Daniel Holway, thirty-six, former Army Ranger gone contract killer, who has several bases all over the world, four weeks ago. LaFarge has lost quite the sum because of some business dealings with Lawrence Miller and Harry Alexander McHill. It went to court, and guess who got the two out of it without having to pay a penny to LaFarge?"

"David Hector Portius II." George and Andi spoke in unison.

"Exactly. LaFarge was livid, which I can understand because the fault was clearly with Miller and McHill, but Portius was a very dangerous shark who could make an old granny look like Freddy Krueger to get what he wanted."

"A perfect motive." George looked at Andi.

"Two weeks before the victims were killed, they agreed on a two-million-dollar fee for the murder of all three men as long as it was 'cruel and painful.'" Shireen scrolled down to a passage that was highlighted in neon pink. "And the day after the killings took place, Holway contacted LaFarge in a private chat telling him the deed was done. Two hours later, LaFarge wired two million dollars to an account in Switzerland."

Andi stared at the words and numbers on the screen, recalling what exactly he had seen at the lake. No matter how much he racked his brain, the insects had definitely shown him two females as the killers, not one male. Because of the input of the moths, he could be sure the information was correct because the pheromones didn't lie and couldn't be interpreted wrongly. Yet here he had written proof that there had been a hit out on the three men currently stashed in Evangeline's morgue, a hit that had apparently been executed and paid for. Something was not adding up at all.

"You said Peter LaFarge lives here in Charleston?" He tried to get his thoughts in order, one thing at a time.

Shireen nodded. "Berkeley County, as you can probably imagine." She tapped some more on her tablet. "Though at the moment he's on a holiday cruise in the Bermuda Triangle. He left ten hours before the money was transferred."

"Shit." George slammed his fist on the table with the panna cotta box, narrowly missing it. "Smart bastard, removing himself from the crime like that."

"He'll have to come back to land eventually." Andi shrugged. It was a pity the man wasn't here for questioning, but not exactly the end of the world. It would draw out the investigation, no doubt, making everything more tedious. "What about the contract killer? Daniel Holway? Is he lying low?"

Shireen changed windows on the flat-screen. "Unlike the rookie broker, Holway is an absolute pro." She must have seen how Andi's shoulders slumped, because she went on, "As am I. It took some hacking and a substantial bribe to people I officially have no affiliation with, and I can't guarantee the information is correct, but I'm fairly sure he's still in the area and has one of his safe houses here. More a safe apartment. It's in West Ashley, on Suntree Alley. I'm sending you the address now."

"Substantial bribe?" Of course George was latching on to the potentially shady part of the miracle Shireen had worked.

"I don't think this is something we should be burdening ourselves with," Andi said, shooting George a meaningful glance. His partner got it, even though he looked as if he had bitten into an entire basket of lemons. To distract George from his internal conflict, Andi turned back to Shireen.

"Do you have any idea why he's still in the area?"

Shireen changed screens yet again, showing another chat. "Because our careless broker has found him another target here and asked him to stay."

Andi took the panna cotta box from the table and held it out to Shireen, very much in the same humble way as George had done. "You are a genius and definitely the best. Could you still keep looking into Tabitha Clemént and Josephine Garr, as well as the wives? I want to be absolutely sure they had nothing to do with the murder." It wasn't what Andi really had in mind, but it was what would motivate Shireen to be extra vigilant concerning them, and it would help if they could finally cross them all off the list.

He and George said their goodbyes to Shireen. After they had checked their weapons and badges, they went out to George's car. While George tapped the address of Daniel Holway's safe house into the GPS, Andi realized that he genuinely hoped the arthropods had been wrong for once. Perhaps there was a perfectly sensible explanation why they had thought it was two women guiding the victims to their deaths and not one man. And perhaps pigs would grow wings and start flying through the air. If there was one thing he had learned in all his years with the *geschenk*, it was that the arthropods were never wrong. They didn't have enough of a self-consciousness to lie, and their senses were so much more accurate than those of humans. If there was a misunderstanding, it always occurred on Andi's end, due to a misinterpretation or simply ignorance. Distinguishing males and females was one of the first things Andi had learned, and after all these years, he knew what men and women looked like to most arthropods, most certainly to those at the lake. No, the solution to this mystery had to be found in the human world, because for the arthropods, things were clear.

They were silent for some time, listening to the classical music coming from the radio. The input Andi was getting from the insects was a low hum he found quite easy to ignore. Probably because he was so preoccupied with this new development.

"Is it possible that you interpreted something wrong?" The faint hope paired with the resignation of knowing how unlikely it was in George's voice mirrored Andi's own sentiment.

"I've been trying to remember every detail about that night, and no matter from which angle—or insect—I'm looking at it, it was two women. One of them was ovulating. That's not something that can be faked or misinterpreted."

"Damn. So what are we looking at?"

"Honestly, I have no clue. My best bet is a freak coincidence. Holway had planned to kill the victims around the time frame they died and simply said it had been his work."

"Aren't contract killers working under a codex or something?"

Andi shrugged. "Two million is two million. And you heard Shireen—the site where they met is bad by reputation."

"No honor amongst criminals?"

"I doubt it."

They fell silent until they reached Suntree Alley. After one drive-by where they scouted out the apartment, George parked at the corner to Moss Beach Alley, which was only two houses down the apartment block where Holway supposedly was. They got out and went directly for the apartment, Andi already stretching his senses. It took him a moment to find the right apartment; coordinating a human-made blueprint with insectoid ideas of space was always a bit of a hit or miss. What gave Holway away was the way the insects saw him as an intruder. Apparently he didn't come often to this safe house, leaving it empty most of the time. Therefore the insects didn't see him as a resident, while all the other people currently in the building were well known by their tiny roommates.

"He's in. Living room, down the hall, kitchen to the left, bathroom for guests to the right." Andi swayed a little when George prevented him from running against a lamppost by yanking him sideways. Being in two places at the same time, with different senses and in various bodies was a nightmare. "He's got lots of weapons, handguns, a rifle, I think a sniper rifle, but that's dismantled, knives, takeout food, he's dressed, wears combat boots, who does that inside the house, bed's not made, more weapons, oil, gunpowder...." He trailed off, tried to get back to where George was leading him with one hand on his lower arm.

"Second exits?"

"A fire escape, window is closed, can be easily broken."

"Okay. Do you think you can manage going through the building to his apartment's main door? The idea of you on a fire escape while your attention is so distracted doesn't appeal to me one bit."

Andi hated to admit it, but George was right. The mere idea of getting on a fire escape ladder and climbing to the second floor where Holway's apartment was while his senses were trying to decide which ground he should be using to put his feet on spelled disaster. "I can manage. Usual sign?"

George nodded. "Two rings."

They parted ways in front of the building, George walking to the back while Andi took the front entrance. He did his best to concentrate on the stairs, clinging to the handrail, which provided some kind of anchor while he still kept most of his attention on the apartment where Holway was cleaning his weapons while listening to the same radio station he and George had on the Escalade's radio. The closer he got, the more information was barraging into him, some of it helpful, some completely useless—

Healthy blood, rich, sweat, oil, appalling, a wound, open, not deep, just a cut, not enough to lay eggs in, the blob was too vital, dirt in the bathroom, mold under the trim in the living room, a leak in the kitchen, not big, too small to be recognized yet, spores of mildew settling under the sink, the pipes in the house were rusty, old, good places to hide, to hatch, stomping, a dead rat in the wall, the corpse dried out, no food, just fur and bones, too dry, water dripping down, forming new paths—

Andi reached the second floor, followed the stream of images coming from his small informants. Holway was focused on cleaning his weapons, which unfortunately meant he was surrounded by means to fight them off. They had to be extremely careful—his phone vibrated twice in his back pocket, the signal that George was in position. Andi took it out, pressed the speed dial and let it ring three times before shutting it off, then calling again, letting it ring two times. *Careful, armed.* He was so glad they had this system to communicate silently. His cell vibrated once. George had gotten the message. Andi got out his weapon and took the safety off before he stepped to the front door of Holway's apartment and knocked.

"Mr. Holway? Charleston PD. Please open the door."

The blob jumped up, adrenaline spiking, heartbeat getting faster, not hastily, alert, two weapons, click, click, silently walking toward the door, too silent to be heard but Andi knew anyway, he was already inside the apartment, he knew where Holway was at all times, the blob raised his hand, gun aimed at the door, two shots, a silencer on the weapon, truly a pro, not drawing attention, Andi could feel the bullets whizzing past, he stepped forward—

"How impolite of you, Mr. Holway. I assure you, all I want to do is talk to you about a contract you fulfilled about a week ago."

The blob shot again, aiming for his voice, and that was enough, another blob was inside the apartment, coming up behind the blob at the door, holding out his weapon,

"Hands up, Mr. Holway, Charleston PD!"

The first blob turning around too fast, his foot coming up, a bang, thumping, two bodies colliding,

Andi shot the lock of the door, kicking it in just in time to see George and Holway, who was easily as tall as George and with at least ten pounds more muscle mass, rolling on the ground, each of them trying to get the upper hand, with Andi unable to get a shot in. Finally Holway got on top, his right fist coming down on George's head. Andi fired his weapon, getting Holway in the shoulder, the ringing of the shot terribly loud in the narrow hallway of the apartment, Holway getting up, firing as well while he made a beeline for the living room and the fire escape. Andi dove to the side to avoid being shot, slammed against the wall, and lost his balance for a moment. George was getting back on his feet when more shots had him ducking again,

The blob in the living room going for the broken window, leaving the same way the other blob had come in, drops of blood everywhere, such a delicious trail, hunger, hunger—

"He's on the fire escape!" George was up now, following Holway while Andi decided to take the stairs and try to block Holway's path.

The blood going down so fast, more drops, food, perhaps larger prey, so much metal, the blood jumping down, running not for the street but in the other direction, the second blob following, hitting the ground hard, the blood reaching a metal cage, going inside, the roof is open, the scents still wafting around, a roar, gravel spitting,

"He had a fucking car back there!" George was coming onto the street, looking furious. His lip was split and his cheek swelling.

Andi started running toward the Escalade. "Come on. He's in a convertible, and he's bleeding and reeking of gunpowder. I can easily follow him."

George broke into a sprint, already getting the keys out. They were inside the car and hightailing it down Suntree Alley. Andi had the presence of mind to put their blue flashlight onto the car's roof while George was pressing the accelerator down to the floor of the car.

The blood was going fast, so delicious but hard to catch, south—

"Turn left at the next possibility."

The car veered to the right when George took the turn into Sutter Alley with more speed than was wise. Andi clung to the armrest in the door, concentrating on the blood and gunpowder that had all the arthropods it passed in uproar. George was on the police radio reporting their status and the need for help.

"This is Detective Donovan. I'm following a suspect in West Ashley. A black convertible, driver armed and wounded. We're currently on Sutter Alley going south."

Andi heard the garbled "Help is on the way" through the police radio over a chorus of—

Blood, hunger, stinks, more blood, prey, blood, blood, hunger—

The mental images guided him. "Turn right, then the next left."

George did as Andi told him, weaving through the thankfully light traffic on William E. Murray Boulevard, racing even faster when they caught sight of the black convertible not half a mile before them. The car was veering left and right, the driver—

The blob was getting weaker, so much blood, dead prey, ideal to lay the eggs, fresh blood to feed from, they just had to wait for the blob to succumb—

—was apparently hurt worse than Andi had assumed. George was getting closer, a siren to their right cutting through the multilayered picture Andi had of their chase, adding another dimension of utter noise to it. The police car came from Babbitt Street, cutting Holway off. Andi was now close enough to see the frantic cranking their suspect was doing with the steering wheel. The car, a shiny Alfa Romeo, the cream interior smeared with blood, did a jerking motion to the left; Holway tried to counter the movement, which had the Alfa Romeo jumping back into its lane like an anxious rabbit before it smashed into the police car blocking its way. The scrunch of metal on metal was deafening and accentuated by the blaring of another siren coming their direction. George brought the Escalade to a screeching halt only a few feet from where the Alfa Romeo was tangled with the police car.

"Suspect is stopped. We need an ambulance here ASAP. Two officers and the suspect were in a car crash, suspect also has a gunshot wound to the shoulder." George radioed their status in before he and Andi got out of the car, their weapons drawn. The other police car arrived on scene, the two officers inside immediately starting to clear the area.

Bang, scrunch, blood, meat, metal, oil, stinking, bad, stay away, food, hunger, enticing, pain, fear, adrenaline, sweat, hunger, gas, don't get close, need to feed—

They reached the Alfa Romeo. Fortunately, Daniel Holway had had the presence of mind to step on the brakes before the crash. The convertible had hit the back door of the police car, leaving the two officers inside shaken up and with a few cuts and bruises but mostly intact. Daniel Holway was slumped over his steering wheel, the airbag a deflated white mass with red sprinkles beneath his body. He had a heavily bleeding wound on his forehead and didn't move. Still, Andi and George approached with caution, having seen what Holway was capable of. In the distance, the siren of the ambulance cut through the air. George reached Holway first and nudged him with his left hand. The killer's body slowly glided toward the middle of the car, Holway doing nothing to stop his own fall. George put his weapon back into its holster when Andi was close enough to keep Holway contained with his gun. Then George started patting the unconscious killer for weapons, finding three knives and one more gun before the ambulance finally arrived. Holway was taken from the car and put on a gurney. George talked to the first responder who was in charge. "How soon do you think he can talk?"

The woman looked at him with her brows almost at her hairline. "I'm aware he's a person of interest for you, Detective, but honestly, I don't think you'll be able to talk to him before tomorrow. That head wound definitely needs stitches, the chances of him having a severe concussion are at almost a hundred percent, and the wound from the gunshot needs surgery. It seems to be a through-and-through, so there's that. I assume you're going to send an officer with him?"

George nodded. "Not just one." He looked at the space where two more police cars had arrived. Andi was already on his way, asking two of the officers to ride with Holway in the ambulance and to not let him out of their sight once he was out of surgery again. They promised to call Andi as soon as the man woke up and to instruct their relief accordingly. Satisfied, Andi watched the ambulance drive away. Another first responder was looking at George's face, treating his swollen cheek and the cut on his lip. Once everything at the site was properly organized with the firefighters starting to tow the cars from the road, Andi and George went back to the Escalade.

"Want me to drive?" Andi offered out of politeness, not because he was keen on getting behind the steering wheel. George just snorted.

"I'd say I'm the better driver, even with the headache from hell."

"Can't argue with that." Andi shrugged, glad he didn't have to suffer through a drive while his senses were still too wide-open to securely determine where the boundaries between his own perception and that of the insects were. "Let's get to my place. You can lie down while I write the report for this." Andi made a gesture meant to indicate everything that had happened since they had set foot in the apartment building.

George didn't argue. He drove them to Andi's house as quickly as possible, the headache obviously getting worse, judging from the way he winced whenever the sun hit the windows of the car in a certain way. Andi could absolutely relate. The moment George had parked the Escalade, Andi was out of his seat and around the car. He opened the door for George, hovering around him in case his partner got dizzy, which was not uncommon with migraines. They somehow made it through the front door, taking off their shoes with careless motions. Andi helped George to the couch in the living room, where the man slumped into the cushions with a soft grunt. The swelling on his cheek was more prominent, the skin already darkening. Andi hurried to get George a bottle of water, two ibuprofen, and an ice pack from the fridge. He always had them there for his own migraines, and it would help with the swelling as well.

"Lay down and rest," he ordered after George had swallowed the pills.

With his partner finally resting, Andi started his laptop to write his report of the events of the day, ignoring his own headache from his active dip into the world of arthropods. It was low anyway, on a level Andi had long ago learned to manage without drugs of any kind. After the report was written and sent, Andi checked on George, who was peacefully snoring on the couch. He then went to the kitchen, trying to figure out a meal he could prepare with what he had in the fridge and pantry before deciding that ordering takeout was the smarter choice. The pizza was delivered around six, waking George with the delicious scent of greasy cheese and salami. They ate in companionable silence, both of them too exhausted to expend much energy into societal niceties they didn't really need anyway. George tried to stay awake for some time after their meal, surfing through the TV channels in the hope of finding something interesting. At around nine o'clock, Andi brought him another round of ibuprofen, helped him to the guest room, and tucked him in after he had stripped down to his boxers and T-shirt. Andi found it comforting to know he was doing something for George for once. He left the door to the guest room ajar, as well as his own bedroom door, in case George needed something from him. With his attention mostly on George's bedroom, Andi pushed the images the arthropods were sending him of the night outside to the back of his mind and fell asleep almost instantly.

18. Mystery Solved

George woke up feeling hungover, which was a shame because he didn't remember drinking anything worth the sluggish condition of his limbs, the wooziness in his head, and the desert in his mouth. The promising scent of coffee lured him into the kitchen after he had made a short visit to the bathroom. Andi was standing at the counter, pouring himself some tea from the kettle George knew very well by now. He came closer. "Good morning."

Without turning around, Andi offered him a mug full of coffee, as black and strong as he needed it on this morning. His cheek hurt like hell, as did the cut on his lip.

"Good morning. How are you feeling?"

George inhaled the roasted aroma of the coffee, which instantly cleared at least his sinuses, before taking a sip. He usually preferred his coffee to pack less of a punch and be more on the smooth side, but for a tea drinker, Andi made an acceptable brew.

"Like I've gone five rounds with a former Army Ranger."

"You did well. And it wasn't five rounds. More like a very intense one."

"At least you shot him."

"I had to defend you."

George snorted, which hurt his lip and cheek. Wincing, he took another sip of the coffee. "Thank you for letting me stay here."

"Are you kidding me? You've taken care of me so often, it's the least I can do. Not to mention you bought me clothes." Andi said it as if that was the best of it all.

"It was my pleasure to go shopping for you, and you were always hurt in the line of duty. Of course I'm looking after you."

"Same goes for you. Are you hungry? I think I have everything for toast with marmalade."

"I could eat. Fighting against a professional killer is exhausting."

"Then sit down." Andi rummaged in some cupboards, pulled out the toaster and a bag of bread from the pantry.

"The strawberry jam is in the first shelf on the right side, next to the raspberry jam and the butter."

Andi raised his head from where he was staring into the fridge. "You reorganized my fridge?" It didn't sound accusing, nor the slightest bit angry.

"Sorry. It was such a chaotic mess." George shrugged, not thinking too hard about why Andi only now realized the contents of the fridge were in new places. He had done that the case before this one. His partner tended to ignore small things, and that was a better explanation than that he simply didn't open the damn fridge door often enough to realize when something was different.

"It's fine." Andi cocked his head. "I can see how it makes more sense to have the jam with the butter." He took all three items out of the fridge while the toaster sent the first wafts of warming bread into the air.

They finished breakfast with minimal crumbs on the table. After a quick shower and another round of ibuprofen, George felt ready to not only tackle driving but also whatever the day would throw at them, hopefully a talkative contract killer.

AT THE precinct they did get talkative, though not from the contract killer but from Chief Norris. She ordered them into her office with a viciously barked, "Donovan, Hayes, here."

"What have we done now?" Andi had his hackles up already.

"We won't have to wait to find out." George closed the door to Norris's office behind Andi. They both sat down in front of her desk, a place George was by now all too familiar with for his taste.

"Can you explain to me why there was a car chase yesterday in one of Charleston's nicest neighborhoods?" Chief Norris yanked a newspaper with a picture of the crash scene on the front from her desk, shaking it so violently it created an actual draft on their faces. "It also made it onto local TV, and there's videos on the internet."

"We were apprehending a prime suspect in the killing of our three victims. The man in question chose to flee, and we had to chase him." George tried to sound as calm as possible despite him simmering inside. The chief hadn't bothered to ask how they were doing, even though his split lip and swollen cheek were clearly visible. The woman just didn't care about them, which worried George more and more.

"A 'prime suspect.'" The chief did nothing to hide her disbelief. "And you let him get away?" While saying this, she pointed her chin toward George's face.

"Well, you know, professional assassins tend to not want to get arrested. They're a bit peculiar in that respect. Oh, and they are trained to kill other people in every way imaginable. Makes it hard to reason with them." George winced. Andi did nothing to keep the sarcasm from his tone, his hard gaze a direct challenge for Chief Norris. As so many times before, George could see her calculating the benefits of throwing Andi out on his ass versus the downsides of doing it. And as every time before, Andi came up on the winning side of that equation. Much to Norris's anger and George's relief.

"I'd advise you to watch the tone, Detective Hayes, but I also know for you this is an exercise in futility. I understand the suspect is in the hospital?"

"He was shot and in a car crash. We wanted to drive over later today to see if he's ready for interrogation." George tried his best to infuse professionalism into the tense atmosphere.

"You think he is your guy?" The chief looked eager and disappointed at the same time.

"We're not sure. All the evidence points to him, though."

"Then let's hope you can close this case today. A success would make the car chase appear in a better light."

It was a clear threat, one George would make sure to mention in his memory protocol. He just wished again it wouldn't be necessary to write one in the first place. "Yes, we're optimistic. Was there anything else?"

"No, you can leave." She waved them off, already turning back to her PC. George held the door for his fuming partner and even managed to guide him to the currently empty break room before Andi exploded.

"That stupid bitch! That arrogant, incompetent, useless waste of space occupying the chair of a chief! I wish we could get rid of her."

"Amen to that." George watched as Andi started pacing like a rabid lion in a too narrow cage. "But if something happens to her, we'd be the first ones they'd look into. It's not worth the hassle."

"Damnation! You're right." Andi sighed. "Another memory protocol?"

"Definitely. I'm afraid we're going to need them." George turned toward the door. "Let's visit Evangeline and Shireen. We also have to call the hospital to see if Holway is awake."

As it turned out, Evangeline and Shireen didn't have anything to contribute. On the upside, the hospital confirmed Daniel Holway was awake and ready for interrogation. They spent another two hours getting the reports and evidence they had gathered so far in order to make sure they hadn't overlooked anything. Around noon, George drove them across Ashley River on the Savannah Highway to Charleston Memorial Hospital where Daniel Holway was treated. They were lucky to find a parking spot almost immediately and went inside.

The officer guarding Holway's room took a look at their badges before letting them pass, a gesture that earned him George's immediate respect. He knew how downright boring guard duty was, especially in a hospital, and how easily a police officer got distracted or lazy about his work. He thanked the young man for being so diligent, which got him a ferocious blush in return.

Holway was handcuffed to his bed with one hand and upright, holding a magazine with the other one. When they entered, he looked up. His eyes narrowed. "You!" he spat.

"Yes, we." George dragged two chairs toward the bed. Andi took the one closer to Holway's feet, making it clear he wanted George to take the lead. George had no problem with that. "You gave me quite the shiner." He pointed at his bruised cheek. Holway scoffed, then winced, reaching for his ribs with his free hand. Apparently the crash had given him some nasty bruising as well. Somehow, George didn't feel a lot of pity for the man.

"And your partner shot me. I'd say we're more than even. Now what do you want?"

"So kind of you to ask." George smiled coldly. "It has come to our attention that you took on a contract for Harry Alexander McHill, David Hector Portius II, and Lawrence Miller. The contractor was one Peter LaFarge. Is that correct?"

Holway's face turned into an impenetrable mask. "I don't know what you're talking about."

"Oh, I think we can help your memory. Detective Hayes?"

Andi had his cell ready, showing Holway the screenshot with the chat between Holway and LaFarge. Holway groaned.

"That fucking idiot! I told him to delete it all! That's what I get for giving a newbie a chance."

"I'm sure you're getting some karmic points for your benevolence, Mr. Holway. Now what we want to talk about is why you claimed the kill as yours."

Daniel Holway furrowed his brows. "Who said it wasn't me?"

Bingo, George thought. This turned out to be easier than anticipated. "We do have our sources, Mr. Holway. Now please elaborate."

Holway stayed silent for a moment, clearly thinking things through. George hated intelligent suspects, but expecting a professional assassin to be completely stupid was naïve. Holway cocked his head. "You know it wasn't me. But you came to me anyway, which means you don't know who did it, and now you're hoping I can help you out."

George did his best to hide his irritation. Easy had just flown out the window. He didn't let that deter him, though. "Your assumption is correct, Mr. Holway."

"So you can't charge me with murder." Holway sounded triumphant.

George allowed a predatory smile to form on his lips. They were entering the negotiation phase. "Actually, we can. Our little conversation here isn't recorded in any way, shape, or form, and we have written proof that you not only entered a contract to kill the three victims but that you claimed the kill and received the payment. Any judge and jury would be more than satisfied with that."

Holway smiled as well, a cold, quick movement of his lips. "But you wouldn't be satisfied. Because you want the real killer."

He leaned back on his pillow. "What do I get for helping you?"

Now they were getting serious. "Apart from being exonerated from killing the three men? We would be willing to put in a good word with the DA to charge you for obstruction of justice and conspiracy to commit murder, asking for a maximum of fifteen years in prison."

Holway made a face as if he had bitten into a lemon. "Seven."

"Twelve."

"Nine." George glanced at Andi, who nodded. He didn't like it, but he knew they had to give Holway an incentive to really help them and tell the truth. Even though they had managed to catch him—with a good portion of luck—everything Shireen had found about him suggested he was a seasoned pro who knew exactly how the game was played. They might have been able to trick him if they had more time, but time was in short supply in this case.

"Fine, we'll do our best to get you nine years. And you tell us everything you know."

Holway nodded, looking way too smug for somebody who was facing time. George also noted the sparks of amusement dancing in the killer's eyes. The man was toying with them. "Deal. Now write it down and sign it." He was also smart. Damn.

Andi got up to get pen and paper. After the terms of their agreement were written down and signed by all three of them, Andi went to copy it. One copy remained with Holway. Since his own cell had been destroyed in the crash, the assassin asked Andi to take a picture of the agreement and send it to his lawyer. It was all tedious, and George got the distinct impression Holway was enjoying it all. Once Holway was satisfied that they couldn't take back what they had promised, he turned into a chatty Cathy, his tone rich with some kind of satisfaction George couldn't understand.

"You're right, I didn't kill the marks. Somebody beat me to it."

"Then why did you claim the kill?" George leaned back in his chair.

"It wasn't an open contract, at least that was the assumption under which I was working. I was made to believe it was just between me and LaFarge. But given what I found out about them during research and observation, I'm not surprised there were others who wanted them dead as well." He shrugged, then winced. No doubt his bruised side had reminded him what a bad idea that was. "Anyway, they were dead. Why shouldn't I take that opportunity? Besides, he wasn't explicit in how he wanted them to die, just to make it cruel and painful. Drowning is pretty cruel and painful, so I decided why not?" He rolled his eyes as if this was perfectly logical, which, in a horrible way, it was.

"You were at their cabin, weren't you?" Andi sounded sly. If he found Holway's behavior strange, he didn't show it.

"I was. After they had been taken. I had planned on strangling them, which can be drawn out quite long, as you may know."

George didn't comment. He saw Andi nodding, though. Holway moved his chained hand a bit, probably to get more comfortable. "After they had arrived on Thursday, I went back to town to get something to eat and prepare for the evening. I figured nobody would miss them before their week away was up, and LaFarge hadn't said I should hide the corpses. Always makes it easier, when you don't have to get rid of bodies." Holway grinned. "Imagine my surprise when I came back to the cabin and they weren't there. It looked like they'd had quite the party, what with all the beer, and I thought they might have gone out on a midnight hunt."

"A midnight hunt?" George couldn't believe it.

Holway shrugged, this time more carefully. "People get the weirdest ideas when drunk. I looked around the cabin and scouted the area around it but couldn't find anything except for tire marks, which ended once they hit the main road. As you can imagine, I was pretty pissed. I stayed a bit longer on site to see if they came back, which they didn't. I came back the next day, and when they were still gone, I started suspecting foul play, which pissed me off even more. I checked with my broker, who swore on everything holy that I was the only one LaFarge had contracted. Then I found out they were killed and decided that I deserved to get a little compensation for my troubles. LaFarge was pretty eager to leave the country for some time, so he didn't look too closely into my claim. Idiot didn't even ask for proof of death and didn't check with the broker." Holway shook his head as if he couldn't believe the stupidity of some people.

"When you were at the cabin, did you notice anything strange?" George wasn't too happy with what Holway had told them so far. No mention of other people or the two women they were looking for.

Holway tapped his chin with his finger. "The only thing that stood out was how the mess didn't fit the amount of alcohol consumed."

"Can you explain that?"

"I don't know if you've ever noticed, but there's several stages when people get drunk. The messy state comes quite late, when coordination goes to shit. The cabin looked as if they had been drinking for at least a complete day, but the number of empty beer bottles was hardly enough to get three men, who I know could stomach their liquor, drunk enough to create such a mess."

George glanced at Andi, who answered in his stead. "That's because the killers used ketamine."

Holway nodded, his expression that of a professional considering the methods of a colleague. "Not like I would have done it, but certainly effective. Getting the first dosage right is a bitch, though."

"You don't think just anybody could have pulled it off?" Finally they were getting something, and George felt a certain relief. It would have stung if they had given Holway a lesser sentence—always provided the DA went with their suggestion—for basically nothing worthy. Not to mention the tirade they would have gotten from Chief Norris—or would get anyway. George wasn't foolish enough to believe otherwise. "Our coroner thought it's just a matter of math and that there's spreadsheets on the web."

"There are. Your coroner is right about that." Holway wiggled on his bed until he was a little more upright. "But in theory everything is easy. In real life, ketamine can be a fickle bitch, especially in combination with alcohol. When it's used as a drug for rape, people tend to not care about how much the victim is aware of. Usually it's the farther gone the better.

The three men were drowned, and the report my hacker got me said their feet weren't bound. Which means they must have walked into that lake, and that means a very careful dosage of the ketamine."

George made a mental note to tell Shireen about a leak in their security system. "You think we're looking at pros?"

"Not necessarily contract killers. Could be a doctor or chemist as well. Somebody who's used to juggling that kind of thing."

"Anything else you can tell us?" George didn't think so but was willing to let himself be surprised, since Holway's mood had obviously improved during their chat.

"Not at the moment. I'll call if I remember anything else."

Strangely enough, George believed the assassin. He did sound sincere. Again he got the nagging feeling that they were being played. "Thank you very much. We would appreciate it."

Holway gave a lazy salute with his nonbound hand before leaning back in his pillow and closing his eyes. They left the room, and Andi turned to the officer guarding Holway. "Be careful. I'm not sure when, but your charge has already made a plan for his escape."

The young officer's eyes widened. "You think so?"

"I'm sure."

George managed to keep his mouth shut until they were back in the Escalade. "Do you really think Holway is going to attempt to flee? He seemed pretty banged up."

"He was way too relaxed and forthcoming for somebody facing trial and prison. There's no way he's going to take that lying down."

"I was under the impression that something was going on. Him already planning his escape would explain a lot. And if he does flee, at least Norris can't blame us. You even warned them."

"Oh, I'm sure she's going to find a way." Andi got into the car. "Let's get back to the precinct. We can go over our list of suspects once more. Perhaps we can find somebody else who stands out." It didn't sound as if Andi was holding out much hope.

"Fun times." George started the car.

19. PRIME SUSPECTS

BACK AT their desks, George uncapped a black marker while Andi opened his drawer. Last time there had been no more pens, but he hoped to find another paper clip. Distracting his hands always helped him to concentrate. To his utter delight, there was an entire box of differently shaped pens waiting for him. He carefully selected one before closing his treasure chest again. "Thank you," he simply said. George didn't even look up from where he was studying the whiteboard with all their suspects on it.

"You're welcome." He lifted the eraser pad and started cleaning off some of the lines without an apparent system, which was symptomatic for this case. When he reached the names of the wives, he looked at Andi. "Are we positive they didn't have anything to do with it?"

Andi unscrewed the pen to get to the innards. "We're positive none of them was at the crime scene. Though I think it's entirely possible they were part of the planning. Probably not together, we have no evidence pointing at that, but one of them? As unlikely as it is, I'd leave them in."

George nodded. Then he took his pink marker to draw squares around the women's names, marking them as possible—yet unlikely—masterminds behind the scenes. "What about the sons? They are involved, though definitely indirectly. Probably more like catalysts than anything else. I'd like to leave them on, though."

"Good idea. Who else do we have?" The spring turned into a straight line in his hands.

"Technically the mistresses of Harry Alexander McHill, though their alibis are ironclad. Shireen sent a final report on them yesterday. I don't know if you've seen it."

"Not yet. What about the sex workers David Hector frequented?"

"Too many. The few he visited twice appear to be clean."

Andi sighed, while the plastic thingy with which the pen could be attached to a piece of paper came apart in his hands. "Which leaves Tabitha Clemént and Josephine Garr."

"Indeed." George framed their names in pink as well. "They fit the bill as perfectly or imperfectly as the wives. And we definitely have to factor in the possibility of another hit contract. Holway seemed to be convinced it had to be one of his fellow assassins. Not every broker is inexperienced or careless, and Shireen is good, but not a goddess."

"Which means all the other suspects with enough money remain on the board. Theoretically it could have been each and every one of them." Andi enjoyed the little grinding sound the plastic casing of the pen made when he started splintering it.

"Yes." George looked resigned. "We need to ask Shireen to go through the finances of each of them, see if there are any suspicious movements, like in LaFarge's case. That way we can hopefully narrow it down. You said it yourself—the kills must have at least cost a hundred and fifty thousand. LaFarge paid two million. I'd say we tell Shireen to look at any transfers between those hundred and fifty thousand up to three million, to be on the safe side. Not everybody has that kind of money lying around, which means we can hopefully cross a few names off the list."

"I feel you." The plastic casing was now a little pile of debris, which left the cartridge. Andi hesitated. Cartridges were messy.

"I've got tissues." George chuckled in dark amusement.

"You're the best!" Andi beamed and attacked the last intact piece of the pen.

Because they hadn't heard back from Shireen, they updated their preliminary reports. Before he met George, Andi had always procrastinated doing this until the very end of a case, keeping track of everything with countless Post-its and random notes. George liked things to be neat, and after their third case, Andi had grumpily admitted to himself that writing the report during the inevitable lulls in an investigation was much better than doing it at the end, where it always seemed like an insurmountable obstacle.

On their way home, George stopped at a deli and insisted they buy the ingredients for a quick pasta dish, because according to him, the contents of Andi's fridge and pantry were "a sad affair." Andi didn't protest, simply made sure he was the one to pay for everything. It gave him the feeling of making a contribution worth mentioning besides just wolfing down whatever George whipped up in the kitchen.

George cooked for them both while Andi went into the garden to get rid of the two piles of dog poo the flies were going crazy about. If he ever caught the dogs—and their owners—who invaded his garden on a regular basis, he wouldn't be responsible for his actions.

Dinner was tranquil, the two of them stuffing their faces with gusto after a long day. Afterward George stayed for a cup of chamomile tea and some college basketball game between two teams Andi had never heard of. George on the other hand seemed to be fully invested, groaning and shouting at the TV as if he were the coach. It gave Andi something to focus on, and by the time George left, the constant humming of *everything* in his mind was down to a soft background noise he could easily ignore. He managed to get into bed and to fall asleep before George's soothing impact lessened, which was more than he could say about most of his nights.

THE NEXT morning Chief Norris called them into her office again, her expression thunderous. They didn't even have time to properly close the door when she started barking at them. "Why wasn't I informed immediately that the case is solved?"

Andi glanced at George, who shrugged before he answered the chief. "Because it isn't solved."

"Your own preliminary reports suggest otherwise, and Miss DuPont's report says she found proof for an assassination contract for the three victims. This looks all very clear-cut to me, Detectives, and I'm wondering why you didn't tell me the moment you knew." Her voice was full of suspicion and anger, and Andi realized the chief honestly thought they were out to get her. He didn't know what annoyed him more, the fact that she judged him and George by her own shortcomings or that she actually went to the trouble to read the reports on an ongoing case. It only confirmed how much she didn't trust them, because she had certainly not done it to be able to help them out. Andi geared up to finally tell her what exactly he thought of her, her methods, and her abilities as chief. He didn't care that this would most probably cost him his badge because he was angry enough to spit nails. Only George's hand on his lower arm stopped him from tearing the chief a new one.

"Our preliminary reports are just that—preliminary. As for Shireen's report, yes, she did find a contract for the three victims on the darknet, and the man we apprehended yesterday was the assassin who took the contract, but he didn't do it. Somebody else beat him to it."

"He confirmed the kill and took the money." The chief's eyes narrowed. "Sounds very obvious to me."

"It did to us as well." George nodded with a serious expression, as if he perfectly understood and agreed with her. "That's why we chased him." What was meant to be a conciliatory gesture to soothe the chief had the opposite effect. Andi could practically see the cogs in her head turning.

"What made you doubt the obvious, then?" The sarcasm in her voice made Andi's hands itch for his gun. Not that he would ever use it on her…. Perhaps he would. Making her disappear would be easy as well, he knew just the right place….

George glanced at him. His left eyelid was twitching a little, a sure sign he didn't like what he was about to do—lie. Because he could hardly tell Chief Norris that the moths at the lake had told Andi it had been two females. For reasons Andi had trouble understanding, George didn't like to lie about his *geschenk*. He had no problems bending the truth out of shape until it was barely recognizable anymore, but he hesitated when it came to telling an outright untruth. In the course of his life, Andi had had to lie so often, it came to him as naturally as being honest.

"When we interrogated him in the hospital yesterday, we realized he didn't know any details about how the victims were killed." The first lie. Holway had said something about his hacker getting him the report. "After we put some pressure on him, he agreed to tell us the truth if we put in a good word with the DA. He even made us write down what we would be trying to negotiate and sign it. Made us send a picture of it to his lawyer as well. Also it's in his best interest to find the real killers, which strengthened our suspicion that he's not our guy."

For a few blissful moments there was absolute silence. A silence during which Andi prayed the chief would never find out that Holway had hacked the coroner's report. Lying was an art, and George still had to learn its finer points. Like keeping information to an absolute minimum and staying as vague as possible with everything he said.

Unfortunately, the short reprieve didn't last. After some quiet fuming, Chief Norris came back louder and more annoying than before. "Let me get this straight. You had a perfect suspect with undeniable proof, in written form, from a site so disreputable every jury would have convicted him for that alone, in a high-profile case you *know* the mayor is pressuring me about, and you promised the man a *fucking deal*? You offered him an out?" Her voice was reaching a higher register with each word.

"He didn't do it. We want the real killer to be brought to justice." George's tone, on the other hand, couldn't have been more collected.

"Do I look like I care? I want this case closed. And you will close it with Daniel Holway as the killer of the three victims. I don't care what kind of deal you made with him, or what information he gave you. I'm going to call his lawyer and inform him it's irrelevant, that the DA won't go for it. You two will write a report stating Daniel Holway was hired to kill the three men, and once the client who ordered the hit is available you will arrest him. End of story."

George opened his mouth to protest, and Chief Norris silenced him with an impatient gesture of her hand. "End. Of. Story. This is an official order. And don't you dare go behind my back again." She pointed at the door. "I believe you have some writing to do."

Again Andi considered risking his career just to have the satisfaction of telling Norris what a waste of a uniform she was. George dragged him out of her office before he had his opening sentences lined up. He did slam the door on his way out, a small comfort he enjoyed.

They went back to their desks, where George got his keys. "Let's get some coffee and tea before you explode."

THEY FOUND a free table at their favorite café, where they ordered tea and blueberry muffins. When the muffins were nothing but a nice memory, not even some wayward crumbs indicating they had once been in existence, George woke his smartphone. He swiped his thumb over the screen a few times, his brows furrowed in concentration.

"The cliff notes. How did the meeting with the chief go?"

Andi groaned. "She ordered us in, started yelling immediately because she somehow thinks we're as rotten as she is and would keep vital information from her. Then she gave us a direct command to ignore the facts regarding the case and declare an innocent man—no, let me rephrase that, declare a seasoned contract killer who isn't guilty of the particular crime we're investigating—to be the killer. She refused to listen to reason or look at the evidence with an open mind, either because she doesn't want to or because she's so ill-fitted for her post she can't even be trusted to work with evidence and insisted we close the case with Daniel Holway as the killer, which leaves us in very much the same fucked-up situation as it was with Castain, forcing us to either ignore evidence or her orders."

George's thumbs were flying over the screen for a few moments longer. When he was done, he put the phone down. "We will have to go behind her back again." He didn't sound too happy about it.

Andi shrugged. "Or we could just leave it be. I'm sure Holway will be gone sometime soon, and finding him again will be very hard. He was the one who claimed the kills, so it's not like we're pinning them on him against his will, and it would solve our other problems as well. The chief would be off our backs, the case would be officially solved, which is good for our statistics, and we could leave this mess behind us."

"I hate myself for even contemplating it." George took a long sip from his tea.

"Why?" Andi cocked his head. He knew George's moral compass was a lot straighter than his own, but he wanted to understand what exactly it was that motivated his partner.

George hesitated, his expression suggesting he was thinking hard about Andi's question. It was one of the things Andi truly liked about George. The man tended to think before he spoke, never taking anything, not even his own beliefs, for cast in stone.

"I can fully understand your reasoning." George nodded at Andi. "Making Holway the scapegoat would benefit us in more ways than one, giving us a break we definitely need. Especially you."

"But—"

"But it just feels wrong. And—I don't even have a word for it. Messy? Unfinished? Loose? Like a tiny little pebble in your shoe, one that is lodged in the seam where you can't get it, but with every step you take, you can feel it, and it's rubbing your skin, creating a blister." George raised his hands. "Damn, now I can understand your frustration when I don't get something you want to explain to me."

"You're not doing too bad. Keep going, as you would tell me." Andi grinned and George relaxed a bit.

"Fine. It's not even that I necessarily believe pinning the murder on Holway is wrong from a moral viewpoint. He certainly has done enough shady stuff to deserve it. I also know not making Holway the scapegoat just means exchanging him with another killer or killers. And his client— well, he did hire a contract killer to get rid of his enemies, which makes him guilty enough. He was willing to kill, and for that alone he deserves what the law has in store for him. And given what the victims have done to others—I know we had an argument about it, but I'm starting to see your point. Whoever did this to them must have had good reason."

"So if it's not your moral compass telling you to keep going, what is it, then?"

"Don't get me wrong. My moral compass, as you call it, does play a role. It's just not the only motivator." All of a sudden, George smiled. It was a bit wicked, and Andi felt a pleasant shiver running down his spine, one he ruthlessly stopped. No need to go *there* when it was already clear George wouldn't be staying.

"Then what else motivates you?"

"The mystery itself. I want to know who did it. If only for myself. What can I say? I'm terribly nosy." George shrugged.

"Not the worst trait in a detective." Andi emptied his tea. It was a good blend, peppermint with an undertone of something sweet and spicy. He had to get it again the next time they were here. "And not a bad reason. In fact, it's one of the few reasons I can accept without question. I'm always suspicious of people who do things for the greater good. In my experience there's always a catch somewhere."

George eyed him with an intensity that had Andi squirming inwardly. "You do things for the greater good," he said with absolute conviction. "And you risk your own sanity for it."

Andi closed his eyes. "I think you have a higher opinion of me than I deserve, George." He looked his partner straight in the eyes. "What I'm doing at the Charleston PD, that's not because I want all those victims to get justice. It's my way to stave off the inevitable, namely me going completely mad. It gives me something to focus on besides the world of arthropods. A reason to come back. If I didn't have that, I'd be long gone by now."

George looked at him for so long, Andi was wondering if he was going to say anything at all or if they would be sitting here until the café closed. When George finally spoke, his tone was gentle, soft. "And I think your own opinion of yourself isn't high enough. I know you keep the pictures of the victims you investigate on your cell. I have seen you working hard to find killers. Hell, I was right there when you brought down Castain and his human trafficking ring. You are compassionate and empathic, and you don't suffer injustice. So what you do helps you stay sane? Who cares? It's the outcome that counts."

"It's never enough." Andi had to avert his gaze. It was never enough. No matter how many cases he solved, how many victims and their loved ones found peace because of what he did, there were always others waiting who were truly forgotten, and the only way of coping was to put the focus off them and onto his own life reality, which was a constant struggle he would be losing some day. Then all justice would be gone because the other world he was linked to, the one he was sinking into each day a bit more, did not know justice or peace. It only knew survival, and the basic instincts, reproduction and death. It was a simpler world on many levels and yet so complicated, with layers no human would ever be able to comprehend, not even one with a *geschenk*, because how could you hope to understand what you couldn't even fully grasp, not the way *they* did, because he didn't see the world through pheromones or the tremors rising up through his legs or the sonic waves in the air or the atmospheric pressure. He didn't breathe through holes in his sides, even though his brain had given him an image of what it thought it would feel like. He didn't share his mind with other humans, though he had an impression of what it entailed. Nothing in his world was real and stable, everything constantly shifting, the only fixed points the corpses whose lives he dissected in order to find their killers, and they, too, were floating by, of no real consequence, at least not to him, not when he thought like them, just saw them as food, no, he needed an anchor. George would be perfect, so reliable, but he would leave, and he would be alone to drown in a sea of information with no end and no sense.

"Andi, hey." George lightly stroked his arm, the touch welcome and soothing, something real in *his* body, not theirs. His partner smiled at him. "There's always more that could be done. It's the reason why there's not just the two of us on this planet. It's not your burden alone or mine. It's a group effort, and you are carrying more than your weight."

The words made sense to Andi, which he found amusing because he had thought he had it all nailed down. George really was a good partner.

"Thank you. I needed to hear that." He got up, winked at George. "Then let's go behind the chief's back."

George made a face. "Yeah. Let's."

20. Gaining Time

GEORGE STILL wondered how he had ended up being insubordinate again. When he had first gotten to Charleston, everything had been so easy, so clear-cut. Work his year and a half, help the chief with a problem, get glowing recommendations, move on and up the ladder toward his goal of becoming chief himself. Now, about half a year into his stint in Charleston, he was not only seriously contemplating staying longer, perhaps permanently, he had also made an enemy of the chief, had himself attached to a partner who was as proud, ferocious, and wildly independent as a street cat while at the same time needed George's protection and help, and he was about to ignore a direct order from his superior—again—to solve a case where he wasn't sure who was worse, the victims or the potential suspects.

His usual morning run had not helped to quiet the swirling thoughts in his head, had only made it worse because once he fell in his runner's trance, they were free to line up, his worry about Andi's mental state front and center, closely followed by Chief Norris's behavior, with the case coming in third. When it was this bad, there was only one thing that helped, writing it all down. George was sitting at his kitchen counter, a glass with his favorite smoothie—apple, banana, pineapple, and spinach—next to the three sheets of paper representing the three most pressing problems in his life. The one titled "Andi" was full in the "problem" column, while the one with solutions was pathetically empty. He had started researching meditation techniques that may help Andi to keep his *geschenk* under control a little longer, but in the light of the last few weeks, George was sure it would only prolong the inevitable, namely Andi losing himself one way or another. By now he was even contemplating suggesting Andi should smoke weed to dampen the effects of the *geschenk*. He had been terrified when he found out about all the potential side effects of seemingly harmless painkillers like ibuprofen and aspirin. The only drug that was safe—up to a certain degree—to take regularly being paracetamol. As much as it galled George, he was still woefully clueless as to how he could help his partner.

He looked at the next sheet, with Chief Norris's name written on it. It presented a different, more positive picture, because George knew how to deal with somebody like her. What would happen once the shit actually hit the fan was by no means certain, but he had done everything in his power to shield himself and Andi as much as possible. With a little luck, this could even be good for his career, make him look determined and capable. *If you still want that career*, the tiny voice at the back of his head chimed in, reminding him of the shift in priorities he was currently experiencing.

The sheet with the case was a mess, with too many question marks at crucial points, and the lure to just accept Daniel Holway as the scapegoat and leave all the chaos, pain, hatred, and sorrow of this murder behind was almost irresistible. George decided not to look too closely at his main reason for pursuing the matter further, which had nothing to do with what he had told Andi. No, George simply didn't want to drop the case after his partner had risked his mental health to get to the bottom of things. He also knew himself well enough to realize how his feelings for Andi were getting more and more muddled, the respect and need to protect his partner interweaving with more personal emotions, some of them healthy and normal, others leading up avenues George wasn't sure he wanted or should pursue. Charleston had been meant to be a stepping-stone, one that was quickly turning into the foundation for a house, to stay with the building metaphor.

George emptied his smoothie, stacked the papers, and got ready to head out. He wanted to go grocery shopping with Andi before they went to the precinct. Both because his partner desperately needed to stock up on necessities and because doing mundane things together helped them clear their heads. The way the case was looking, they needed clarity more than anything.

ANDI WAS still sleeping when George arrived at his house. After he had let himself in, George went to the kitchen to prepare breakfast, only to be hampered by the lack of food. In the end he had to settle for the usual tea and coffee plus two lonely slices of toast he managed to make edible by smearing them with the remains of the butter he had bought more than three weeks ago and roasting them in a pan. The strawberry jam would provide the sugar Andi needed to brave the grocery store until George could get something more substantial into his partner. In the car the plain bagel was waiting to be consumed as well. Andi always ate the bagel either in the car or at the precinct. Bringing it into the house didn't work, as George had learned by now. Andi was very peculiar about his eating, and so far, this quirk was the only one George hadn't managed to somehow tie back to the *geschenk*. It seemed to be an independent character trait, one George valued because everything else about Andi was so tangled up in his *geschenk*, it was impossible to tell where the lines between Andi's coping mechanisms and his true personality ran.

Andi shuffled into the kitchen with a yawn, his dirty-blond hair hanging around his face, making him look extremely hungover. George held out the cup of tea.

"Good morning. Did you sleep well?"

Andi took the tea, smelled it with closed eyes. "Mmm. Good morning to you too. I slept well, thank you. Housemates were fairly quiet. They love it when you come, by the way."

"They do?"

"Yeah, associate you with food. Me too." Andi took a sip of the tea while George tried to determine if his partner was making fun of him or if he was serious.

"What do I look like to them?" George was curious.

"To the mosquitoes you're delicious, because your blood is so healthy. They like the scent. For the silverfish and spiders, you're a calming presence, you move steadily, you don't disturb the ground or shake the air, you exude calm. To the moths and ants and termites you're this multilayered blob made of color and mass, something they can identify easily because you're here so often, part of the world, not an intruder anymore, safe, comfort, you always lose crumbs and bits, feeding time, the car stinks, not you, you smell of something good, sandalwood and citrus with a hint of orange and cinnamon, warm, delicious, it clings to you, some kind of aftershave, I think, makes me feel cozy." Andi stopped his ramblings to look at George. "Sorry," he said with a lopsided smile. "Got carried away."

"No, no, it's fine. I asked." George pushed the plate with the toast in Andi's direction. "Eat up."

Andi took the first slice, bit into it with a crunching sound. Little crumbs flew everywhere, making George think of tiny mouths—mandibles?—hungrily consuming them, little legs clicking toward the food, racing to be the first…. He shook his head. It wasn't a good idea to go down that road.

One of them had to remain firmly in the world of blobs. There were things to be done, obstacles to be overcome. George cleared his throat.

"Before we drive to the precinct, I thought we could do some grocery shopping at that nice little store we always pass on the way to your house."

"You want to go grocery shopping with me?" The disbelief in Andi's voice made George rethink his proposal immediately. Had he gone too far?

"Uh, yes?"

"Why?" The genuine interest Andi expressed reminded George how unpredictable his partner was.

"Because while I have no problem doing it for you, I'd like to know what brands and stuff you prefer."

"Brands?" Andi looked puzzled.

"Uhm, you know, food brands? Take butter, for example. Do you prefer the real thing or margarine or the stuff that's completely vegan? If you want the real thing, are you a salted butter kind of man? Which is the brand you grew up with? In my family, we're all conditioned on Kerrygold. My mom and Griffin, my oldest brother, prefer it salted, while Dad, Daniel, and I like the unsalted version best. In a pinch, we'll accept Anchor, while my cousins on my mother's side swear on Organic Valley. You see, there's lots of options for butter alone, and so far, I've made you eat all the brands I prefer. What kind of butter did you grow up with?"

Andi's mouth stood open until he closed it with an audible *clack*. Then he mulled George's question over with an expression so serious, as if the fate of the nation hinged on his answer.

"I can't say I have too many fond memories of my past, let alone regarding food." He took a sip from his tea, avoiding George's gaze. "Food was way down on my list of priorities, and I have to admit, I never paid close attention to it."

Andi put the tea mug down. Before George could say anything or start crying at the sadness of it all, Andi continued. "I do remember my gran always had butter in a white-and-purple package. I think there was a piece of grilled fish or meat on it?"

"Ah, your gran had excellent taste. That's Shurfine you're talking about. We can definitely get that."

"I thought you preferred Kerrygold?"

"Yeah. But you like Shurfine. It's your fridge."

Andi furrowed his brows. "Which you fill most of the time. Besides, I'm not sure I would even taste the difference."

"Can I tell you a secret?" George winked like a conspirator in a bad movie.

Andi nodded.

"It's not so much about how something tastes. I'm not saying I wouldn't recognize my favorite butter, mind you, just that it's not about the taste but the familiarity of the package, of having something of your childhood spilling over into your adult life. Kerrygold reminds me of the past."

"Which makes you happy."

"Yes, it makes me happy." George smiled.

"Then we go for Kerrygold. I want you to be happy, and perhaps I can learn it from you? Associating taste with something familiar and cozy? Adopt your happy, so to speak?"

George had to get up abruptly and put his coffee mug in the sink, because now the tears were dripping like crazy out of the corners of his eyes.

"Don't be sorry for me, George. You know I hate that." Andi's voice was softer than his words.

"I'm not feeling sorry for you." George did his best to get a handle on his emotions. "I just can't stand the thought of somebody being deprived the chance to be dependent on certain brands of food. I mean, how can you go through life not supporting one brand while abhorring the other?"

"Uh—easily?"

"We can't have that. We're going to get you fixed on a few brands right away." George gathered the remaining dishes to put them into the dishwasher before he grabbed his keys. "Let's go to the grocery store."

An hour later they were unpacking all the good stuff, starting with Kerrygold butter (unsalted, of course), peanut butter from Smucker's (the creamy kind, George hated crunchy and saw no reason to give Andi the chance to latch on to something he didn't like), Nature Nate's honey, and Kellogg's Frosted Flakes. George had felt a bit bad about practically steamrolling Andi with his own preferences and had let him decide on milk and bread, only to realize his partner took whatever came first in the row. Such irresponsible shopping George couldn't allow, so he took charge again without a bad conscience, guiding Andi none too subtly to what George thought were responsible and sensible food choices. He could already see that it would be a work in progress for the foreseeable future and found he didn't mind. When everything was tucked away, they drove to work.

21. Ripples in the Net

As soon as they entered the precinct, Andi could tell, not only by the agitation of the arthropods but also by the nervous hum in the air, that something was wrong. He just hoped the chief hadn't gone nuclear because they had again done something she didn't like. Then again, if it had been about them, the whole precinct wouldn't be in uproar. They reached the first floor with the bullpen, where things were even more hectic. George had the presence of mind to stop one of the officers rushing past and ask her what happened.

"They haven't reached out to you?" Her eyes were wide with horror. George shook his head.

"No. For what?"

"Daniel Holway escaped custody this morning at eight o'clock."

George looked at Andi, who just shrugged. "Told you so."

The officer hurried on, paying them no more attention. Andi followed George to their desks, where they were promptly met by Detectives Mescew and Gentry, two of their colleagues Andi could at least tolerate.

"There you are. About time." Detective Sandra Mescew smiled at them, taking the sting out of her words. The sharp lines around her eyes and mouth told Andi she'd had one hell of a morning. Her usually meticulous bun was loose, longer strands of her thick black hair framing her face while some of the shorter ones stuck up in all directions. She actually resembled the pictures of Medusa Andi had seen in a book about Rome, not that he would ever dare say it to her face. She was an excellent detective and a better shot than Andi.

"What's going on?" George nodded at her and her partner, Tobias Gentry. He, too, looked stressed, the dark circles under his eyes blending with his beard. At forty-eight he was one of their senior detectives with a cool head in a crisis. He wasn't the most ingenious detective, but what he lacked in imagination he made up for with sheer determination and a love for detail that would have made Andi kill him, had they been partners. As it was, Mescew and Gentry were a good team with a solid solving rate. Andi wasn't surprised they had been tasked with catching Daniel Holway.

"As you've probably heard already, Daniel Holway, your main suspect, escaped from the hospital this morning. Apparently he had help, but we don't know any specifics yet. Shireen is already looking at the video footage, trying to find out how he did it and where he could have gone. Where have you been all morning? The chief has been asking for you."

I can imagine, Andi thought. Out loud he said, "We've been trying to tie up some loose ends." There was no need for anybody to know their loose ends were about the right brand of butter. Andi still didn't understand the concept. "I assume you're in charge of the escape scene?"

"Oh yes. What a joy." Mescew made a face. "The chief said the case was closed, so you can take over now since this is your suspect?" The hope in her voice made Andi smile. Chasing escaped suspects was usually a bitch.

"Actually no. As I said, there are still some loose ends we have to tie up. We do appreciate your help and hope you'll find Holway as soon as possible." Andi kept his voice and face blank, trying to sound as professional as possible. The problem with detectives, though, was that they were a suspicious bunch to begin with, and Mescew had known him since he started at the CPD. She was neither blind nor stupid, much to Andi's annoyance.

Her eyes narrowed. "I'm not going to ask, so you don't have to lie to me, but if you don't tell us to stop working the moment you've done whatever you're going to do, I'll personally wring your scraggly neck. Understood, Hayes?"

Andi nodded gravely, not wanting to aggravate her even more.

George just shrugged. "Where's the chief?" he wanted to know.

"In her office screaming at officers through the phone," Gentry answered. If his tone was supposed to sound neutral, he was doing a terrible job. Chief Norris didn't have many fans at the precinct, certainly not with the more experienced officers. Perhaps she would have been more lenient with Andi if her standing as chief with the entire precinct were better. Those were idle thoughts, though, because the fact was she had a hard time, she could sense the resentment directed at her, and she had chosen Andi as the outlet for her frustration.

"Then it's probably best we don't disturb her. What do you think, Andi?"

Andi was more than happy to avoid Chief Norris wherever he could. "Why don't we go see Evangeline? Perhaps *she* has some good news for us."

"I heard that," Detective Mescew grumbled.

"Hey, I didn't blame you, did I?"

"Not in so many words. Get going, Hayes." Gentry was suppressing a laugh, much to the annoyance of Mescew, who socked him in the shoulder. The way the man winced, he was probably getting a nice bruise.

Andi and George left them to their bantering in favor of descending down to Evangeline's kingdom. Today, she had her stunning black hair up in the messiest bun Andi had ever seen, including the one Mescew was sporting at the moment, the tattoos on her face looking too dark on her pale skin. Apparently, she had pulled another all-nighter, always working hard to bring justice for those who could no longer claim it themselves.

"*Talofa lava*, Andi, George. Though I heard it's not such a good morning after all." She raised one thick, perfectly shaped brow.

"Good morning to you, too, Evangeline. And no, we've seen better." Andi smiled at her. "Rough night?"

"Don't get me started. Suspected murder which turned out to be a mass suicide with four victims." She shuddered. "And they didn't go easy on themselves."

Andi knew better than to pry further. It wasn't his case, and if Evangeline wanted to share more, she would do so without prompting.

"I was about to send my report to you yesterday when they were dumped in my lap."

"You've found something?" George sounded hopeful.

"*Loe*. I don't know how you always know what to look for, and I certainly don't care what kind of sacrifices you made to whatever dark deity you're serving, but I *did* find your silk protein. It was a miniscule trace preserved in a pocket formed by a piece of cloth and the chains, keeping it from dissolving in the water."

"And?"

Evangeline raised a brow. Their gazes remained locked for a moment before she gave up with a huff. "And the silk protein wasn't the most interesting I've found. The cloth it was on wasn't from the victim, and it also carried some skin cells, of which the DNA is currently running through all databases I have access to. It's from a female, by the way."

"You're the best." Andi smiled at her. Unknown female DNA in a place where it could have only gotten when the victim was chained strengthened their theory about another, unknown player and affirmed what Andi had gotten from the arthropods.

Evangeline took his praise by slightly inclining her head. "I've also come up with a suitably scientific explanation how I found the silk in the first place, since it didn't pop up in the overall sample tests I made. If you crack this case, I'm going to write an article about it."

"Whatever pleases you. Can you send us the report? This is going to help us a great deal."

"*Loe*. Consider it done." She turned in the direction of her office, the dismissal clear, but neither Andi nor George took offense. Evangeline was a hardworking woman who had just given them another puzzle piece to solving the case. The least they could do was respect her privacy when she wanted to be left alone.

"What do we do now?" George opened the main door of the precinct, to which they had gravitated without talking about it. Neither of them wanted to stay in there any longer. Not with the chief so obviously on the warpath.

"Until Evangeline hopefully gets a match on that DNA, we might as well drive to the hospital, see if I can't get a feel of where Holway went."

"I'm not sure that's a good idea," George stated while he opened the door on the driver's side of his Escalade.

"Don't worry. I have absolutely no intention of going deep. I'm just going to listen to the general hum. Perhaps we'll be lucky." Andi sat down in the passenger's seat, leaning his head back.

"Yeah. Lucky." George didn't sound too hopeful.

22. By a Hair's Breadth

As it turned out, George had been right to be pessimistic. All Andi could discern was that somebody who looked like a nurse but hadn't belonged to the hospital had wheeled Holway out of the hospital and to a car when he was supposed to have been getting an X-ray. How the fake nurse had ditched the two cops on watch duty, Andi couldn't tell because the overall excitement made it hard to pick up any details. Once Holway was in the car, the arthropods had lost interest because he was out of reach and moving too fast, which was the end of what Andi was able and willing to discern, much to George's relief.

They were almost back at the precinct when the call came. Andi fished out his cell and put it on speaker as soon as he had taken a look at the screen. Detective Mescew's voice came through slightly distorted over the background of a moving car.

"We've found Holway. He was spotted in the Goose Creek area by one of our beat officers. He followed him to one of the old houses at the end of Mapleridge Drive. Holway is hiding there. We're on our way."

"Meet you there in ten." While Andi ended the call, George changed lanes and raced toward Goose Creek. Memories of their first drive there came to his mind. He and Andi had just been paired up and had been called to investigate the murder of a woman, which eventually put them on track to the human trafficking ring led by Jake Castain and Clayton Harris. Their first case together. George felt a little nostalgic thinking about it.

They reached Mapleridge Drive, and he slowed down so as not to alert Daniel Holway. Several police cars were parked out at the curb, Detective Gentry waving them over. He was wearing a bulletproof vest, his badge clearly displayed on the leather belt around his waist. He looked more than ready to spring into action. As soon as they were both out, Gentry started rattling off the facts while leading them toward the back of an abandoned house. "He's hiding in the last house on the street. You'll see it as soon as we reach the corner. The beat officer who recognized him followed him here and has been watching the house with his partner until we arrived. Holway is still in there. The heat cameras show he's on the second floor. We already have the building surrounded and are ready to go in."

They reached the corner, and George got his first view of the house. It looked almost identical to the one they were hiding behind, the high grass on the front lane barely obscuring different items of trash such as old tires, a toilet broken in half, and an entire pile of pipes in various sizes. The door looked to still be quite solid; the windows were nailed shut with planks of chipboard. All in all, a sad though not uncommon sight in this area. Out of the corner of his eye he saw Andi stiffen.

"It's a wonder that thing is still standing."

Gentry turned toward Andi. "Surely it can't be that bad? I mean, it looks relatively solid compared to some of the others, and Holway is in there...." He trailed off when he saw the expression on Andi's face. Detective Mescew stepped next to him. She had been watching the house through a pair of binoculars.

"How bad is it, Andi?" Her voice was calm, as if they were talking about the weather, not something Andi shouldn't know by simply glancing at a building that showed no glaring signs of decay. At least not if the normal laws of the world applied. It was something that always puzzled George anew—even though Andi kept his distance to all his colleagues, most of them were willing to follow his lead even when things were in no way clear-cut. George didn't know if it said more about Andi's personality or the underlying willingness to believe in some higher power that seemed to be inherent in human beings.

"Too bad to send anybody in, least of all an entire group of police."

"How do you want to do this?" Mescew didn't question Andi; she didn't discuss. She simply *trusted* him.

Andi closed his eyes for a moment. "Surround the house but keep a healthy distance, especially on the southern side. That balcony is a death trap. George and I will go inside and try to drive Holway outside."

"Fine by me. Be careful." Mescew turned to Gentry, who nodded and started barking orders into his radio.

George touched Andi's upper left arm. His partner smiled weakly at him, the familiar lines of exhaustion around his eyes and mouth already deepening, indicating he was inside the house with at least half his mind already. George wasn't happy about it, because this was the third time within less than a week Andi was consciously deepening his contact to the arthropods. Knowing how stressful this was, George was already mentally preparing for a good excuse to get Andi back home as soon as they had Holway.

"It's fine, George. I can get us through unharmed. I think." Andi had obviously picked up on George's worry and misinterpreted it. George didn't bother to correct him. They had more important things to do than wasting Andi's precious mental capacities on such petty things.

"I trust you."

"Good, let's get going." Andi got out his gun and took the safety off. "Stay behind me and only tread where I do."

"Roger that." George checked his own weapon before following Andi toward the house. His partner's gait was a bit wonky, no doubt because he was trying to remember that the body he was using had only two legs instead of six or more. He didn't try to hide their approach, which told George that Holway didn't know they were coming. George did his best to keep his attention on his surroundings while at the same time being alert to where Andi stepped and what he was saying, a constant stream of words coming from his lips, the only way he could share what he was feeling and sensing. It was stringent, meaning Andi had—at least for the moment— enough mental distance to just translate and not slip under the current. How long he would be able to maintain that distance was anyone's guess, and George was ready to catch his partner should he fall. Just dividing his focus on four things at the same time was taxing for George, and he didn't want to contemplate what Andi had to endure every minute of every day.

"Left wall is unstable, earth underneath it soaked through because of a burst water pipe, foundation sagging, wood just sawdust, mold everywhere, eating away at the structure, termites, a huge colony, the queen heavy with eggs, so many soldiers and workers, no, don't get distracted, Andi, you need to know where it's still safe, focus, open the door, Holway is upstairs, in a room close to the sagging wall, need to be careful, ceiling is broken, just held by plaster, careful now, the planks are rotting away, need to stay at the wall, not here though, one step to the middle, three forward, back to the wall, try to get your foot on the very edge, no weight to the side, here are the stairs, don't touch the banister, stay away from it, not too close to the wall, the anchors are lose, half in the middle, careful, slowly, damn, he's heard us, he has a weapon, quick, need to get upstairs, the floor is not as bad as the stairs, hurry, he's trying to flee, no, don't go there, it won't hold, not when you run so fast, slow down, damn, it's breaking, breaking, stay at the side, back down, too dangerous, no, he's going for the balcony...."

George was already carefully but quickly retreating the same way they had come up half the stairs when he heard the sickening crunch of wood and plaster slowly caving in, the sound getting louder, more insistent, more threatening, like the rumble of an avalanche racing down the mountain. And like an avalanche, the noise was deafening when the ceiling broke, crashing into the first floor. Among the sounds of breaking wood and shattering tiles, George heard the pained screams of a human being, and for a terrible second, he thought he sensed the meaty thump of a body hitting the ground or being squashed, but that couldn't be, not over the cacophony of sounds surrounding them. They made it safely down the stairs, and George let Andi squeeze past him to get them outside before the entire house collapsed on their heads. Andi moved fast, with an urgency that had George staying sharp at his partner's heels. The moment they were through the main door, Andi jumped in a bid to get as far away as possible. George followed his example, and not a second too soon, because behind him, the noise tripled, accompanied by a sighing sound, as if the house was happy to be finally put to rest.

George rolled through the brownish grass, careful not to squish Andi, who was lying on his back, panting. One look back at the ruins they had just escaped from, and George knew it would take a miracle for Holway to still be alive. Why on earth the man had chosen this house as his hiding spot was beyond George. Then again, he himself had thought it was still fairly safe. He shuddered. If it hadn't been for Andi, they would have gone in there with at least a half dozen police. George didn't have to be a seer to know the outcome would have been devastating. He slowly pushed up on his elbows when Gentry and Mescew came running toward them. Mescew kneeled down next to Andi while Gentry offered George his hand to pull him up. When he was standing, George turned to where Andi was now sitting, his eyes closed, in obvious pain.

"My head is killing me."

"Let's get you back to the car. I have more ibuprofen there." George helped Andi up and kept an arm around his waist while he briefly talked to Mescew and Gentry. "Can we leave this to you? I need to take care of Andi."

Mescew glanced at the pile of debris that had been a house only minutes before. "I don't think Holway is going anywhere. If he's still alive, which I very much doubt. We'll report this and tell the chief you were in the middle of it all and had to take the rest of the day off."

"Thank you." George started leading Andi toward the Escalade. His partner was leaning on him heavily, his body slightly shivering.

"There you are, sit down." George helped Andi into the car, where he immediately went for the glove department to get the ibuprofen. He didn't even bother to wait until George had opened a water bottle; he simply swallowed them dry. George hurried to get into the driver's seat and start the car. The drive back to James Island seemed to take an eternity, though in reality it couldn't have been more than twenty minutes. Andi looked half passed out in the passenger seat, his head lolled to the side as if he didn't have the strength to keep it up. Getting him inside the house was difficult enough to make George grateful for the weight training he was doing. By the time he had Andi stripped down to his underwear and on the bed, he was sweating from the strain. Andi just slumped into the mattress with a groan, left it to George to pull the cover over him. When George turned toward the door, Andi called after him.

"Are you staying?"

"Of course." George smiled when Andi grunted happily and went to sleep.

BREAKFAST WAS a silent affair, Andi obviously still suffering from mental exhaustion and a headache. Experience had taught George that all his partner needed in this stage was quiet, some tea, and something plain to eat, hence the toast with butter (Kerrygold, unsalted, thank you very much) and apricot jam (some unknown-to-him brand but edible, if a little too sweet for his taste) for George while Andi was nibbling on just the bread. He stopped at their usual Starbucks to get more tea and coffee and a bagel for Andi who, at this point, was starting to show some interest in his surroundings besides groaning when the light hit his eyes the wrong way. When Andi bit into his bagel with a contented sigh, George risked asking him a question that had been bothering him the entire night.

"How come there were still arthropods in the house?"

"Huh?" Either Andi was too distracted with filling his stomach, or he really didn't understand what George meant.

"Yesterday, at the house. You said it was close to collapsing, and you knew exactly where to tread, which means the arthropods knew it as well. So why didn't they leave long ago?"

From the corner of his eye, George saw Andi staring at him as if he had lost his mind.

"You're serious, aren't you?"

"Yes?" George wasn't sure why, but suddenly he felt stupid. Andi took a sip from his tea, then cursed a little because it was still too hot.

"They didn't leave because everything was ideal as far as they were concerned. Arthropods have no concept of the future or the integrity of buildings. Everything I said in the house was how they saw it, translated into what it meant for us. For them it was some version of paradise until it wasn't. End of story."

"Damn. I was applying human standards to a completely different form of life—again." George would have thumped his forehead against the steering wheel if they hadn't been in the middle of traffic.

"Happens to the best of us. Don't stress it."

"But I do. I'm a detective. I should know better than to impose my own set thoughts on something else. I should be more open." George wasn't entirely sure why it bothered him so much; perhaps it was the stress of the case or the fact that he had started to think he understood the world Andi lived in, only to realize he was still very much an outsider.

"Man, I think you're pretty open, considering what you put up with from me. Don't be harder on yourself than I am."

"You're never hard on me."

"Because you buy me clothes and feed me and put me to bed when I'm too exhausted to think clearly." Andi was absolutely deadpan, and it yanked George out of his low.

"Fine. I get it. No being too hard on myself."

"See how easy it is?" Andi tried another sip from his tea, and this time it seemed to be the right temperature because he followed it with a huge gulp.

George maneuvered the Escalade into the parking lot, using the familiar task of trying to find the perfect spot to calm his mind for the storm that would surely descend upon them the moment they entered the precinct. Gentry had written him a short text the day before that they had found Holway dead under the debris, and Chief Norris had tried to call them first on his and then on Andi's cell at least five times. He had put both phones on mute, because he had been too drained to deal with her. It wouldn't endear them to her, but having narrowly escaped a collapsing house was a valid reason to take half an afternoon off. Besides, George had realized he had lost all interest in playing nice with the chief.

The moment they entered the bullpen, Chief Norris was on them like a vulture on a cadaver, bellowing at them to come to her office. Even though she was seething, she seemed to have decided to try a new tactic, because once the door was shut and George and Andi had sat down, she simply stared at them without saying a word. It was kind of childish and stupid. Andi had no problem with people *not saying a thing*. George wasn't even sure his partner was aware that the silent treatment was supposed to make him feel uncomfortable and nervous, and George had two brothers and an overly dominant mother. Nothing Chief Norris could dish out came even close to what he had endured during childhood.

It was funny, really, the three of them sitting in the office, none of them saying a word. After about five minutes, Andi obviously decided that just sitting around was a waste of his time and started checking his texts. George had to summon every ounce of self-control he possessed when he saw the nervous tic starting in Chief Norris's left eyelid. It was one of the first lessons George had learned from his mother—only play the silent game when you're absolutely sure you're going to win it. Otherwise you look like an idiot. Norris started tapping her fingers on the desk.

"Don't you have something to tell me, Detectives?"

George looked at Andi, who put his phone away. He decided to play along. "Yes, indeed. Yesterday we received some new and highly interesting information from Dr. Melcourt regarding the case. We're still waiting on a possible DNA match from various databases. We also helped apprehend Daniel Holway, who unfortunately died in the collapsing house he had been hiding in. We made a narrow escape and are fine, thank you for enquiring."

Chief Norris stared at him as if he had been talking in a completely different language. "You went against my express orders, let the murderer of Harry Alexander McHill, David Hector Portius II, and Lawrence Miller escape and die, let yourself be led astray by whatever Dr. Melcourt has found, and had the nerve to ghost your direct superior for an entire evening. I'd say this is more than enough for me to suspend you for a month!"

"That's what you threatened us with during the Castain case." Andi sounded absentminded, as if Chief Norris was nothing but a nuisance to him. George was almost sure he was doing it on purpose.

"It's what superiors do when their detectives don't follow orders," Norris snapped.

"We were right concerning Castain." Still, Andi appeared unfazed.

"What do you mean?" Chief Norris's voice had a dangerous edge now, one George didn't like in the least. He also didn't like the gleam in Andi's eyes. His partner was finally ready to confront the chief. George hastened to interfere, shooting Andi a warning glance. If they were going toe-to-toe with their superior, George wanted more time to prepare in advance, not being thrown into it like a lobster into boiling water.

"He means that we've shown we're capable of thorough work and that you should perhaps consider trusting us to know what we're doing." It wasn't as smooth as he would have liked it to sound, but in any case, it was better than anything Andi would have said. "I'd also like to add that we didn't have anything to do with the escape of Daniel Holway, who was in custody with our colleagues. What Dr. Melcourt found puts an entirely new spin on the case and exonerates Daniel Holway, as little good as that does him now. And as I just told you, we barely escaped a collapsing building yesterday and needed to get some rest. Now, if you don't want anybody else to clean up the mess this case currently is, I'd suggest you let us do our job."

Chief Norris stared at them for a long time, her eyes glinting in silent fury. He was right and she knew it. She could, of course, suspend them and hand the case to somebody else, perhaps even pin everything that went wrong on them, but it would draw even more attention to the case, increasing the chance of it looking bad for her.

"Get out."

George had no inclination to stay a second longer than absolutely necessary in the vicinity of this woman who seemed intent on ruining him and Andi for no reason George could see. They left quickly for their own desks. Behind the relative privacy of the two whiteboards, George slumped into his chair.

"That's another memory protocol in the making."

"No need this time," Andi informed him.

"What? I'd say we definitely need it."

"No." Andi grinned and held his phone up. "I recorded it all."

George stared at his partner in a mixture of awe and horror. "If she had realized—"

"She hasn't. I was looking at my texts, remember?" A small smile flashed on Andi's lips, there and gone again. It reminded George that his partner was more than just a man who listened to insects. He was also a damn good detective with nerves of steel.

"Can you send it to me? We need to save it on our private laptops as well."

"On it." Andi started thumbing his phone while George woke his PC. He had several mails, one of them from CSI, which surprised him because analyzing samples and running them through databases usually took longer than a day. The person sending the report stated they had bumped their case up the moment they heard of Holway's escape and that several tests were still ongoing. What they did have already made George smile. The cloth on which the silk and DNA had been found was a generic brand, no spectacular new insights there, but the DNA was matched to three other murder cases, one of them in the US, the other two in France and Belgium respectively. All three murders had been high profile and therefore entered into the databases of Interpol. At the crime site in Belgium, traces of DNA of a second female had been found, perfectly matching what Andi had told him about there being two women involved.

The next good news was that the silk protein Evangeline had found on the piece of cloth matched the samples from the house. The case was finally taking on a more defined shape in front of his eyes, and George couldn't have been happier—except for Chief Norris's erratic behavior, but George was determined to address this issue as soon as possible.

The rest of the day they spent knee-deep in paperwork, writing reports about every step they had taken so far, about apprehending Holway and how they had witnessed his death, and getting all their ducks in very neat rows, just the way George liked it. Andi did complain loudly until George appeased him with lunch at their favorite Italian restaurant, which bought him an afternoon of blissful silence only interrupted by the clicking of the keyboards. Granted, they still had to find out who had sent the two assassins, a task that gave George an uncomfortable pulsing between his temples, but they were at least sure that the persons who killed the victims had been identified. In a way. George had no illusions about how impossible it was to find professional assassins, especially if there were no names and faces attached to the DNA. Their case would no doubt be entered into the databases of Interpol and the FBI, and nobody would fault them for not finding killers who probably had left the country right after fulfilling their contract. Still, they needed to find out who had given the order to have the three men killed, and the list for that person wasn't as short as George would have preferred.

23. Closing In

THE FOLLOWING two days they had a medical examination because of the house that had almost buried them—Andi didn't understand why they had to go because they were obviously fine, apart from some minor scratches—and a meeting with the resident psychologist to make sure they hadn't suffered any trauma—how could they; the house had missed them, and they were still alive. They finished all the paperwork and kept brooding over the whiteboards, trying to eliminate as many suspects as possible. Because assassins weren't cheap, they were able to thin the crowd considerably, weeding everybody out who didn't have the financial prowess to be part of this game. It still left plenty of suspects, quite naturally because of the circles the victims had frequented. Andi was willing to bet his money on some business rival, while George insisted on keeping the wives on the list as well.

George was busy compiling the complaint against Chief Norris. Andi was the first to admit that he wasn't well versed enough in precinct politics to understand the finer points of what George was doing. If it had been just him, he would have gotten it all out in one huge confrontation with her directly. According to George, this was not how such matters were handled because of the potential risks Andi hadn't even thought of. He was content to leave it all to his partner, offering his input only when asked and ready to stand beside George when he decided to make his move.

Chief Norris kept her distance, not bothering them in any way. Andi was grateful for the reprieve, though he knew it was just the calm before the storm.

On the third day after the confrontation with the chief, they got surprising news from the Narcotics unit. Dominic McHill had been found dead in his house the day after Holway died. According to the coroner, McHill had died because the heroin he had injected into his arm had been laced with a combination of rat poison and fentanyl. His already weakened body and heart—the condition of his liver suggested he'd been an alcoholic for at least eight years, if not longer—hadn't been able to deal with the potent chemical mix and simply shut down. There were no traces of a break-in; the needle with the lethal dose was found next to his body and didn't show any fingerprints besides his own. It was another coincidence in a long line, though this one was the first Andi was willing to accept because he had sensed how sick Dominic McHill was. There was a chance his death was somehow connected to the case—Andi and George agreed it was about fifty-fifty—and they planned on looking into it as soon as possible. First, though, they had been summoned by Shireen, who was quite excited when George and Andi greeted her.

"I'm still wading through tons of information, and let me tell you, the deeper I get, the uglier it becomes. I did find something about Tabitha Clemént and Josephine Garr you might be interested in."

Andi saw George furrowing his brows. They had taken the two women off their list because a) Andi knew they hadn't been the ones at the lake, b) they didn't have the money to hire somebody to do the killing for them, and c) it simply didn't sit right with them to harass these two victims further, even if they didn't know anything about how Andi and George were conducting their investigation. Andi still wanted to know what exactly they had planned to do at the cabin, but not urgently enough to dive deeper into the minds of the arthropods there, especially if it didn't contribute to them solving the case.

"And that would be?" George had a way of intonating his sentences that made his true feelings perfectly clear. In this case wariness paired with a dose of annoyance. They had way too many suspects as it was. Shireen ignored the subtext with her usual cheer, tapping on her tablet with the energy of the Duracell bunny.

"We already know the two left Harvard and went to Yale after the rape and subsequent intimidation by Portius, Dyson & Partners."

"Yes." Andi looked at the screen where a list of names appeared, some connected through black lines. "They were lucky enough to get a scholarship there as well."

"Oh yes, they did." Shireen's eyes were sparkling with excitement now. "They applied at several foundations who give out scholarships, and with their grades, they were considered by three of them. The interesting bit is which of these foundations chose them."

The picture on the screen changed; the lines were now white, and one of the names was prominent. "Aquarius Foundation. They're picky about who they take on, and people like Tabitha and Josephine are not on their usual list." Shireen made a disgusted face.

"Let me guess—the usual list doesn't contain women or people of mixed heritage." The words poured like acid from George's lips.

"Mixed heritage, African American, Asian American, female, queer, all reasons to not be chosen by them. And yet they got the scholarship. Guess why."

"Shireen, please," Andi groaned.

"Fine. If you insist on being a spoilsport...." Shireen pouted briefly. "I'm not entirely sure this is the reason they were accepted, but the legal counsel for the Aquarius Foundation is Gartner & Partners, and Gideon Gartner is a member of their board. Coincidence? I don't think so."

George whistled. "That's interesting indeed. I didn't peg Gideon Gartner as so conservative, though."

Shireen shrugged. "That man has his fingers in many pies. His law firm also regularly donates to the LGBTQ youth shelter in their neighborhood, and every lawyer in his firm has to take on one pro bono case per year for people who can't afford a high-priced lawyer, which means they defend a lot of nonwhite people every year. If you ask me, Gideon Gartner likes to be on top of everything. The Aquarius Foundation has many rich, influential donors, many of whom have employed the services of Gartner & Partners."

Andi stared at the screen with the names of firms, companies, foundations, and charities, all of them interwoven and connected through a list of recurring names. He wasn't surprised to see the names Miller, McHill, and Portius as well. A caterpillar's weave indeed, with no hope to ever find the starting point. "Can you keep looking into Gartner?" It was a hunch, something his gut instinct told him to do, and Andi trusted his unconscious more than his senses, which were quite unreliable, as he knew only too well from his connection with the arthropods.

"Will do. Whatever I find, I'll text you. Now, shoo." Shireen waved them away, already concentrating on her screen again. George and Andi turned toward the door. George was already reaching for his car keys in the back pocket of his jeans. "We're going to visit a lawyer?"

"We're going to visit a lawyer."

THIS TIME, the building where Gideon Gartner's law firm was located wasn't freshly fumigated and the arthropods had returned, most probably in vaster numbers than before, something humans didn't seem to understand. If the infestation was on a normal level, it made little sense to fumigate because the then empty territories were like magnets drawing even more creepy crawlers in. As it was, the house was teeming with everything from silverfish to roaches, spiders, flies, mites, and pill bugs. Their vast numbers gave Andi a multilayered picture with so much more dimension than what he had seen with just his human senses. The first thing he realized once they were led into Gartner's office was the silk protein clinging to the handlebars of his wheelchair. Because he was distracted, he let George take over the conversation.

"Detectives Donovan and Hayes! What a pleasure to see you again. To what do I owe the honor?"

Interestingly enough, Gartner really was happy to see them. There was no spike in adrenaline or anything. Just the general pheromone signature indicating contentment. He must have felt completely safe, and Andi could see why. Shireen would have to find a lot more than just a possible link between Gartner and two victims of the three sons of the men who had made him a victim, and wasn't that sentence an ugly summary of the entire case? Until Shireen found more about Gartner and his possible connections, all they had was the silk protein Andi just sensed. And there was no way they would ever get a warrant for that.

"Well, Mr. Gartner," George lifted his right brow in a conspiratorial manner. "We had to investigate two women who briefly were suspects for the murder of McHill, Portius, and Miller, and imagine our surprise when we found out they got their scholarship to finish their studies at Yale from a foundation you're a member of."

Gartner tapped the side of his nose.

"You mean the Aquarius Foundation."

"Yes, the Aquarius Foundation, who granted a scholarship to two women of color, something it has never done before or after. Women who had been raped by the sons of the men who put you in a wheelchair."

"Well, I heard of their plight back then and decided to help where Portius, McHill, and Miller had chosen to intimidate."

"That was very generous of you." George's entire body language projected calm and laid-back. It was a trick that often loosened the tongues of suspects. Andi doubted it would work on Gartner, though. The man was a veteran hardened in countless battles in court, no doubt knowing all intimidation tactics in the book and some that were only passed on from lawyer's mouth to lawyer's ear. It was worth a shot, though.

"Not really. As I already told you, I was fortunate enough to profit from the horrible turn my life had taken. I only thought it just to help others as well. Spreading the goodness, so to speak." Gartner opened his arms wide. Andi almost believed his philanthropist shtick. The man was good.

"By mentoring two women who might one day help you get your revenge on the men who put you in a wheelchair." George was fishing, and his words didn't match the way he was lounging on the chair, which was exactly like he wanted it to be. Gartner smiled broadly, obviously not falling for George's trick.

"Life works in mysterious ways, don't you agree, Detectives?"

"Yes. And sometimes its workings are downright sweet, aren't they?" George smiled as well. Andi wasn't sure if this was him still trying to play Gartner or if he truly meant it. Andi was leaning toward the second, because fooling the lawyer in front of them was close to impossible.

"Yes, it is." Gartner made another broad gesture with his hands. "Is there anything else I can help you with?"

"No, thank you for your time, Mr. Gartner. Have a nice afternoon." George got up and Andi followed, nodding toward Gartner. He was sure they had found the caterpillar who had woven the impenetrable cocoon, but it was too well hidden beneath countless threads to be caught. Or at least it thought it was too clever. Perhaps Shireen would prove it wrong.

In the car, George stared ahead for a moment before he started the engine. "He's involved, isn't he?"

"Definitely. There was silk protein on his wheelchair. The same as on Josephine, Tabitha, the two female assassins, and the victims. He did have contact with either one of them or perhaps all, and I bet he's up to his ears in this whole case."

"Any chance we can prove it?"

"Depends on Shireen and what she's able to find. I wouldn't get my hopes up. He's had an entire lifetime to plan his revenge."

George groaned. "I hate this."

"That we probably won't be able to get him?"

"That too. No, the fact that one of the theories we discarded as too unlikely turns out to have been accurate."

"We didn't know, we couldn't know, and we followed logic. Logic isn't always right, as we both know." Andi wasn't happy about the turn of events either, but there was no way they could have approached the case differently, and if Gartner was as thorough as Andi suspected, it wouldn't have done them any good. The outcome would have been the same.

"Let me ask Shireen if she has found something else. If not, I suggest we drive by Dominic McHill's house to see if there was foul play involved in his death or if we can leave it to Narcotics."

George was in agreement, and after Shireen had told him to have a little more patience, they drove to Thrasher Drive. Dominic McHill's house was still taped off, which didn't hinder Andi in the slightest. One quick dip into the minds of the arthropods revealed McHill had indeed been alone when he had taken the lethal dose of heroin. Nobody had forced his hand, nobody had been there, and Andi wondered who would mourn his death. Somehow he didn't think Sophia McHill would be overly sad. He closed his eyes for a moment, wondering how this tangle of toxic ties they had unearthed during their investigations would resolve itself. He wasn't very optimistic it would do so at all.

"Nobody was here when he died. Doesn't mean it wasn't murder, doesn't mean the H he bought wasn't laced on purpose. Nothing we can prove one way or another. The report from Narcotics says his dealer is known for diluting his merchandise. I'm inclined to write this off as a tragic accident." Andi shrugged. "Well, a foreseeable accident. Let's call it a day. Our own reports are mostly done, Gartner won't go anywhere, he's too experienced to panic, I have no desire to see the chief again today, and I'm hungry."

George nodded. He seemed almost relieved that there wasn't a new lead to be found. Andi could relate. "Let's get takeout at that Indian place and have a nice meal on your veranda. Sound good?"

"Sounds perfect." Andi grinned happily.

THE CURRY was wonderfully spicy, the mango lassi cool and soothing in comparison, the raisins in the rice easy to find and remove, and the paneer just the right kind of soft. Andi leaned back in his lounge chair, completely sated and ready for a nap. George reached for his beer, staring into the garden.

"We have to decide what we're going to do about the chief."

Andi sighed. "I was under the impression you already knew what you wanted to do."

"I do. Doesn't mean I'm not going to discuss it with you, especially since it's probably going to affect you more than me, depending on how things go."

"Explain." Andi had a pretty good idea what George meant. He just thought it a good idea to have it all spelled out once before he decided to bring even more drama into his life—and drama it would be, there was no doubt.

"This was the second time she basically told us to tamper with a case to make her look good. During the Castain case, she even took the case from us. I have it all in written form, our latest interactions a lot more detailed than what happened before. Plus we have the official reports, so there's little she can say to get out of it. Things are pretty clear-cut in our favor, but Chief Norris didn't get to her position by being stupid."

"Could have fooled me," Andi interrupted, which earned him a grin from George.

"Granted, she hides it well. Anyway, she has the means to make things ugly for us, depending on who IA is going to believe more."

"Which means there's a good chance they're going to look into all our cases."

"And not just ours. If things go really south, they might start sniffing through all your cases." George took a sip from his beer. "Are you absolutely sure they're all above suspicion?"

Andi hesitated, thinking back on all the cases he had solved. Most of them had ended with the culprits behind bars, and only a few had been too flimsy for the DA to succeed.

"They won't be finding anything in the reports, if that's what you mean. I've always been extremely careful." He hesitated. "And I think the accumulation of instances where my gut instinct was spot-on can be explained away with me being very intuitive, or so I hope."

"Sounds solid." George was playing with the label on the beer bottle, ripping tiny pieces of paper off the glass. "Or as solid as it can get."

"You're not sure what to do?"

After a long silence, George answered, "No. I want to get rid of her because at this point this isn't merely about you and me anymore. She's willing to tamper with cases for her personal gain or out of spite against us, which is not a desirable trait in somebody who's in charge of an entire precinct. Her inability to differentiate between personal and professional life makes her unfit to be chief. And then there's you." George sat up in his chair and stared directly at Andi.

"Me?"

"Yes. I feel responsible for you, not just because you're my partner, but also because I really like you, which has never happened to me before, and because you need somebody in your corner."

Andi opened his mouth to object, but George wouldn't let him. "You've helped so many people at great personal cost, and I can see how it's getting worse. I don't want to add to that burden by starting a war with the chief."

Andi snorted. "In case you haven't noticed, we *are* at war with the chief. And I'd rather do the final battle against her with the prospect of things getting back to normal afterward than stay in this precarious situation we have now where everything we do can be potentially used against us. You said it yourself—she's not stupid, and I bet you my house she's already gathering evidence against us. If you think we have enough to get rid of her before she can launch an attack, I'm all for doing it."

"I never realized you can be so violent." George raised his bottle in Andi's direction. "Grumpy and antisocial, yes, but not downright violent."

"I only let it out when needed. Too much hassle, usually." Andi shrugged. His belly was comfortably filled, demanding to rest, and George's presence helped him keep the world of arthropods at bay. As far as Andi was concerned, the evening couldn't get any better.

"Fine. You're right, of course. I'm going to lodge the formal complaint tomorrow."

Andi closed his eyes. "Do that. It's going to be okay. You'll see."

"I'll make it so." George sounded determined. Andi let his voice wash over him, chasing away all the bad and giving him a rare moment of peace. He just wished it could go on forever.

24. THE CATERPILLAR'S COCOON

AFTER THEIR talk the evening before, George felt better about his decision to go against Chief Norris. Even though he still felt the weight of responsibility, having heard Andi's pragmatic take on things had helped him gain perspective. The first thing he did in the morning before he started making breakfast was send the file he had compiled to IA. In a way it was freeing to have it out of the way. Now he could concentrate on closing their case, even though he had given up on putting *all* of the culprits behind bars.

The precinct was unusually quiet, at least compared to the last few days, what with all the drama surrounding Daniel Holway's escape and death. Gentry and Mescew were at their desks, greeting them with nods. Andi didn't waste time to get to their whiteboards, staring intently at all the lines and names while murmuring something about a caterpillar's cocoon. George was curious, so he asked him about it. "Don't you mean a spider's web?"

"No. That wouldn't be so complicated. One net, one spider in the middle or to the side, waiting to strike. This case is a lot more intricate."

When George only looked at him blankly, not understanding what this explanation had to do with caterpillars, Andi pinched the bridge of his nose. "The caterpillars of the ermine moth weaves a huge net to hide under. It can cover entire trees and protects the caterpillars from predators while they are eating. It's huge, way bigger than anything a spider could weave, and intricate because it's done by many, and it's perfect for hiding. Basically what Gideon Gartner has done with this case. Though he did have a solid base to work with, considering what charming individuals our victims were."

Andi was right, George realized with sudden clarity; the entire case was a multidimensional web with the victims at the heart and the predators partially out of reach, hidden behind layers of years and trickery. The image frustrated George to no end while he sat down at his computer.

Over the course of the night, some new information had trickled in from various sources. Timmy Delain had sent them a notification about Tamara Portius having successfully fought her husband's will. It seemed she had found the contract between her father and her husband about two-thirds of the money belonging to her. Apparently it was clear-cut enough for Portius, Dyson & Partners to refrain from fighting it, which meant the whole ordeal had ended well for at least one participant. Two, because George was sure Theodora had feathered her own nest just like she claimed, and she surely wasn't too upset about her husband's death. Sophia McHill was now free of her husband, but she had also lost her son. Andi had mentioned he didn't believe she would grieve, an assessment that probably stemmed from his less than stellar experiences with his own mother. No matter how distant mother and son had grown, George was sure Sophia felt the loss of her child. It was something he had to believe in, because when mothers stopped mourning their sons, what kind of world did they live in? A final report from Narcotics stated they had arrested the dealer who had sold Dominic the laced heroin. The batch had killed two more addicts the police knew of and probably a few more they would never hear about. There was still a bad aftertaste for George when he thought how beautifully the timing lined up, but sometimes, on very rare occasions, what looked like a duck was really a goose. He wondered if geese could be eaten with dumplings and *blaukraut* as well.

A text from Shireen had them walking over to her space, where she greeted them with a serious expression. "I have news, and you won't like it."

George felt his shoulders sagging. The morning was off to a wonderful start. "Give it to us."

"I looked into Gideon Gartner again, this time combing through everybody and everything related to the case." She tapped her tablet and the flat-screen on the wall came to life, showing another net, this one even more elaborate than the one on their whiteboards.

"As I've already told you, Gideon Gartner has his hands in many pies, just like the three victims, though he's a lot more careful and discreet about his less savory endeavors, so to speak." She waved her hand around, making her bracelets clink. "On the other hand, one could argue this is normal in the circles he frequents."

"You're sounding very posh today, Shireen." Andi didn't take his eyes off the screen while teasing her.

"I'm just trying to give things a little polish." She flipped Andi off and turned toward George. "Anyway, I found things. Many things. Unfortunately, it's just crumbs, and they're not leading anywhere, least to the witch's house."

"You mean out of the woods?" George was confused. Shireen had a knack for getting her metaphors mixed up.

"No. The riches were at the witch's house. Why would we want to leave the forest?" She sounded as if she couldn't believe he was that dense.

"Could we stop with the fairy tales, please? Shireen, do we have something or not?" Andi did his usual impression of a hedgehog with a sore nose.

Shireen's shoulders slumped a bit. "I'm sorry, we don't have enough. Besides the glaring fact that he's in a wheelchair because of Portius, Miller, and McHill, I can tie Gartner to the three victims and the crime in several indirect ways, but nothing a good defense lawyer wouldn't blow right out of the courtroom. Nothing a DA would risk using for that exact reason. If it even made it to court."

"Tell us anyway." George wanted to know. Perhaps there was a way….

"First of all, I took a closer look at the scholarships for Tabitha Clément and Josephine Garr, the ones they got for Yale. They were definitely paid by Aquarius Foundation, but I have no evidence whatsoever that Gartner somehow intervened on their behalf. The way they make it look, the foundation helped Tabitha and Josephine because of their excellent grades, which is valid because the two were at the top of their classes. They were also the only nonwhite, nonmale students ever to receive a scholarship from Aquarius, but again, I can't tie that back to Gartner. It's completely circumstantial."

"Okay. First dead end. Go on." George did nothing to hide his frustration. They might be able to talk to somebody at the foundation, but with things being so far in the past, witnesses were hardly reliable, not to mention hard to find. And even if somebody did talk, what would it prove? That Gideon Gartner was a philanthropist? Not the image George wanted a jury to get of him.

"I also found a connection to Peter LaFarge, the man who put out the hit on the three victims. One of his companies was a client of Gartner & Partners, though not him personally."

"Doesn't mean he didn't know him." Andi sounded grim.

"No, it doesn't. Which brings us to the contract I so conveniently found on the darknet."

"The way you say it makes me think something is very wrong." George looked at her. Shireen's expression was grim.

"I think I was supposed to find it, because for somebody who was careless enough to let me hack him, he surely is damn good at vanishing without a trace. If I had to make a guess, I'd say our newbie broker never existed in the first place. The timing works as well. I mean, what are the chances of me finding a kill contract so shortly after the victims died?"

"You mean this was meant to throw us off track? That Daniel Holway and Peter LaFarge were tricked?" George could easily believe it. A genius move, letting the police find a professional killer to blur the trace of the real one. And it would have worked perfectly hadn't it been for Andi and his army of informants.

"The longer I think about it, the surer I am." Shireen furrowed her brows. "That Holway was greedy enough to take the money without having made the kill must have made the person who cooked this up very happy. And come to think of it, finding him the first time was a little too easy as well. As if somebody had prepared the information for me to find. I know—" She held up her hand. "—everybody makes mistakes, but in hindsight, I shouldn't have been able to trace him so quickly. The offer of another contract was probably a ruse to keep him in the city long enough to give us a realistic chance to find him. I mean, having a suspect at large is one thing, but having said suspect behind bars? Perfect."

As much as George hated it, Shireen was right. If Holway hadn't escaped, he was sure Chief Norris would have done everything in her power to make him the prime suspect regardless of what Andi and George said, effectively erasing the traces of the real killers. If it weren't for Andi, they wouldn't have found the DNA of the female on the chains and would have never known who did the actual killing. It was beautiful, if nauseating.

"Did you find any recent connections between Gartner and Tabitha and Josephine?" George saw the answer in Shireen's defeated look even before she shook her head.

"No, they were either super careful, or the thing with the foundation really is just a coincidence."

"You don't think so?"

"No. There are too many of those connecting back to Gartner. But as I said, nothing solid. No money to be traced, no contracts or documents, nothing. If he really is behind all this, he did a marvelous job of hiding all the evidence. Or not creating any at all."

"Nothing that would get us a warrant." Andi sounded resigned.

"No. Sorry."

"It's fine, Shireen. You did your best. Gartner is just very good at this. He had his entire life to plan his revenge. Perhaps you could try and find that second contract on the darknet? That would be helpful." George patted her arm, ignoring her furrowed brows, which told him not to get his hopes up. As it seemed, hope was all they had left in this case. He turned to Andi. "Back to the whiteboard?"

"Back to the whiteboard."

"WHAT DO you think, should we pay Gartner's home a visit?" George was playing with the cap of one of his markers. Andi was sitting on his desk, staring at the names and lines.

"Of course we will, but I don't think anything will come of it. He definitely wasn't there when the three victims were killed, so there's nothing with which we can tie him to the murder. And the silk protein on his wheelchair is circumstantial at best. It could have come from anybody using a lotion with silk protein in it. That's how miniscule the traces are. I just know it's the same because…." Andi trailed off, clearly trying to find words George would understand. "The ratio of silk and DNA and other things is the same. That's how I know it wasn't some random person. Anyway, it's nothing a test could show. It's definitely not enough to get us a warrant, especially since I don't see how we can explain that we just happened to get a sample from the wheelchair."

"Yeah, I can see how that wouldn't go over well. Hell and damnation!" George wasn't one to swear, but this situation warranted it. He stared at the whiteboard some more, hoping it would offer some divine insight, but as was typical for whiteboards, it just stood there in a Zen-like state. George put his marker back down. "Let's go now. Perhaps we'll be lucky. I mean, Castain was stupid enough to have evidence at his house."

"Yes, but Castain was a self-entitled, arrogant, foolish prick, whereas Gideon Gartner is a cunning old fox who had *decades* to plan this whole thing."

"Everybody makes mistakes?" George tried.

Andi just shook his head. "I'm afraid not." He grabbed his jacket from his office chair. "Let's go anyway."

They had just reached the door leading out of the bullpen when it opened and Bill Waters, the DA for Charleston, stepped inside. His graying hair was standing up in odd angles, he was wearing khakis and a polo shirt that did nothing to hide his trim physique despite his nearly sixty-two years. *Must be all that golfing*, George thought when Waters's sharp gaze landed on them.

"Detectives Hayes and Donovan, the men I wanted to talk to."

And there went their trip to Gideon Gartner's home. "DA Waters, how can we help?" He gestured for the man to follow Andi, who had already turned and was striding toward one of the conference rooms at the back of the bullpen. Waters waited till they were inside the smallest and George had closed the door.

"The murder with the three victims. Big thing." Waters started pacing around the five tables forming a U.

George looked at Andi. They had finished their reports the day before, including the ties Gideon Gartner had to Tabitha and Josephine. He was surprised Waters had already read them. Then again, the case was huge, with great impact for the city, losing three rich and influential men. Of course it took precedence.

"Yes?" George talked while Andi just stood there, watching Waters.

"You exonerated the prime suspect, this Holway guy, who would have been a very convenient culprit because he's dead. Would have spared me a lot of trouble." Apparently Waters had taken a page from Chief Norris's book, or so George thought until the DA kept on talking. "I know you wouldn't have done that without good reason, and the DNA from those other murder cases proves you were right." Waters was looking directly at Andi, which George would have taken as an offense if he hadn't known that Waters knew it was Andi who provided the things he needed. These two had known each other for almost as long as Andi was a detective. "Tell me something good, Hayes. Tell me there's a chance we can nail the bastard who gave the kill order."

Andi slowly shook his head. "Not this time, Waters. I'm sorry. All we have is circumstantial at best."

"Fuck." Waters slumped on one of the chairs. "This is not looking good." He rubbed his face with his right hand.

"Will this fall back on you?" George knew it would ultimately fall back on him and Andi, but the DA always had a part, especially in high-profile cases that made the news.

"Don't worry about me. Or yourself. I'm going to spin this to show the Charleston PD is so good, they even find connections to international crimes. Strictly speaking, the case is federal anyway because the killers are obviously operating internationally, no matter how high the odds are for the contractor being from here. Or would it fall to the CIA? I'm not sure. Jurisdiction could be complicated here. As far as I heard, the only reason the FBI hasn't knocked on your door yet is because they are so woefully understaffed, they can hardly man the hot cases. Something that's been brewing for what, ten years, I think it said in the report about the first murder with the female DNA, is at the very end of their list of priorities. It would be wonderful if you could find anything that's not circumstantial." Waters tapped his chin with his right forefinger.

"I'm sorry, Waters." Andi looked the man directly in the eye, his voice conveying how serious he was.

"I'd say it's fine, Hayes, but we both know I'd be lying. I'm afraid I've gotten too used to winning, thanks to you." Waters shook his head. "You make it easy for my office most of the time. Perhaps it's a good thing we have to take a defeat sometimes." A weak smile graced Waters's face. "I've got to go. If you find anything helpful, inform me immediately, okay?"

"We will." Andi nodded in both confirmation and goodbye. Waters left the conference room with his head held high and the confident stride people expected of him.

"There goes the old warhorse." The hint of affection in Andi's voice made George turn toward him. His partner had never indicated he felt anything but his usual indifference for Waters.

"You like him?" He must have sounded incredulous because Andi chuckled.

"Come on, George. I do like some people, on occasion. You, Shireen, Evangeline. It's not that surprising."

"I just never suspected Bill Waters to be part of our illustrious circle."

"What can I say? I like variety." Andi was now grinning broadly.

"I'm not sure if you're pulling my leg or not." George shook his head. He liked seeing Andi carefree for once. "You still up for driving to Gartner's home?"

"Yes. Let's get it over with."

GIDEON GARTNER'S house was a beautiful Southern Belle with the typical columns on the generous porch and a balcony wrapping around the entire second floor. It was painted a vibrant orange, which looked gorgeous among the tamer beige, light yellow, and white of its neighbors.

The location downtown also meant they could simply take a stroll around the neighborhood without drawing any attention when they sat down for a break on one of the benches along the walkway. George had given Andi two ibuprofen and made a mental note to do some additional reading on pain medication. His partner wasn't taking the heavyweights, but George already knew swallowing them in the quantities Andi did wasn't good, even if they were prescription free.

The bench was only a few feet from the driveway of Gartner's house, which meant Andi didn't have to stretch his senses too far. George slung his arm around Andi's shoulders like a lover would, leaning close to him, both as a cover for anybody who might be too interested in them as well as to be close enough when Andi started talking so that nobody else would hear. It also gave George the opportunity to keep Andi stable once he dove into that world beneath their own that was so alien to George. Leaning in, he could smell a hint of the chamomile soap Andi used. The odors of the city mixed with the remnants of the tacos they had had on their way to downtown, layered with Andi's natural scent, which George found more fascinating than he had any business doing.

Andi took a deep breath, put his head on George's shoulder in a rare gesture of openness, and started talking, translating what he was seeing.

"It's loud, so much noise here, all the time, thumping and screeching and pounding, so many blobs, dogs, cats, the gardens here are too clean, not many places to feed, to hide, to live, barren, almost, the houses are good, old, many nooks and crannies, rotting wood, decent hiding spots, the house is quiet most of the time, only four blobs there, two always cleaning, taking the food away, one producing food in the kitchen, what a great place, damp spots, a bit moldy where the pipe has been leaking, not many plants, a room full of books, more dust, the wood tastes good, I need a place to lay the eggs, silverfish in the bathroom, many of them, happy, healthy, thriving, the cellar's dark and damp, perfect, tiles on the floor, new, there's a skeleton behind one of the walls, too old, nobody knows, no food, just bones, ignore it, the thumping is hollow here, not so bad, I'm so tired, hungry, need to build a new net, the colony is getting too big, we need a new nest, not here, the ground's too hard, no way to build more tunnels, the space behind the wardrobe is perfect, so many, prey, I kill one of them, they're so easy to catch with their many legs and I'm poisonous, sated, nothing there, the breeze in the bedroom is too strong, I'm sleeping, found the perfect spot, everything's liquid, the skin is too tight, I need, I need, I'm gone, where am I, where is, who was I, gone, gone, dripping, changing, turning, away, away, so deep—"

"Andi! Come back! I need you here!" George was squeezing Andi's side, trying to shake him out of his trance. This time, Andi reacted fairly quickly, his gaze focusing back on George.

"Man, I hate that."

"Everything all right, Andi?"

His partner shuddered. "There were some caterpillars undergoing transformation to a butterfly. It's so weird, being all liquid while knowing you're not."

George could only stare. "I don't think I want to even imagine that."

"Trust me, you don't want to feel it either."

"Then let's ignore it in favor of the skeleton you said was in Gartner's wall. Did you mean that literally, or was it just a euphemism for finding something we can get him with?" George very firmly focused his thoughts on this information.

"Sorry, as much as it galls me to say it, but that skeleton has been there for a long time. Gartner bought this house ten years ago, correct?"

George furrowed his brows. They had done their homework on the house during the taco break. Well, Shireen had done the homework and sent it to them. "I think it was eleven. How old are the bones?"

"Hard to say. At least twenty years, if not older. I could find no traces of memories of a giant feast, which means it's been so long the resident arthropods have forgotten all about it. And something big like that tends to leave a huge impression."

"What if the house has been fumigated at some point? Wouldn't the memory be gone as well?"

"Not necessarily. It depends on how far in the past the incident was. Let's say the person was killed by Gartner and he put the corpse behind the wall, then fumigated the house a few months later. Even if all the arthropods died—which is unlikely in a house with a cellar like that—the event itself would still be recent enough for the new arthropods to register as something big. The bigger the timespan between the kill and the fumigation, the greater the chances for the memory of the kill to fade."

George felt a headache coming his way. Andi had explained how the memory of arthropods worked—which was completely different to human memory, sometimes a lot more accurate, at other times even hazier than the recounting of college students high on weed and drunk from cheap beer. "How can you tell the length of the timespan?"

"It's not a science. Lots of it is experience, plus guesswork. There's an ant colony living under the porch. The nest is getting too small for them, and they need to expand. As you know, the memory of social insects is a lot more precise than that of solitary insects. That colony has been in the house for at least fifteen dead spaces, and they can't remember the kill, which means they weren't there when it took place. This in turn means the skeleton has been there for at least twenty years if not more, taking into account that the counting of the dead spaces is always tricky and more of a plus/minus two or three thing and the fact that it takes a body a year to decompose if it's placed in soil. Behind a wall in a cellar, I'd say it takes longer. We'd have to ask Evangeline for detailed information. There are no clothes on the skeleton anymore, and they only start decomposing after about a year when the chemicals the body produces begin eating away at them. So I take the fifteen dead spaces the ants have memorized, add two more to be on the safe side, then three more to take into account that for the ants not thinking the skeleton was a big thing, it had to be nothing but bones when the colony started, which makes twenty years in total. If we were to decide we want to know who the victim could be, I would start looking into the history of the house, going backwards from 2000."

"Which we are not going to do because we can't explain how we knew about the bones in the first place."

"Welcome to my world." Andi groaned and leaned more heavily on George's shoulder.

"Did you sense anything else? Anything you didn't mention?"

"No. Nothing incriminating."

"Fuck."

"Yes, fuck. Can we go home now? I'm tired." Andi made no move to lift his head from George's shoulder. With some difficulty, he managed to heave his partner up. Because Andi seemed to be in a cuddling mood, another indicator of how stressed he was, George kept his arm around Andi's shoulders while they strolled back to the Escalade, all the time trying to not think about how right it felt to have Andi there.

They were just passing a quaint little café that had George thinking he could use some caffeine, when Andi suddenly tensed in his arms. Not sure what was going on, he followed his partner's lead, turning slightly so that Andi's back was toward the café. The sudden brush of Andi's lips on his couldn't have surprised George more if it had happened in front of the chief in the precinct. Andi mumbled into his mouth. "They're here. Fucking *here*."

George tightened his arms around Andi, doing his best not to be obvious while trying to take his surroundings in.

"Who is here?" he whispered back, sharing his breath with Andi.

"The killers. It's them. Silk, and the blood is right and rich and one is a little older, the other related, so healthy, not ovulating this time, it's the same silk, the same combination, it's them."

George didn't question what Andi was telling him. Instead he walked him backward toward the wall of the café next to the huge window, chuckling softly as if they were a couple deeply in love. *And wouldn't that be nice?* The thought flashed through his mind like lightning, there and gone, superseded by the need to catch their killers who seemingly had been served to them by fate.

"Where are they?"

"Inside, they're just getting their coffee."

"Have they seen us?"

"No, they're focused on the pastries."

"Good, let's take a seat here. I'll go inside to get us some coffee, see where they'll sit down. You get Forard here."

He led Andi to the next free table, which was away from the window, in a shadowy spot. To keep up the cover, he gave Andi a peck on his lips before he went inside. The café was moderately full, mainly tourists looking for some refreshment. To the trained eye, the two assassins stuck out like sore thumbs. They were Caucasian, sitting in a corner from where they could view the entire room, especially the exits, their body language relaxed. The cups with the coffee in front of them were steaming; they both wore bright summer tunics with shorts and flip-flops. If they had realized George was a threat, they weren't showing it. George didn't risk tipping his hand by staring at them too long. Just a casual glance, as one might give a room while waiting for an order. Then he took out his phone, again doing what people usually did in waiting situations, thumbing through it to see if Andi had sent a text. There was just a thumb up plus *ETA 10*. Ten minutes until Forard would be here. George opened a game of Mahjong on his cell, finding it easier to really play something instead of simply pretending.

After he got his coffee and Andi's tea, not making any small talk besides the usual pleasantries, he went back outside where his partner was waiting. Andi's gaze was unfocused; he was undoubtedly keeping an eye—eyes? Antenna? Legs? Smelling organ?—on the two women inside. He wasn't saying anything, clearly concentrating, which meant George could relax a bit and instead start worrying about the situation at hand. There were too many people here, and he doubted the two women would come with them willingly. He hadn't seen any obvious weapons, not meaning there weren't any. In fact it would be stupid to assume the killers wouldn't be armed. Hell, Holway had worn three knives and a gun while cleaning his other weapons. While he was still mulling over how to best approach the situation, Andi's cell vibrated. George reached for it when his partner didn't give any indication that it had even registered with him. It was a text from Forard.

We're here.

George looked around but couldn't see anybody. Good.

Not sure how to proceed, he typed.

What does Hayes say?

George poked Andi until he looked at the screen George was showing him. After a moment, he started to type.

Suspects inside at back. Two exits additional to entrance. Go to back, windows at bathrooms need to be covered. We go in and pull a stupid police stunt, make them run. Position two people at entrance.

A thumbs-up appeared. George had to admit the plan wasn't bad. Making the two assassins run—or rather try to leave unobtrusively while the two bumbling cops tried to find somebody—was the likeliest way to avoid any casualties among the civilians.

When the *In position* text appeared a few moments later, Andi and George got up, taking out their badges in the process. They entered the café as loudly as they could, Andi going to the first table on the right while George went to the first on the left, introducing himself as a detective and asking if they could help him with an ongoing murder investigation. He heard Andi doing the same song and dance, and in the corner of his eye he saw the two women, both of them almost as tall as he was, one blond, the other with chestnut hair, getting up and calmly walking toward the bathrooms. He waited till they were out of sight before he thanked the two confused men for their help. Andi was already on his way over, almost tripping over a chair. George was at his side in a flash, gripping his elbow to steer him while he whipped out his cell with the other hand, hitting the speed dial for Forard's cell. As soon as the call connected, he held it next to Andi so Forard could hear what his partner was saying.

"They're in the bathroom, preparing to go through the window at the very end. Careful, they have knives and two guns, wait till both are out, there's a hole in the fence leading to the house next door, cover it, it's big enough to slip through, don't let them go too far right, there's a car behind that tree, open, try to herd them toward the left, the wall is solid, the top full of shards, somebody wants to keep the doves away, foolish, they don't care about shards, but blobs do, the three men from behind the trash need to make their move now, yes, very good, you've got them, no, be careful, the knives, so quick, she's reaching for the gun, the shards, blood, delicious blood, smearing on the wall, duck—"

George ended the call when he heard a gunshot at the back, indicating the two contract killers were resisting arrest. They quickly made their way outside, in time to see Forard trying to wrestle a gun from the hand of the blond while two of his men were trying to herd the brunet woman against the wall. It wasn't going well. Two other men were on the ground, unconscious, at least George hoped they were. There were no signs of too much blood on them suggesting they were dying. Another gunshot resounded, plaster falling from the wall where the bullet had hit, followed by an angry bellow from Forard and a clattering when metal hit stone. George dove forward to get the weapon before the blond had a chance to retrieve it. Forard was on his back, gasping. The pained yelp of another man had George redirecting his focus to the brunet woman, who had managed to fell one of her attackers. The remaining one was hesitating, merely following her along the wall without engaging. The blond, who had managed to evade Forard's other man, was now next to her partner. Both of them had knives, and the brunet was taking another gun out of her purse, which she had taken up from the ground in a quick maneuver. George heard the telltale clicking of a gun being cocked, this time at his back. Andi's voice was steady, cold.

"Drop your weapons."

Both women tensed; George could see them weighing their chances. They weren't as bad as George would have wished. Four of Forard's men were down for good, the two who were still standing were positioned right and left of George, and Forard himself was back on his feet but swaying slightly. He did have his gun out, though George wasn't sure if that would do them any good. These women had proven impressively that a few SWAT members weren't a problem for them. George steadied the weapon he had taken from the ground, aiming at the brunet. Andi talked again.

"I said drop your weapons."

There was a waver in Andi's voice. From the corner of his eye, George could see his partner was so tense he was close to snapping, meaning he hadn't been able to close the connection to the arthropods before shit hit the fan. It also meant Andi knew a lot more about the mental state of these women than George or anybody else could deduce from their body language. He risked a direct glance at Andi, who had his weapon firmly trained on the blond.

"Don't. It won't do you any good."

George's body reacted before the words truly registered in his brain. It was something about the way Andi angled his body, nothing anybody else watching him would have seen, just something George knew and recognized because he had spent so much time getting attuned to his partner's body language. He fired a shot at the brunet, aiming for her right shoulder, forcing her to drop her gun. A second shot rang out, followed by a scream of pain and the glittering of a knife bouncing on the ground. Andi had taken care of the blond. Forard and the two SWAT members surged forward, Forard going for the blond while his partners got the brunet in handcuffs. Both women were cursing up a storm in a language George thought might be Croatian, but he wasn't sure. They were both wounded, the blood smearing their brightly colored tunics, small puddles forming at their feet. Andi had hit the blond in her right leg. She was still standing, though, spitting on the ground when Forard dragged her toward the gate that would lead them out of the backyard. By now they had a healthy crowd of spectators, who George tried to fend off while the two women were led away. A siren close by told him backup was on the way, and once the beat officers arrived, they hastened to fence the scene of the crime off.

"Hayes. Another hunch?" Forard didn't even raise a brow when he approached them. He was favoring his left leg, and George could see a bruise forming on his forehead. The blond had obviously not held back.

Andi shrugged, leaned heavily on George. He had been exhausted before, but now the dark circles under his eyes made him look like the realistic impression of a skull. George would have loved nothing more than to take his partner home and put him into bed. With the catching of the two killers, that wasn't in the cards. What he could do was divert some attention from Andi to Forard's wounds and himself.

"Not this time. We saw them entering the café and got a glimpse of one of the guns when the blond one paid. We thought it was a good idea to keep an eye on them because they acted suspiciously. I wouldn't be surprised if they had planned to rob the café. How are you doing, by the way? When you went down, I thought she got you hard."

The first part was completely bogus, and Forard's skeptical look said as much. The second was a thinly veiled attempt to derail Forard, and the leader of the SWAT team was kind enough to let it happen.

"I'm fine. Nothing a few days of rest won't cure. I'm a bit more worried about Millner and Beaumont. The paramedics said they would be okay, though."

"I'm glad to hear that. And thank you for coming so quickly. Without you—" George shook his head. "Well, without you, I think we all can imagine what would have happened."

Forard didn't comment, just slapped George on the shoulder, wisely realizing Andi would probably fall over if he did the same to him.

"I wouldn't be so sure about that. Hayes tends to have aces up his sleeves when you would expect him to draw a blank. As far as I'm concerned, this is another successful arrest, that's all I care about." George nodded, acknowledging Forard's silent promise to back them up.

"Thank you for that. We have to get to the precinct now."

"Yeah, see you there." Forard waved and went into the café, probably to get himself some caffeine. After he had collected two blood samples from the ground, using a handkerchief and stuffing it into the plastic it had come in, George turned to Andi, who had somehow managed to stay on his feet.

"Come on, Andi. We need to go." George guided Andi to the Escalade, not liking the ashen color of his partner's skin. "Will you be all right?"

"Yeah. It's going to take a while to get the DNA from the blood and match it to the case. We should use it to find a plausible explanation as to why we want the DNA tested when all we suspect the women of is a possible robbery."

"Well, the way they leveled four SWAT team members should be incentive enough to look at them more closely. And if anybody gets suspicious, we keep it simple. We have the blood, it's only natural to look at it."

Andi massaged his temples. "That's actually a good idea. No sense wasting evidence, is there?"

"No. Anyway, once it's clear who they are, the FBI will be here in a flash, understaffed or not, and hopefully nobody's going to ask too many questions why we looked at the DNA."

"Certainly not the FBI. They will only care about the solve."

"And claim it for themselves." George had worked with the FBI often enough to know this.

"Another reason why they won't question how we found out. That would just mean more investigative work they don't have the resources for. And why would they waste what they don't have on a case that's already solved?"

"Sometimes human laziness is a good thing." George started the Escalade and drove them back to the precinct.

25. CLOSING A CASE, OPENING A CAN OF WORMS

As GEORGE had predicted, the FBI showed up in Charleston the moment CSI got confirmation of a DNA match with not only their murder case but the others with the previously unknown DNA as well. The blond who had provided the blood through the wound in her leg was the one whose DNA had been found in connection with the other cases. The second woman's DNA matched the sample from the one case where the police had found two traces. Both women carried false ID and refused to cooperate. They didn't even ask for a lawyer, instead waiting until the FBI appeared. Andi and George didn't get to interrogate them; the honor fell to a seasoned FBI agent who saw to it that nobody could listen in on his chat with the women. When he was done, he told Andi and George that the women— still no names, which made Andi suspect the FBI either knew them or had plans for them—had gotten the contract to kill Lawrence Miller, Alexander McHill, and David Hector Portius II through a broker called Swallow. They claimed they hadn't known there was another contract out for the men and that the stipulations for the kill had been very clear. Originally, the customer had asked for the men to drown while fully conscious, but when they had gotten to the cabin, the three victims had been dazed by ketamine, which finally confirmed what Tabitha and Josephine had done at the crime scene. Though what they had had in mind would remain a mystery because Andi had no inclination to go after them. Not looking a gift horse in the mouth, the assassins had taken the men with them, using their own ketamine spray to keep them docile. Apparently they always carried it for close-up kills, never knowing when it would come in handy. And since they knew the water would dissolve any traces of it before the victims were found, they didn't see why they shouldn't make their work easier. If anything, they were pragmatic. The reason why they had been in Charleston so soon again after having left it right after the assassination was because they were passing through on their way to another contract.

Andi sensing them in the café had been a stroke of sheer luck, one George said they more than deserved in this crazy case.

With the actual killers whisked away by the FBI, the official explanation being they were internationally wanted, which had the nice side effect of making Andi and George's work shine even more, Shireen concentrated on finding the broker, Swallow. She even managed to hack the person and find the payment—two point five million—for the kills. The money had traveled around the globe before it landed in Swallow's accounts, but Shireen managed to trace it to a company Gideon Gartner had a share of 40 percent in. Combined with all the other circumstantial evidence they had found, Gideon Gartner was arrested. He made bail after the initial twenty-four hours.

One of Waters's attorneys gathered everything they had and presented it to a judge, trying to convince the woman to admit the case to court. When Gartner's defense attorney was done shredding everything the attorney had presented, the judge threw the case out and Gideon Gartner was a free man again.

Andi wasn't entirely sure how he felt about it. The cop in him wanted everybody involved in the murder to pay, while another part of him, the one that saw justice as a prickly bitch, applauded the man for having executed his revenge so perfectly. Why Gartner had waited so long to kill his tormentors would remain a mystery, but Andi was sure it had to do with how the murder had been planned and executed—being able to erase or blur all the traces leading to him.

The news of Lester Miller being arrested for a case of fraud with one of his customers didn't help their case but was interesting enough they mentioned it in their final reports. Timmy Delain looked closely at the case, eager to impress Shireen. He found out the customer who had brought the charges against Miller was the son of a cousin of one of Gideon Gartner's partners. Interestingly enough, he didn't use the services of Gartner & Partners but turned to another law firm who did have ties with Gartner, but only in a professional capacity. It was another threadbare lead Gartner's lawyer had snipped with some well-placed words.

When they got the information that David Hector Portius III had been evicted from his office, Andi wasn't even surprised anymore. Again Timmy dug deeper, finding out David Hector III was absolutely inept when it came to handling money and had made some bad investments that had come back to bite him in the ass. Since he didn't have an office anymore and word of his precarious situation had gotten around, he was at the end of his rope. His house had been confiscated, as well as his car, and if there wasn't a miracle, he would end up on the streets. His mother, Tamara, hadn't shown any interest in helping her son, though that could be because she apparently was on a cruise through the Mediterranean at the moment. Peter LaFarge had been clever enough to leave the cruise ship when it anchored at the Bahamas, which didn't extradite people to the US. More than two-thirds of his money was distributed between Switzerland, the Bahamas, Ireland, and Monaco, which made freezing his accounts in the US more a gesture of principle than actually having an effect. Andi was a bit torn about the whole thing. He would have loved to see LaFarge pay for his crimes. On the other hand, the man had been nothing but a pawn for Gartner, which made his escape feel somehow justified. Andi wished Interpol and CIA good luck getting him, knowing he wasn't anywhere near their top ten list of dangerous people to catch.

George seemed to be content with how everything had played out because he was now fully focused on their showdown with Chief Norris.

She hadn't spoken to them since their last confrontation, not even to congratulate them on their impossible solve, and both Andi and George were waiting for the other shoe to drop. They had a meeting with somebody from IA this afternoon at Andi's house where they could speak freely. The officer, one Luke Gelman from Spartanburg, had suggested they meet outside the precinct, and Andi didn't know if this was good news or bad news. George had bought some groceries on their way to James Island and was currently preparing tea, sandwiches, and cookies for when their guest would arrive. Andi found it a very British thing to do but wasn't sure if mentioning it was such a good idea because George's father was Irish, not British. Pondering on the relationship between Brits and the Irish conveniently kept Andi from questioning why he liked having George in his house so much.

Two hours later, Luke Gelman arrived in a beige Dodge so nondescript it practically screamed "cop car in a cheap TV film." The man himself was pleasant, a little shorter than Andi, with dark hair, gray eyes, and a friendly smile. He eyed the sandwiches and cookies hungrily and with a rueful pat to the little belly protruding over his trousers.

"I really shouldn't," he said with a sigh before he took one of the sandwiches, ham and egg, cut in neat triangles, and with the mayo-mustard sauce George did so well. After Gelman had devoured the sandwich and drunk some of the lavender tea, he went straight to the point. Andi had to concentrate on what he was saying because the arthropods in the house were in an uproar over the intruder disrupting their usual tranquil routines. Especially the silverfish were appalled by the acid stink of the nail polish Gelman used against the nail fungus on his toes. Something about the chemical set them off like nothing Andi had ever encountered. Another fact to file away in his ever-growing library of sensory images. Thankfully he was doing better again, managing the impressions he was getting, though his control was still thin and ready to snap. He only hoped it would keep getting better, and not revert back to what it had been only a few weeks before.

"First of all, I want to stress that everything we talk about here is strictly confidential. I have read everything you've sent me, Detectives, and I can understand why you decided to take such drastic measures. Chief Norris's behavior is concerning, and we're currently looking into her affairs. We haven't talked to her yet, but you need to know that she submitted a formal complaint about you as well, citing insubordination." Gelman took a sip of his tea. "You don't seem surprised."

George shook his head. "Not really, no. It's the way she works. And the way our last confrontation went, I would have been surprised if she hadn't taken any measures."

"I see. Now, before we start, let me make two things very clear." Gelman put his cup down. "First, we always try to keep cases like yours as discreet as possible to protect the image of the police force as a whole. Which means we try to find amicable solutions before things escalate."

"So you're some kind of mediator?" Andi asked.

"Yes. If mediation fails, everything will go the official way, though I pride myself in saying I'm usually successful in finding compromises that leave everybody just mad enough at me to forget about quarreling with each other." He grinned at that, and Andi's respect for the man went up more than a few notches. Judging books by their cover—or toenails in this case—really was unwise.

"Now let's talk about the current situation. I did some research on you two, and to be honest, I don't understand why you aren't the chief's golden boys. Your solving rates are so impeccable, every precinct would be proud to have you. And that last case was brilliant."

Andi glanced at George, who cleared his throat. They had talked about how much they would reveal and decided that honesty was the best way. Of course they wouldn't mention Andi's *geschenk*, but George would tell Gelman everything else, starting with the deal he made with Chief Norris when he first came to Charleston.

"Our, or more precisely, Andi's solving rates are kind of the root of the problem."

Gelman straightened on the sofa. "How come?"

"As you surely know, I transferred to Charleston PD roughly six months ago. On my first day, Chief Norris asked me into her office and told me I would be partnering with Andi. She also told me to find out how Andi solves his cases in exchange for a glowing recommendation for when I left Charleston."

"And you agreed?"

George shrugged, winked in Andi's direction. "Why not? It wasn't what I had expected, but I couldn't find anything inherently wrong with it either. I would be working with Andi closely anyway, and if I found anything, well, then I had a direct order to report. It was kind of a gray area. Plus, I had the chance to make a positive impression on the chief, which is usually a good idea."

Gelman nodded. "What did you find? I expect it wasn't what Chief Norris suspected?"

"She wasn't happy, if that's what you mean. Our first case was the trafficking ring we busted."

"Castain and Harris. Nasty business."

"Yes. It was a horrible case with leads drying up left and right. We were able to get results because of Andi's contacts everywhere in the city and because of his very accurate instincts. In the beginning I had some trouble trusting his gut feelings because I myself work with a more evidence-based manner, but I learned to see his instincts as something that gives us pointers in the right direction. Anyway, Chief Norris wasn't happy when I reported back that there wasn't anything sinister going on with my partner. Since that first case, our relationship has deteriorated steadily."

"She did suspend you from the Castain case."

"Yes."

"Because you ignored her order of leaving Castain alone."

"Yes."

"Why did you do that?" Gelman sounded genuinely interested, a good trait in somebody who regularly stepped into volatile situations. George nodded at Andi, who took over.

"We knew Chief Norris wanted Castain to be left alone because he worked for the mayor, who didn't want a scandal so close to election. All evidence we had, though, pointed to him. At the time we weren't sure if he was one of the ringleaders or just involved in some manner, but it was clear he was part of it, and leaving him alone wasn't an option." Andi told the white lie smoothly, thinking of what an ordinary detective would have known at the time when Norris had suspended them. Gelman had apparently no problem believing Andi.

"I see. You were spot-on, cracked the case, recommendations all around."

"Yes."

"Then why is she so fixated on you?"

Andi shrugged. "I honestly don't know. Could be because Chief Renard, her predecessor, told her to leave me be."

"He didn't have a problem with you working alone? Or with your solving rates?"

"Chief Renard is a pragmatic. I made him look good, he didn't complain."

"A wise man, it seems." Gelman leaned back on the sofa. "I'm going to be honest, gentlemen. We're in a kind of pickle here. You have given me enough condemning material to start an official investigation, which very likely would end with Chief Norris being removed from her position."

"Which is not what you want." George sounded resigned with a hint of predatory awareness Andi had learned to recognize as his partner being close to pouncing on his prey.

"It's not what the higher-ups want. You know how it is, Detectives, the public opinion of the police is bad enough as it is. Removing an African American chief of police from her post, here in the South, is going to cause a huge stink. One we would like to avoid if possible."

"We get that. What do you suggest?" George leaned forward in his seat.

"It's something we haven't done often, but it has worked every time so far." Gelman seemed to brace himself for the backlash coming from them. "I will come to the precinct as an agent from IA, officially to get a feeling how the corps as a whole works. I'll be nosing around, accompanying detectives on their cases, talking to people. There's going to be a lot of talking. And during those talks, I'm trying to smooth things over. It works remarkably well, because as an outsider with a clear mission, nobody expects me to do something completely different instead."

"And the catch is?" George asked.

"The catch is you have to agree to it because the complaint has come from you. If you say you don't want to try it, you want to go official immediately, I have to do it."

"What happens if what you're proposing doesn't work?" Andi thought George was rightfully suspicious.

"Then it becomes official. With the difference of an additional witness." Gelman gestured at himself.

George looked at Andi. He was calm. The arthropods weren't picking up any stress from him. He was leaving the decision to Andi, showing him without words that he was fine with whatever Andi decided. Andi thought about it for a moment. He usually liked to have things out of the way, but Gelman was right. There was more at stake than just their internal problem with Chief Norris. And he loved his work; he loved the police. Protecting it was more important than a triumph over the chief. He looked at Gelman.

"We try it your way. If it doesn't work, I reserve the right to say 'I told you so.'"

"Duly noted." Gelman smiled and got up. "I'm leaving you to it, gentlemen. See you in the precinct soon." He shook both their hands before George showed him out of the house. The moment the door closed, the arthropods quieted down, left Andi with just a soft hum at the back of his head.

He helped George clean up the living room and kitchen by eating the rest of the sandwiches and all the cookies. They didn't talk until George had opened two bottles of beer and they were sitting in the recliners on the back porch, watching the sun making its slow descent behind the horizon. The arthropods of the dusk were waking, filling his senses with more than just what his human ears and eyes and nose could detect.

"I think we're doing the right thing." George clinked his bottle with Andi.

"I think so too. And what choice did we have, after he so politely put a gun to our heads?"

"He's good at playing games, I give him that." A smile appeared on George's face. "It's in our favor, I think. He's not going to be fooled by Chief Norris."

"Let's drink to that." They both took a swig before they stared into the darkening garden in companionable silence. After a while, George suddenly stated, "I don't like it."

Andi glanced at him, saw just enough of his expression to conclude he wasn't talking about Gelman, which only left one other topic.

"That we couldn't nail Gartner down?" he guessed.

"Yes." George took another swig of his beer, his movement almost angry. "I know it doesn't bother you as much, but I think he should pay for his crimes." George didn't sound confrontational, just resigned.

"You're wrong. It does bother me. In a different way than you, obviously, but that's because my view on justice is—" Andi hesitated, searching for a word he knew didn't exist and settling for a poor substitute instead. "—blurred."

George looked at him. "Blurred?"

"I can't describe it better." Andi lifted his bottle to his lips. "You are a good cop, George, a great detective. Your moral compass is very firmly set and maintained by a family who deals in law enforcement one way or another. Me, I know how lacking our law is. I see and feel and sense and, gods, sometimes even taste how lacking it is. I know justice is for a few select individuals, and I'm trying to raise their numbers, but it's not even a drop in the ocean." Andi closed his eyes for a moment, almost got tangled in the joy of a few moths fluttering around a porch light. "Three deaths for three ruined lives. It's not ideal, it's not how I *want* it to be, but it's something I have no problem accepting."

George stared at him for a long time. Then he reached over to Andi's lounge and placed his right hand on Andi's. It was warm and comforting and just what Andi needed. "You know what the worst is for me? How completely I get you. Also, I don't want you to think you have to censor or justify yourself. I can live with us having differing opinions on the matter." He grinned ruefully. "I admit it's mostly because I know you'll do your job anyway, but also because you help me gain perspective—as I hope I do to you."

Andi sighed, enjoying the warmth seeping into his hand from where George's fingers touched it. "I do respect your viewpoint. And I admire you for it. I guess I'm not a good enough man to feel compassion for victims who have been offenders all their lives. It's good to have that kind of balance."

George squeezed Andi's hand lightly. "I wouldn't call it compassion. Those three men were complete and utter assholes, no arguing that point. I simply want to believe that justice is free of any passion—because how can it be just otherwise?"

"Good question." Andi looked at their joined hands, which were becoming blurs in the thickening darkness. "But how can there be justice if passion isn't taken into account?"

George made a grunting sound and raised his bottle to look at it closely. "I think there's something wrong with the beer. We're being all philosophical and shit."

Andi laughed. It felt good when George joined him, distracting from the seriousness of their conversation.

"I guess we better drink more of it. Next stage after philosophical is happy singing, I think."

"Ugh. Thanks, I pass. Singing and me don't mix well. And I assume you like your eardrums. Let's have some ice cream instead. It's supposed to cure all ailments, isn't it?"

Andi slowly got up. Their fingers slid apart. "Let's find out."

XENIA MELZER grew up and still lives in rural Bavaria, where not much of anything happens – an escaped cow or some lost tourists now and then, nothing truly mysterious or even scandalous. For that reason, trying her hand in some mystery of her own seemed like a good idea. Xenia has also recently discovered she's demisexual with a dash of asexuality thrown into the mix, which opened her eyes to a lot of things and gave Andi and George, the two main characters in the Andi Hayes Mystery series, their special spin. In addition, a fascination with insects of all kinds provided her with the real detectives for the story. Xenia loves NCIS, snuggling with either her husband or her horse – the children don't keep still long enough – and crocheting, the latter a newly discovered hobby.

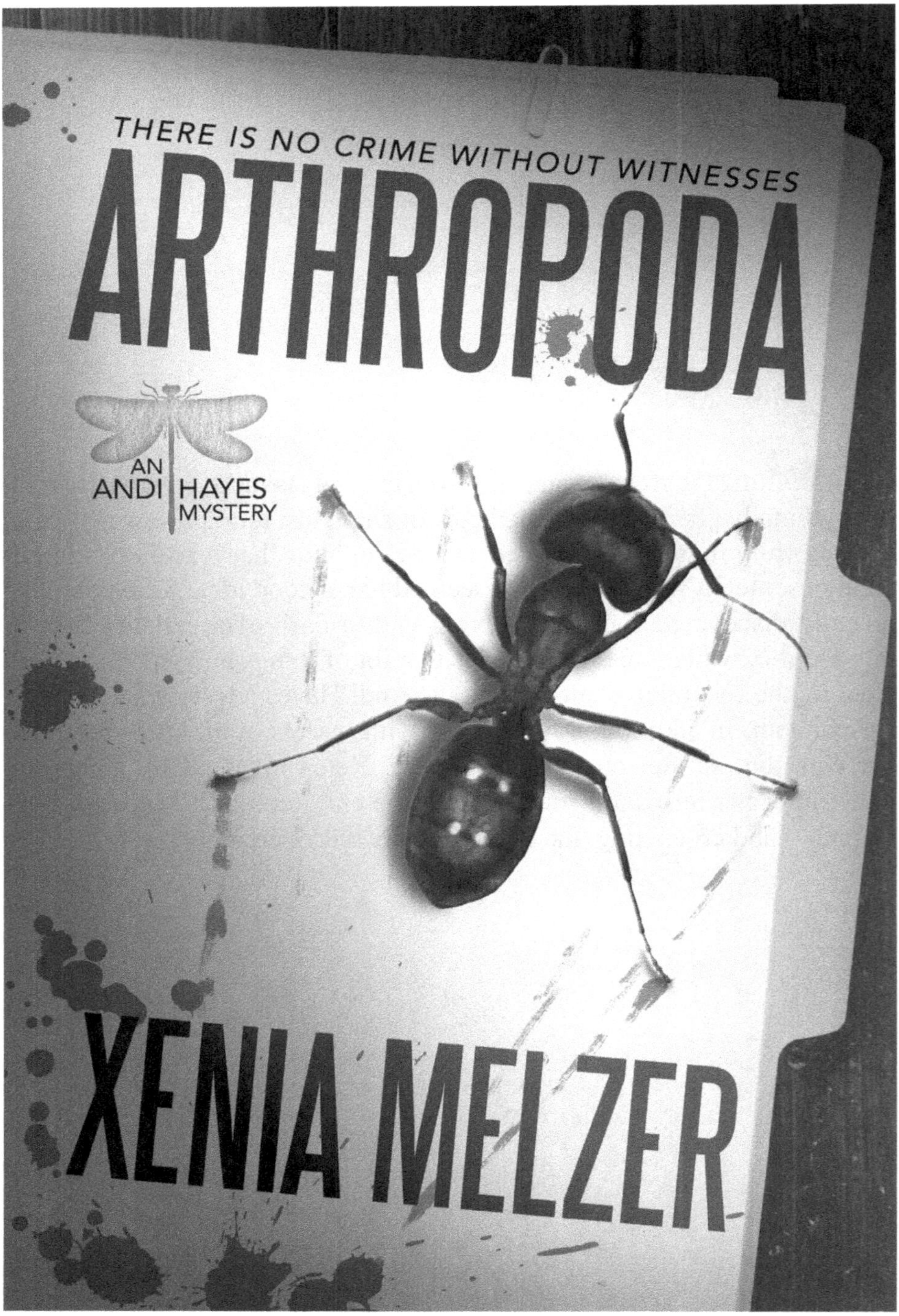
THERE IS NO CRIME WITHOUT WITNESSES
ARTHROPODA
AN
ANDI HAYES
MYSTERY
XENIA MELZER

An Andi Hayes Murder Mystery

Detective George Donavon doesn't plan to stay in Charleston long. Skeptical and by-the-book, he's on the fast track to the top, and he won't let anything derail his career. Especially not Andrew Hayes, his grumpy, awkward new partner—and not the chief's secret order to find out how said partner solves even the most difficult cases.

George and Andi can't agree on anything except their mutual dislike, but when three dead girls turn up at a storage unit, they must put their differences aside before the suspected trafficking ring claims another victim.

There is no crime without witnesses. Andi knows George suspects his always-right "hunches" point to corruption, but he doesn't care. All that matters is catching a killer… and keeping his secret. But with leads on this sprawling conspiracy drying up, he has no choice. He just can't let his partner find out how he's getting the information.

Andi's on the verge of losing his life, his mind, and his career. He could take George down with him…

If the violent criminals who are always one step ahead don't get to them first.

www.dsppublications.com

CASTO

GODS OF WAR

XENIA MELZER

Gods of War: Book One

All is fair in love and war. Renaldo has lived happily by that proverb his entire life. But he has finally met his match, and he's about to discover how unfair love and war can be.

When demigod and warlord Lord Renaldo takes a beautiful stranger captive during an ambush, he is delighted to have found a distraction that will keep him entertained during the upcoming siege. Little does he know, Casto is keeping more than just one secret from him. Slowly, Renaldo gets sucked into a turbulent roller-coaster relationship with his mysterious prisoner, one that begins with hatred and soon spirals into a whirlwind of conflicting emotions. And when it seems that things can get no worse, an old enemy stirs right in the heart of his home.

Determined to keep Casto by his side, Renaldo has to find a balance between the capricious young man and his own destiny as a ruler and god to his people.

www.dsppublications.com

LOVE
AND THE
STUBBORN
GODS OF WAR: BOOK II

XENIA MELZER

Gods of War: Book Two

All is fair in love and war. By now, Renaldo has found out the hard way how utterly stupid this statement is once you've met your match. And Casto won't give an inch in their ongoing war for love.

After a tumultuous start to their relationship, Renaldo and Casto seem to have finally reached calmer waters. But just when Renaldo starts getting comfortable and thinks he can relax, things get out of hand again. His old enemy, the Good Mother, is dangerously close to defeating the divine brothers by reaching out to what is most dear to him. Casto still clinging to his stubborn pride is all the plotters need to drive him and Renaldo apart. Burdened by the secrets of his past, Casto fights with everything he's got not only to save his life, but also to secure his future happiness. Facing the destruction of everything they have built together, Renaldo and Casto must choose between pride and love.

www.dsppublications.com

For more
great fiction
from

DSP PUBLICATIONS

visit us online.

WWW.DSPPUBLICATIONS.COM